ANGEL FOOD AND DEVIL DOGS

৵৶

Liz Bradbury

LESBIAN MYSTERY BOOKS

ALLENTOWN, PENNSYLVANIA

ANGEL FOOD AND DEVIL DOGS

**Lesbian Mystery Books
is an imprint of Boudica Publishing Inc.
Allentown, Pennsylvania**

To purchase copies, or for further information
visit our web site:
www.boudicapublishing.com

ISBN 0-9800549-1-5

Printed in the United States of America

First Edition

For Patricia Sullivan
Rowing in Eden today. Wild nights forever.

The author wishes to acknowledge:

Patricia Sullivan, for the enormous amount of work she has contributed to the production of this book in ways too numerous to mention, Jean Rubin for her advice, vast knowledge and painstaking scrutiny, Don Kohn, of Kohn Engineering for his expertise on fire, fire safety and sprinkler systems, Genevieve Goff for advice and editing, Miriam Lavandier for Spanish translations, Steve Libby of Gaydar Magazine for publishing early excerpts, Gail Erich for insight, suggestions, editing, and catching the big mistake, David Rosenbaum, Ann Warde, and Michael Pastore for publishing advice and Kate Mulgrew for inspiration.

And readers: Laura Gutierrez, Sarah Kersh, Melinda Kohn, Bob Wittman, Frank Whalen, Chenoweth Moffatt, Barb Loch, Dennis Bradbury, Kristen Buckno, Elizabeth Goff, Beverly Morgan, Sara Niebler, Roberta Meek, and Christine Gaffney, for their help and suggestions.

Chapter 1

"Maggie Gale," I said to the prison security guard. Attorney Sara Martinez and her law partner Emma Strong followed me through the check in. They both greeted the guard by name and got a genial response compared with the flatline I'd received when I'd flashed my private investigator's license. When I'd been a cop, I knew everybody at the jail, but those days appear to have passed.

"In here," Sara said, leading us into one of the lawyer/client conference rooms. Sara Martinez is my younger sister. Today though, she was my boss.

Fenchester City jail smelled of disinfectant, sweat, and despair. Not necessarily in that order. With a table that looked like it had been clawed by wild animals, this room sported the additional aura of raging fear. We sat and waited in plastic chairs.

Sara and Emma looked crisply professional and at the peak of fashion, even under harsh fluorescent lights. I was wearing a polo shirt and jeans. My private detective undercover uniform and what I wear most days, whether I'm working or not. I'll never reach the peak of fashion. I don't even know where the flatlands of fashion are. But I was fairly sure the fluorescent light was making my pale skin tone look as green as my eyes.

"You've known Mickey for a long time, Maggie, but I don't think you understand how hard it is to get a direct answer out of him. He's sweet and gentle but he's kind of a problem child," said Sara.

"He's accused of rape and murder, Sara, *problem child* is an understatement," I countered.

"But he's innocent and that's what you're going to prove, right?" asked Emma. She took off her glasses and eyed my shoulder bag with the same eagle gaze that made tough witnesses cave on the stand.

I'd called them to meet me at the jail because I had some new evidence. Emma and Sara were two of the sharpest lawyers in Pennsylvania. Mickey would never understand how lucky he was to have them on his side, and pro-bono no less.

Emma said, "I just got the notification that his arraignment hearing's next Monday. That gives us six days to get the charges dismissed or at least get him out on bail."

"I think I've found something to punch a hole in the prosecution's case." I pulled a large manila envelope from the bag and laid it on the table.

"What?" asked Sara, her dark eyes flashing with excitement. "Is it good? Tell!"

But I was interrupted by a guard leading a thin childlike man into the room. Mickey Murphy pushed his matted blond hair away from his face. His eyes were red and swollen, his nose raw from sleeve wiping. According to a social worker's report, he'd been crying almost constantly since the police had nabbed him. He was in serious trouble. Just two weeks after he'd been *transitioned* from a halfway house for adults with mental disabilities into his own tiny apartment, his next-door neighbor, a young social worker named Daria Webster had been found dead. She'd been raped and strangled. Circumstantial evidence tagged Mickey as the prime suspect.

When Mickey looked up and saw Sara and Emma, a happy smile transformed his entire presence. He was more than just relieved to see them, he was thrilled.

"Hi, hiya, hi!" he rapid-fired loudly.

"Do you remember us Mickey?" asked Sara gently.

"Huh? Oh yeah, yeah...She-ra and Wonder Woman? That's right... right?" he said wrinkling his brow, then grinning.

Sara and Emma weren't fazed by Mickey's obtuse identifications. It's just my opinion mind you, but Sara, while hot looking in her own right, doesn't favor She-ra, and Emma, while also quite fine, wasn't exactly wearing a star-covered body suit.

Sara explained, "Mickey likes cartoons, he likes people to call him Mickey Mouse." She turned from me to Mickey, got his full attention, then said deliberately, "Mickey, this is Maggie Gale, you've seen her before, she's our... your private detective. She finds out things. She's helping us with your case."

"Maggie Gale? Gale... I can name you Storm, cause Storm is a superhero and helps people. She-ra and Wonder Woman are the best superheroes and they are like, the best lawyers right?" He pointed at Sara and Emma with both hands. They glanced at me and couldn't keep from smiling at my incredulous expression.

Sara said smugly, "She-ra is the protector of Eternia, you know."

"Oh, right, of course," I snorted softly.

Mickey was mulling over my new moniker, looking down at the tabletop. He said to himself, "Storm... from the X-men, but there's another superhero named Storm, he's a man, he fights bad guys, but he likes girls, do you think people might get them mixed up?" Mickey looked up with a puzzled face.

"Perfect," murmured Sara.

Emma said, "You know what, Mickey? Maggie fights bad guys and she likes girls, so I think it would be OK if you call her Storm even if people get the two characters mixed up. She has to ask you some questions and you need to answer very carefully."

Mickey nodded seriously, turning in his chair to me.

"I hear you're a pinball wizard, Mickey," I said simply. His comfortable expression stiffened to wariness.

"Um, yeah, so?"

"Mickey, she's on your side, like Storm. OK?" said Sara, who probably also wanted to say...*so?*

"Yeah, Storm." Mickey was nodding, paying full attention again.

"The police say that the day Daria died, you had a lot of bruises on your legs. Remember?"

I was hoping Mickey would recall the day of the murder, when cops interviewing the neighbors found Mickey's door standing open and him hiding in his underwear in the corner of his tiny bedroom. The cops had seen a dozen finger and fist shaped bruises on his thighs and figured they were defense wounds. They pressed Mickey and he'd blurted a vague confession.

Mickey looked at me sideways and finally squeaked, "I don't... but I didn't hurt Daria. I would never hurt her."

Everyone who knew Mickey felt he was innocent, but prejudice against people like Mickey outweighs the opinions of friends. The public was desperate to feel safe, so Mickey had been arrested.

The fight for Mickey's freedom rapidly became an uphill battle. Mickey told Sara and Emma that he couldn't remember the day of the murder at all. Which was probably true, because while his cognitive ability fluctuated between an 8 to 12-year-old level, Mickey's extremely selective memory was that of a child of 4. He retained certain items with incredible clarity, but he forgot scary things he didn't want to remember.

"Look at this." I put a flyer from the envelope on the table. It was an advertisement for the pinball convention that had been in the middle of downtown Fenchester the day before the murder. Then I pulled out two 8 by 10 glossy photos. One showed rows of pinball machines set up at the convention. The other featured a single blazingly ornate machine. Sara and Emma stared at the pictures. Mickey's eye glazed over with toy lust.

"Did you play these machines?" I whispered. Mickey stared at the pictures and then slowly looked up at me. "This one, *The Slam-meister*? Did you play it?" I pointed to the picture of the four-legged electronic monster with five garish levels and ramps. Its name, lettered in flashing lights, glared off the page. "What was your best score?"

"Seventy-five thousand six hundred twenty points," Mickey rattled off, "the best score of anybody. I won, but I..." he froze.

"They told you at the half-way house not to spend your money on pinball machines, didn't they? They said you couldn't live on your own if you skipped work and used up all your money to play? Mickey, it's OK for you to tell us, it really is," I coaxed.

Mickey pushed his hair out of his eyes with his wet sleeve and nodded. Then he stared back at the machine. "I used to play at the bar on the corner, but they told the owner not to let me. This was different; it was only for one day. So many machines, and this one... nothing's like it, and I got the best score. I remembered I wasn't supposed to play. So I left, and then I forgot. I didn't want nobody to know I played the machines..." he said in a far away voice.

Emma said softly, "Maggie, what's the point of this?"

Sara leaned in, "He played the day before, not the day of the murder. We can't use this as an alibi."

"Yeah, I understand that," I said, "but look..." I reached into the envelope and took out five more photos. "I went to a pinball convention in York yesterday to get these. Everyone was packing up, I got there just in time." I put the glossy photos on the table. Three men and two women, each had towels covering their underwear, but the bruises on their upper thighs, in the shapes of fingers and fists, showed plainly. Everybody had at least a dozen of them.

Sara grabbed a photo and stood up. "These bruises are just like the ones Mickey had. The ones the case is built on. Are there bruises on their hips and stomachs too? Who are these people?"

"Pinball wizards. If you want to win, you can't just hit the flippers, you have to use body English, you have to nudge...well, you practically have to hump the machine. I've seen these people play. It's physical. Bruises from thigh to waist. It's an occupational hazard. Mickey played hard, he won, and he must have been bruised from it. Even if he can't remember, fifty spectators saw him get the top score. I have the names and contact information of a dozen people who were in Fenchester for the convention. They'll testify they saw Mickey play, and they'll also testify about the physical marks of pinball competition."

Sara nearly shouted with exasperation, "But why hasn't anyone come forward? All the newspaper articles..."

"Because Mickey used his pinball name, didn't you buddy, not Mickey Murphy, not even Mickey Mouse, your special name?" Mickey hadn't been listening to a word we were saying. He was still staring at the photo of The Slam-meister. I touched his shoulder. "You use a different name when you play pinball, don't you Mick?"

"Oh yeah, my pinball name. I'm Mighty Mouseman when I play pinball," chimed Mickey obliviously.

Sara and Emma slumped back in their chairs, their expressions showed unmistakable signs of relief. The unexplained bruises had even shaken their confidence in Mickey's innocence. That was all gone now. They were already recalculating their defense strategy.

"Mickey," said Emma gently, "do you remember now, the day the police came?"

Mickey looked up blankly. "Huh? Um, Chief O'Hara, Batman and Robin, and The Sandman... he's one of Spiderman's enemies, he shot me... I hate him..." Mickey trailed off.

"Nobody shot you Mickey. We want to know about the bruises on your legs, remember getting bruises on your legs from playing pinball?" Sara asked evenly.

"I guess that's what happened," said Mickey in his best effort to please. All of us looked at Mickey, each understanding that his defense would have to come from us, because he couldn't defend himself.

After a long moment, Sara and Emma stood up. This was the hardest part of their visits with Mickey. "Mick, we have to go now," said Sara in her softest voice.

"Can I go too? I really want to go home, please?" His desperation was painful to hear. Tears streaked his cheeks again.

"No, I'm sorry honey, but maybe in a few days. We'll work hard on it," Sara squeezed his shoulder. Mickey tried to look brave as we filed out. I saw Emma give him a tiny pack of Kleenex as I slipped through the door.

When we were out on the sidewalk, Sara hugged me. We all took pro-bono cases for people who couldn't stand up for themselves, but this one was special. Mickey lived right in our neighborhood where he bagged groceries at the local farmer's market. We'd known him since he was a teenager, when he was found by a neighbor sitting on a park bench all alone in Washington Mews. His family had moved away and left him behind, because their legal responsibility to look after him had ended the day he turned eighteen.

"Will this be enough?" I asked as Emma took her turn hugging me.

"We'll certainly be able to get bail for him now. Maybe we'll be able to convince the judge the prosecution really has no case against him. We still have time to build his case. Frankly, even though this is a terrible place for him, he might be safer in here than out on the street. He really shouldn't be by himself. After all, the person who killed Daria is still out there, and deep down, Mickey knows who it is." Emma looked up at the blank façade of the jail building, then shivered and pulled her coat tighter.

"You'll save him. Heck, you're superheroes, you can get him off!" I insisted.

"She-ra and Wonder Woman. He converts everyone to cartoon characters. He always remembers the name, but usually forgets why he chose it in the first place," said Sara putting her arm through mine as we walked against the frosty winter wind to Emma's car. "We have a better chance now... not much of a case without the bruises. But still, Mickey did vaguely confess and Daria Webster was killed. Until whomever really did it is caught, Mickey'll be the top suspect." A biting cold gust cut off the rest of the conversation.

"Can't DNA evidence help Mickey?" I asked Sara in the car, "it was a rape after all."

"There wasn't any semen. The Medical Examiner thinks the perp probably used a condom."

"Oh, right," I muttered sarcastically, "like Mickey would think of using a condom and then carefully dispose of it, but forget to put his pants on when the police came to talk to him."

Sara went on, "There's some blood evidence under Daria's fingernails, but only a trace. The lab will take weeks on it. Mickey's confession made the blood DNA a low priority. We'll press for the test results and we'll try to get the confession thrown out. Hey, and we have some new information. The marks on Daria's neck indicate a cylindrical object pressed against her windpipe choked her. The police found a heavy marble rolling pin in her kitchen sink, in a pile of dishes. Possibly the murder weapon, they're still testing it, but no prints. Daria must have been doing the dishes when she was attacked. The sink hose was draped in the sink; there was water all over the floor. The police searched for other physical evidence, but Daria hosted that office party in her apartment earlier that day. Two dozen people were there. They'd played charades and Twister. There was DNA everywhere..."

"I'll check each party guest, maybe one of them did it," I suggested.

"Well, we'll get a list, but each one you rule out makes the shadow of doubt narrower and spotlights Mickey. It's not our job to find the killer, only to get Mickey off." Sara paused looking out the window, I knew she was considering the arguments she and Emma would use at Mickey's hearing, she went on, "Of course, if you could find the real killer..."

"I'm not sure I could do that without ruling any of the others out," I considered.

"I bet Storm could find the killer, or would she be too busy chasing women?" teased Emma.

"Woman-chasing in a fair match? Storm, She-ra or Wonder Woman?" I posed the names for consideration.

All three of us called out laughing, "Wonder Woman!"

"And don't you forget it," Emma declared as she turned into Washington Mews. "Maggie, I hope you didn't mind my explaining to Mickey that you like girls..."

"Yeah, like I'd mind. Geez Emma, I'm as *out* as a lesbian can be."

"I know, I know... of course it's been a while since you had a girlfriend..." Emma ribbed.

I changed the subject, "Does Mickey choose superhero names for everyone?"

"Nope," said Sara. "Only Justice League types like us get to be superheroes, the rest are just plain cartoon characters."

"Halle Berry was so hot as Storm in the X-men but I don't even know who the male Storm is, what does he look like?" I asked.

"He wears caveman clothes and is kind of huge like the Hulk but not green," said Emma.

"I can't believe you know that," Sara muttered.

"I don't look anything like that! I'm in pretty good shape. Does Mickey think I'm a Hulk type? I'll have to go on a diet..."

"Your body's fine, but you have the dullest wardrobe in Fenchester," said my beloved but annoyingly accurate sister. "Mickey's nicknames don't have to do with how you look, they usually have something to do with your name. Yours was easy. Gale - Storm, get it? Wonder Woman is *Strong*, and even She-ra kind of sounds like Sara, and then he throws in the fighting for justice stuff, but that's secondary. Some are impossible to figure out. He calls Farrel Case *Fur Ball*. She has no idea why, and by now neither does Mickey."

Farrel Case is my best friend. We happened to be passing the rowhouse she and her partner Jessie Wiggins own in the Washington Mews Historic

District. Emma swung into a parking spot in front of the four story converted factory building that houses Martinez and Strong, Attorneys at Law and Gale Investigations, Inc. By an extraordinary set of circumstances, I own the whole building. I've converted the third floor loft into my living space. I'm sporadically working on the fourth floor, but I had to take some time off from construction to actually earn a living. That's one of the bummer things about self-employment; you actually have to work to make money. Of course Mickey's pro-bono case, while morally satisfying, wasn't exactly a cash cow.

We piled out of Emma's car and Sara punched in the code to the keyless entry system. We can change the combination whenever we want without having to worry about replacing keys. We have other security precautions as well, even building-wide video surveillance with monitors in the offices and my loft. Lawyers and investigators often have enemies. It's a byproduct of the legal eagle and beagle business. We climbed the stairs to our second floor offices.

At a desk in the small reception area, our shared secretary Evelyn Quaid chirped, "Emma, you have an ACLU board meeting in forty-five minutes, and..." she glanced at a memo, "Ingrid called and left a message on your voice mail." Emma scrambled into her office without a word and slammed the door. Sara howled laughter.

"Who's Ingrid?" I asked Sara.

She caught her breath, pushing her dark curly hair back into place. "It's what she calls the new girlfriend, and the name fits, she looks just like Ingrid Bergman."

"Yum."

"She's a flight attendant," Sara continued as she shrugged off her coat, "she flies to Paris several times a week, it's thrown Emma's schedule off completely. She actually goes on dates at 3:00 AM and gets to the office by 9:00 AM."

"How's that affecting her work?" I smirked.

"It's improving it!"

"Sara, you're due in court in thirty minutes and Maggie," said Evelyn, "you have a message too. It's from President Bouchet. He wants to see you."

"Evie, you make him sound like the President of a country... is he?" I reached for the memo.

"Oh... well... I guess he might be," said Evelyn slightly confused, "but he called from Irwin College."

Sara called after me as I headed for my little office next door, "Gracias, querida, bien hecho."

"De nada," I called.

Sitting behind my desk I thought about Mickey. He was so alone. His family had found him too complicated, too different from them, too hard to understand. They'd moved away, leaving him behind in a lonely world to fend for himself.

I looked slowly around my office, from the big windows overlooking the rooftops of Washington Mews, to my private investigator license, which I'd hung up less than a year ago, to a painting I'd done in art college. Next to the painting was a five-year-old photo of me in Fenchester City Hall, receiving my promotion to police lieutenant.

On my desk were two smaller pictures. The one of me on my eighth birthday sitting between my mother and father in an amusement park in western New York State was the last picture taken of my mother. She died just a few days later. She'd been an artist and taught me that the harder a problem was, the more unconventional the solution might have to be.

A prime example of my mom's problem solving skill was my name. When family pressured my parents to name me after a wealthy yet unpleasant Aunt, Mehitabel Arrabella Gale, Mom and Dad regretfully conceded. Covertly, my mother crafted the plan to call me Maggie, using my initials, M. A. G. for inspiration. Ultimately the wealthy Aunt didn't cough up. Turned out she had debt up to her eyeballs. But my nickname stuck.

The other picture on my desk is of me when I was eleven, surrounded by my new family. Three years after my mother died, my father married the brilliant, wild, and often hilarious free spirit, Juana Anita Martinez. We not only added Juana to our family but her daughters, eight-year-old Sara and three-year-old Rosa. I learned to speak Spanish fluently from my new mother and sisters. I also learned I didn't have to be sad and lonely any more.

I shook myself out of this little reverie and placed a call to Irwin College. The president's secretary put me on hold.

"This is Max Bouchet," said a deep booming voice over the phone a minute later. "I hope you can help us Ms. Gale. We have a problem here at Irwin College, and you've been recommended to me by... well, let's just say it was someone in the police department. I'd rather not talk about this over the phone, so if you're free this afternoon at 1:45..." I agreed to meet him at his office in the Administration building.

Dr. Max Bouchet was the new President of Irwin. He'd only been there about two months. He hadn't even been formally installed. Like many college presidents, Bouchet was a corporate guy. The bottom line is the line a college president must toe these days. Some businessmen can pull it off. Others struggle with the academicians from their very first minute on campus.

The newspapers had been full of how Bouchet was a major young CEO who had recently sold his successful company for an obscenely large amount of money. He could probably buy Irwin lock, stock and barrel, with enough Benjamins left over to live happily-ever-after in a palatial tropical paradise. Yet, Bouchet had applied for the Irwin leadership job because he said he was devoted to learning and knowledge. He had a doctorate in economics.

Bouchet also was one of very few African American private college presidents in the US. Probably the only one who also happened to be a multimillionaire. And he'd just called me to come and see him about a problem. How cool was that?

I thought I already knew what Irwin College's problem was. Just a few days ago there'd been a suicide there. Sad to say that while suicides on college campuses are tragic, they're not all that rare. Overworked, under pressure students, fueled by drugs, alcohol, teen hormones, and depression, sometimes choose the one-way express to oblivion. Colleges keep the frequency of these tragedies quiet so tuition-paying parents don't get cold feet about sending their fragile progeny away from the nest.

But this campus suicide was different. It had been a faculty member, Dr. Carl Rasmus, who'd jumped from a six-story building. It was still making the local front page days after the body had been discovered. The police were still, *declining to comment*, on the circumstances, but the local press and TV had a load of read-between-the-lines innuendo.

Sara and Emma had both briefly served with the late Carl Rasmus on the Pennsylvania Gay and Lesbian Committee on Performing Arts. Though they hadn't known him well they'd felt his death personally. I could talk to them about Rasmus later. But now, I went on-line and searched all the local newspapers for information.

Rasmus had been an Assistant Professor in the Music History Department. Music History was a relatively new program at Irwin, but then Irwin College was so old, anything less than 100 years was considered new-fangled. On Rasmus's last birthday, he'd been thirty.

He was in his fourth year of teaching at Irwin and nearing the odious period of a tenure review. According to the papers, he'd finished his doctorate just two years before and had actually published quite a bit; he was well liked and had made significant contributions to the College. Of course, this was all being said about him after he was dead, in the *don't speak ill of* period.

The papers mentioned that Rasmus was an expert in 20th century American composers and that he played the piano, oboe, and the clarinet. He was single, hard working, and had been blind from birth. I reread that part because it was a surprise. Nothing had been mentioned about his blindness on the TV news. Even Sara and Emma hadn't mentioned it. I wondered how he got around his disability when it came to reading and grading student's work. In fact, campus communication in general, now almost completely done via email, must have been very complicated for someone who couldn't see.

Just two days ago an article in the Fenchester Daily News said Rasmus had left a detailed note on his computer indicating his reasons for taking his own life, but the text of the note wasn't included.

Chapter 2

The edge of Irwin College has been just two blocks west of Washington Mews since about 1860. For more than a century before that, it was in the middle of town in what's now the Fenchester Historical Society building. Irwin College was one of the first ten colleges in the United States and probably the very first dedicated to art and architecture.

You'd think there'd be soaring experimental architecture cantilevering all over the place. There's a little of that, and a little over-attention to Neo Rococo detail in some of the 19th century buildings, but all in all there's an almost anal restraint in the designs and ornamentation of most of the structures. It's as though the designers had a desperate fear of creating something that would someday be outdated. So they stuck to the tried and true principles of design and beauty: the arithmetic mean, the properties of scale and balance, elements that occur in nature, but not too natural. Maybe a good school motto for Irwin would have been, "Form Follows Function As Long As It's Beautiful, Simple and Not Too Ostentatious," which, when you think about it, is not a bad plan.

Not too ostentatious...until you look closely. There's attention to architectural detail in the placement of every brick and the planting of every shrub. The proportions of the windows in relation to the façades of even the most mundane buildings are painstaking. Only a couple of Irwin's structures are ugly or cheap looking. The rest are gems.

I walked the four blocks to the Irwin Administration Building, not because I wanted the exercise, but because in the middle of the day, finding a parking place there would be like finding room for a king-sized bed in a sardine can. People going to Irwin actually parked in my block. So even though it was December and wet, gray, and cold out, I grabbed my shoulder bag and took to the slush covered sidewalks.

I was wearing a heavy polo shirt, fresh black jeans, a wool blazer, and my new squall parka. The parka had a spiffy lined hood in case I needed a hat, and special lined pockets strategically placed for optimum hand-warm-ability. I really liked this jacket.

Winter in small Eastern cities can seem particularly grim on days like this. Regular municipal street sweeping ends in November. Fewer homeowners sweep sidewalks in the cold. Casually dropped litter or over-spill from trash pick-ups accumulates. People stay inside. In winter, the city looks best at night when sundown hides the grime and trash, and holiday lights twinkle.

Irwin College has many confusing buildings, pathways, gardens and monuments, but it's easy to find the Administration Building. It's dead center in the half circle drive off Washington Street, in the main area of the campus. Even better, over the door is a huge polished granite sign with gilt letters that says Administration Building. Its marble steps were no longer in the pale gray sunlight, so puddled slush had turned to ice. It felt slick as I made my way up to the double glass doors.

In the middle of the lobby was a huge donut-shaped reception desk. In the donut hole a student sat on a stool eating an apple and reading a textbook laid open on the counter. Her long straight hair fell forward making a hair-sided pipeline to the book pages. She'd grown her own cubicle.

I considered asking for directions, but I couldn't bear to break her concentration. The sign next to the elevator said the President's office was on the fourth floor. The doors were open, so I rode up.

The elevator opened into what was definitely a rich guy's domain. My shoes sank deep into the luxurious carpet pile. The hall was decorated with real art from the College's permanent collection. I stopped to admire a large Peter Milton etching of a cat sitting on a garden wall. Opposite it was a Robert Rauschenberg silk screen and a Louise Nevelson pressed paper serigraph. This stuff was original, no offset litho reproductions here. Impressive.

The hallway ended at a perpendicular space, which formed a wide reception area. On the far wall were several doors. I figured the one with the reception desk in front must be Bouchet's office. The receptionist was studying a piece of paper. She looked about twenty, had fluffy blond hair and a figure that would kindly be called plump and cattily be called porky. Inexpertly applied make-up tried but failed to make her seem older.

"Maggie Gale?" she squeaked. When I nodded, she said with sincerity, "I'm sorry, President Bouchet is on the phone. He asked if you could just wait for a few minutes. Would that be OK? Would you like some coffee?"

"No thank you...Ms...?" I extended my hand. Her blue eyes widened. Nobody ever asked who she was.

"Connie Robinson," she said shaking my hand.

I smiled back. I took off my jacket and hung it up on a coat rack in the corner and sat down in one of the chairs lined up against a wall of windows. From there, I could see the entrance to the stairs in front of me. To my right was Connie at her desk. To my immediate left were double doors with a sign that read, Large Conference Room.

The beige wall-to-wall carpeting ran from the elevator throughout the reception area. On top of the carpet in front of Connie's desk, were two beautiful, handmade Asian rugs. Rugs like these were a special passion of mine. Each was about five by seven feet. One was a late 19th century camel hair Afshar, probably from Southern Persia. It had a beautiful dark blue field with a red geometric diagonal pattern. The other was a Heriz silk, of about the same age, with an intricately patterned medallion in the center. The corner of the Heriz was flipped over as though it had a mind of its own.

A sign on one of the other doors to the right said, Miranda Juarez, Assistant to the President. It opened and a small capable looking woman in her late forties, came toward me with her hand extended.

"Ms. Gale? I am Miranda Juarez, President Bouchet's assistant," she said with a strong Latino inflection, a firm handshake, and a confident manner. "We are just waiting for two other people to arrive for a quick meeting in President Bouchet's office. Then he would like you to meet with a larger group in the conference room."

I heard the elevator ding. Two people came down the art-lined hall. First came a man about thirty years old with thick blond hair parted in the middle, a ruddy complexion, and a huge handlebar mustache. He tugged on his mustache with one hand, trying to balance a load of loose papers in the other. He had *nerd-alert* stamped all over him.

He and the woman who came after him, must have come directly from outside because he had on a puffy down jacket and she was wearing a tailored dark tweed coat and red scarf. When the nerd-alert man got almost to the reception desk he dropped the papers. They scattered all over the floor at his feet. He dove down on his hands and knees and began pushing the papers into a pile. The woman in the coat, Miranda, Connie and I all moved to help him, but he waved us away by flailing his arms.

He was humming and grunting, "...in order...all right...data reports..." Occasionally he giggled softly. He managed to gather everything and stand.

I focused my attention on the woman in the tweed coat. She was one of the most attractive women I'd ever seen, maybe not classically beautiful, but extraordinarily... gee, I couldn't think of a word... maybe *fetching*.

She turned and looked at me directly, then smiled mostly with her eyes. My breath caught in my throat. Auburn hair framed her face with an inward curve. The brisk December afternoon still showed in pink tinged cheekbones glowing softly against alabaster skin. Her blue-gray eyes held a fascinating spark. And I had the vague feeling I'd seen her before, quite a while ago. She was pulling off her gloves and saying in a deep, incredibly sexy voice, "Miranda, I hope we're not late."

Miranda Juarez was saying, "Dr. Anthony, how was your trip?"

The door to the President's office opened. President Max Bouchet leaned out and said, "Oh good, you're all here. Please come in." The messy papers guy was closest so he went in first. The rest of us followed. Miranda Juarez closed the door behind her.

President Bouchet was about 40, trim but not thin, with short hair and a neatly cut beard. His skin was dark brown and so were his eyes, which seemed very shrewd. He was also much shorter than I'd imagined him. 5'6" tops. But what he lacked in stature he made up for with a booming, James Earl Jones voice.

Bouchet called to the receptionist, "Ms. Robinson, when the others come, please unlock the door to the conference room and ask them to have a seat. Thank you." His engaging voice had risen up like a thundering kettledrum, with just a touch of pretentiousness. He offered his hand to me.

"Ms. Gale, thank you very much for coming on such short notice, I really appreciate it. I think you'll be suited to this undertaking."

"I'm interested to hear what this is all about Dr. Bouchet," I replied.

Dr. Anthony was taking off her coat. The nerd-alert man sat, trying to sort the papers in his lap, dropping more in the process.

Bouchet's office was even more impressive than the reception area. He had an Isabel Bishop painting of a New York crowd scene hanging on the wall behind his desk. The desk itself was a slab of polished wood with butterfly wedges in the distinctive style of George Nakashima. There were a few pieces of paper on the desk, a gold pen, and a simple wood frame with a picture of an attractive woman.

"Have you all met?" asked Bouchet. There was head shaking so he said, "This is Maggie Gale. Ms. Gale is a private investigator who comes highly recommended by the police to give us some help with regard to Carl's... death." He turned and said, "This is Dr. Kathryn Anthony, she is working on a series of important projects this semester and she also teaches a graduate seminar and... is advisor to some Ph.D. candidates. Is that right?" he asked her. "Have I included everything Kathryn?"

"Yes Max, that covers what I'm doing quite well." She reached out to shake my hand firmly. She was captivating. "I'm very glad you're here Ms. Gale," she said. She looked deeply into my eyes and convinced me she meant every word. It made me feel a tad weak, which I managed to hide. I think.

"A pleasure to meet you, Dr. Anthony," I said. She seemed to be about to say something else, maybe, *Please call me Kathryn,* but she was interrupted by Bouchet.

"And this is Bartholomew Edgar," said Bouchet turning to the nerd-guy. "I've asked Bart to bring along some information for you, Ms. Gale. Bart is Assistant Dean in charge of personnel."

It was impossible for Edgar to stand or shake hands because he was holding the papers in his lap. Instead he said, "Hello," with one giggled, "hee," then bobbed his head like a nervous chicken.

"Bart has just been to the airport to pick up Kathryn. She's been representing Irwin College at a week-long conference in London. She very graciously consented to come here directly from the plane for the meeting we'll be having in the conference room."

Dr. Kathryn Anthony said, "Max, I promise I'll give you a full report on the London conference later, but now I have some very good news. I just received a call from the Governor's Task Force on Higher Education. The grant we've been working on for the satellite campus in Blue Mountain County is approved. But..."

Bouchet broke in jubilantly, "Excellent, how wonderful! ...I'm sorry, you were saying?"

"It's just that I must get to Harrisburg to talk to the Governor about a press release. He wants to be live on the five o'clock news..."

"Kathryn, that is better than good news, and really due to all your hard work. But you just got back, you must be so tired," said Bouchet sincerely. She should have been wiped from jet lag, but at the moment she seemed pumped.

"Max, could you do me a great favor? I have to leave very soon. I'll only have to be in Harrisburg for about an hour, but the four-hour round-trip drive might be too much for me. And I need to write the press release on the way. So I was hoping you might be able to arrange for someone to drive me there?" I was watching her. In fact, I could barely take my eyes off of her. She looked hopeful, but when Bouchet glanced toward Bart Edgar, I saw a flash of panic cross her face. Bouchet saw it too.

Miranda Juarez, who had been standing by quietly through the entire conversation, turned to Bouchet saying, "I could call the limousine service. I think they could get a car here in fifteen minutes. Especially if we mention that this is a meeting with the Governor."

"Yes, excellent idea Miranda," he looked relieved and so did Kathryn Anthony. Miranda left to make the call.

"Max, thank you so much, this will make it much easier for me. I'm sorry I'll have to miss today's meeting. Please give everyone my regrets. Perhaps you can fill me in later?" Kathryn Anthony said to Bouchet as she stood. "As it is, I just have time to go over to my office and get the grant outline."

She turned to me and gave me her hand again, "Ms. Gale, I hope we have another chance to meet soon," I certainly felt the same way, but she was in a hurry so all I did was nod and smile.

"Kathryn," said Bouchet, "I will need to tell you about today's conference. When you get back tonight, I know you'll be very tired, but please give me a call at home so I can fill you in, say about 9:00 PM?"

Was this guy full of himself or what? She'd just flown back from England, swung a multi-million dollar grant, rushed to this meeting, has to whip out to Harrisburg to make the College look good with the Governor by actually writing the press release herself... and Bouchet wants her to call him as soon as she gets back? And he's even telling her what time?

"Of course Max, I'll talk to you then," said Dr. Anthony as she left.

Bouchet turned to Bart Edgar and said, "Bart, I just need to speak to Ms. Gale alone for a few minutes."

Edgar did that head-bobbing thing again, his huge mustache flapping like seagull wings, but he didn't make a move to leave.

Bouchet said patiently as though speaking to a four year-old, "...so Bart if you will just leave us now and go into the Large Conference Room, we'll be there shortly."

The penny dropped. Edgar squashed his papers together with both hands and made his way to the door, miraculously getting through it without dropping anything else.

Bouchet and I watched him leave with *car accident* fascination. When the door closed Bouchet dropped his administrator persona and said in honest exasperation, "He's always like that."

"Really?"

Bouchet nodded incredulously. "His great aunt is one of the most generous contributors to the College. I guess he's a small price to pay..." Bouchet sighed and leaned back in his chair. "I'll have to fill you in quickly because the others are already waiting and they aren't a generally patient lot. As you probably know, last week Carl Rasmus died. It's been a terrible blow to the

College community. Everyone has been affected. We've had counselors in to
work with the students, and even some of the faculty. Many people cared
deeply for him. Are you familiar with what was in the papers?"

I nodded.

"The police presumed it was suicide, with good reason. There was a note
on Carl's computer detailing his...unhappiness and fears and also blaming
several people on the Tenure Committee for his problems."

I nodded again.

"I'm sure you've read that Carl was blind. His disability rarely got in his
way. In fact, he was able to bring a unique perspective to his work because he
was... differently abled, as some people say." Bouchet paused, then went on
choosing his words carefully. "Carl wrote the note on his computer in his
office. His computer was off-line at the time. The computer even indicated
the time the note was written. Three witnesses confirm that Carl was alone in
his office and his were the only fingerprints on the keyboard."

"But something has happened to suggest this might not have been
suicide?" I suggested.

"The autopsy report. A contact in the Coroner's office called me
specifically to tell me about it, for which I'm grateful. Carl left his office on
the second floor of the Music History building and took the elevator to the
sixth floor. He seems to have opened the outside door of a small west side
balcony with a key. The key was left in the door. He climbed over the railing,
which is about four feet high, and jumped...but..."

Bouchet paused again to look out the windows to his left. The view
included the Music History building. We could both see the sixth floor
balcony where this all took place. It was eerie. Bouchet went on, "But the
coroner says there are bruises on Carl's back and the back of his legs. He hit
the railing very hard on the way over. The thing is..."

"The bruising doesn't make sense if he killed himself?"

"Right," said Max Bouchet, "and the inquest is public information. The
press will jump on the physical inconsistencies. And they'll revel in what was
actually in the note. Carl blamed others for his distress."

"Who's mentioned in the note?"

"Those whom you are about to meet, the people on the Tenure Review
Committee. They'll be furious, because much of the note is absolutely untrue.
The press may not make it clear that Carl's note is unfounded. It could hurt
these people's careers..." sighed Bouchet.

"So you want me to find out why Rasmus was being unreasonable and if
this really was suicide or murder," I said, "and if he was murdered, you'd like

me to find out who the murderer was. And you want me to do it before the inquest information is made public?"

Bouchet was beginning to smile. "Guess this is a tall order?"

"Regardless," I said in a businesslike way, "it's what you want me to do. Dr. Bouchet, you have to understand, I can't shield anyone for the good of Irwin College..."

"I know that," he broke in. "Look, I'm new in town and this has been dumped in my lap. I guess that sounds shallow. I'm very sorry about Carl, I didn't know him well but he seemed like a good man and I'm sorry he's dead, but I'm most concerned with the health and safety of the rest of the College people right now." He shook his head a little. "I'm used to success. I have a lot of money. What I want is to be able to concentrate on making the College the best it can be. I can't do that with a cloud of doubt and fear hanging over the whole campus. So, I'm proposing that I will pay your salary personally. That way I won't have to get Board approval, which frankly would not only take too long, but would probably be impossible. Will you do it? What are your terms?"

I explained my fee then added, "I'll give you a detailed accounting of how my time is spent and what the expenses are. If I'm answering solely to you, then I'll give you a daily report, if you want."

"Fine, and I'd also like to propose that if you are able to find the answers you just listed before the inquest, which is next Tuesday, I'll give you a bonus." He mentioned a figure that would easily buy a very, very nice car, "Frankly, I don't know whether that's a good *deal* for you or not?" he asked with eyebrows raised.

"It's a great deal. I work hard on cases and I don't need the extra incentive, but since you offered, I'll take it. Because as you said, this is a tall order. I have a contract form here and I'll need a retainer. And one more thing, I am going to ask tough questions of everyone. Since you're hiring me, people will blame you if they think I'm being ruthless or rude. Do you still want to do it this way?"

"Yes, I do," he said. We shook on it. Then I pulled out the contract and filled it in, including the part about the bonus. He signed it and gave me a retainer check. I gave him a copy of the contract and my card.

"A few things..." I said seriously, "were there fingerprints on the key to the balcony door?"

"Too smudged to distinguish."

"I want to see the note, not just a copy. I'll need to see Rasmus's office and have the freedom to talk to everyone who could possibly have any information. Do you think you can get the police to let me see the computer?"

"I'm not sure if they took the computer out of Carl's office or not. Until we can find out, here's a copy of what Carl wrote. Bouchet handed me a sheet of paper. This is what it said:

To all:

It is impossible to live this sordid life. I know that homosexuals are often murdered by other homosexuals or otherwise die a slow painful death from AIDS, which is God's punishment for immorality.

The Tenure Committee: Knightbridge, Roth, Carvelle, Getty, Anthony, Harmon, Cohen and Smith have done nothing but encourage me to continue in this meaningless existence while they laugh at me behind my back because I am a blind homosexual. I know I will not receive tenure and that I am morally corrupt and alone. Killing myself is punishment for my sins.

Carl Rasmus

Grim and sad. And it sure wasn't one of those notes from mystery fiction that was really written to mean something else and then just misinterpreted by the cops. I stashed the copy in my shoulder bag.

"You're going to tell these people what this note says... today?"

"I have to. It'll be out in the papers by the middle of next week. These people may feel they need to defend themselves. Listen," Bouchet said, dropping all pretense, "I have to admit, I'd really like to be the one who solves this problem. It's intriguing and if I didn't have to deal with the fall out, if this wasn't all so lamentable, I imagine untangling the clues could be interesting."

Whenever someone⁻ suggests solving a murder is *interesting*, it always makes my bullet scars itch. "Uh huh," I said, dubiously.

"Don't worry," he said reassuringly, "I'm not going to get in your way. If this was a murder...Christ...I'm a suspect. I guess anyone is, if they had the opportunity... Carl was arguing one way or another with everyone on the Tenure Committee. I'm still checking but as far as I know not one of them has an alibi. None but Kathryn Anthony. She was in Seattle at the time."

I was absurdly elated that Kathryn Anthony wasn't the murderer.

"Look," Bouchet went on, "Kathryn is on the committee. She knows everyone fairly well, but though Kathryn's been part of the Irwin faculty for years, she's been on an *Exchange of Faculty Touring Program*, set up by the

United States College Cooperative System, the CCS - EFTP they call it, until last September. I trust Kathryn, and I think she might be able to help you."

"Are you going to order her to be a snitch?"

"No, no, no. Not at all, it's not like that," he boomed, "she's just someone who could give you simple information, like who's who. She doesn't have a full load of classes and her grant activity is mostly done for the year..."

"So you're volunteering her time?" I said dryly.

He nodded his head with a deep chuckle, "I'm a bastard when it comes to that kind of thing, and it's even worse than that, because she's my friend. I've known her since grad school. I won't tell her anything else except that you might want to talk to her, how would that be?"

Well, that was true. I did want to talk to her. In fact, a little voice in my brain suggested I ask her on a date, if she were so inclined.

Bouchet looked at his watch. "Time to face the lions."

Chapter 3

As Bouchet and I walked out of his office toward the open door of the large conference room, we were joined by Miranda Juarez, who handed me a piece of paper, "I have made a list of the people you are about to meet. It includes their titles, contact information and job responsibilities on campus," she explained.

"I asked Bart Edgar to make up that list for Ms. Gale," said Bouchet to Miranda pointedly.

Miranda gave him an *Oh, please* look. To me she said, "I am sure you will need other information. Do not hesitate to ask." A model of efficiency. The kind of assistant everyone needs to get all their work done for the good of humanity with time left over to achieve their dreams.

The conference room contained an oval table big enough to seat twenty. One end was near the door we'd come in. The room was freezing. Six people were already seated. Some still had their coats on.

The left wall was floor to ceiling windows with a remarkable view of the half-round drive and more of the campus beyond. I could see the balcony where Carl Rasmus plunged to his death from here, too. Was it just my fertile imagination or were the people around the table avoiding that view. Bouchet took the nearest chair and indicated that I should sit next to him. Miranda Juarez sat to Bouchet's right.

"Miranda," said Bouchet, "why is it so cold in here? Please, turn up the heat." Miranda got up silently and fiddled with the thermostat. Bouchet looked at his watch. I glanced at the clock on the wall. It was almost 2:15 PM. Connie Robinson came in balancing a tray of soft drinks in bottles and cans. She put the tray on a little table at the far end of the room.

"Ah, thank you Connie." Bouchet raised his voice and said expansively, "Here are the beverages you all enjoy." He sounded condescendingly *Lord of the Manor*. He was back to the *Mr. President* persona. Was he trying to hook these folks with free sodas?

He turned a little and watched Connie come in again with a plate of cookies, which she put on the table in front of us. They were Pepperidge Farm! Wow, top dollar. Hey, I'm a ho for good cookies. I was hooked. I scooped up a Bordeaux and a dark chocolate Milano.

The two women and four men already seated got up and went to the back table to get their soft drinks. Bouchet, Miranda, and I stayed in our places. There was quite an array of drinks but just one per person. There was a bit of soft-drink gridlock, because the space near the back table wasn't very roomy. After each of the folks had finally snagged their pleasure, remaining on the table were, a can of diet cola, and bottles each of iced tea, Cafalatte, Lifeline Organic Juice, and spring water. Bouchet turned to me and asked if I wanted anything. Of the things left on the table, I chose the water. But when Bouchet called my order to Connie, she brought me a water from the reception area. I guessed the water on the back table was for someone else.

"Still a little early," said Bouchet. "Whom are we waiting for?"

Miranda Juarez, ever the efficient assistant said, "Dr. Georgia Smith and Prof. Daniel Cohen."

"And Kathryn, I believe," said a precise-voiced, older woman sitting to my left. She looked sharply at me. I'd seen her many times before in the Mews. She had long gray hair pinned up in a coil at the back of her neck and skin tanned from years of outdoor exposure.

"Kathryn did make it back in time, but she had to rush to Harrisburg, so she won't be attending," said the President. Someone exhaled. I couldn't tell whom.

A man with flaming red hair, sat just beyond the imposing woman on the left side. I recognized him now as Jimmy Harmon, Irwin's one nationally famous professor. Even at the young age of 42, he had an amazing body of successes to his credit. He'd created two classic Broadway shows that were destined to be performed in high schools and little theater forever, but could pull in crowds on Broadway with each revival. He'd written a pop TV theme and composed a rock opera. He had also recorded some of the greatest collections of American folk music to date and written about them in an engaging yet scholarly way. He was dressed in wild mismatched clothes, including bright orange overalls that echoed his "I Love Lucy" hair color.

He said excitedly, "To Harrisburg? Has the satellite grant gone through?"

"Yes, yes it has. Kathryn is helping the Governor with the press release," said Bouchet.

Everyone seemed pleased. I heard someone say, "Well, that is wonderful news."

I took out my small laptop computer and opened it on the table. I put the list of people Miranda Juarez had given me on top of it and quickly typed the names into a spreadsheet.

A man and woman entered the room. Miranda had indicated the late people were Georgia Smith and Daniel Cohen, so I checked off their names.

There were now eleven people at the table counting me. Bouchet didn't pull any punches as he began the meeting, "There has been a very serious development regarding Carl Rasmus's tragic death."

Heads shot up. Bouchet had everyone's full attention. He explained in a general way that the autopsy did not fit well with the original presumption of suicide. He added that information from the coroner's inquest would be made public sometime next week.

"We have planned a memorial service for Carl on Sunday, in the College Chapel along with the regular service at 11:00 AM. It will help the students... and the rest of us deal with the shock of Carl's death by celebrating his life. I hope you will all attend." He made it clear that absence was not an option.

"And there is something else as well," said Bouchet. He turned to Miranda and she handed him a sheaf of papers that he passed around to everyone. "This is a copy of Carl's suicide note. It may be made public as part of the inquest evidence. As you can see, everyone on the Tenure Committee is named and Carl blames us all and himself for his unhappy life and untimely death."

As everyone scanned the note, I heard the words, "Slander, libel, obscene, preposterous, ridiculous, and crap," said with various intonations and emphasis.

An expensively dressed man at the end of the table said, "Max, this is really too much," in a pompous way. Georgia Smith's eyes glistened.

Bouchet said, "Yes, I know, what Carl says here is unfounded and untrue. And what he says about himself is... odd. That coupled with the facts of the autopsy has brought me to a decision." He indicated me. "This is Maggie Gale. She is a private investigator who comes highly recommended. I have hired her to get to the truth of this matter. She will be..."

A black-haired woman in round-rimmed glasses sitting at the far right end of the table stood up. According to the list she had to be either Dr. Amanda Knightbridge or Dr. Rowlina Roth-Holtzmann. She interrupted angrily with a German accent, "Max, really, of this you cannot be serious," she eyed me. "This is not the cops and robbers. Carl killed himself, there is no mystery. He was an unfortunate young man with demons. He could not..."

"Rowlina, please hear me out," Bouchet commanded in a semi-roar. Dr. Rolina Roth-Holtzman bit back the rest of her words and flopped back into her seat.

Bouchet resumed in a quieter yet still commanding rumble, "Yes, there are many reasons to believe that Carl's death was exactly as it seemed, but there is now room for doubt. There must be a very careful investigation, more careful than the police are willing to undertake."

"May I ask," said the imposing woman to my far left whom I could now identify as Dr. Amanda Knightbridge, "has the Board approved this investigation?"

"Yes, Amanda, you may ask and no, they have not. I have hired Ms. Gale on my own and will be paying her fee personally. In some ways that may not be the correct *procedure,* but the Board will not meet for another month and a half and that is too long to wait. I believe if you all think back carefully you will remember that Ms. Gale worked on a case here at the college a few years ago. She solved the problem of the thefts from the technology department. She was a police lieutenant at the time." He stopped speaking and looked around the room.

Amanda Knightbridge nodded, "So, this is Ms. Gale? I was on sabbatical at the time but I remember some very glowing accounts of her success. I can see why you are putting this in her hands."

Bouchet nodded gratefully to Dr. Knightbridge, "I appreciate your cooperation. Ms. Gale will be interviewing each of you," he said, "please introduce yourself and briefly explain your position at the college," he gestured to me to continue.

I said before anyone could express further shock, "I'd like to speak to each of you in person over the next two days, my time is flexible so if you can tell me now when I may come to see you, that would help."

"Very well," said Bouchet, "I've already introduced myself so we'll go on to Miranda." He looked to his right. Miranda Juarez gave her name and title. She mentioned that she was not on the Tenure Committee but I wanted to speak with her anyway, so we agreed on 9:00 AM the next day.

Next around the table was Daniel Cohen the Head of the Fire and Safety Engineering Department. He was tall, about 55, and had curly gray hair. He wasn't fat, but he'd have to be careful counting the carbs. His intelligent ruddy face was noncommittal. He seemed comfortable and casual in sport jacket, tie, and khaki pants. He'd taken off his overcoat when he came in and hung it on the back of his chair. He explained the function of his department, making it clear, in an understated but slightly long winded way, that it was a significant part of the College, that impacted fire and safety codes throughout the Country. Cohen checked his list of appointments. He suggested 2:00 PM,

Wednesday and explained that his office was across the street.

Next up was Bart Edgar who seemed to have forgotten we'd just met minutes before. At the time, I'd labeled Edgar a nerd. The label still fit but I was appending, inefficient and incompetent to the description. I couldn't believe anybody could be such a dolt. Maybe it was an act, covering up the wry intellect of a Shakespearian fool? Yeah, right.

Edgar explained at length that he was not on the Tenure Committee, then attempted an explanation of his job. He did this all in unfinished sentences, with the logic of a frictionless puck. The more uncomfortable he felt, the more he giggled. While Edgar snickered his way through his narrative, I looked around the room and noticed several of the men tugging their collars. The women were doing the female equivalent; they were looking at their nails.

Sparking universal relief, I interrupted Edgar myself, "Do you have any time free to speak with me?"

Edgar began shaking his head, "Time... um, there's a meeting..."

I asked, "Before or after the meeting?"

He looked at his calendar, then said, "I could email you?"

I said, "You mean you have no time before or after your meeting?"

He stared at me. Then he looked down. "2:00 PM?" he suggested. That was the time Daniel Cohen had just arranged. I glanced at Cohen who had his hand over his eyes and was gently shaking his head.

I said to Edgar, "How about 3:30?"

"3:30 *PM*? he asked.

Resisting the urge to scream, *No, you idiot, 3:30 in the morning!* I just nodded. 3:30 seemed to be OK, because he began to bob his head and mumble affirmative noises.

Cutting to the chase, Miranda Juarez turned to me and said rapidly, "Bart's Office is on the third floor of this building, room 310." I nodded and typed it into my schedule. People around the room sighed quietly in relief.

The last person seated on the right side of the table tersely introduced herself as Dr. Rowlina Roth-Holtzmann. The Germanic accent was still strong but less strident. Her hairstyle was Edith Head, complete with bangs and a jet-black dye job. Nobody her age, which was mid-fifties, has hair that color. In fact nobody of any age has hair that color. It looked like the tip of a black magic marker. Her face was powdered white and she was thin as a stick and hunched up like a crab. Rowlina Roth-Holtzmann looked like the kind of person who'd always feel cold. She was still wearing her coat, though it was unbuttoned. It was very dark gray wool and way too big for her.

"Between 4:00 PM and 5:00 PM tomorrow I have time. I am not free after 5:00 PM. My office is in the Architectural Design building, of which department I am the Chair. The building is called also Fenton Hall."

While everyone was looking at Rowlina Roth-Holtzmann, I stole a look at Jimmy Harmon. I'd heard he was a kind, sweet and a bit wacky guy. But at this minute he had an expression that would sour chocolate milk and it was aimed at me. Scowling there in his odd clothing and flaming red hair he looked like a bad dream circus clown. Since no one was watching me but him, I stuck my tongue out at him. His demeanor changed immediately into a silent horse laugh, which was charming, but a dramatic mood swing.

Jimmy Harmon's pale skin would sunburn in a second, even faster than mine. His black-rimmed Buddy Holly glasses looked cool on him, but his nose was runny. He didn't seem sick though. I wondered if Harmon was a nose candy connoisseur.

He sniffed and said unnecessarily, "I'm James Harmon, the Head of Music History. My office is in the Music History Building. You'll probably want to see Carl's office, so let's go over there after this meeting. We can talk and you can see the scene of the cri..." He stopped, looking sincerely shocked. He shook his head mumbling, "Shit, I'm sorry."

I said, "OK, Mr. Harmon, we can do that. Thank you."

Dr. Amanda Knightbridge was next around the table from Jimmy Harmon, watching him with obvious maternal concern. Yet there was a transcendental depth in her eyes. As her expression faded into polite attention I flashed on seeing her in the summer, tending the Mews' Rose Garden, decked out in an elaborate gardening hat and smock. I'd imagined she was just a neighborhood character who didn't have anything better to do than pick Japanese beetles off American Beauties, but according to the list, Dr. Amanda Knightbridge was the Chair of Irwin College's Art and Architecture History Department.

She said simply, "Thursday at 10:30 AM? My office is in Clymer Hall, that's 320 College Street." But there was an intensity about her that briefly filled the room. She nodded once, then focused on Georgia Smith, who was next along the table.

In her mid-30s, Dr. Smith was younger than the others. She'd slipped off her winter jacket and put it in the chair next to her, then taken off a wool hat and patted her Dorothy Hamill wedge hairstyle into place. She was wearing a functional beige colored *wash-n-go* polyester suit, which contrasted in style to the yin-yang pendant and woven feather Indian necklace she was wearing around her neck. She also had uncut crystal earrings that dangled almost to her shoulders.

Up until this moment, Georgia Smith had been intently reading over the copy of Carl Rasmus's suicide note. When she felt the attention in the room shift to her, she looked up. Her eyes were shining. "Karmetic sign..." she murmured touching her feather necklace. Not everyone was close enough to hear her; Amanda Knightbridge put her hand on the young woman's arm. Georgia Smith focused, said she was the Assistant Dean who coordinated Freshman Studies, then flipped open her electronic calendar and offered Thursday at 10:00 AM as the first time she had free.

"I have freshman conferences every half hour," she explained. "I'm sorry I don't have an earlier time... and I don't know if I can give you any information." As attention shifted along the table to the next person, Dr. Georgia Smith picked up Carl's note to read it again, touching her necklace absently.

"I'm Leo Getty, Dean of Students," piped the next person. His tone was far less formal than all the others. He was wearing a baseball cap with the College's name on it, and a bright orange knit shirt. He said with an open hand gesture, "I'm free almost anytime tomorrow. My office is one floor below this, next to Bart's. Room 308. I liked Carl a lot. I'll help anyway I can."

Dr. Leo Getty was the first one to say he liked Carl and wanted to help. Everyone who'd already spoken realized they should have said that too, and probably now felt like crap. Getty had a classic Pennsylvania Dutch face, big hands, and a load of pent-up energy. I figured him to be about two years from retirement, but not wanting to go. He fiddled with his empty soda can and the papers in front of him as he spoke.

"11:00 AM tomorrow then?" I suggested.

Leo Getty smiled and said, "I remember the work you did when you were here before." He said to everyone, "This gal and the rest of the cops really pulled the College's *you know what* out of the fire," he turned back to me, "it's too bad you left the police force, the city needs good cops. Yeah, 11:00 will be fine, I'll see you tomorrow."

Sitting between me and Dr. Leo Getty was Dr. Skylar Carvelle. What a total suck up. He faced Bouchet and said pompously, "And of course Max, I cared a great deal for Carl and will help you, the College and, uh, Miss Gale, in every way possible..." At about 45 Carvelle was something of a dandy. Definitely *designer* from collar to socks. His skin was so evenly tanned, it must have been airbrush. His hair and carefully trimmed mustache were tightly styled. He was wearing a full-length soft black leather overcoat which probably cost more than every article of clothing I'd bought in the last decade. He smoothly stood up to take it off, as though modeling.

Topping off the presentation was affected speech. Carvelle sounded English but wasn't, in a William F. Buckley / Madonna kind of way. Oddly, he also reeked of cheap aftershave, which didn't really go with his image. Maybe it was coming from Leo Getty or Jimmy Harmon. It was so strong it filled my nostrils like the laundry detergent aisle at the supermarket.

He turned to me and said unctuously, "I'll certainly have several inside pieces of information to share," and then he actually winked at me. Carvelle insisted he couldn't meet until Thursday because he had to be in Philadelphia all day. "I'm the head of the Art Department," he said by way of explanation. How that explained being in Philly, I couldn't figure. He indicated 9:00 AM and made a point of saying he would have to come right over from the gym.

I looked at my full calendar for the next two days. Plenty to do. First I'd go with Jimmy Harmon to see Rasmus's office, then I'd go back to my office and do some preliminary checking on all these people before I met up with them in their own lairs.

President Bouchet stood and said sincerely, "Well, thank you all for coming, I deeply appreciate your cooperation."

Most of the people moved slowly to the door. It was a little after 3:00 PM. Not too long for a meeting of academics. There was still work time left in the day.

Leo Getty stopped in the reception area to talk to Skylar Carvelle, but Carvelle seemed in a hurry to go. Daniel Cohen was standing near Miranda Juarez's office door talking to her and President Bouchet about some kind of new State safety requirements. Georgia Smith was still sitting in the conference room staring at the copy of Carl Rasmus's note.

Getty and Carvelle moved apart. Carvelle seemed ready to bolt for the elevator but then I saw him duck into the men's rest room. Amanda Knightbridge and Rowlina Roth-Holtzmann had pressed the elevator button. Jimmy Harmon was with them. The elevator dinged. The three of them got on and the doors closed. Getty missed the elevator, shrugged, and took the stairs.

Bart Edgar came out of the restroom in a hurry, darting back across the reception area. Georgia Smith finally stopped reading Carl's note, gathered up her things and was nearing the door when Edgar ducked past her, speeding back into the conference room.

Georgia Smith was standing in the conference room doorway, looking toward the President, Miranda, and Daniel. She seemed lost in thought. Over

Georgia Smith's shoulder I could see Bart Edgar at the far end of the conference room. He bumped into a chair, and then kneeled on it, straining to reach over the chair's back for something on the rear table. And then it happened.

There was a blinding flash. Then a deafening boom. Followed immediately by an explosion of bright orange flames bursting out the conference room door. It blew Georgia Smith into the air toward me and the President's office. When she hit the floor she was screaming and kicking her legs. Her clothes were on fire. Green-blue flames enveloped her body giving off an eerie alien glow. Now everyone was yelling.

Things seemed to slow down. Scenes registered in stop action, like a flickering old time movie with half the frames left out. In that split second I wondered if an electrical short had caused the fire, or if it was terrorism. I saw Daniel Cohen run down the hall. He yelled, "Fire! Get out now! Use the Stairs!" He grabbed a wall-mounted fire extinguisher and hit the fire alarm.

After only a tiny moment of hesitation I saw Max Bouchet run into his office. He shouted, "Miranda, get the extinguisher from your closet!"

I saw myself... running toward Georgia Smith. For a tenth of an agonizing second I looked around desperately for a blanket to smother her burning clothes. Then I was covering her with the silk Asian rug that had been in front of Connie Robinson's desk.

In the next moment Connie Robinson leapt over her desk to help me. Georgia was no longer on fire but she was screaming in agony. Her legs were hideously black. I couldn't tell what parts were skin, but I could smell the intermingling odors of smoking plastic and burnt flesh. In the few seconds of flame, some of Georgia's synthetic no-iron clothing had melted onto her body. Thank the long dead Persian carpet makers that their rug was silk and not polyester too.

The fire alarm was blaring. I jumped up and looked around. Smoke was billowing into the reception area from the conference room. The crackling sound of burning became a roar.

Daniel Cohen was using a fire extinguisher at the entrance of the conference room. In a second he was joined by Max Bouchet who had his office extinguisher. The room was filling with an acrid black fog. The synthetic fibers in everything from the drop ceilings to the last-forever-wall-to-wall were giving off a horrible choking stench. Flaming globs of molten acoustical tile were falling from the ceiling like buckets of burning mud. Wherever they landed, the carpeting burst into flame.

There were pools of fire all around the room, mostly at the far end. And then I saw Bart Edgar's body on the floor partly under the distant end of the oval table.

I could see through the dark smoke that much of the floor area around the table was burning. At that instant a glob of ceiling tile fell to the floor inches from Bart's body igniting the carpet next to him. Cohen and Bouchet had managed to put out the fire nearest the door, but the area around Bart was too far for their extinguishers to reach.

Miranda Juarez was running from her office carrying another small extinguisher. Connie Robinson had produced a bucket of ice from somewhere and was sliding it on Georgia's legs while trying to pull her toward the stairs. The electrical system failed, the lights went out, but emergency lighting blinked on in seconds.

I grabbed the small extinguisher from Miranda and pulled the release in the handle to activate it. I yelled, "Get out!" at Miranda who turned toward the stairs. Skylar Carvelle peeped out of the men's room. Without hesitation Miranda grabbed him and pulled him toward the exit.

I pushed my way between Cohen and Bouchet and threw myself through the doorway under the table. It was the only area not in flame. I commando crawled under the table keeping my nose to the floor where the freshest air was supposed to be. As it was, the air was a terrible mass of stinking roiling smoke and scorching heat. I held my breath.

I reached Bart and sprayed him with the extinguisher. I grabbed his collar and dragged him the rest of the way under the table, dodging a piece of flaming ceiling tile as it fell on his shoes. I sprayed him again with the extinguisher putting the tile out. He still wasn't moving.

I dragged him most of the way to the door by crawling backward and pulling his arms. My lungs felt about to burst and my eyes stung. Bouchet crawled up beside me as Cohen covered him with his extinguisher. A glob of molten ceiling tile hit my shoe, bounced, and set the hem of my jeans on fire. Cohen bent down and put me out with his extinguisher. Then he crawled forward to help us.

Just as Bouchet, Cohen, and I got Bart to the edge of the table near the door, the sprinkler system went off. The flames died down in seconds and the air quality cleared a tiny bit. We dragged Bart out and Cohen slammed the door to the room. Spray from the ceiling system and my own stinging tears ran soot into my eyes and made me shake my head like a Labrador retriever.

I rolled Bart flat on his back and leaned my ear to his mouth. "He's not breathing," I shouted. I heard Daniel Cohen yelling... then a deafening crash of shattering glass. Fighting off the urge to cough, I pulled Bart's chin down, pinched his nose, and blew with all my might into his mouth. Daniel Cohen crawled over to compress Bart's chest. Bart took a big gasp, coughed and sputtered, then began to breathe on his own.

Fire truck sirens filled the air. There must have been dozens of them outside. I was coughing now, unable to stop. Firefighters and EMTs began to flood into the space. I rocked back out of the way so they could work on Bart. Others were helping Georgia. The next thing I knew, I was outside in a truck with an oxygen mask over my nose and mouth.

My face was hot and my hair singed, but I figured I wasn't burned or they would have rushed me to the hospital. Other ambulances were driving away. I was sure Bart and Georgia must be in them. I desperately wanted to know if they were going to be all right. All sorts of people stood around asking what happened in what sounded to me like incredibly stupid voices. Paramedics were questioning me about my condition. I let them. I answered by nodding or shaking my head.

I saw Max Bouchet. He was refusing to get in an ambulance, pushing off the EMTs. I took off the oxygen mask and stood up. The paramedics didn't want me to, but I told them I had to talk to that guy. I pointed at Bouchet.

When he saw me, he smiled. I did too. We were OK, and we were both happy about that. Bouchet's pinstriped jacket and power tie were gone, his shirt, beard and hair were thick with soot. His handmade black Gucci shoes were whitish gray with ash. I probably looked pretty bad too. I looked down and saw that my black suede mocs were in the same condition. Of course these shoes had cost me $19.50 on sale at Sears while Bouchet's had probably cost him about what I'd paid for my first car.

I pointed to the ambulance truck and said to him, "Get in, we have to talk... right now."

He scanned the chaotic scene, nodded once, and got in.

Chapter 4

President Bouchet and I couldn't say much on the way to the ER. In the ambulance we'd been tossed around like dice in a Yahtzee cup all the way to the hospital. Luckily it was only 12 blocks.

They rushed us into separate examining areas with a curtain between us, to wait. They'd do a few tests, monitor our vitals, and a doctor would come in, take a look at us and tell us to go. Then they'd charge our insurance companies a thousand dollars each... probably more.

In the curtain-walled room on my other side was Georgia Smith, she was screaming in pain. In between screams she was refusing the painkillers. I opened the curtain and made my way around to her head, keeping out of the way of the emergency workers, I leaned and spoke evenly in her ear. "Georgia, let them give you the drugs. It will allow you to reach a different level of consciousness; that's where you need to be right now."

She heard me and it registered. She bit her lip and nodded. Her lip began to bleed. I turned to the nurse with the needle and said, "She'll take the drugs now."

Max Bouchet had frantically tried to call his wife on his cell phone, but inside the hospital he couldn't get a clear signal and they wouldn't let him go outside to make a call. It was making him a basket case. I could hear him arguing. I yanked open the curtain to his space and said, "Max, chill," like a dog command...*Rex, sit*. Bouchet's expression of anger and frustration broke like a cloud and he smiled.

I said, "By the way, from now on, after what we've been through, I'm calling you Max. You can call me Maggie. I insist. And if my insurance doesn't cover all this, I'm putting it on my expense sheet." Which reminded me that I still had Bouchet's check in my shoulder bag, but I didn't know where the hell my shoulder bag was. I didn't even want to consider what might have happened to my laptop.

"Maggie," he said simply.

"Don't tell the medical staff, but I must have passed out for a few minutes, because I don't know what happened between getting Bart Edgar out of the room and ending up outside with an oxygen mask on. Can you fill me in?" I asked quietly.

Now that he had something to do, he seemed less agitated. He took a deep breath. His voice rumbled up like he was telling a theater of people a bedtime story. "Well, let me see...yes I think you did lose it for a while. I think you held your breath for about 2 minutes while you were dragging Bart out and that must have made you light-headed." His rich tones were carrying all over the place. People in the waiting room could probably hear him.

I hissed insistently, "Will you keep your voice down...geez, they'll hear you!" I paused to listen but no one came in. "OK, go on, but keep it down." I made one of those palm down pushing gestures. And then put my finger to my lips, making the international symbol for *Shhhh!*

We sat in two chairs, he said in a whisper loud enough to hear across a ballpark, "You were sitting on the floor breathing well, but I noticed you had a glazed look. The medics pulled you aside. One talked to you and you stood up and walked out with him. If you were *passed out* then, you did a great imitation of someone who was fine."

"What happened to Bart?"

"The EMTs took him and Georgia downstairs on stretchers. Georgia was talking, well, screaming really. Bart wasn't talking, but he was alive. They put an oxygen mask on him. I'm sure they rushed him to the burn unit...Damn, I want to call my wife...what if she hears about this on the news!" Bouchet punched his hand for emphasis.

To get him focused again I asked, "What about Daniel Cohen?

"Oh, Daniel's fine. Just dirty and tired. They may have him here to check him." Bouchet looked around as if he might be somewhere in this examining enclosure with us, but we just hadn't noticed him. Stupidly, I looked around too.

He continued, "Oh, here's something else...just seconds after the EMTs took over for you on Bart, Daniel yelled that we needed fresh air in the reception area. He picked up one of those chairs by the window. He yelled, 'Stand back!' Then threw the chair at the glass, but it just bounced off. So get this..." Bouchet was smiling shaking his head, "Connie Robinson runs in out of nowhere and grabs that marble stand that was next to her desk. The damn thing must be close to two hundred pounds. She hefts it in the air and hurls it five feet into the window. Smashing the glass completely... All our jaws dropped open." Bouchet chuckled, "Oh man, you should've seen the look on

Dan Cohen's face. It went from incredulity to total admiration in one second. And before that, did you see her with the ice for Georgia? When we got outside, I asked her how she knew what to do and she yelled that she was a Girl Scout! You know, I'm gonna have to give her a raise."

Something was going on at the nurse's station. I opened the curtain. It was Miranda Juarez. In a tone of concern and relief Miranda called, "President Bouchet, are you all right? I am so glad to see you." There was genuine emotion in her voice, as she walked toward us. "And Ms. Gale..."

"Miranda, are you all right? I need to know what's happening," said Bouchet emphatically.

Miranda Juarez snapped into her efficient assistant role immediately. Her hair didn't even seem mussed. She actually took out a small steno notebook and flipped it open. "First, I want you to know that I called your wife."

"Thank God," sighed Bouchet rubbing the back of his neck in relief.

"She was on her way here when I got her. I told her you had not been seriously injured in the fire because I had seen you standing and talking with the EMTs outside. I hope it was all right to say that to her?"

"Yes, yes, I really appreciate it. Thank you so much, Miranda."

Miranda nodded and went back to looking at her notes, "The news people are outside. They want a statement, and I think you should speak because if you do not, it will be...harder for you to..." she hesitated.

"It will be harder to keep media speculation out of the story. Yes, I see," finished Bouchet.

Miranda merely nodded.

"All right, I'll speak to the press, but first I need to know if there is any information on Bart or Georgia's condition."

"Alive, but very serious. I have contacted Georgia Smith's husband Adam Smith already and he is here. I found that Bart listed Alicia Wellington as his Aunt. I contacted her, she is in Palm Springs." There was a note of surprise in Miranda's voice. She didn't bother to ask if this was the same Alicia Wellington the new library wing was named after.

"Very well, tell the TV crew I'll go on the news live, and then let me know when they want me. I need to get cleaned up and I need to speak to Ms. Gale for a minute." Miranda Juarez didn't have to be told anything twice. She left the emergency area to return to the press.

Bouchet immediately faced me and said, "What do you think? What was this?"

I said simply, "I think it's related to Carl Rasmus's death, but I don't have any idea why."

Max Bouchet said, "Well I can't say that to the press but yes, it could be. I'm doubling your bonus. Find out who did this and stop him..." then as an after thought he said, "or her?"

Miranda came back in to say the press people were ready. She had a clean suit jacket for Bouchet. *Where the heck did she get that, does she carry his clothes around in her car?*

"Oh, and Ms. Gale," said Miranda, "I brought your shoulder bag." She had my brown leather bag under her other arm. She handed it to me. I could see that my laptop was in it. I could have kissed her, but I was too dirty.

Someone burst into the emergency room. It was an attractive African American woman in a business suit with a look of distress so palpable it hurt my heart. She began to say something to the desk nurse but then she saw Max Bouchet standing next to me.

"Oh, Max!" She rushed to him. They hugged and kissed for a full minute. She was so overcome she couldn't speak except to cry, "Oh, Oh."

Bouchet made consoling noises then looked into her eyes and said in a strong direct voice, "I'm all right Shanna, really." Then he said to me, "Maggie, this is my wife Shanna Allen." He turned back to Shanna and gestured at me, "Maggie's a hero."

I shook hands with her and said, "Max is too, but he has to go on TV right now so he can tell a thousand parents their kids weren't hurt."

It was the right thing to say. Shanna Allen nodded and went into the waiting area with Bouchet. Miranda followed. I heard Max talking to the press. He was in his element. He managed to convey that everything was safe and well at Irwin. Anyone watching would be completely confident that President Max Bouchet was in control. This guy should be the president of a country, I thought, he should be the President of this country.

A minute later the doctor came in and told me my chest x-ray had shown no smoke damage and I could go. I was glad that Miranda Juarez was a model of efficiency, because now I had my cell phone.

Outside I called Sara's cell but it was on voice mail, so I left a message saying I was all right. My sister Rosa was out of town so I figured I could call her when I got home. I called the office where Evelyn told me both Sara and Emma were in court. Evelyn said, "Where are you?"

"Evelyn listen carefully, I'm at the hospital, but I'm OK." Evelyn said, *Ohmigod,* several times as I explained what happened.

I still needed a ride home. It was 14 blocks on a dark December night and I didn't even have a scarf. In fact, my new jacket, hanging on the reception room coat rack, was probably ruined. Another expense account item. Damn,

I'd really liked that jacket. I called my best friend Farrel Case. Before I could even get past, "I'm in the hospital..." Farrel and her partner Jessie were on their way to pick me up.

Both Farrel and Jessie leapt out of the car to hug me after they pulled up at the hospital. Farrel, who is taller than I am, a little over-weight but strong looking in a traditional old time lesbian way, and Jessie who is smaller, slighter and quieter than Farrel, kept asking me if I was all right and I kept saying yes. It was a pain but it's also nice to have friends who really care.

I was in the front seat with Farrel driving. I was telling them the story of the fire like I was on a rollercoaster and had to be finished before the ride was over, still on a rush from a successful life saving situation. Cops can begin to crave this sort of thing because the adrenaline high is addictive. Half way through the second recounting, Farrel rolled down the car window. I barely noticed the freezing air blasting in.

She shouted over the icy wind, "Do you know how bad you smell?"

"Why? What do I smell like?" I asked, because I really couldn't tell.

"Like a burning pile of used tires," said Farrel.

"Not even *new* tires?"

"No, definitely used," said Jessie who was sitting in the back seat holding her nose.

"Maybe with a bucket of model airplane glue mixed in," said Farrel.

"Uh huh," said Jessie, "and there's a little essence of ...what is that...?" she sniffed, "industrial solvent?"

"Yes, exactly," said Farrel.

"Yeah, OK, I get it. Take a shower when I get home," I said.

Farrel said, "Take two."

"You'll never get that smell out of your clothes," said Jessie.

I looked down. I was streaked with soot and tar-like stuff. "I'll trash 'em," I said decidedly. "I wonder if I can save the shoes?"

"No," said Farrel and Jessie in unison.

When we got to my place, Jessie made me dinner while I took a shower and put on clean clothes. I was starving. While I ate a broiled mushroom and red pepper sandwich with a generous layer of Jarlsberg cheese, I told them the story of the fire all over again until they insisted I talk about something else. So I told them about meeting all the people on the Tenure Committee. Farrel, who teaches woodworking and furniture design at the College, knew most of them already.

"I'm sorry about Bart and Georgia," said Farrel. "However, I have to say, Bart is one of the stupidest guys I've ever met. He's a disproof of the Peter

Principle because he's risen way, way above the level of his incompetence. Does that sound too mean, since he just got hurt?" I shrugged so Farrel rolled on, "Amanda Knightbridge always seems to perceive things. She's nice, but she can be uncanny. Georgia Smith is kind of odd. I think she takes her job very seriously and does it well, but she's so naive about life!"

"Explain," I said.

Farrel ran her fingers through her short gray-blond hair thinking, then said, "She's a good person and all, but I think Georgia wants to be perceptive like Amanda Knightbridge. Georgia thinks you get that way by being all new age and mystical. She goes on vision quests and fasts and meditation retreats. Her current husband Adam seems like a nice guy but I think Georgia wants a Svengali. She's looking for the *answer.*"

"What's the question?" I asked half humorously.

"Georgia doesn't have a clue. Enlightenment could bitch slap her in the face and she wouldn't recognize it."

I told them about meeting Kathryn Anthony.

"I've met her at the college. She's really something, isn't she? Kind of electric, and that voice! Do you think she's gay?" Farrel asked.

"I was going to ask you."

"Why don't you ask her?" said Jessie intelligently. "What does she look like?" We described her and Jessie said, "I think I've seen her in the neighborhood, she might live in one of the apartment houses, the Hampshire or Dakota."

"Let's *google* her," Farrel said.

I got my laptop, plugged it in and searched her name. "Lot's of women's studies stuff...and work on gay and lesbian history in one of her on-line bios...seems promising."

Jessie said, "Why don't you just ask her?"

Farrel and I scanned the list of articles, then Farrel turned to me and said, "You could always ask her."

Jessie slapped her forehead, "I just said that twice!" Then she muttered, "Nobody listens to me."

"Because it's more fun to sleuth," I said yawning. "Hey, don't you have to go to a show in North Carolina sometime soon?" It was only 9:00 PM but I was suddenly very tired.

"We were packing when you called," said Jessie. "It opens Wednesday."

I shook sense into my head, "Wednesday's tomorrow! When are you leaving?"

"Well, you called..." said Farrel.

"Oh my God, you have to go now!" I looked at my watch, "You'll have to drive all night!" Like many antique dealers, Farrel and Jessie just did high volume shows. They packed up their stuff, set it up at a show for a few days, sold stuff, bought stuff and then packed it all back up and came home. Sometimes the shows fit in between Farrel's classes. Sometimes Jesse did the shows on her own.

They reminded me that Cora Martin, their elderly next-door neighbor, would be looking after their black cats Griswold and Wagner, but I'd have to shovel their walk if it snowed. Cora was also an antique dealer, but usually did different shows. They often took turns watching each other's pets. Cora had a yippy little dog named Cynthia.

I thanked Farrel and Jessie profusely. Before they left, Farrel took me by the shoulders and said very seriously, "Are you sure you're all right?" Farrel is ten years older than I am and Jessie is almost 20 years older. I consider them part of my family, they feel that way too.

"Yeah, I'm OK, thanks," I said hugging them both.

A few minutes after they left, the phone rang. It was Sara.

"Are you all right? Do you want me to come over? Were you hurt?" she asked.

"I'm OK, but I was right there. I'm a hero. I saved people...but now I'm totally tired." I yawned again wanting to hang-up, but Sara made me tell her the whole story.

"Maggie this all sounds very creepy. Do you think Carl was murdered?"

I said yawning again, "Maybe...that's what I'm supposed to find out..." I yawned again, even bigger this time, I was crashing. "Look, would you call Rosa and Emma and tell them I'm OK?" (Our sister Rosa is a court reporter, she'd be hearing about the whole thing in no time from people at the courthouse.) "I really am very tired and I don't feel that great. Don't tell her all about the case though. Should we call Mom?"

"Mom's in Thailand..." said Sara conversationally.

"Mom's in Thailand!?!" I jolted back. My stepmother was always full of surprises.

"Yeah, *spur of the moment* trip, two days ago."

"Well, I guess I don't have to worry about her hearing about the fire on the radio...*yawn*." By now I could barely stand, I really needed to go to bed.

"Right." Then Sara said with sincere concern, "Are you sure you're OK, querida?"

"Uh huh, just sleepy...coming off an adrenalin high. Have you...*yawn*...done anything about Mickey?" *Huge yawn.*

"I'm working through the arguments for his arraignment, *yawn,* geez Maggie, you're making me yawn! Go to bed querida, I'll talk to you tomorrow."

I went into the bathroom and noticed it smelled a little like a pile of used burning tires. The odor came from the shoes I'd left on the floor. I put my shoes in the trash bag I'd thrown my stinking clothes in and carried it downstairs to the curb. It was bitterly cold. The dark sky was cloudless. I looked up at the stars for a minute and took a deep breath of arctic air, which did nothing to cure my exhaustion. My smoky lungs ached. I made a wish on one of the stars. I always do that when I take the garbage out. I went back upstairs and stumbled into bed. I fell asleep immediately and slept for five hours. Then, I was suddenly wide-awake and very hungry. I got up and made a peanut butter and jelly sandwich and ate it at the kitchen table looking out the windows over the Mews. Going over the day, I tried to remember each thing that happened before the explosion.

I thought about Carl Rasmus falling six stories through freezing December air to the cold hard sidewalk.

I went back to bed. On the edge of a dream I could hear Dr. Kathryn Anthony's alluring voice. I just barely sensed her handshake again.

Chapter 5

When my alarm went off at 7:30 AM, I was stiff and sore and my lungs hurt when I took a deep breath. I took another shower because my hair still smelled like burning tires, albeit *new* burning tires. After the shower, I seemed to be stink free. I wore Nikes because my work shoes were now in a landfill somewhere and my leather jacket because my parka was undoubtedly a melted stink sponge, unfit for human use. I also brought along my 9 mm Berretta. I don't always carry a gun. It's too easy to kill people with them. However, my profession requires heat. I have licenses and as a matter of fact, I'm a good shot. I got a medal for marksmanship when I was on the force. Whether the explosion at Irwin yesterday was an accident or not, I was packing a burner.

Miranda Juarez waved me to a seat when I arrived to interview her at 9:00 AM. She was using Bart Edgar's office, because Edgar was still in the hospital. Miranda was on the phone.

"Si bueno, pero es importante que tu vayas a las classes todos los dias, hijito...Si, mañana. Si, para la cena. Hasta mas tarde, querido."

She was speaking to a child, probably her grandson, telling him he had to go to school every day, and that she would be having dinner with him soon. From her tone, she obviously loved this child very much. She hung up.

"I'm glad you're here Ms. Gale, the President wanted me to give you this as soon as you came in." She handed me a small piece of paper. It said Daniel Cohen had been speaking at a conference in Virginia during the time Carl Rasmus died. Bouchet was letting me know that if Carl was indeed pushed, Professor Daniel Cohen had an alibi.

"This is Bart Edgar's office. I dislike not being in my own." Miranda gestured at the papers in the corner. "Those were on his desk. I feel guilty just moving everything to the floor, but I will go through all the papers and get them in order."

I opened my mouth to make a comment but she sighed, "Please do not say that you are sure I will be able to straighten out all of Bart's..." she waved over at the papers. "You will be the sixth person to have done so this morning."

I nodded sympathetically, "Bart does seem to have...issues. Anything new on his or Georgia Smith's condition?"

"First thing, I must tell you that Dr. Leo Getty will not be free for your appointment this morning. He must attend a meeting. He asks to meet you this evening in his office after 5:00 PM." I nodded as I changed my schedule on my laptop. "I will relay the confirmation to him. Yes, you are right," Miranda agreed, "Bart has...as you say, *issues*. I had no idea how he got to this employment level, until yesterday." I understood her meaning; nepotism was the glue that held Bart in his job. "Georgia Smith's injuries are more serious than Bart's, however, both were very lucky. Especially lucky that you were willing to risk your life."

I shrugged like Gary Cooper, but skipped saying, "Tweren't nothin."

She went on efficiently, "Georgia Smith received third degree burns, her synthetic clothing melted onto her skin. The burns are very serious but they do not cover much of her body. The back of her right leg was the most injured. She is in extreme pain and under heavy sedation." Miranda shook her head, then went on quietly, "It will be a long recovery, months, and there is risk of infection."

I nodded, "Anything else?"

"The firefighters think it may have been an accidental gas explosion from a pipe in the wall. Fire reached almost everything..."

"How was Bart able to dodge the impact of the explosion?"

"Shielded by something, perhaps..."

"Yes," I said thinking back, "I saw him." I formed a mental picture of yesterday. "Bart was reaching toward the back table, but he was kneeling on a chair, leaning over the back of it."

"Ah, well, he frequently chose the illogical way. It appears choosing the illogical way saved him this time. And he was wearing an all-natural fiber shirt. His arm...it was burned, but not like Georgia's. It turns out Bart is allergic to synthetics, so he does not wear them."

"He was unconscious...not breathing."

"He was thrown back. He had a concussion. He was very lucky that you, President Bouchet and Professor Daniel Cohen got him out when you did. It may have been the fumes that caused him to stop breathing, the CPR you performed was critical to his rescue. As it is, he may have to take several weeks off to recover. He will need therapy for the burns on his hand."

"Do the fire inspectors or the police have any more theories?"

"They were here much of last night but they say nothing yet. Do you want to go up there? " she asked, glancing at the ceiling.

"Where's Max Bouchet?" I asked.

"His personal office, in the President's mansion."

I paused then asked, "Would you say Bart's mistakes make people angry?"

"No hay duda." It was the Spanish idiom for, *No doubt about it.* Then her eyes widened and her veneer of composure slipped. "You think someone may have been trying to...to ...kill Bart Edgar...because of some stupid thing he did? It was an accident, was it not?" she asked incredulously. "I find this hard to comprehend."

"Ms. Juarez, isn't what happened yesterday and what happened to Carl Rasmus, generally hard to comprehend?"

She pulled herself together and said, "Yes..." she thought for a moment, then began again slowly, "last month Bart was working with a fundraising committee with Professor Jimmy Harmon. It had to do with the preservation of old time music from the...is it *"Ozark"* Mountains?" She pronounced it Oh-sark.

"Ozark," I said with more of a zee sound.

"Ozark," she repeated. "Bart had volunteered to be in charge of invitations. This was to be a $1000 dollar a couple black-tie event. Professor Harmon gave Bart all the information written on a sheet. All Bart had to do was give the sheet and the design to the printer. But he did not. For some reason he rewrote the information into an email. As time got closer, Professor Harmon asked Bart if he had checked information with the printer. Bart said yes, which was not true."

She went on, "The printed invitations, which were embossed and goldleafed, were reviewed at the next meeting. The date and time were wrong. Even the name of the event was misspelled. Professor Harmon was furious, he called Bart names, he moved to hit Bart, but others restrained him. Professor Harmon walked out of the meeting and called out that they must cancel the entire performance."

Huh, quite a shadow on Jimmy Harmon. I asked, "Have there been other people...?"

"Yes, many. It is Bart's job to provide each of the departments with enrollment data to project costs and apply for state reimbursement. Every Department Chair has had strong words with Bart due to serious mistakes in his data. You see, these mistakes make the Department Chairs look inefficient. Most produce the data themselves, now."

"Can you tell me if any of the other Tenure Committee members have had problems with Bart Edgar?"

"Ms. Gale, he irritates everyone."

"How does he irritate you?"

She paused looking at me, then said honestly, "He volunteers for jobs he does not have time to do and then either does not do them, or makes a mess of them. At the same time, he excuses his poor job performance by saying he was busy doing the things he volunteered to do. Frankly, I think his best choice would be to claim disability from these recent injuries."

I nodded. "What can you tell me about Carl Rasmus?"

"Dr. Rasmus did his work, he was pleasant, but just a few months ago he began to change. He became rude and I guess you would say paranoid. Then he would calm down again. He yelled at people and accused them of odd things. He sent very rude emails."

"Was any of this directed at you?"

"No...well, one mass email he sent to everyone in Administration and the Tenure Committee. Very bitter. That was just a day before he killed himself."

"How well did Carl type, I mean, was it possible that some of the email he sent or received was just poorly written or had typos...?"

"Yes, that can happen. Someone writes I *can* go, when they mean to say I *cannot* go...but the tech department set up a voice translation system for Dr. Rasmus. He could talk into the machine and it would write his words and read them back to him. Quite amazing, really. He had the technology to know just what he was writing. The words were not mistakes. They were from a very angry and sad man."

"Do you know anything about his personal life?"

She paused searching her data bank brain, "Not really." She seemed disconcerted that she hadn't been able to answer a question fully.

"Do you remember where you were when Carl killed himself?" I was planning on asking everybody this question.

"Oh...I..." she reached for the desk calendar and flipped to the previous week. "Yes, I was in Becks County, arranging for the production of the next College Catalog at the printer in Doonestown. I left at 12:30 and returned at 6:00. I went directly home, as it was so late."

This was not a great alibi for her. If indeed Carl was murdered, she had a window of time.

"The drinks Connie Robinson brought in on the tray, what was the procedure for that?"

Miranda Juarez was unfazed by the change of subject, she said, "President

Bouchet has just started that. He feels that the personal attention makes people feel valued. Everyone who regularly attends a meeting has already indicated what his or her beverage preference is. We have a small refrigerator in the storage room next to my office. Connie gets the list and fills the tray with the choices of those attending."

"What's your preference?"

"I usually have water in a bottle but I left it on the tray. I'd just had coffee," she added as an after thought, "the President drinks iced tea."

"President Bouchet told me there had been witnesses near Carl Rasmus's office on the day of his death..."

"Two students and a graduate assistant," said Miranda Juarez. "I have their contact information here."

I glanced at the sheet she handed me. The undergrads were: Caitlyn Zale and Mike Jacobsen. The grad assistant's name was Jack Leavitt.

"I'd like to look at the top floor now."

She gave me the keys. I left the well-lighted office and climbed the stairs to what was now a burned-out disaster scene. The reception area was a shambles. The police had sealed the conference room with a piece of yellow tape across the door. I didn't really think the thin piece of plastic would keep anyone out, but I couldn't imagine why anyone would want to go in. It stank. Would I ruin another of my clothing ensembles, just by absorbing the smell, the way one's clothes do in a smoky bar?

Looking in the conference room, I had a flashback. When I'd been in graduate school, a small house I'd rented with friends caught on fire during a rainstorm from an electrical short in the attic. Luckily, we were all out for the evening. One of my roommates, Adrienne, had a girlfriend who was quite a bit older than the rest of us. Come to think of it, she was the age I am now. I digressed for a moment wondering why a 35-year-old woman would want a 19-year-old girlfriend, but that wasn't the point of the flashback.

This "older woman" had given Adrienne a gift of a spice rack, complete with two dozen bottles of assorted spices. The rack hung on a wall in the kitchen but the girlfriend was over protective of it and constantly insisted Adrienne and the rest of us not *waste* the spices by using them. It became an in-house joke, but we did painstakingly conserve them, thus making all the food we cooked consistently bland.

After the fire, the fire department let us back in to salvage what we could. When I went into the kitchen, I called to Adrienne that we didn't have to worry about saving the spices any more. She asked why. I pointed. Not only was the spice rack gone, so was the entire wall it had been hanging on. The wiring in the kitchen wall must have ignited too. When we looked up, the ceiling and roof were gone as well. There was a moral in there somewhere about the spice rack, but the real lesson was: Fire Is Scary.

In a way, the Irwin Administration Building conference room now looked more horrifying than when it was actually on fire. Maybe because I had more time to think about it. A large section of the ceiling was gone. Tarps covered the torn open roof. The fire department must have cut it away to be sure the fire was out. Part of the back wall behind the table where the drinks had been was now just a large hole with twisted metal behind it. Everything in the room was black and sooty. Splintered furniture parts stuck out at odd angles like greenstick fractures. File cabinets lay on their sides. Shards of glass crunched under my feet. Another tarpaulin hung over the broken window area, but a sharp December breeze buckled it into the room. The wind was stirring up rank odors and wet grit.

It was easy to see how the fire had spread. The pattern of blackened scorch marks resembled a childlike charcoal drawing of the sun. The irregular rays generated from a round blackened area at the back table.

The chair Bart Edgar had knelt on was lying on its side. The back was charred, its plastic arms melted. But the area directly above the chair was fairly untouched, as was the area where Bart had fallen to the floor. The phrase, "gods protect little children, drunks and fools," seemed particularly apt.

Nighttime temperatures were forecast to drop below freezing. Puddled water on the rug would be ice before dawn. I marveled that I hadn't seen more water damage to the ceilings of the floor below, but then Bart's office wasn't under this part of the building.

In a heap on the floor next to the coat rack, was my once beloved parka, filthy and stinking of burnt rubber. I left it there. Good thing my good gloves hadn't been in the pockets.

The reception area window was smashed where Connie had tossed out the marble stand. I pulled the tarp to one side, interested to see if the stand was still on the ground below the window, but it was gone. Good thing it didn't hit anybody. My mind segued for a moment to Carl Rasmus's dead body on the sidewalk.

I had hoped looking at the fire scene would give me some profound insight. It didn't, except the fire pattern seems more like a wide slash than a blow out. I took out my laptop and rested it on Connie's not too dirty desk. I made a few notes about events leading up to the explosion. I also noted that Miranda didn't have an alibi for Carl's death and that according to her, Jimmy

Harmon had tried to punch Bart. Miranda was a fount of information, maybe I should have quizzed her about Kathryn Anthony... *so Miranda, does Dr. Anthony live with anyone?* But then, Jesse Wiggins voice echoed in my mind, Why don't you ask her?

When I returned the keys to Miranda, I noticed that half the pile of Bart's papers on the floor was gone. It was nearly 11:00 AM.

Chapter 6

Since Leo Getty had rescheduled, my next appointment was with Daniel Cohen at 2:00 PM. Plenty of time to walk home, check some things in my office, look over my notes, then hop in the car and speed over to Sears to replace my dearly departed jacket. I wore the new parka to the meeting with Cohen.

I was a little early, so I darted over to the Student Union and snagged a pre-made sandwich of Swiss cheese and lettuce on a hard roll. Not many choices left by nearly 1:50 PM. I mused that my choice for a meeting beverage would probably be a Stewart's Root Beer in a glass bottle. Stewart's would always win my vote in a blind taste test. I thought again about Carl Rasmus. He'd had such a promising future...he died too soon. At that moment, I made a promise to Carl. I would solve the case and ring out justice, in his name. It sounded like a folk song, but I meant it.

Daniel Cohen's building was on the other side of Washington Street facing the Administration Building. The Environmental Safety Building had soaring angles, projecting cantilevers, and all the outside surfaces were mirrored glass or polished steel. I liked the irregular negative space it created. The inside lobby felt vast, because there was a spectacular outdoor view in every direction. Pipes running along the ceiling were polished sculptural bronze. There were bright lights and splashy colors, with giant posters and even some neon. It had the feel of a high style mall, which must have made many teenaged students feel at home.

Professor Cohen's office door was painted red. Inside the secretary ducked her head into the door behind her desk when I explained who I was, then said genially, "Go on in." She seemed happy and enthusiastic. Maybe it was reflection of the way Cohen ran the department.

"Nice office," I said taking in the glass wall view, then eyeing at a shaped canvas painting by Frank Stella on the wall by the door.

"Yeah, it is isn't it?" he smiled. "The painting's part of the College's permanent collection. I don't even want to know what it's worth. More than my house, probably. Have a seat." The chair was a museum reproduction of Le Corbusier's "Wassily" chair, made of steel tubing and leather.

Cohen was casually dressed in a sport jacket. He was the kind of guy you instantly thought of as a dad who'd fix your car or hang up a basketball hoop in the driveway. There were playful models of 1940s trucks on a shelf and neat piles of papers, folders and documents on almost every other surface in the room. A photograph of two attractive women, probably his wife and daughter, was on the desk. There was also a large computer with a huge monitor.

Daniel Cohen's ruddy round face broke into a warm smile, he reached out with one of his large meaty hands. He and I suddenly felt a comradeship that neither of us expected. We'd faced death as a team just the day before. It was like we were part of the Justice League. I smiled too, gripping his hand for a moment with both of mine.

"You were at a two day conference on fire safety in Virginia at the time Carl fell from the balcony?"

Cohen chuckled, "I guess giving a keynote address in front of 500 people is a pretty good alibi."

I said directly, "I think the explosion had something to do with one or more of the bottles that were on the back table of the conference room. But, you're the fire safety expert, what do you think?"

"Me too," he said simply, but then he began to digress into the way fire inspectors work and that he shouldn't jump to conclusions.

"Daniel," I stopped him, "I'll bet you have some pretty strong opinions about what happened already, and you probably trained all those fire inspectors yourself, didn't you? Have you spoken to them?"

"Confidentially?" he asked. When I nodded he went on, "My guys, who happen to be on the fire team called me. Some of the State guys just want to chalk this up to a back flow gas tank leak, but that's not how it started, not what I think anyway. My guys on the inspection team say there was accelerant in one or more of the bottles on the table and Bart managed to tell the police at the hospital that there was a bang when he lifted a bottle. The cops aren't taking him seriously though."

"I saw him."

"What?" he asked with raised eyebrows.

"I saw Bart pick up the bottle... Well, I saw him reach for it. I couldn't really see the bottle."

"And there was a bang? "

"Yes, well...there was a flash and then a bang," I said slowly.

"Good, then that fits. I think that when Bart picked up one of the bottles, the movement somehow triggered or detonated a small explosion."

"Before the fire started?" I asked typing the information into my laptop.

"See, all over the internet, you can easily buy baby M-80s. It's not legal to buy the old fashioned M-80s any more, but you can buy fireworks that have just under 50 grains of blast powder, anywhere. The old M-80s were really dangerous, they were equal to a quarter stick of dynamite, but 50 grains still gives a real kick," he explained. "The bottle exploded and the flaming accelerant in the bottle splashed across the room. There was a tiny pocket of natural gas in an old pipe in the wall. It wasn't connected to anything any more, but it exploded too, from the heat from the fire. The pipe was secondary though, it was the bottle that caused the damage. That's what I think anyway."

"How could the bottle go off just because someone touched it?"

"It's not too hard. There are detonators for sale on the Internet. Even a homemade device wouldn't be too complicated for someone to fashion. It just has to make a good spark. Static electricity or a battery in a sham bottle base. The spark would ignite an immediate fuse made of something like flash paper, which would touch off a couple of M-80s. The bottom of the bottle would explode and the liquid and fumes that were in the bottle... it would have to be flammable, like gasoline or lighter fluid, even paint thinner... would be ignited. If it was compressed in the bottle, liquid would be propelled all over the room. That room itself was a fire hazard, way too many flammables, those old ceiling tiles certainly weren't up to the current code, and the carpet was so incendiary, it might as well have been kerosene..."

"This bottle bomb...would it be hard to make it?"

"Unfortunately no. Look," he swiveled his computer screen toward me, "I found this at a site called: blowitupquick.com."

I shivered involuntarily. It was a mechanical drawing of a plastic soda pop bottle with a detonator and directions on how to make it. "This is really creepy. Could anybody do this?"

"It would be very dangerous. Fumes can easily ignite... some of the fire inspectors combed the room for hours looking for detonator parts. All they found was a little watch battery. I think a tin foil pressure switch with a flat battery could have made the spark that set off the M-80s." He paused thinking, then went on, "I didn't answer your question... yeah, anybody could make this. So I guess the next question is: Who would do it?"

"Let's just think about who *could*. This is the time frame...Max Bouchet told Connie to unlock the door to the room when the tenure committee began to show up...”

“Yeah, they're a lot of confidential files in that room. The doors have to be locked all the time,” Daniel explained.

I nodded, then took the list Miranda Juarez had given me out of my shoulder bag. The paper smelled like the fire. “When I came into the room: Bart Edgar, Dr. Rowlina Roth-Holtzmann, Dr. Leo Getty, Dr. Skylar Carvelle, Professor Jimmy Harmon and Dr. Amanda Knightbridge were already there. Then Miranda Juarez, Max Bouchet, and I came in together. After that Connie Robinson came in with the drinks on a tray and put them on the back table. She left, then came back in with a tray of cookies. Everyone in the room got their respective drinks except me, Bouchet and Miranda. Connie brought me a water from the reception area. You and Dr. Georgia Smith came in after that, but neither of you got your drinks.”

I paused, he nodded. I continued, “After everyone was done getting drinks, there were five bottles left on the back table.”

Cohen interrupted, “Were they all plastic bottles?”

I formed a clear picture in my mind of the back table. “Yes. There was, a water, a Diet Coke, a Cafalatte, some kind of organic juice, and an iced tea.”

Cohen said, “The Diet Coke was for me, I always have that, but since I'd come in late I didn't get it.”

“Could someone have set up the bottle bomb and then left it in the refrigerator so that Connie would put it on the tray without knowing it was explosive?” I asked.

He glanced at the sky through the glass ceiling. Then he turned to the bomb diagram and ran his fingers through his curly hair a few times.

“Nope.”

“Why?”

“Too volatile. That is if we're presuming it went off with Bart just picking it up. Connie couldn't have taken it from the fridge, put it on the tray, carried it in on the tray, picked it up again, and then set it on the table without setting it off. No way.”

“What if Connie knew it would blow up, could she have carried it in carefully?”

I'd surprised him with that one. Connie didn't seem like the type. On the other hand she'd been amazingly decisive and capable during the fire. He finally said, “Yeah, I guess, she could have been careful to hold the bottom on and keep the contact in place, if she's known...” He suddenly looked shocked at what he was saying. “Oh ...no... look, I'm not saying I think she did it! We have no idea what really happened..."

"But if the bomb was in a bottle, then the *bomber* would have had to carry the armed bottle carefully to the back table, put it on the table and then take away the corresponding bottle Connie had brought in, along with their own drink."

"Seems tricky to do," said Cohen imagining the scene. "I wasn't there when people were carrying their drinks back to the table, did you see anyone acting strangely?"

I thought, then shook my head, "Under this theory, we're talking about; Connie Robinson, Rowlina Roth-Holtzmann, Skylar Carvelle, Jimmy Harmon, Amanda Knightbridge, and Leo Getty."

"Oh God, I can't believe any of them would try...wait, there's one more," suggested Cohen.

"Who?"

"Bart."

"Would he blow himself up on purpose?" I asked incredulously.

"Well, maybe, or he could have been trying to take the device away and it went off... or..." Cohen put his chin in his hand and though for a moment, "or, he could have intentionally been trying to injure himself..."

"Why?" Then I saw his point. "You mean to be in a position to get disability rather than getting fired? That would be so risky! It would be stupid to attempt it."

"Bart shielded himself with the chair, but yes, it would have been stupid. However, if you ask most people, they'll tell you that Bart's not exactly the best tuned truck in the bay, he's clumsy too."

"But then that would be saying an idiot did this job and whoever did this at least was careful and paid attention to details and wasn't clumsy," I said.

"I don't think that describes Bart," Cohen said dryly.

I nodded, "OK, cross out Bart. Too bumbling. But heck, the whole room went up in flames. It injured someone in the doorway! If the *bomber* was in the room, he or she could have been killed. Seems stupidly risky."

Daniel Cohen was in his element now. He explained, "Amateurs rarely gauge the amount of explosives they need correctly. They almost always over dose. I'd guess this psycho, whoever he or she was, had planned to just kill the person picking up the bottle. As a matter of fact, if you read this schematic and the directions here on the screen," he indicated diagram, "it says this device is for targeting one person you want to get rid of without collateral damage. It's a ridiculous claim. This was a fire bomb after all, with fire anything can happen...and it did."

"This has been very helpful, Professor Cohen," I closed my notebook.

"Wait...about Carl, I'm going to be frank, I'm a PFLAG dad. Know what that means?" he looked at me closely.

I nodded and smiled, "Yeah, my parents are too."

"Thought so. Look, I would have said, from what I knew of Carl ...that it's hard to believe he'd write that note. He didn't seem like the kind of a guy who hated himself, even with those erratic emails recently. Maybe he was on drugs or something that made him not himself. It all just doesn't make sense."

Chapter 7

It was a little after 3:30 PM when I finished with Daniel Cohen. I'd given him my card in case he had more ideas.

Twenty-five minutes to get over to Fenton Hall to meet Dr. Rowlina Roth - Holtzmann. I had a feeling, based on her general lock-step attitude, that she wouldn't tolerate lateness. First though, I wanted to ask Connie Robinson the receptionist, some quick questions.

I took a short cut to the Administration Building by bisecting the half circle drive. It was getting colder. The sky had turned gray and heavy. A yellowish cast of waning afternoon light made the campus seem surreal. No question about it, Frosty the Snowman was on his way.

As I got near the door to Miranda's temporary office I heard two voices, both tense and angry, coming from inside. One was Miranda's.

"You must leave. I do not want you to come here again," said Miranda. The fear in her tone surprised me.

"You think you can tell me what to do?" sneered a man's voice, "I tell *you* what to do. Understand!"

Miranda shrieked. I sprang into the room. A middle-aged man was twisting Miranda's wrist, her face showed pain, but when she saw me, an even more painful look infused her features.

The man was ugly with rage. When he saw me he dropped Miranda's arm, and wheeled on me. "What're you looking at, bitch?"

Miranda's mortification was evident. Her dark even skin tone blanched. She'd been uncomfortable with this man in her office, but a witness made her utterly humiliated.

The man was an inch or two taller than I. His skin was wind-burned red from long hours outdoors. His greasy light brown hair was uncombed, and he looked way beyond the point where *needed a shave* would adequately describe the condition of his face.

I stepped in close to him. He stank of stale whiskey, bad breath, and unwashed clothes. "Time to go," I said in a low no-nonsense voice.

"Oh yeah?" he taunted, a master of repartee.

"Yeah," I said catching his wrist and twisting it behind his back. I spun him around and pushed him off balance toward the door. He did a stumble run trying to right himself, but fell, catching his shoulder painfully on the frame. He hit the floor in the hall, whacking his knee again against the far wall.

Someone down the hall poked his head out of an office to see what was going on. Two maintenance workers, a man and a woman both in coveralls, advanced from the elevator.

All these spectators made this cowardly bully think more rationally. It wasn't just him against one small woman any more. He elbowed his way through the crowd, heading for the exit. We could hear his uneven footsteps echoing down the stairs.

I moved back into Bart's office, closing the door behind me. Miranda was sitting behind her desk. She didn't look up.

"Who was that?" I asked softly.

Miranda slowly raised her head, a portrait of deep chagrin. "My ex-husband. He...he comes around here sometimes. I have told him not to. He needs money. He has not been able to find a job, it is not his fault..."

My mouth fell open. I couldn't believe this capable woman was sticking up for that asshole. Her self-esteem and assurance were gone, replaced by a part of her she normally hid.

"What's his name?" He wasn't Latino, so I figured Juarez might be Miranda's birth name rather than her married name.

"Cedrick Sheldon Druckenmacher. He prefers to be called Shel," she said it as though his preference was the priority.

"He comes around ...frequently?"

Miranda just shook her head. She didn't want to talk about this at all. She wanted to pretend it hadn't happened. She was straightening papers on her desk in an efficient way, doing her best to repress the last few minutes.

"Miranda, there are places that support women who are treated harshly by..." But Miranda shook her head again, and I realized that right then at least, there was no point in pushing Miranda about Druckenmacher. She was too desperate to act as though it hadn't happened, too practiced at denial. So I said, "I'd like to speak to Connie Robinson about a few things that happened yesterday. Do you know where she is?"

"Connie went over to the President's house to take him some papers. Then I think she was going to go home. Is there something I may help you with?"

said Miranda crisply, desperately relieved that the subject had changed.

I'd wanted to ask Connie about the beverages but since she wasn't there... "I need to take another look upstairs and I'll need the key to the storage room, too." Miranda handed over the keys.

It was even colder up there than before, and the high stink of decay was stronger. The power was still off, no electricity, no lights. Luckily not the entire bank of windows was covered by tarps, but the rapidly setting sun was creating deep shadows. Fortunately the storage room had a window, so I could see without a flashlight. It was relatively clean and neat in there. The fire and its aftermath hadn't touched it.

I opened the refrigerator. The inside of it was warmer than the air in the room. No little refrigerator light came on. It was full of drink containers of every type. Every kind of soda, from cream to quinine. There were open twelve packs of diet and regular Cokes. There were juice boxes in all flavors, two unopened three-packs of Cafalatte, and a six-pack of Stewart's Root Beer in bottles! I could have asked for one of those, who knew? There were bottles of water, both local and *designer spring*. Opened six-pack cartons of Lipton Iced Tea and Life Line Organic Juice were on a lower shelf. There was milk and half and half. There was even Grape Nehi. Were there actually people who drank that stuff?

No wonder Connie needed a list. On the counter top was the tray. I imagined her staring at the list then reaching into the fridge to get each bottle she needed.

It was so quiet in there. No electricity, no white noise. No buzz of fluorescent ceiling fixtures, no constant refrigerator hum. Two copy machines sat noiselessly in one corner. The hands on the electric wall clock by the window were frozen at 3:09.

Snowflakes were falling past the window outside. The President's office and the big conference room faced south. The storage room was on the north side of the building, overlooking the campus quad.

I took a few steps closer to the window to watch the silent white flakes drift four stories to the ground below. I could see a few people scurrying along the sidewalks, wrapped in coats or jackets, heads down against the swirling wind. Coming from the far end of the quad were a man and a woman walking toward the Administration Building. They stopped at a sidewalk intersection and stood talking as the snowflakes floated around them.

The man's flaming red hair identified him immediately as Jimmy Harmon. The woman was Dr. Kathryn Anthony. I felt the recognition of her physically.

It was a curious feeling, pleasant and uncertain at the same time. Even from this distance I could feel how attractive she was. Her movements were graceful; fluid hand gestures, smooth nods of her head. I watched as she and Harmon spoke. He was waving his arms dramatically. She was shaking her head. They both laughed. As they did, she momentarily touched Harmon's arm. They each turned. Harmon went to the right. Kathryn Anthony went to the left. I watched her as she disappeared into a building.

I suddenly became aware that time was passing and I would be late if I didn't tear myself away from the window and the view Kathryn Anthony was no longer in. I locked up, went back downstairs, and gave Miranda Juarez back the keys.

"Do you always give Connie a list of what drinks to bring everyone?" I asked quickly when Miranda looked up from her keyboard.

"Yes, that is the process. Actually, Tuesday was the first time we used the new drink policy."

"When people were getting their drinks at the back table, did you notice any of them doing anything out of the ordinary?"

She thought a moment. "No, I can't...some people took longer than others, but I couldn't say who did so."

"Did you send out an email asking people what they liked to drink?"

"Yes, exactly, and we were surprised that almost everyone answered. Some people asked for odd things, others wanted just the regular: Coke, Pepsi, water, that type of thing. One person asked for chocolate milk. That struck me as very funny, I think it was Professor Harmon. When we had everyone's preference, Connie went out and purchased a supply of each. It took her an entire day to do it."

"Have you noticed anyone hanging around the storage room in the last few days, who didn't belong here?" I watched her as she considered the question.

"No," she answered after a moment's thought.

"I'd like to get into Carl Rasmus's office later this evening. Do you have the key?"

"No, the President had the room padlocked. He has the only key."

"I'll go over to the President's house later, right now I need to know how to get to Fenton Hall." As Miranda Juarez wrote down Bouchet's private number on a card, I noticed the pile of Bart's work in the corner was now completely gone. She gave me concise directions to Rowlina Roth-Holtzmann's office in the Architecture Building, I said thanks and burned shoe rubber to get there just in time.

Chapter 8

Dr. Rowlina Roth-Holtzmann stood outside the Architectural Design Building smoking a cigarette. It was snowing, cold and getting dark. She had her *too-large* coat on and a fox fur hat that was more like a muff with her head in the middle. Her severely cut black bangs fringed the reddish fox, outlining her face. Her lipstick was a red slash against her powdered white skin. The cold made her draw in, shoulders hunched, arms folded like crab claws. She propped her elbow on her wrist to hold her cigarette just inches from her mouth.

"We will speak out here. The building is *smoke free*," she said as though *smoke free* was an abomination.

"OK," I said incredulously. I flipped up my parka hood. The dropping temperature threatened teeth chattering. I fought to relax my jaw. There's no dignity in sounding like a wind-up plastic novelty.

"Though you have done successful work for the College before, I am not in favor of this investigation. It is the President's money though, and does not come from our budgets. He has asked that I cooperate, so this I will do," snapped Dr. Roth-Holtzmann.

"Carl Rasmus, let's talk about him..." I asked not bothering to correct her statement that I'd worked for the College; I was on the police force then, not working for the College.

She said in her best imitation of a female Eric Von Stroheim, "It is cold, I must go in." She threw her cigarette butt on the ground, savagely grinding it with her heel into the snow alongside a dozen others that were equally smeared with red lipstick. It was OK to make a pile of disgusting garbage, but God forbid it would smolder a second in a puddle of slush. Geez, what a neurotic.

I followed Dr. Rowlina Roth-Holtzmann into the building. It was a magnificent example of 1930s period Bau Haus style, probably designed by one of the top German Bau Haus designers, Walter Gropius maybe. Every detail in the building was form following function, from the polished wood window handles to the geometric carpeting, even the lettering on the office doors displayed careful mechanical simplicity.

Rowlina Roth-Holtzmann bee-lined to her office. As she shook off her billowy coat and sat behind her desk, I noticed a leather couch designed by Eileen Gray against one wall and a small "Wiener Werkstatte" ceramic head of a young woman in the bookcase. Rows of large books lined one wall and a huge flat screen Mac computer sat on her desk. Beside the desk was the biggest color printer I'd ever seen. There was a very small original Leonora Fini composition of collage and watercolor on one wall. Well, at least she has good taste, I mused.

A family picture of young Rowlina and her parents hung on the wall in one corner. There was no image of the illusive Mr. Holtzmann. Hmm, interesting.

"I did know Carl," she resumed still sounding mechanical, "when he first came here he seemed a nice hard working young man, regardless of his lack of sight."

Implying that lack of sight could make him a not-nice young man or not hard working? I wondered.

"It was recently that he began to act in a strange way," she went on, "he sent emails that were ill-advised. When I asked him what he meant by one of them, he became angry. It required that I argue with him. It is all very hard to understand." She said the last words in a softer voice, shaking her head.

"Do you remember where you were when you heard that Carl had died?" I tired to be casual. She seemed so edgy; I hoped she wouldn't gather the implication.

"I received a call at home from Max Bouchet late in the day, he told me of Carl's death. I had returned home from a conference the day before. I was tired so I worked at home that day rather than coming into the office."

No alibi, I thought.

"What did you think of the suicide note?" I asked.

"He should not have blamed other people for his circumstances. It does no good."

"And the rest of it?" I pried further.

"Strange... In all the time I knew Carl, I never once heard him mention God. Certainly he never mentioned sins. He did not seem to have any discomfort. He did not feel he had to..." She stopped, avoiding the next word.

"Hide?" I said simply.

She stared at me for a long moment, and then said, "Yes, he did not feel he had to hide. That must have been his undoing."

"We're talking about sexual orientation, right?" I said trying to clarify.

"Sexual orientation?" she repeated as though not understanding the term. Strange she didn't know it, it's in every anti-discrimination statement on every Irwin personnel document.

"Sexual orientation means whether a person is homosexual, heterosexual or bisexual. Everyone has a sexual orientation," I explained.

"I am a married woman!" she said insistently, "I have no sexual orientation, I am married!"

Huh? Oh, I get it, I said to myself. Worried I might think she's a lesbian. What I did next wasn't really the best interview technique, but she was irritating me, so I goaded her internalized homophobia by saying... "How long *have* you been married Dr. Roth-Holtzmann?"

"One year," she said looking away nervously. "My husband lives in Los Angeles."

I wanted to shout, An unconvincing beard, living 3000 miles away! But that was her problem and I still had other questions, so I asked, "What beverage had you requested for the meeting?"

"I...Oh...I had Schweppes Ginger Ale, 10 ounces, in a glass bottle, which I poured into a glass with ice." She pulled the red shawl more tightly around her.

"When we were all in the meeting, do you remember getting up to get your drink?"

"Yes, my 10 ounce Schweppes Ginger Ale," she repeated nervously as though I might erroneously imagine she's had a 12 ounce Schweppes.

"Do you remember anyone acting strangely when they got up to get their drink?" I asked.

She thought for a moment, "No, there was no one in front of me in the queue." Then as an afterthought she said, "But...I do remember, that there was an odor... the smell of solvent. Slight, but I noticed it several times. Some type of cleaning fluid for the carpeting? Perhaps that is what made the fire spread? Why are you asking this?"

"When did you smell it?"

"I am not sure. I do not have the most successful sense of smell, due to allergies."

Yeah, right. Couldn't possibly be due to her smoking like a coal furnace.

She said nervously, "I was in the elevator with Leo Getty and Amanda Knightbridge. We heard the fire alarm. I was afraid the elevator would stop. I have a fear of small places. When we got outside, the fire trucks arrived. We saw the flames." Clutching at her shawl, she asked fearfully, "What was this?" Rowlina Roth-Holtzmann was wound more tightly than a broken Baby Ben. No wonder she smoked like a chimney.

I asked, "Do you have any reason to be afraid for your own safety, Dr. Roth-Holtzmann?"

A look of pure terror flashed over her face, then it was gone. She drew herself up, "No, I have no more reason to be afraid than anyone else in these uncertain times." She said it like something she'd rehearsed.

"Here's my card in case you think of anything else," I said standing.

On my way out, I noticed the metal sign next to her office door with her name on it said, "Dr. Rowlina Roth." The *hyphen Holtzmann* had still not been added, even after a year. Bet that pissed her off. What's the point of a beard marriage if you can't even get a sign to advertise it?

Dr. Rowlina Roth - Holtzmann needed a hard-nosed shrink who'd kick her butt out of the closet, but there was something frightening her beyond Carl's death and the explosion in the conference room. Something more personal. I wondered if she needed protection.

Chapter 9

Dr. Leo Getty was sitting behind his desk eating a huge roast beef sandwich with lettuce, onions, and tomato on a Kaiser roll, when I got there for our appointment at 5:00 PM.

"Maggie!" he called expansively, "come on in, sit down, sit down. Just grabbing supper, didn't get much at lunch, meetings with parents all day." He stood, still holding the sandwich in his left hand, brushing Kaiser crumbs off his shirt with his right. He wiped his hand on his pants before extending it to me. I shook it. He acted genuinely glad to see me.

"Want some of my sandwich? Chips? Hey listen, how are ya, OK? What'd they do to you in the hospital? It was something what you did. Were you a Brownie Scout or what?" he chuckled.

His office was much larger than Bart's. Besides the standard file cabinets and desk, there were tables covered with computer equipment. Monitors, towers, scanners, a large workhorse laser printer, manuals, and a ton of electronic stuff I couldn't identify. On the wall was a chart for a football pool and a Penn State Football poster with the schedule of this year's games. On the floor in the corner were a pile of footballs, some deflated, some seemed smaller than regulation size, and a patch kit and mini bicycle pump.

Getty sat in he the middle of it all. Without the baseball cap he'd been wearing yesterday his straight gray hair was visible. Thick, silver and cut in the shape of a helmet. Hydrant hair with a touch of Moe Howard. To finish off the hydrant impersonation, his 5'7" stocky frame was sporting a bright yellow tracksuit with the college logo on it. He reeked of *straight guy cologne*. Old Spice? Aqua Velva?

"I'll pass on the sandwich, but thanks. Dr. Getty, I want to ask you about Carl Rasmus, but let's just touch on what happened yesterday, first."

"Shoot," he said leaning back in his swivel chair while he took a huge bite of sandwich. Then he said around it, "Call me Leo. Really, it's OK. Look, I'm concerned about all this..." He waved his arm, not able to think of what to call *all this.*

"You're the Dean of Students, right? Are you also in the Athletic Department?" I asked as an icebreaker.

"No, no, I used to coach college football at St. Bonny's in Hadesville, and I still coach Pop Warner in the fall." He gestured to the mound of beat up footballs in the corner. "Gotta fix those up for the kids for next fall, but here I just do administration stuff. Love the game though," he said enthusiastically.

I smiled, "Start with Bart Edgar..." I was booting up my laptop to enter his impressions.

"Excuse my French but Bart's a screw-up...don't get me wrong, I'm sorry he's hurt ...but Holy Mary, the guy can't make a spreadsheet, remember data, compile stats...he was always coming in here asking me to help him get his computer working. Sometimes he just forgot to turn it on! Forget about loading software. And sometimes," Getty was warming to his whine... "He'd screw something up so bad, it would take an hour to fix. Usually I helped, but I was beginning to tell him I was too busy. The thing is, he'd just wait until later and ask me again. Can't figure why he still works here...nope, notta clue. Hey listen, have you heard anything about Georgia?"

"Well, she has serious burns on her legs, but I guess the doctors are cautiously optimistic that she'll recover."

"Oh, geez, well thank God for that, right? Georgia's a nice gal, good with the kids, the students I mean. I knew her first husband, Jacob Elliot. Jake's a good guy. Between you and me, I think she'd have been better off with Jake."

"Why?"

"She has two kids and Jake's their father. He could have went away lots of times, but he stayed with her, then *she* left *him*." Getty shook his head.

I tacked to, "Remember the drinks that Connie Robinson brought in to everybody?"

"Yeah?"

"What did you have?" I asked.

He hesitated. A wave of something passed over his face then he was back to Mr. Affable, "Me? I always have an ATreat. Any flavor. Cola, grape, orange. You thinking someone was drinking something hard?"

"A can?"

"Huh, oh, yeah, a can of ATreat, why?"

"Just trying to keep track of everything. Think about the room and the people getting their drinks. Do you remember anyone carrying more than one bottle?"

"Nope." He paused frowning then looked up and laughed, "You think somebody swiped someone else's drink?"

"What did you do after the meeting ended?"

"Right after? I..." he looked at the ceiling, scratching his head, "I asked Carvelle about some freshmen orientation event, and," he screwed his face up with thinking effort, "oh yeah, I missed the elevator so I took the stairs. The alarm started when I was almost to the bottom. I got outside, then all hell broke loose."

I nodded and made a note, "You mentioned you liked Carl Rasmus. How well did you know him?"

"Oh, I knew Carl for years," said Getty tipping back in his chair, "When I was coach at St. Bonny's, Carl's family lived in our neighborhood. I knew him from a kid. My boys knew him in school..." Getty tossed his head at two photos on the wall near his framed Ph.D. diploma. The pictures were of average looking guys with wives. One had a little girl; the other had a boy about four and a baby.

"Yeah," said Getty proudly, when he noticed me looking, "those are my boys, Leo Jr. and Arnie and their families." He beamed, but I didn't want him sidetracked by the excitement of having his DNA carried on to the next two generations.

"So you knew Carl's family in Hadesville?"

"Went to the same church as us. That kind of thing. He was always blind, didn't have a dad. He did music. It's a shame what happened. He was very unhappy. He told me that several times..." said Getty trailing off, "but you know, a man needs to work things out, even a person who's crippled like Carl. Well, I don't know. I'm just a sports guy who wants to help kids get through college."

"Carl seemed down to you?"

"Depressed. Unsure of himself. Unhappy maybe. Hey, I'm not very good at this, maybe a psychologist could explain better. You know, I don't get a lot of this stuff about depression..." he laughed, "I mean, if somebody came to me and said they're tired all the time and had no energy, I'd tell 'em, lay down and take a nap. Not go spend a year in therapy! I guess that's *politically incorrect* to say. People can take charge of their own lives if they want to, people have free will...but they have to want to. Carl didn't seem to want to. I think that kind of a college professor can be a bad influence on students. Students can be easily influenced."

I nodded, "Yes they can. ...Did you ever get the feeling Carl Rasmus would kill himself?"

"Between you and me, Carl always seemed unstable. I'd known him forever and he'd done some darn abnormal things...I mean even for a blind kid," said Getty candidly.

"What?"

"Huh?"

"What? What did he do as a kid that was abnormal?"

"Oh," Getty ran his fingers through his hair, thinking back. It took him awhile to start talking again.

"Yeah, well, OK, how can I say this... when Carl was a kid he did bad things and other kids would join in with him. He was always doing that. A what-a-ya-call-it... instigator. He got thrown out of school for it," said Getty.

"Carl was thrown out of school? High school?" I said with surprise.

"Yeah, that's what I heard."

"Do you know what high school that was?"

"Uh...Hadesville High, I guess."

"So then what happened to him? Did he go to another school?"

"Well, I kinda lost track and we moved here about that time..."

I made some notes to check into this.

Getty went on, "Irregardless of his past though, Carl made it into a good college and then, you know, did well in college, he got advanced degrees. He got the job here..."

"But then he killed himself..."

"Yeah, that was a shame," said Getty unable to keep emotion out of the last words.

"Do you remember where you were when you heard Carl had killed himself?"

"Huh? Oh, yeah... I spent the day at the football field. They were bringing a bunch of high school kids in for try-outs. I always sit up high in the bleachers and watch that. It's great to see what the new kids can do... wait a minute...are you asking this...to see if I had some kind of alibi or something?" he said with agitation. "I think you're off the track. Carl's note...it was suicide. You know about that, right?"

I nodded. "Dr. Getty, I'm asking everybody where they were that day. It's nothing personal. About the note, what do you think about it?"

"I just read it, yesterday... I guess when a person thinks that way, then they must be pretty depressed. I wish he would have talked to me...I could have talked him out of the whole thing, if he'd just listened."

****

Getty didn't have much more to say. The wind and snow had picked up as I trekked the two blocks to The President's Mansion, a freestanding 1890 Victorian with about twenty rooms that were mostly used for entertaining.

Through the window at the side of the door, I could see Max Bouchet coming past a grand staircase in stocking feet and padding over the polished oak floors to open the door himself. He ushered me into his office, which was to the right of the foyer. Logs were glowing in a fieldstone fireplace. I stood in front of it to counter the outdoor chill.

Over the fireplace was a very old portrait of one of Irwin's first Presidents. According to a small bronze plaque, it was done by one of the Peale family. I was hoping for Angelica, but it turned out to be by the father, Charles Wilson Peale.

There was another guy in the room. Bouchet did introductions.

"This is Captain Harry Dearborne. Harry this is Maggie Gale, I've hired her to help investigate what is happening..." Bouchet gestured with his arm to indicate all that had happened over the last few weeks. Dearborne raised an eyebrow at my involvement. He shook my hand anyway.

"Harry is leading the State Investigation Team," rumbled Bouchet formally. "Harry was sent by the Governor to talk over his findings with me and the local fire inspectors and police." Max Bouchet was letting me know that the State's fire expert was actually reporting to him first, not the local or even state police.

"Harry please tell Ms. Gale what you just told me?" Bouchet said in a polite yet demanding tone.

Dearborne, a big bear of a guy except for the shaved head, was not happy with the idea of talking to me. He wasn't in uniform, but he might as well have been. He wore a nondescript dark suit, white shirt, and Government Issue shoes. He wasn't used to dealing with civilians. I figured he didn't even like talking to Bouchet, much less a *private dick dyke*, but his compulsion to follow orders, and Bouchet's command of the situation, won out.

"We have determined that the incendiary occurrence was precipitated by a small explosion related to a natural gas pocket of non-natural origin in or around the posterior wall of the effected area," pontificated Dearborn in a higher than normal voice for a man of his size.

"How did you determine that the explosion came from a gas pocket and not something else triggering the pocket, like possibly one of the bottles exploding?" I asked. As my internal voice yelled, *why are you ignoring the other facts?*

Dearborne looked at Bouchet who nodded his head. Dearborne plainly didn't want to tell me, but he had to. I had a barely controllable urge to say *nyah nyah, nya nyah nyah*. Luckily, as a trained law enforcer of professional and natural origin, I was able to keep myself in check.

"Well, Miss Gale, there are still one or two other theories pertaining to the origin of the fire. The team found pieces of plastic from a bottle-like-container, both melted and of a non-melted condition, strewn randomly around the area of concern. However, the consensus of the team is that the plastic bottle-like-container pieces, resulted from the wall exploding and propelling said bottles about the room. That is the official position at this time."

"But, was there any evidence of fire accelerant?" I already knew from Cohen that some of the fire guys had found pretty strong indicators the fire was set, but Dearborne seemed to be rewriting scientific history, he must have been a devotee of the far right approach of a certain Federal Administration. Was this guy stupid or just lazy?

"If we find any evidence that indicates there was accelerant in any of the bottles, it is possible that that could lead us to the conclusion that the incident may have been foul-play generated," he said in a confident voice.

My inner voice was screaming, *duh !!!* "Well, surely there would be no other reason for fire accelerant to be in any beverage bottle," I suggested evenly.

He stared at me for a few seconds and then said, "We have not determined that information at this time." I told my internal voice to shut-up because it was giving me a headache.

"Captain Dearborne has to get back to Harrisburg. He'll be leading the rest of the investigation from there and will be back in the area in the next few days. More lab information will be coming in soon, isn't that correct Harry?" said Bouchet.

"Yes, we will access a formal report on Tuesday."

Bouchet walked him to the door.

When Bouchet came back in the room I said sarcastically, "Incendiary occurrence? ...Any other substance strewn thusly in that manner?"

Bouchet chuckled, "Yes well, all professions have their extremes."

"You got the Governor to make that guy answer to you, Max?" Bouchet nodded, I said, "Just how much money did you give to the Governor's campaign?"

Max laughed, "It's good to be rich."

"Uh huh...well anyway, if Dearborne is really telling you the truth about his investigation..." I began.

"I'm confident that's the team's conclusion," nodded Bouchet.

"He's wrong Max, I spoke with Daniel Cohen, the evidence points to a bomb in a bottle," I filled Bouchet in on how Cohen figured the bottle bomb worked and our theory that it was probably someone in the meeting who set it.

Bouchet groaned, "Shit," in a low thundering voice, then asked, "Who did it?"

"Well, seven people went to the back table of the conference room, but we can probably eliminate Bart who doesn't have the wits or nerve to do it. So that leaves six. Rowlina Roth-Holtzmann, Jimmy Harmon, Skylar Carvelle, Amanda Knightbridge, Leo Getty, and Connie Robinson. But this is just a theory, Max, the whole thing could be completely wrong," I insisted.

"What about me, am I a suspect?" asked Bouchet.

"You didn't go to the back table, but you did arrange to hold the meeting, so I guess you're not completely off the map."

Bouchet nodded smiling, "I'm glad you're not letting me off the hook, just because I'm paying you."

"Look Max, this is very serious, we're talking about a killer on campus. I think you should close the College down."

"Maggie, that's a huge decision based on a guess. Most of the students are already gone for the holidays and all of them will be off once Carl's funeral is over, for now, we'll stay open." Bouchet had obviously already made up his mind and clearly he wasn't going to change it. Not right now anyway.

I sighed, "I need the keys to Carl's office. Was the note left on a laptop or desk computer?"

"Carl had both. The suicide note was on the desktop. It's a huge system. The police only took the keyboard to check for fingerprints."

"If the laptop is still there I'm going to take it with me," I said, "I'm sure the police have already gone over it. Tomorrow or Friday I want to go speak to Carl's parents in Hadesville."

"His parents aren't living. He was brought up by his mother, however, she died several years ago," said Bouchet. "Carl has a sister and a brother in Hadesville. They've agreed to the memorial service for Carl here at the College. The coroner hasn't released Carl's body yet, but the brother and sister said we could bury him here in Fenchester when the time comes."

"Will they inherit anything?"

"No, we've just found out Carl did have a will... most people don't. It leaves everything to some kind of organization." Bouchet lifted a note pad from a stack of papers. "It's called Rainbow Youth Symphony of Washington.

We're researching it to find the address. The group won't get much, but of course that depends on what you consider *much*. Carl didn't have a good deal in the bank but there are some death benefits through the college. A year's salary and I think another ten grand, plus a portion of what was in his TIAA CREF retirement and probably anything in his credit union account."

"Well, that must be fairly significant," I suggested a ballpark figure.

"A little more, but not much higher. Still, if you don't have anything, it's a considerable amount for a little not-for-profit. This organization must be very small. They don't even have a web site."

At 8:00 PM I promised Max Bouchet I'd keep him up to date on anything I found out, then took the keys to Carl Rasmus's office and began the trudge through the deepening snow.

Chapter 10

Jack Leavitt scared the crap out of me when he emerged from a dark corner of the second floor recording studio in the Music History Building. This skinny guy in a sweat shirt and ratty jeans, with shoulder length dark hair, gold rimmed glasses and a pallor that was punctuated by a little acne, was either the Music Department Grad Student, or the ghost of music studio past.

Carl's office was off the large recording studio. As I stood in front of the padlocked door, Jack Leavitt made it clear he'd admired Dr. Carl Rasmus. He also gave me some information I hadn't heard. I asked him if *everyone* had gotten along with Carl, Leavitt said...

"Well the students did but, I did hear him yelling at someone on the phone, once and one time he got really angry at Jim Harmon. Right in front of a class."

"Really...what did he say?" I asked him.

Leavitt thought about it and then said, "Um... that Jimmy was a cheat or something like that. Jimmy tried to reason with him. Carl shouted. Jimmy put his hand on Carl's shoulder, Carl pushed Jimmy away. All of the sudden, Jimmy looked like he was going to hit Carl. I was sitting right there so I said, 'Jim, stop it.' Jimmy kind of shook his head and calmed down and then walked right out of the room."

Leavitt had been there on the day Carl died. When I asked him to tell me exactly what happened he said: "I came in at noon, that's my regular time. I brought all the control room panels back to default settings. About 20 minutes later, Mike Jacobsen and Caitlyn Zale came in. They're students. Caitlyn was going to sing and Mike was going to do the tech. Mike's homework really. Caitlyn was just helping him out...Caitlyn and Mike started to work. She was singing some pop ballad kind of thing, she has a great voice. After a while, maybe about 20 minutes later, Carl came in. He had his cane open. I could hear him tapping it. Caitlyn had to stop singing because

Mike was picking up the tapping. Carl said he was sorry to Mike. Um...then...Carl asked if I was there and I called out to him. He said, 'hi.' Then Carl went in his office."

Leavitt told me that even though the doors to the offices were supposed to be soundproof, they were really only about 80%, which made Jimmy Harmon *postal* when he was trying to make a recording because sometimes sounds from Carl's office got picked up. Also anytime Carl opened his door, it spoiled a recording session.

Leavitt told me that no one came in to see Carl, but he suddenly remembered..."Carl may have gotten a phone call."

"Really?" I asked with interest, "you heard it ring?"

"I didn't," explained Leavitt, "but Mike stopped the recording because he heard ringing over the mics. They're pretty sensitive. I'm not sure of the exact time, but Mike would know."

I made a note to check this with Mike Jacobsen, especially because Leavitt told me that Carl left his office just after the call. Leavitt went on to describe the chaos that ensued after Carl's fall from the balcony. He ended it with..."I keep remembering the last time I saw him, Carl got in the elevator and...waved...just by holding his hand up, like this." Leavitt raised his hand, palm out, not moving it, "And the doors closed and... I didn't say goodbye." He became quiet.

I asked Jack Leavitt to stay while I took a preliminary gander at Carl's office in case there was anything in there I needed him to explain. It was free of the typical paper clutter of most offices, since Carl had no use for hard copy files and written memos.

"You came in here on that day?" I asked as I took in the office space.

"Yeah, I brought him some CDs that students had dropped off, some completed projects ...assignments," he said.

"Was his computer on, did he have the screen turned on?"

"Uh huh."

"What was up on it?

"Um, a blank text document."

"A text screen ready to type on?" I suggested.

"Yeah, or one that he could talk the text onto, using the Voice Transcription System. His mic was set up."

"Could it pick up someone else's voice?"

"No, the program's really amazing, it only recognized Carl's voice. It took a long time to set up. Dr. Smith helped him."

"Dr. *Georgia* Smith?"

"Yeah, she'd come in every few weeks and update it for him. It's easier for a sighted person to do that, because they can read the words that are coming out on the screen to be sure they're right."

I made a note of that.

After Leavitt left, I poked around the computer music hook ups, electronic piano keyboards, digital speakers, and the large microphone in the middle of the desk next to the phone.

The computer typing keyboard was gone, the police had taken it to check for fingerprints. I found an extra one in a different office, plugged it in, then booted up Carl's computer and scanned his files. I reviewed Carl's suicide note, it was the same as the hard copy Bouchet had handed out.

In the top drawer of the desk, I found a very powerful laptop computer next to a nearly full box of Devil Dogs snack cakes. I opened one of the plastic packages of Devil Dogs and sniffed it while I copied all of Carl's written files and program information from the desktop onto the laptop. The snack cakes were a little stale, but as I hadn't had dinner, I ate the whole package of three. I didn't think Carl would mind.

I managed to open the Voice Transcription System program and accessed the files. I copied them onto the laptop; the voice transcription software was already loaded into the laptop.

The Voice Transcription Program would read any text out loud in a voice selected by the program user. One would read any text to the tune of "Happy Days Are Here Again." Why would anybody need that, I wondered. By using this program, Carl could *read* all his student's papers by just having the computer convert the text to voice or musical sound. He could hear emails using it and he could check his own typing to be sure he hadn't made mistakes. This was one of the ways it was possible for him to function in a college full of sighted people.

Carl could also use the program as a text translator. He could talk into a mic and the words he said would come out as text. Cool. I looked around the room to see if there were any software manuals with directions on operating that program. The software books were all in a stack in the corner. They weren't anything Carl could use, but if he had a problem, the College tech guys could come in and access them.

I found the one for the Voice Transcription Program and flipped through the five hundred or so pages of *simple* directions. There was no way I could figure this out tonight. It was getting very late.

I couldn't access Carl's email without his password. I gave guessing it a shot, trying a few dozen combinations of letters and numbers that might have been important in his life, but no dice. I looked around his desk to see if he'd written it down. *Mental head slap.* He was blind, *stupid.* Maybe he had a Braille reminder. If he did, it wouldn't do me any good. It was almost midnight. I put Carl's laptop and the software manual in my shoulder bag, left Carl's office snapping the padlock back in place, then passed through the large dark recording studio en route to the elevator.

I decided to go to the top floor and see the balcony where Carl Rasmus met death. The elevator door opened into darkness on the sixth floor. Carl had killed himself in the middle of the day, but it would have been darker for him than this was for me. The balcony Carl Rasmus fell from was reached by a pair of locked French doors off the hall. I didn't have the key. Peering through the glass, I could make out the four-foot cement railing that probably bruised Carl's legs.

Could it be that he'd just rode up there and jumped? How did he even know there was a balcony there, anyway? Where did he get the key? How did he know there wasn't a huge awning under the balcony that would break his fall? The whole thing seemed implausible. If someone had pushed him, though...I looked up and down the hall.

All the killer would have to do was push him off, then walk over to the stairs. There were plenty of ways to get out of the building. Killing a blind man wouldn't have been that hard to do...but Carl had left a suicide note in a locked room ...and that I couldn't explain.

Chapter 11

I walked home. The snow had stopped and the wind was less than a whisper. The city lay quietly nestled under a white blanket. I was carrying Carl Rasmus's laptop, which I may have removed from his office illegally, but I'd take my chances with that.

I remembered watching Kathryn Anthony talking in the Quad, I realized that I'd had a pang of jealousy when I'd seen her gently touch Jimmy Harmon's arm.

You might be sweet on that girl, I teased myself.

The small parking lot in front of my building had already been plowed out by the maintenance service. They'd done a fairly good job, but the space they made through the snow pile to the building entrances was pretty narrow. I had to turn sideways. Sara would complain to the landlord, and the landlord would be me.

I was planning to work out for about an hour, have a bowl of Jessie Wiggins' homemade chicken soup and then go to sleep as fast as possible. My 9:00 AM meeting with Skylar Carvelle was coming up fast.

I gathered the mail in the foyer and trudged up the stairs to my loft, but when I reached the second floor landing I noticed a note with my name on it taped to the door of my office.

All it said was, "Maggie, List on Evelyn's desk."

Inside Martinez and Strong Law Offices, I scooped up two sheets from the front desk. A handwritten note from Sara on one of them said, "Maggie, please run this list. It's from Daria's party."

The list had about 40 names. How did Daria ever fit that many party goers into her tiny apartment? Apparently Sara wanted me to send this list to my fact checkers to see if any of these people had been charged or convicted of violent acts.

In my own office, I faxed the list off with a note of explanation and my pin number for the service. I made a notation on my calendar. Credit results should be back by Friday evening. More extensive information would take longer. If any of these people had been guilty of rape or sexual assault in the past, it could help get Mickey off. The whole procedure only took about ten minutes. I locked up and resumed my climb to the third floor.

I'd finished converting my loft to living space a few weeks ago. The hard work to get it done over the last six months had paid off and I was unabashedly proud of myself for the way it had come out. Fun to come home to it, but right now I was a little too tired for full-fledged appreciation.

As I unlocked the door a nagging feeling I was forgetting something tickled my conscience. In the back of my mind I knew there was something else I was supposed to do. What was it?

I hung my jacket on a peg near the door and sat down at the kitchen table, staring off into space. Visions of Kathryn Anthony clouded my concentration. Even after everything that had happened yesterday and all the information I'd gathered today, I just kept coming back to the way she'd looked at me when we'd met. Maybe it was all my imagination, but the look in her eyes seemed very personal.

I wish I could call Farrel and talk to her about all this, I thought.

It was too late to call her though ...too late to call Farrel and Jessie and besides... they're away doing an antique show. Oh shit! They're away and it snowed...and I have to shovel their walk! I couldn't believe I'd forgotten. I'd even reminded myself when it started snowing. What a moron. Now I'd have to go back out in the cold. Damn!

I put my new parka back on, grabbed my keys and leather gloves, and went back out into the night.

Farrel and Jessie lived on Washington Street on the south side of Washington Mews. In fact, they have two rowhouses next to each other that they joined into one. When you live in Washington Mews, you ultimately succumb to the *propriety police*. Mews people can be painfully rule-oriented. It's like a cult. It's considered impolite to leave snow on the sidewalk in front of your house in Washington Mews. So the Mewsians, including Farrel and Jessie themselves, lobbied City Council to pass a law that requires all residents of the historic districts of the city to shovel their walks down to the pavement within 24 hours of the snow stopping. There's even a $35 fine.

Because Farrel and Jessie have two houses combined into one, they could get a $70 ticket! Even more serious, was the danger of the disdain of their neighbors. A disdain meted out in side-ways glances and turned up noses. It could be a stinking black spot on their reputations for years.

There are a lot of gay and lesbian families in the Mews, and they often seem to be the most insistent on rule following. Gay and lesbian homeowners who began buying and restoring Mews homes twenty years ago had rescued this neighborhood, like so many historic areas all over the country.

The snow had just stopped a few hours earlier. If I could get there before too many pedestrians walked by, I could get the four or five inches of powder off the sidewalk before boots trampled it into an icy packed down mass.

What the heck, I shrugged, half and hour of rapid shoveling and I won't have to work out. I glanced at my watch. It was 1:10AM. There shouldn't be anyone out at this hour on a Wednesday night, just *after hours* folks like vampires and guys like Herman Munster.

It was just over a block to Farrel and Jessie's house from my building. By the time I was half way there I'd decided a vampire would be flying rather than strolling and that Herman Munster had that hot-ride-hearse, so the sidewalks would probably be empty.

Things seemed different in the Mews, like a world apart. I stopped for a minute to appreciate the rare beauty of the snow. It was clean and pure white. A bright full moon had risen in the southeast in counterpoint to the rest of the night sky, which was as soft and dark as black velvet. Overhead was a shoal of a thousand stars. It was impossible to look at any point in the northwestern sky and not see a dozen tiny dots of light. Some were beacons in the recognizable patterns of constellations, others almost too small to discern individually, were like a fist full of shining grains of sand flung by a Greek god onto an inky background.

The old-fashioned streetlight globes on their ornate copper columns were dimmed by little white caps. Bushes and tree branches seemed dusted with talcum. Every car parked along the sidewalk sported a new white ragtop. The snow on the park lawns in the center of the Mews was as smooth as fondant icing. The deep powder muffled every sound. Even my own footsteps made only a quiet chuffing as I moved along.

Farrel and Jessie keep a snow shovel in their foyer from November until April. I had keys to their house. Though Cora Martin was taking care of their cats, Cora was not expected to shovel. I'd do her walk as well.

After letting myself into the house, I had to disarm the burglar alarm quickly. This is a stressful job because a loud beeping ticks off the seconds you have to enter the special code before the alarm decides to let out with its screaming horns, buzzers and sirens. I managed in time. The alarm system in my building is much easier to use. Much more forgiving.

I petted the jet-black cats as they wound around my legs.

"Hi boys."

Griswold said, "Merf."

Wagner said, "Ow."

I grabbed the shovel and went back outside and began to toss large fluffy scoopfuls aside. There was no wind at all. It was still and quiet. The only sound was the scraping of the shovel as I cleared down to the pavement. Inside, Griswold and Wagner jumped to the front sill to watch me. I waved to them. Griswold stretched his paws over his head on the window glass as though he was waving back.

Just three cars went by during the forty-five minutes I worked. I stopped and leaned on the shovel for a time to gaze around at the job I'd done to see if it would pass Mews muster.

Down the street, I could see someone coming toward me on the sidewalk from the east end of the Mews. I could tell it was a woman by the way she moved and by her silhouette against the unshoveled snowy sidewalk, behind her. She'd passed 11th Street and was just a few houses away. Before I could possibly be sure on an intellectual level, I knew in my soul it was Kathryn Anthony. My heart began to race and I strained my brain to think of something charming to say. She might remember me, or she might think I was some late night crazy, armed with a big garden tool. In instances like this, when hoping to impress, it's always best not to scare the person to death by popping out of the dark, wielding something that could be mistaken for a giant ax.

Her face was turned toward the center of the Mews. No hurry, just moving steadily along. As she got nearer she passed under a streetlight. She was wearing her calf length dark tweed coat and her red scarf wrapped once around her neck, then tossed over her shoulder. No hat, hands in her pockets, boots with a medium heel. She must have been wearing a dress or skirt because I couldn't see pant cuffs below the hem of her coat. This was a pretty formal outfit for what must now be about 2:00 AM. Maybe she'd been on a date and was just coming home. I had mixed feelings about that.

She was fairly close when she turned and saw me. There was no one else on the street. She hesitated. Then she saw the shovel and figured I must be a Mews homeowner on a late night quest to fulfill my civic shoveling responsibility.

I said, "Good evening Dr. Anthony, it's quite late for a moonlight stroll." Oh crap, what a pompous thing to say. Don't be a jerk, stop trying so hard, my internal voice yelled.

She stopped, smiled, tilted her head to the side a little and said, "Oh, please call me Kathryn. Nearly two o'clock in the morning is no time to be

formal. It's very late for shoveling sidewalks too...is this where you live?"
she said looking up at the house, in a voice that caused my stomach to flutter.

I looked too, like I had to see whether it was my house or not. Geez, take a
deep breath and stop being an addlepated teenager.

"No, it belongs to some friends of mine. I promised I'd shovel their walk
while they were away, and I didn't think I'd have time tomorrow."

She nodded and took some steps nearer, then said, "It's not really too cold
is it? It's so still." She paused to look again toward the center of the Mews.
Then she said with a tired sigh and a hint of amusement, "After a day like
this, I just needed to go for a short walk and I couldn't resist seeing the moon
on the crest of the new fallen snow."

"Tough day?" I asked leaning on the shovel, trying to be calm and not trip
over it.

"Boring, frustrating, tedious, parts of it were pointless... Oh! I sound like
such a malcontent," she laughed.

"Are you just coming home? Now? From work?" I asked in amazement.

She shrugged, "I had meetings all day. Tonight, I was reading graduate
thesis proposals in my office. I wanted to finish because I just couldn't go on
with them for another day. So I stayed late."

"Is this a solitary walk?" I asked gently.

"Are you done shoveling? Would you like to walk with me? You're
welcome to."

I thought dramatically, Is the sun hot? Did the Titanic spring a leak?? Are
the worst homophobes, conservative ministers who cruise men's rooms???
But I answered evenly, "That would be nice. Just let me put the shovel back
in the house."

Chapter 12

I sped up the steps, leaned the shovel back in its place in the foyer and patted Griswold and Wagner goodbye.

Griswold said, "Merf."

Wagner said, "Ow."

I tried to re-arm the alarm efficiently, but set off the blaring horn for a split second. It gave off one piercing whoop, which probably woke everyone in the Mews. I hoped, since it was only one honk, that maybe all the Mewsians would think they had had a collective epiphanaic dream and then all go back to sleep.

When I got back outside, Kathryn asked in surprise, "What was that noise?"

"Um noise, you mean like an earsplitting blaring horn? I didn't hear anything," I replied with a grin.

"Uh huh," she laughed, "I didn't either." Dimples made her amused face radiant. My God, she was gorgeous, I could barely stand it.

"I'm not very good with their house alarm. They just changed it to a more *sophisticated* system, which, as far as I'm concerned means more complicated to use. The Wolf Alarm 5000 Company monitors it. They should change their name to the Cry Wolf Alarm." We both turned in the direction she'd been walking and continued along the sidewalk side by side.

She said, "I just talked to my father on the phone yesterday. He keeps getting telemarketing calls from security alarm companies. He was so pleased with himself, he told me he'd hit on the perfect foil to their sales pitch. When they say they want to sell him a burglar alarm, he tells them he's against them, and when the salesman asks him why, Dad says, 'Because I'm a burglar'."

I laughed. "Where does he live?"

"Portland...Maine, near my brother."

"And your mother?"

"I don't hear from her much, she lives in Georgia."

Her tone signaled, don't go there, so I didn't say anything but, "Uh huh."

We were at the middle of the western end of the Mews. There was a beautiful rowhouse with a grand piano visible in its dimly lighted front window. On the far wall, over an ornate fireplace, was a dark Pre-Raphaelite painting with a tiny spotlight over it. We both stopped to look, as the owner had obviously wanted passersby to do.

"The piano looks like it wants to be played," she said, "I wonder if anyone ever does, or if it's just an ornament...there's no music on it."

"Do you play?"

"When I have time. I don't get many chances to play an instrument like that though. It's not exactly something you can tote around with you."

"Maybe you should take up the harmonica?"

"Probably a good idea... or maybe the kazoo," she laughed lightly.

"Or the sweet potato...what's the other name for that?"

"Ocarina?"

"There you go...handy for purse or pocket...but not quite the same tone as a baby grand." We walked a little more slowly, looking at the facades of other 100 year old homes. "Are you living in a Mews rowhouse?" I asked.

"Oh, I wish. I'm subletting an apartment in the Hampshire from a faculty member who's on sabbatical. I had to get a place in a hurry and I needed something furnished, so I took it for a semester with an option for next semester if I choose."

"Do you like living there?"

"It's OK," she said conversationally. "The building does have charm. Vintage Nick and Nora Charles. The thing that's most odd is living in someone else's space. Every bit of the place is covered with Joe's things, and he has a lot of them. Every inch of wall space, every bookshelf, every drawer and closet has his sensibility. He does have good taste, but they're not *my* things. Which makes me feel like..." she paused trying to think of the right word.

"A guest? An intruder? An accidental tourist?" I suggested.

"Well, all of the above...but, I shouldn't complain, it's not bad. I guess I'll probably be there next semester too. In the summer I can look for something else."

"Irwin will be going on winter break soon, will you go away?" I asked deeply interested in her reply.

"I don't usually go anywhere for the holidays ...it never seems to work out. Going to Maine in winter is rarely a wise move. I get about four weeks off. I might go someplace warm, just to break the winter up. I lived in California for much of last year and I'm not used to this weather yet. I'd like to go walk on a warm beach somewhere, but I'm not a sun worshiper or anything like that. I get sunburned too easily."

"Fair skin. I can see why you'd avoid the sun. I do too. My sisters, well, they're actually my stepsisters, can sit on the beach for hours and they never get anything but a lovely tan. I just scorch. ...Northern Florida is comfortable in the winter. My friends Farrel and Jessie have a place there."

"I've heard it's nice, I'll try it some time, but I have to admit, I've been in so many airports in the last few months, I'd rather not fly anywhere for a while," she said earnestly. "In fact, after all the flights I've had to take, I'd be happy if I never flew anywhere again."

"It sounds like you've been moving from place to place for a long time. Are you going to stay in Fenchester now?"

"I think so. I've been traveling for years, and it was interesting, but I don't want to travel for work any more. I guess I'm just getting too old for it." She said the last part with an amused tone as though she'd just figured it out. That she planned to stay in the neighborhood made me absurdly happy, even though I knew very little about her. We were starting to walk east on the north side of the Mews now. We were only two blocks away from the Hampshire apartment building and closing fast. This stroll was going to end too soon unless I calculated a stalling tactic.

"Let's walk over to the Monument," I suggested gesturing across the street. Washington Mews is a two by two block square with four distinct quadrants. They include an arboretum and a bocce court. Dead center is the Soldier and Sailor's monument honoring Civil War veterans. It's an impressive memorial, one of the few in the country that honors both armies.

Life-sized statues of men in Union and Confederate uniforms occupy the first level. Steps ascend several more levels to the base of a typically phallic obelisk that's etched with quotes from presidents, generals, and poets. On the highest level, four park benches face each compass point. I swept the snow off a bench when we reached them. We sat under the Gettysburg Address facing east toward the moon.

"Top of the world," she said softly, without any sarcasm. Because it did feel that way. The snow distorted the landscape, making everything seem even and smooth. The contrasting dark shadows cast by the bright moonlight created a surreal depth like a black and white photo with no gray tones.

"I'm channeling DiChirico," I said thinking of the surrealist painter famous for odd shadows and dramatic perspective.

She turned toward me resting her arm on the back of the bench, propping her head against her gloved hand. She looked incredibly beautiful. The cold tinted her clear porcelain skin slightly pink at the cheekbones. The bright moonlight brought out the auburn highlights in her hair and the dark blue in her eyes.

She said, "I talked to Max Bouchet last night, he told me everything he could. He said you were heroic!"

"Did he tell you about Daniel Cohen and Connie Robinson?"

"Daniel's quick thinking in fighting the fire and Connie throwing that marble pedestal out the window? Wasn't that something? And the look on Daniel's face when she did it? He told me about that too," she said shaking her head lightly, imagining the scene.

"I'm sure Max Bouchet didn't mention his own heroics. He took a huge risk to save Bart."

"No, he didn't tell me that, what did he do?" she asked with interest.

I told her about Max crawling under the table to help pull Bart out of the fire, finishing with, "He was amazing in the press conference. I was very impressed."

"Max is an impressive man. I've known him a long time... but, what a terrible thing to happen to Bart and Georgia...I feel so odd about it. Almost guilty that I only escaped it all by luck." She looked thoughtful and concerned, "Max says Bart and Georgia will be all right but I've heard Georgia was very seriously burned. Is Max being honest about their recovery or is he trying to be the up-beat positive administrator?"

"She's in intensive care. Burns can be tricky. I think Bart will be fine, but it's hard to tell about Georgia. She's young and strong, she has that going for her."

"What really happened? Can you tell me?"

Max Bouchet was sure that Dr. Kathryn Anthony was not a suspect in Carl Rasmus's murder. He was probably right. The strongest evidence pointed that way, but before I talked about the case with her, I needed just a little more information from a few other people. Soon we could discuss the whole thing. But now just wasn't a good time to talk about murder and arson. We were alone together in the moonlight. First encounters are rarely cast in such a romantic setting. I really would be a fool to spoil the moment with a discussion about crime.

"It sounds like Max Bouchet told you everything about the fire. As for the rest of it, I have to get some more information before talking about it...I'd like to discuss it with you later in the week though. In fact, I'd really appreciate talking to you about it tomorrow afternoon or maybe Friday, after I've had a chance to collect a few more pieces of information? For now though, let's skip talking about work..."

"All right then, I won't ask you any work questions now." She paused for an instant considering me. "I'm free late in the day on Friday. Tomorrow the only time I have free is lunchtime, but someday, I'd like to ask you if your job is anything at all like being Nancy Drew."

I laughed, "It's more like being Joe Friday, especially when I was actually on the police force. All that stuff on Dragnet that seemed to be so painfully slow and boring, really is painfully slow and boring, even more so. I haven't been a *P.I.* on my own for that long, but so far it does seem to be a little more interesting than being a police officer. Probably because I get to pick the cases I want to work on. On the other hand, there is the actual question of earning a salary... which is much more regular when you're a union cop. Were you a big Nancy Drew fan?"

She was listening to me intently. We were sitting fairly close. The air was clear and crisp. I could smell a hint of, I guessed Chanel. I should do a study on the scents of perfume. It would be impressively Sherlock Holmesian if I could tell exactly what perfume still wafted at a crime scene. It could also be impressive to women I might want to date. It had been a very long time since I'd had a date. It had been even longer since I'd been this fascinated by anyone. Be a detective, I said to myself, find out if she's a lesbian. That's the task for the evening. If she isn't, then at least you can stop wasting your imagination. Yeah, I said to myself, find out if she's gay, and then if she is...set a date to see her again. This was good, I'm task oriented, now I had goals.

"I just have to ask you one more thing," she said, "are there a lot of suspects?"

"Sometimes, I've had cases with no leads at all, and it's hard even to find anything to investigate. This is not one of those cases. There are plenty of suspects," I admitted.

"Do you think I'm a suspect?" she asked curiously.

"Oh my...should I?" I asked smiling.

"Shouldn't you? Trust no one..." she said in a Mata Hari accent and then smiled back.

"See, you must have been a Nancy Drew fan to say something like that! Or maybe Hercule? To answer your question, I think you have a pretty good alibi. Being in Seattle during the first death and in a limo on the way to Harrisburg during the explosion..."

"So you've already investigated me? I *was* a suspect, before?" she asked wryly.

"Trust no one," I replied in a deep voice.

A half smile appeared, as though she was about to say something very provocative. It made her face even more intriguing. She said, "Well, for what it's worth, I didn't do it."

"Good, that narrows it down. You have just made my job twelve and a half percent easier."

"I still might have important information though. Don't you want to *interrogate* me?"

She'd made it sound so suggestive that I was barely able to steady my voice when I answered, "Is that something you'd like me to do? What do you imagine it would be like?"

She raised her eyebrows a little, paused and then answered in a deep tone, "I'd bet you'd be very good at it. I'm sure you'd know exactly the right things to do, to encourage someone to respond...in a satisfying way. Tell me how you...do it."

Maggie, I thought to myself, I believe this woman is flirting with you. I smiled back, inclined my head a little and continued the game, "Some investigators have a deep and pressing need to work very quickly and sometimes that can be...exciting...but I feel the best way is to go very slowly and explore every avenue...seeing to every detail... meeting every need... for the entire experience to be...intensely gratifying for everyone involved," I said in a low voice.

"So, you like to take your time? Pay attention to all the nuances? Were you best at being the good cop, or the bad cop?" she whispered into the still night.

I answered slowly, "I can be very good, but I'm better when I'm bad..."

We were staring into each other's eyes. She tipped her chin down a bit but still kept eye contact. She made a humming noise. Very sexy, like a soft anticipatory growl.

After quite a long moment I said, "It's gotten quite a bit warmer out here hasn't it?"

She laughed deep in her throat. Then she shook herself a little.

"What made you go into law enforcement?" Kathryn asked using a much less sensual tone. She'd taken charge of setting the direction of the conversation. The game was over...for now anyway.

"I didn't start out with that in mind. I decided to apply for the police force because someone I knew needed the help of the police and what they got was inadequate. I wanted to fix that, which was idealistic and naive, but I did get a lot of experience. I'm glad I'm on my own now, but I don't regret my years on the force. However..." I said, "this is still too much like talking about work, let's talk about something else."

"How about if I ask you this, do you know any people who work at Irwin?"

"Sure, Farrel Case is my closest friend, she teaches woodworking and furniture design. Um...Charles Majors in the Art History Department, he's a good friend too..." I mentioned some others, then thought for a moment, "and Judith Levi, she's retired now but she was an English Professor. Then there are all those people who teach there and live in the Mews. I didn't know Amanda Knightbridge directs the Art History Department until yesterday, but I've been saying hello to her in the Mews for years."

Kathryn was looking at me with full concentration. She said purposefully, "I've heard you knew Susan Fuller, when she was here for the exchange program with the Slade?"

"Yes, I knew Susan then. That was several years ago, I was still a cop." I didn't add that I'd had a torrid affair with Susan Fuller. It'd been full of hot scene playing sex that featured her fascination with my handcuffs. It went on non-stop for five days, then ended because she had to go back to England. Fun while it lasted, something to think about erotically, but not the kind of thing to build a future on.

"Do you know her?" I asked innocently.

"We've never met, I've read her books...Is she a lesbian?"

Huh, that was direct. Well, Susan isn't closeted; she speaks about being a lesbian in her lectures and on her web site. So I certainly wasn't betraying a confidence by saying, "Yes she is."

Kathryn Anthony paused a beat, and then she asked, "Are you?"

"Yes, I am. Are you?"

"Yes," she said slowly, and there was that sexy half smile again.

Hey, how about that, I congratulated myself, am I some detective or what!?! Of course I had to admit that I didn't have to do a lot of tricky ferreting to deduce the lesbian thing. Maybe I should just pose yes or no questions all the time... I could just ask suspects, "So, did you embezzle the funds?" Or, "Did you bomb the conference room?" And maybe they'd just answer, yes. Think of the time I could save! Perhaps I've been going about this private eye stuff all wrong.

Anyway, I checked off number one on my list of tasks for the evening. I was pleased with myself and damn pleased with her answer. Now for the second task...arrange to see her again. But maybe first I should be sure she isn't already involved with somebody. That would be a bummer. She'd been pretty darn direct in the last round. I figured I could serve the next volley.

"Are you seeing anyone?"

"No," she said simply, she turned and looked up at the moon. "Even though I've been part of Irwin's faculty for years, I've traveled so much that I really don't know many people here in Fenchester." She turned back to me. "How about you?"

Back into my court! She might be better at this than I am. I still couldn't tell yet if she was interested or just had a very direct, provocative manner. Maybe she flirted with everyone. Maybe she was just nosy. Can't blame her for that, God knows I'm a snoop.

"No, I'm not seeing anyone." I looked steadily back into her dark blue eyes, in this light; it was impossible to see any separation between her irises and pupils. It was stirring and also a bit disconcerting. After a moment she turned and looked out over the Mews again. The light from the moon illuminated her face, highlighting her cheekbones. Have I mentioned I'm a sucker for cheekbones?

"But you have lots of friends here..." she said still looking at the Mews, "so, what do you do for fun?"

"That's a complex question," I said with amusement. "Fun is relative. Right now I've been working with friends to rehab my living space. I make art. I volunteer in the summer at the Latino Community Center, teaching kids crafts. As far as entertainment goes I like the standard things, including an occasional walk in the moonlight, although they're fairly rare... putting it that way my life sounds pretty dull, except the moonlight walks part."

"I don't think it sounds dull, I'm glad you didn't say watching Monday Night Football."

"I hate football, I'm not much into organized sports," I laughed. "Do you think they'll make me turn in my dyke card?"

"I hope not, then I'd have to, too." She shifted gears again, "Were you *out* at work?"

"Very. I did pro-gay activism in the union and on the force and it got a lot of press. It was needed at the time and is probably why I don't work there any more. One of the reasons anyway. It's a long, somewhat unpleasant story. Doesn't suit this atmosphere. Let's just say that I'm out as I can be and proud of it. How out are you? "

She sighed, "I've done political work...and I edited a book about lesbian artists. I was the advisor for a University Gay/Straight Alliance. I've served on the Governor's committee for higher education as a representative of the gay community and..." she paused to think, "oh and I've been in public forum discussions on same-sex marriage that were televised in Pennsylvania and New York ... and in California too. I figured as a tenured professor with a fairly understanding family, if I can't be an out advocate, then how could I expect anyone else to be one?" She was speaking passionately. I admired that kind of attitude, which made me glad the subject had come up. I certainly could never have much respect for someone who was closeted. She seemed to feel the same way. The passion brought a glint to her eye that was seductive all by itself.

"Has it ever been a problem for you, being so out?" I asked recalling the harassment I'd received from some of my *brothers in blue* when I was on the force.

She nodded, "Sure, when I was on television debating in favor of Gay/ Straight Student Alliances, I got a dandy series of hate mail, and I got death threats after a same-sex marriage panel."

"Did they catch the perp? As we say in the business..."

"They didn't even bother to look," she said sardonically.

"I'm sorry you had to go through that."

"It was something I chose to do. Frankly, I don't respond well to threats, they made me double my efforts."

"So I guess I don't have to ask whether you're out to all your friends?"

"Seems to be a given for both of us," she said as I nodded affirmation. "It's a shame but, I actually know some gay people even today who are closeted to people they consider their closest friends. I know this one lesbian who spends most of her time with another woman who is so homophobic that she spews vitriolic anti-gay hate language constantly."

"Uh huh, and the punchline: They're secretly in love with each other and the stress and frustration of that has made them bitter bigots instead of a happy family of loving partners," I said.

"And they both teach at a women's college!"

"You're kidding, is it a religious college?"

"No, no, it's actually a fairly liberal school..." she said in exasperation, shaking her head.

"Internalized homophobia..." I shot back.

"Yes, exactly," she said in rapid acknowledgment.

We both paused. I smiled saying, "You know one of the great things about being a lesbian is that you get to argue with people you agree with."

"The trouble is, not everyone agrees. I'm afraid I have a tendency, when I feel I'm right, to expect everyone else to see it my way."

"You're stubborn about it?"

"Well, sure, but I'd change my mind if I'm presented with good evidence to the contrary," she insisted.

"Does anyone ever come up with that?" I teased.

"Yes...well, sometimes," she said with amusement, "maybe."

"You're a Taurus aren't you," I don't usually dwell on astrology stuff, but this was a revelation that hit me like divine prophecy.

She just smiled in response.

"No, come on, it's true isn't it? When's your birthday?"

"April 29th," she admitted.

"Ah ha, said the detective!"

"Am I that stubborn?"

"There's nothing wrong with standing by your convictions."

We both took a moment to look out again over the Mews; the moon was higher above the horizon. The moon shadows had shortened. It was very beautiful, an uncommon scene in a place we both saw every day.

I turned back to her and asked, "What was your major in college?"

"American Literature."

"Recite something for me."

"Hm?"

"Recite a poem or something that speaks to the stars, or the moon, or this snow covered scene."

"You want me to perform?" she asked in mock incredulity.

"Sure, show me you got your money's worth from your undergraduate education. Memorized poetry was made for special moments like this, don't you think?" I asked gently.

"Um..." she hesitated.

"I'm sure you can do it. Where did you go for your Bachelor's?" I asked.

She paused as if embarrassed... "Smith."

"Oh well, now you have to do it, and you have to choose a New England poet," I challenged.

"OK I'll play, but since you brought it up, I think you should go first. Where did you go to college?"

"I went to The Baltimore University for the Arts for my BFA, and Midwestern Institute of Art and Technology for my MFA and I don't mind going first..."

She was clearly surprised. She'd almost done a double take. In the world of fine art academia both those schools were at the top of the pack. She was impressed and fueled up to spar. A hint of competitive spirit came into her eyes. I'd said the right thing, but I also knew that this evening was going to have to come to an end soon. For one thing, it was getting really cold again.

"All right ...um, something to the snow then?" Looking out over the wide expanse of white, I recited:

"Who shall declare the joy of the running!
   Who shall tell of the pleasures of flight!
Springing and spurning the tufts of white heather,
   Sweeping, wide-winged, through the blue dome of night.
Everything mortal has moments immortal,
   Shift and God-gifted, immeasurably bright.

So with the stretch of the white road before me,
   Shining snow crystals rainbowed by the sun,
Fields that are white, stained with long, cool, blue shadows,
   Strong with the strength of my horse as we run.
Joy in the touch of the wind and the sunlight!
   Joy! With the vigorous earth I am one."

"That was nice," she said sincerely, "must have been an Imagist...Amy Lowell? Does she count as a New England poet if she did most of her writing in Europe?"

"Amy Lowell was from Brookline, Mass, the heart of New England, and I get extra credit because she was a lesbian."

"So now it's my turn? I'll have to try to get extra credit too. And maybe I can offer something to the snow as well." She gathered herself for a moment and then with her mesmerizing voice she recited:

It sifts from Leaden Sieves --
It powders all the Wood.
It fills with Alabaster Wool
The Wrinkles of the Road --

It makes an Even Face
Of Mountain, and of Plain --
Unbroken Forehead from the East
Unto the East again --

It reaches to the Fence --
It wraps it Rail by Rail
Till it is lost in Fleeces --
It deals Celestial Vail

To Stump, and Stack -- and Stem --
A Summer's empty Room --
Acres of Joints, where Harvests were,
Recordless, but for them--

It Ruffles Wrists of Posts
As Ankles of a Queen --
Then stills its Artisans -- like Ghosts --
Denying they have been --

While she was speaking, I had to acknowledge that she had such an intoxicating voice, she could have been reading a laundry list and I'd want to listen. Even so, the piece she'd chosen seemed exactly right for the scene. Better than mine. When she was done, I grinned, "Emily Dickinson, how perfect."

We looked into each other's eyes for several long moments. The silence between us wasn't uncomfortable. She was considering me with her head tilted to the side again with a slightly predatory look in her eyes. I liked the way it made me feel.

The clock tower on the Zion Church at the far end of the Mews struck the hour in snow muffled tones. "It's 3:00 AM, I have an appointment in a few hours. I have to go home, but I'd like to see you to your door," I said.

"You don't have to," she said standing up.

"I really want to talk to you about Carl Rasmus and also what happened in the conference room yesterday. I need someone in the college who has an objective viewpoint on people...if we could meet for lunch tomorrow..."

She was quiet for what seemed like a long time. I immediately knew I'd said something wrong. There was a dissatisfied look in her eyes, or maybe it was suspicion. She said stiffly, "I don't want to be in a position to accuse anyone."

"Kathryn, I just want you to tell me things like -- This guy teaches printmaking and he's married and about 40 years old. You don't have to tell me whether or not you think he's capable of murdering someone. After all, the whole thing may have nothing to do with the college at all."

"So you want background...? "

"Yeah."

"Can't the college supply that?" she asked flatly.

"Not completely, because records don't always include general personal information ... due to affirmative action requirements," I explained way too mechanically.

"We could have spoken about this all now..." she said impatiently as we walked down the steps. I was beginning to understand. She was thinking that the only reason I was chatting her up was to get information for the case.

I touched her arm, slowing her down. I said softly, "Yes, we could have, but that wouldn't have been nearly as...pleasurable. It was far more interesting to talk to you about other things. I enjoyed it. How frequently does an hour like this pop up in life?" I said gesturing back to the monument, as we crossed the street. "How could I waste it talking about things we could discuss any time?"

She turned to look at me, a hint of a smile returned to her face. We were almost to her building.

"So... lunch tomorrow?" I asked hopefully.

She paused to think. "I have a grad seminar at 10:00 AM. It ends at 1:00. Then I get about an hour for lunch. Then, I have a series of dull meetings in the afternoon and into the evening. We could meet in the cafeteria for lunch at a little after 1:00?" We seemed to be back on an even keel.

We were on the sidewalk facing each other in front of her building. I said I'd meet her at 1:00 PM in the Student Union. I had fulfilled all my self-appointed tasks for the evening and was feeling pretty smug.

There were two long low steps to the entrance of the Hampshire Apartment Building. Behind the glass doors to the lobby I could see a dim light where a doorman was probably watching the late, late show. The light on the elevator panel was just visible.

"Where are your windows? Are they on this side?" I leaned back to look up at the front of the building.

She seemed to hesitate, then said, "There, on the third floor."

I looked where she was pointing. No lights on, but I could see the outline of the windows. Everything seemed hushed. I could hear the muffled sounds of a few cars several blocks away, but we hadn't seen one drive along any of the Mews streets in all the moments we'd been together.

Time slowed down. I felt the warmth of her body near mine. She stepped up on one of the steps, and then turned to face me. It made her a few inches taller than I. I pulled off my gloves and stuffed them into my pockets.

"Thank you for a wonderful walk, it was the highlight of my day," I said as I extended my hand. She pulled off her gloves too. She took my hand in both of hers and held it. Her hands were warm. Mine was too. I could feel a humming electric current between us.

"Warm hands..." she said.

"But I'm unlucky at cards." We both laughed. She still held on, looking down at me from the step.

OK, I thought to myself, I'm not sure what's going on here, are we having a *moment*, or is she just being polite? I put my other hand on the outside of hers. I had a second to consider whether kissing her might be a good move. I thought of something else.

"One more poem by Emily Dickinson, to say goodnight?" and then I recited something I'd been saving for years, just for this very moment:

Meeting by Accident,
We hovered by design --
As often as a Century
An error so divine
Is ratified by Destiny,
But Destiny is old
And economical of Bliss
As Midas is of Gold --

When I finished, a few seconds went by before she took a breath and whispered, "Take a step forward."

I moved up to the step. She leaned down slightly and brushed my cheek with her very soft lips, then whispered near my ear, "I'm looking forward to seeing you again," and then she let go of my hands and was gone.

Yipe... yeah that was a moment all right. I had to shake myself to stop standing there like a dolt. Geez, I hope she didn't glance over her shoulder and notice I was frozen in place with my mouth open.

I turned and began to walk west to my building. Everything had been so perfect. Even though I could still feel the sensation of her lips on my cheek and her breath in my ear, I was beginning to wonder whether what had just happened was all a dream.

I walked up the south side of the Mews. When I got to the part of the sidewalk I'd cleared in front of Farrel and Jessie's house, I stopped. I turned around slowly and looked back at the Hampshire Apartments. I could see the line of four windows Kathryn had said were hers, on the third floor. Now, a dim light was showing in the far left one. I wondered if she was standing in one of the darkened windows watching me. I turned and continued on up the sidewalk, but the prickly excited feeling that she may have been watching, pleasantly tickled the back of my neck all the way home.

Oh man, it is really going to be a let-down if any minute now the alarm rings and I find I'm dreaming this, I thought to myself. But I wasn't dreaming...and that wasn't the last *moment* I was to have with Dr. Kathryn Anthony.

Chapter 13

Thursday morning, I got up just before 8:00 AM but was mighty sleepy. I'd tried to go right to sleep the night before, but I lay awake for a long time...thinking. I should have been sorting through the facts on Carl Rasmus. I should have been trying to figure out who set the firebomb, but all I could think about was Kathryn. She'd kissed me. She'd whispered in my ear. I wondered if in her apartment in the Hampshire building, she'd laid awake too.

I showered and dressed. The phone rang. It was Bouchet. He told me that both Bart and Georgia could probably talk to me in the hospital today, but that Georgia was on heavy pain meds. I scarfed coffee, toast, and OJ and sped out the door, fast walking to the Fine Art Building, making it there by 8:55 AM.

The building where Skylar Carvelle had his office was just beyond the Environmental Safety Building but it was older, taller, and grander. In my opinion, this was the kind of building Irwin College did best. The exterior architecture sported Ionic columns and a bas-relief frieze of scantily clad dancing women having a great time allegorically representing "The Arts." There were cement lions at the base of the entrance stairs, huge cement and polished brass handrails, and twelve foot high, cast bronze, double doors. It looked like an 1890s bank or maybe the town hall in a Jimmy Stewart movie.

Inside were several full size reproductions of Greek and Roman statues with late Victorian applied fig leaves. There were marble floors, slate window frames, and large architectural details everywhere. Voices echoed against the thirty-foot high ceiling. I spent a few minutes looking around, taking it all in. People had felt the grandeur of this room for over 120 years, it was impossible not to.

Carvelle wasn't in yet. His assistant (it said "Assistant to Dr. Skylar Carvelle" on her name plate, but had no other name) looked like Cloris Leachman overacting a tyrannical secretary to the hilt. Her attitude dial was set on *vexed.* She sighed deeply as though everything was designed to make her day more complicated. She suggested I take a seat, eyeing me up and down judgmentally. Maybe she didn't appreciate my casual *couture.* She was dressed to the corporate nines.

Dr. Skylar Carvelle's office was as ostentatious as his designer wardrobe. The carpeting and furniture must have cost a fortune, but weren't remarkable for form or comfort. There was a wonderful Mark Rothko painting on one wall, however, and a cluster of Edward Weston photos on the other. These too must have been from the College's collection. The Rothko was certainly worth twenty times my yearly salary...on my best year.

Connie Robinson stepped into the office carrying a stack of folders. She had on a puffy white dress, tightly belted at the waist. She squeaked nervously to the Leachman look-alike, "Miranda Juarez asked me to bring these to Dr. Carvelle. Miranda wants me to tell her as soon as I've delivered them to him. They're confidential."

Carvelle's Cloris clone sighed deeply and said, "Dr. Carvelle hasn't arrived yet."

Connie saw me, smiled a little, and nodded hello. She turned back to the Cloris clone and said plaintively, "He's not here? Miranda told me that I have to give these to him." Connie didn't know what to do. Getting no help from Cloris, she turned to me for guidance.

I stage whispered, "Call Miranda, tell her that Carvelle isn't here and ask her what to do."

Connie nodded rapidly, looking relieved. She turned back to Carvelle's secretary who sighed deeply while motioning toward a side table, "You can use that phone over there."

Connie was dialing Miranda when Jimmy Harmon and Leo Getty came into the office. I heard Connie say over the phone to Miranda, "Ms. Gale suggested I call you..."

Jimmy Harmon asked Cloris, "Is Carvelle here?"

Getty caught sight of me and became expansive, "Maggie! Hey, how's it going!?!" He was wearing an orange knit shirt today, but he still looked like a fireplug. Jimmy Harmon nodded at me. He was wearing green overalls and a shirt with bright yellow ducks.

The phone on Cloris's desk rang. She said, "Dr. Carvelle? Where are you? Yes, she's here..." Then she glared at me, and with a sigh that literally puffed out a lock of her hair, said, "Dr. Carvelle would like to speak to you." She pointed to the extension Connie had used.

I asked, "Which phone should I use?" Just to see if I could make Cloris sigh hard enough to blow some papers off her desk.

When I picked up the phone, Skylar Carvelle sounded distinctly nervous. "Ms. Gale?" he swallowed, and then went on, "I...I...have something to talk to you about, but I don't want to come into the office."

I wanted to say, Why don't you just tell me what it is? But awareness that everyone in the office could hear my every word made me just say, "OK."

"Please... come to my house," he said urgently.

"OK," I said.

He gave me the address. It was in the new upscale General Hunterton development on the far western edge of Fenchester.

"Fine, Dr. Carvelle, thanks." I was trying to be discreet, but for want of other entertainment, all attention was focused on me.

Harmon was already saying to Cloris, "It sounds like Skylar isn't going to be here for a while. Have him call me when he comes in."

Getty nodded and told Cloris virtually the same thing. Connie was balancing the massive stack of folders as she made for the door.

We left in a row, then executed a five car chain reaction as Rowlina Roth-Holtzmann bumped into Jimmy Harmon, who was leading the line and not paying attention.

Getty screeched to a halt, shouting, "Whoa there."

Connie stopped and I just managed to keep from plowing into her. *The Marx Brothers Go To College.* We all mumbled apologies. I ducked around the crowd and made it outside without further mishap.

I hurried home to get my van because Carvelle lived at least 6 miles away. It was nearly 10:00 AM. My appointment with Amanda Knightbridge was for 11:00 AM back at the College in Clymer House. I didn't see how I could make it in time, so I pulled the Tenure Committee contact list out of my bag and entered Knightbridge's office number into my cell. She answered it herself, in her clear precise voice. I explained that I wouldn't be able to make the 11:00 AM meeting but asked if we could reschedule for 3:00 PM.

She said, "Unforeseen things do come up. We must all strive to be flexible. I shall see you later today." Then she said more deliberately, before hanging up, "Please, be careful, Ms. Gale."

"Be careful?" I questioned the dial tone.

I reached home in ten minutes, then wove through downtown traffic to make it to the General Hunterdon condos 15 minutes after that. This place had been so recently built, the landscaping trees still had price tags on them. Cars whizzed by on the main road, but inside the actual development the lanes were deserted. This whole synthetic neighborhood had the odor of formaldehyde off-gassing from cheap particleboard construction that belied the self-conscious effort to make the place look opulent and upper-crust. Jessie Wiggins says that because these overpriced houses are so cheaply made, they'll be the slums of the future.

There was a general feeling of *nobody home*. In front of the condos were parking spaces, but no cars. The snow had been cleared by a plow that had driven perpendicular to the empty spaces, piling the snow in a high mound in the last space. There were probably garages in the back. Skylar Carvelle's unit was at the end of the row. I walked up the shoveled sidewalk. My footsteps seemed loud, causing me to tiptoe unconsciously.

When I got to the door, I looked for the doorbell button. Then I noticed the door was ajar.

Chapter 14

A door wide open in December, when the temperature is less than 30, is a bad sign. I reached in my shoulder bag and took out my gun, then pulled my sleeve over my other hand to avoid spoiling fingerprints in what I sincerely hoped was *not* going to be a crime scene.

"Dr. Carvelle?" I called, pushing the door open. Maybe he was just taking a shower and forgot to close the door, I hoped. *Yeah, sure, right.*

No sound of water running, no sound of anything. No lights on. The living room had big windows, but the overcast sky wasn't helping the place seem cheerful. I moved cautiously with my gun held in both hands, arms extended, like a cop on TV. I moved straight ahead through the open floor plan. No one in the decorator furnished living area. I circled to my left returning to the front of the place through the fancy dining and kitchen areas.

Back in the foyer, I stepped quietly to the right. There was a room with a door slightly open. I pushed it with my elbow.

Dr. Skylar Carvelle was lying on the floor of his home office face down. He was wearing a velour forest green warm up jacket and matching sweat pants. The outfit didn't go with the wet red stain that had flowed from his smashed skull onto the plush off-white carpet. A large Steuben glass bird, smeared with blood, lay on the floor beside him. I touched him...no pulse. Skylar Carvelle was dead, yet his body was warm.

I stood up fast. The killer could easily still be in the condo; this was no time to let my defenses down.

I stepped back into the corner of the room and faced the door with my gun ready. Flipping out my cell phone, I called the direct number of Police Lieutenant Ed O'Brien. Ed was a strong union guy and a friend of mine. He was smart and savvy but didn't seem that way, which was one of his greatest assets. I trusted him.

"Ed? This is Maggie. I'm at a condo in the Hunterdon Development. Number 1259. Dr. Skylar Carvelle called me to meet him. When I got here, the door was open. Carvelle's dead body is on the floor."

Ed cut in, "Shit, Maggie, the killer could still be in the house!"

"Yeah, I know, so get over here."

"Be right there," he barked, not wasting time to say anything else.

I put my cell back in my pocket, then moved slowly out of the room and down the hallway to the right. There was a door that was probably a coat closet. I stood to the side and opened it. Three coats, two jackets, no killer.

The hall now angled 90 degrees to the left. A small door on the right was ajar. I pushed it open slowly. Powder room. No killer.

Farther down the hall I could see a bedroom. There was no place to go beyond that. If the killer was still in the house, he or she was in there. I leaned to look down the hall into the room. A shot broke the silence. The bullet ripping along the wall just over my head. Plaster dust floated in the air. I shot back to let the killer know I could, then flattening myself against the wall. I crouched down. A step closer and I'd be framed in the doorway as the perfect sitting duck. Another shot pierced the air. This one went wildly down the hall nowhere near me. I heard metal sliding on metal and then the sound of running footsteps. I moved slowly into the bedroom.

Faint police sirens were getting nearer. Good, I needed back-up.

The square bedroom held a large bed, a leather covered sofa and a pair of dressers. Sliding glass doors to outside were pushed open wide enough for someone to sidle through. I moved to the door and looked out. Footprints in the snow made for a group of trees directly behind the condo. I heard the distant sound of a car engine and a squeal of tires. I stepped out and ran for the trees, brushing against a snow covered yew branch dislodging powdery clouds that sifted into my collar. Beyond the trees was a roadside where a car could easily have been parked. Nobody there now, and no sign of witnesses.

Back at the condo the place was teeming with cops. Ed O'Brien yelled, "Let her in."

"No, no," I called back, "the killer shot at me from in there. Get these people out of the room; there could be all sorts of evidence on the carpet. Ed shooed everybody back out the door and closed it.

I told Ed what I could, but I didn't mention who might have overheard my phone conversation with Carvelle. That was all circumstantial, anyway. We didn't talk about whether this murder was related to Carl Rasmus. The Rasmus case was considered a suicide and the cops were treating the explosion at the College as a gas pipe accident.

Ed rubbed a hand over yesterday's five-o'clock shadow, considering the murder scene. He said, "Here's the *Who Wants To Be A Millionaire* question, why did the killer do it with a candlestick in the conservatory... I mean, why use a paperweight when he had a gun?"

I looked around the over decorated room for a minute, noting a drawer open in Carvelle's faux Empire desk, "I bet the gun's Carvelle's. Carvelle must have known the killer and let his guard down."

I moved to where Carvelle must have stood and said, "He turns his back for a second, the perp snags the first handy thing." I pointed to a light ring of dust on a bookshelf near the door where the glass paperweight must have been, then mimed grabbing the glass bird and swinging it. "Then drops it, spies the gun in the open desk drawer, grabs it when he or she hears me at the door... The perp has a gun now." I sighed thinking about the killer in a practical way. Before, the weapons were a balcony and a complicated firebomb. Now, murder would be as easy as squeezing a trigger.

Ed and a tech guy I didn't know, talked to me for a long time about each move I'd made in the condo. They wanted me to come right to the station to give a statement, but it was 1:25 PM. I was supposed to meet Kathryn 25 minutes ago!

"Shit," I said, "I have to go." I told Ed I'd give him my statement later. He reluctantly agreed. I sped to Irwin, calling Bouchet on the way to tell him about Carvelle's murder. Bouchet immediately clicked into administrator mode, beginning a plan to correctly deal with the situation,

****

I finally found a parking place a block from the Student Union. I ran into the building and scanned the room. It was 1:52 PM according to the digital clock on the wall. *Damn.*

Kathryn Anthony was sitting with three guys at a table on the far side of the cafeteria. Two were grad students, the other was Jimmy Harmon. She had a plate in front of her. On it was a purple cabbage leaf garni and an orange rind. There was an empty Cafalatte bottle next to her. She was laughing at something one of them had said. She looked wonderful.

I crossed the room, pulled out a chair at her table and sat down. I was out of breath. She looked at me. She didn't exactly frown, but annoyance flashed in her eyes. I had a feeling I might have to pay dearly for my tardiness.

I said, "I'm sorry I'm late. I have a note from my mom...?"

The other guys laughed. She leaned back in her chair and said flatly, "I'm sorry you're late, too." The frost was evident. The guys even felt it. I practically shivered.

Jimmy Harmon was smart enough to stand up and say hastily, "Good talking with you Kathryn, see you later," and scram. The students were more dense. They stayed. I looked at them. I looked at her. She sure wasn't going to help. Lunchtime was over and I'd missed it.

If the students hadn't been there I would have said, "If you want to punish me severely, I'll do anything to make it up to you." Kathryn unconsciously squeezed her shoulder near her neck to ease a tense muscle. Great, I'd stressed her out. Now I felt guilty for that, too.

"Are you free later today?" I asked tentatively.

She shook her head and said dryly, "No, I'm not."

Damn, I thought again. I asked a trifle pathetically, "Tomorrow?"

She tilted her head to the side and looked deeply into my eyes for a moment. I could feel it to my toes. "You have a good excuse?"

"Very."

"Later in the day tomorrow?" she suggested, thawing a tiny bit.

"What time?"

"Later in the evening, I'll be in my office."

"I promise I'll be there."

"Hmm," she said quietly.

She stood up and said to everyone, "I have a meeting, nice seeing you all." She glanced one last time at me and left.

Geez, she's tough, I thought. Well, I really did have a good excuse. Whatever happened, I'd better damn well be on time tomorrow.

Chapter 15

Dr. Amanda Knightbridge's office, at 320 College Street in the middle of the Irwin campus, was easy to find because College Street is clearly marked and runs all the way through town. Clymer House, with its brick four story facade, slate block entrance steps, and six pane over six pane window frames, was a perfect example of Federal style architecture.

Inside, directly in front of the entrance, was a wide staircase with hardwood threads and risers. The railing was hand carved with grapeleaf ornamentation. I went closer to it to see if the twist balusters were hand carved as well.

"The entire balustrade was handmade," said Dr. Amanda Knightbridge coming to my side.

"Chestnut?"

"Yes, yes it is," she nodded approvingly. "Won't you come into my office Ms. Gale?"

"This building must pre-date the college?" I asked conversationally.

"Well, yes and no," said Dr. Knightbridge, in her element. "Irwin College was founded in 1769, by the wealthy Irwin family. This building was built that year, but of course the College wasn't on this site then. This was the family home of James Clymer who was the son-in-law of Walter Irwin and the brother of George Clymer, one of the signers of the Constitution. George Clymer was President of the Philadelphia Academy of Art, and James was the first President of Irwin College. There's a portrait of James by C.W. Peale in the President's house."

"Yes, I saw it yesterday."

"Did you?" she said smiling, "James Clymer willed this house and land to the college. When the college outgrew its original site downtown in the 1860s, the directors of the institution proposed to build on this site. They kept the house and built around it. Much of the design was influenced by Jeffersonian planning though less grand, of course."

"Because James Clymer didn't have slaves to build it?"

"Yes, yes, well, I feel that's why. I'm doing research for a paper exploring that very point," she said pausing to face me again. "This house has some wonderful details. There are majolica tile fireplaces in every room. The tiles are Minton..."

Amanda Knightbridge went on talking as we entered her fascinating office. The furniture was Windsor and Sheridan. There was an early pictorial baby quilt hanging on one wall, and a Revolution era handdrawn map of Lenape County on another. Somehow, I could tell these things weren't part of the College's collection; they belonged to Dr. Knightbridge personally. An engraving of botanical specimens caught my attention. I looked at it closely.

"Is this by Maria Sibylla Merian!?!!" I was sincerely awed.

Amanda Knightbridge was very pleased, she said, "Why yes it is. From one of her later botanical studies, still of the 1600s though. A little early for the room but... how do you know of her work?"

"Grad school research. I was interested in her travels. So fantastic that she could travel to South America to do botanical studies while Pilgrims were still barely scratching out an existence in New England," I said looking more closely at the engraving.

She sat on a small couch. I sat in a wingback chair opposite her. Tucking a strand of long white hair back into the bun pinned at her neck, she drew her long Cardigan sweater more closely around her, folded her hands in her lap, and focused on me intently.

"Skylar Carvelle has been murdered," I said without preamble.

Her expression sharpened with concentration. "How do you know this?" she asked concisely.

"He asked me to come to his home this morning. When I arrived, I found his body. He'd only been dead a short while."

"You knew it was murder?"

"Yes."

She didn't ask how I knew, instead she asked, "Is this tied to the explosion and Carl's death?"

"I think so, but I may be wrong. Dr. Carvelle wanted to speak to me about something he didn't want others to overhear, and he seemed very nervous. Can you imagine what he might have wanted to say?"

"How very distressing, how very distressing," she said shaking her head and looking down at her hands, then she went on, "Skylar is...was...the type of man who enjoyed knowing secrets and telling them to others. It made him feel powerful, I suppose. He was very observant and sometimes he pried. He also had an excellent memory. All important skills for a gossip. Perhaps he knew something, but, I can't imagine what. I don't find that type of conversation amusing, so Skylar rarely shared anything he deemed important with me," she said shaking her head again, but she was more than distressed; now she was angry. "Will the police stop this killer?" she demanded.

"You're presuming what happened in the conference room was deliberate, Dr. Knightbridge?"

"Was it not? Ms. Gale, I don't know what the police are choosing to do, but surely you are perceptive enough to see it as more than a coincidence, especially now, after Skylar." She stared at me for a long moment, then said, "This is a complicated problem. Creative thought is needed." It sounded like something my mother would have said.

Amanda Knightbridge continued, "I was just on the phone with Miranda Juarez regarding Bart and Georgia's condition. I'm relieved that the doctors believe they both will recover."

"How did Georgia get along with Carl Rasmus?"

"She worked on a grant project with him. She also helped him set up some of his computer programs. She cared about him as a friend, I believe, and she was hurt...no, maybe it would be more accurate to say she was *confused* by Carl's irrational behavior."

"Irrational because he acted in an angry way? Or because he was rude?"

"We can all be rude..." she thought for a minute, "have you noticed that since the advent of email, people get into disagreements much more quickly? The time it takes to write and send a real letter tends to dilute rudeness, speaking on the phone allows compensation for emotion, but rapid email is too easy, too remote, a medium loaded with opportunities for miscommunication," she went on, "it was Carl's anger that was irrational. He seemed to be a very nice young man. A little unsure and perhaps too trusting at times, but a good person and a sound teacher. Then suddenly he seemed to have huge sweeping mood swings. Sweet one moment, then hateful. As though he had two separate personalities in conflict."

"Can you give me an example?"

"Yes...one day, Carl and I had coffee and talked about a National Public Radio presentation that we had both heard. Everything seemed fine with him. However, when I got back here, there was an email from him saying he felt I had been patronizing him because he was blind and it went on to say curtly he wished not to speak with me ever again. I was shocked. So I called him in his office. I asked him to explain his email; he asked me why I was concerned. He sounded sad and depressed and I think also confused. He told me he had other things to do and then hung up on me. That was just a day or two before he died. I think..." she paused considering, then shook her head.

"What? What do you think?

"I'm not sure exactly what I think about it all. Let me consider it further. Are there other things you wish to ask me?"

"Did you see him on the day he died?"

"No, I didn't."

"Where were you at the time?"

"Where was I?" She gazed at me with piercing gray eyes, then nodded once, "ah yes, I see. Let me check." She got up to refer to the date book on her desk. "I was in this office all day until 5:00 PM. My secretary was here for most of the day as well. She goes to lunch at 1:00 PM and comes back at about 2:00 PM."

Which meant Amanda Knightbridge didn't have an alibi for Carl Rasmus's death. Changing the subject I asked, "Do you think someone may have been angry enough at Bart Edgar to plan to kill him?

"Kill Bart? Because he is incompetent? No, probably not. There are many incompetent people in the world. Have you read any of the Dilbert comics by Scott Adams? They stem from genuine stories about incompetent people in offices. Everyone knows someone like that. Unfortunately, incompetent people are not rare, but, Ms. Gale, I don't think Carl's death could have much to do with Georgia and certainly nothing to do with Bart."

I pulled my laptop from my bag and opened it, scanning the information I'd collected so far. "During the meeting in the conference room, what kind of beverage did you have?"

"Eve's Apple Juice. I like the small bottles."

"What do you remember about people getting their drinks?"

A very serious look came over her face. Perhaps she understood the implications and now she was replaying the scene in her mind. She took a deep breath. "Well... I couldn't see everything because in most instances their bodies hid the table, but ...Lina Roth took a very long time pouring her bottle of ginger ale into the glass. Jimmy Harmon also took a long time. Skylar spent some time finding his selection and then got a glass and ice cubes. Leo was standing behind him waiting and he became impatient because Skylar was taking so long. Leo didn't take as long, he popped his soda can open on the way back to his seat. At that point Daniel and Georgia came in and the President started the meeting. One more thing, I remember the odor of petroleum."

"A strong smell?" I asked with interest.

"No, just a whiff. Frankly, Jimmy Harmon was drinking a grape soda. I dislike that strong synthetic grape smell. There were other odors too that masked the petroleum smell, but it was there."

"Other odors?" I tried to remember the other smells.

"The cookies, coffee brewing in the outer office, someone's cologne, I would have sworn I noticed Kathryn Anthony's perfume in the hallway..."

This woman was good, we never got a witnesses like her when I was a cop. Her opinions made sense too, I asked, "What did you think of Carl's suicide note?"

"Quite simply, I do not believe he wrote it."

"You seem quite sure."

"The things said in the note were stupid. Carl was not a stupid man. The 30-year-old myth about homosexuals being murdered by homosexuals. Carl was a scholar. He based his opinions on facts and research not antiquated rhetoric."

"There are some people who do hate themselves because they're gay."

"Educated young people, who do not have religious pressures and overbearing parents, rarely develop these deep hatreds of themselves these days," she said dismissively.

"So how do you explain how the suicide note got onto Carl's computer when he had a closed system?"

"I cannot explain it, but its existence is a puzzle, not a fact. *You* must figure it out."

I was a bit startled by her insistent tone. She was nodding at me. I went on, "May I ask, Dr. Knightbridge, where you were earlier today?"

"When you called to say you were not coming at 11:00 AM, I joined Kathryn Anthony's morning seminar. We went from there to lunch at the Student Union, at about one o'clock. I sat with Kathryn and some students. I left to come back here at about 1:45."

"Do you have a car?"

"Well, I suppose one could say I have. It's a Volkswagen Beetle. Not the new kind, it's many decades old. It's in my garage, but I haven't driven it for several years."

The seminar was a good alibi, it also alibied Kathryn. If Dr. Amanda Knightbridge was telling the truth, and it would be easy to check, she seemed to be cleared. At least regarding Skylar Carvelle's murder.

She leaned forward, "May I ask *you* some things?

"Yes, but I may not be able to answer."

"Have you spoken with Kathryn Anthony?"

"You mean about the explosion and Carl's death?"

"No, I mean in general."

"Yes, I've spoken with her...in general."

"Do you feel she is attractive?"

"Huh?" I said stunned.

"Are you attracted to her? Personally?"

"Why do you feel you need to know that, Dr. Knightbridge?"

"Ah, well... I think you would complement each other," she said as though she had simply suggested a wine to have with dinner.

Chapter 16

As I walked down College Street, my mind wandered to Amanda Knightbridge's suggestion that Kathryn and I would complement each other. Maybe I could spin control my unpunctual behavior by getting Dr. Knightbridge to call Kathryn and tell *her* that.

Instead, I called Jimmy Harmon's office. His secretary told me Professor Harmon was in the recording studio and that he planned to be there all night. Good, I'd go to the Music History Building as soon as I made a few other calls.

The hospital told me that Bart Edgar had been discharged. Georgia Smith was still in very serious condition. She could have visitors if her family agreed, but only for very short periods.

I also called the dorm number for Mike Jacobsen the student who'd been recording music just before Carl died. He said I could come and see him anytime tonight.

First things first. I headed directly to the Music History Building. Instead of taking the elevator, I walked quietly up the stairs. I didn't want Jimmy Harmon yelling at me when the elevator noise screwed up his recording session. When I got to the second floor, there were five musicians packing up their guitars, fiddles and music and pulling on their coats.

Jimmy came out of the recording booth, saying distractedly, "That was great everybody, I think we're all done for today." Harmon stared through me for a minute then turned his back and headed back to Jack in the booth.

"Jimmy, I'm not leaving until we talk," I said sternly, "so turn off whatever part of your brain is concentrating on doing something else and listen to me."

His shoulders slumped. "OK," he said resignedly, "just let me tell Jack he can leave." When Jimmy came back, we each took a chair in the empty circle.

Jimmy Harmon had opportunity: he was at the meeting and could have put the bottle on the table, he was in Skylar Carvelle's office where he was able to overhear that I was on my way to Carvelle's condo. He also had some level of motive: he had a hell of a temper and had almost hit both Carl and Bart. So I might be talking to the killer in a deserted building all by myself. I should have been more concerned, but the thing was, I liked him. He seemed like a nice guy. On the other hand, what do I know from guys? Kathryn Anthony's voice rang in my mind... " Trust no one."

"What did you want to see Skylar Carvelle about this morning?"

"Huh, oh God, um...he had some projections of next year's enrollment..." Harmon's voice trailed off.

"Jimmy, where did you go after Skylar's office this morning?" I asked sharply.

"Oh geez. I drove home. My kids were in school. Linda was out. Skylar's dead... I don't have an alibi, go ahead, and type my name at the top of the list."

I did.

"How about when Carl died?"

"I was in my office on the fourth floor of this building listening to a series of recordings with headphones. When I have the headphones on, I can't hear a damn thing. Even though the police and rescue workers were swarming all over this building, I didn't know Carl was dead until late in the day."

I watched him carefully as he spoke, his red hair seemed limp and he sniffed, like he had the tail end of a cold. I asked, "What did you drink at the meeting in the conference room?"

"What?" he said looking up. He seemed disoriented.

"Your drink at the meeting, what was it?"

"OK, look," he hesitated. "There's...I..." He stopped and slapped his forehead, then started again, "See how my nose is running?" He pointed at his nose, in case I didn't know where it was, then he took out a purple handkerchief and blew, making a honking noise that would have impressed Harpo Marx.

I nodded. I figured he was about to admit to cocaine.

But he said, "I have terrible allergies. My nose runs constantly even at this time of year. In the spring and fall I'm miserable. A few months ago, my allergy doctor gave me a new prescription medication for pollen, animal hair, dust, mold allergies...it was supposed to cover everything. I went along with her because I really needed some relief." He sniffed, then blew his nose again. It looked red and sore.

"So?"

"It worked great but... serious side effects. Made me forget stuff and cranky. More than cranky. Edgy, quick to fly off the handle. You probably heard about me and Bart, I almost hit that asshole. How could anyone be as incompetent as that guy? But it was my fault too. I should have double-checked the invitations. The medication was making me forget everything. Hey, normally, I would never have assigned an important task to Bart. Why take the risk when there are a dozen other people who would have done it right?"

I didn't say anything. He was looking at the floor, talking more to himself than to me.

"The same kinda thing happened between me and Carl. He came in during a recording session. The noise ruined the take. I got so mad I almost... I almost hit a blind man just because he'd opened his door." Jimmy Harmon was shaking his head. There were tears in his eyes.

"Didn't you realize you were over the edge then?"

He looked up and nodded. "I finally told my wife what I'd done and she said I'd been acting strangely ever since the new allergy medication. So I called my doctor and she said she'd just gotten a bulletin that day cautioning physicians on the side effects of this medication. So I stopped taking it. My nose started running right away, but I felt in a fog for days, still do."

"Who's the doctor? I want to speak to her."

"Call her now," he said immediately. He looked at his watch. "She has evening appointments on Thursdays."

He gave me the number from his cell and I called. The doctor named the meds and apologized to Jimmy again. She even gave me a web site to check all the information. It all sounded legit to me. Jimmy Harmon seemed remorseful about his behavior, but so what if it was the drugs that made him into an angry kook. Angry kooks may be more likely to be killers than average guys.

"So, back to the soda at the conference room, are you saying you don't remember what you had?" I asked.

"No, I couldn't remember what I was *supposed* to have. I thought I'd ordered Yoohoo. I could have sworn ...but there wasn't any Yoohoo on the table. My brain felt so fuzzy. Then I saw the Grape Nehi. Real Americana. You know...every GI from Gomer to Radar? So I chose it. Nobody said, 'Hey, that's my Nehi!' So I took it back to my seat. Amanda said it was foul smelling and I thought so too. I didn't drink much."

"Before and after you were getting your drink, did you notice anyone acting strangely while they were getting theirs?"

"You mean other than me?" He laughed sardonically, wiping his nose on his handkerchief, "Um, honestly I was so hopped up, I wouldn't even drive my car. I called my wife to come and get me. Let's see, other people...no, I can't think of anything. Oh, wait; Skylar had a funny look on his face. Rolina Roth took forever to pour hers...she's always like that. Maybe that was my imagination."

"Is there any other reason you had for fighting with Carl Rasmus?"

"Why?" said Harmon shortly.

"Why? Because he's dead, that's why! Did you?"

"No. Look, Carl accused me of all sorts of things. He sent me outrageous emails..." A look of anguish flickered over Harmon's face.

"Do you have copies of any of them?"

"I delete things like that ... I'm sorry, I have work to do. Is there anything else?"

"Yeah there is. Carl claimed people on the tenure committee had slandered his work. Why would he say that?"

"I can't think why he would be so upset. Would you think a guy like that would kill himself just because he felt a little depressed or unhappy?"

"I didn't know him. What do you think?"

"I think about him everyday. I'm so sorry he's gone," said Jimmy Harmon shaking his head miserably.

Chapter 17

Fenchester City Hospital was twenty blocks away. Too far to walk in the cold December darkness, but a quick drive.

The lobby was classic hospital modern: glass, neutral carpeting and phony plants that looked real. Bright colored framed prints dotted the walls. To the right was a gift shop laden with things people in hospitals didn't want or need, at obscenely high prices. Where else can you buy an eighteen-dollar magazine?

I asked the woman at the desk where Georgia Smith's room was.

"Name?" she chirped. She had beehive hair, tons of make up and cat-eye glasses. I looked around to see if there was a candid camera from some low budget reality show focused on my face to capture my dubious reaction. This desk lady had to be an actor. But no, she was just the hospital desk volunteer... from another decade; or maybe another planet.

"Georgia Smith," I said slowly and clearly for the second time. She checked her list. Because Georgia's condition was so serious, the desk woman had to call somebody to check on what to do with me. Georgia's husband Adam said my visit was all right with him.

Hospitals used to be repositories of constant noise. Imagine an old movie or TV show about doctors saving lives at *St. Something*. Drama or comedy, there was always a non-stop soundtrack of public address system pages: *Calling Doctor Howard, Doctor Fine, Doctor Howard.*

That's pretty much history these days. Doctors, nurses, even aides, all have pagers on silent. The glaring lights are gone. Hospital lighting is *diffused*. Sometimes the hallways are even carpeted. Although the surface harshness is mostly gone, there's still the desperate battle between life and death. Death often wins. For many people, the worst moments of their lives are spent in a hospital, no matter how quiet or tastefully decorated it is.

On the third floor, Adam Smith, Georgia's husband, met me at the nurse's desk. Someone must have told him about my using the rug to smother

Georgia's burning clothes. Adam shook my hand, thanking me sincerely, and then he started crying and hugged me.

"Take deep breaths," I told him.

In an average week, Adam Smith was probably a good-looking guy, but now he looked like hell. He obviously hadn't slept for days, which was one reason he couldn't control his tears. A tumble of emotions showed simultaneously in his red-rimmed eyes. His sandy blond hair was uncombed and oily, his clothes were a mass of wrinkles and he needed a shower, badly.

"She's going to be OK," I said consolingly.

He nodded and began to cry again, but stopped after two sobs and said, "Yes, she is. I...um...you want to talk to her? She's under heavy sedation, she sometimes says things that make sense, but then other times..." he looked off into space vaguely.

"Adam, you need to go home and get some sleep."

"I can't, I can't. I have to be here in case she wakes up. I don't want her to be alone."

"Where are her sons?"

"They're home now. They'll be back at 7:00 PM."

"Is there anyone else in the family who could be here...?"

He shook his head absently.

"If I could get someone here, would you go home and sleep?"

He just stared at me.

I said firmly, "You'll be of no use to her if you make yourself sick with exhaustion." He nodded slightly.

A nurse let me dial 9 on the hospital phone to get an outside line. I called Amanda Knightbridge and told her that Adam Smith hadn't slept in 48 hours. She suggested she come to the hospital immediately to sit with Georgia while Adam went home to rest. I told her I'd get Georgia's sons to pick her up. Adam gave me their number. I got hold of them and told them to swing by Washington Mews to pick up Amanda Knightbridge.

Adam and I went into Georgia's room. There were monitors and tons of equipment I couldn't begin to identify, but everything was turned off. The lights were low. The room was quiet.

Georgia lay in a high hospital bed on her stomach. There was some kind of frame under the covers that held the sheets above her legs like a tent. There was a chair placed at the end of the bed so she could see and talk to someone without having to lift her head. I was glad I couldn't see her legs. I didn't need another mental image like that.

"Sit down, she can see you better. She's on a constant painkiller drip,"

Adam said inclining his head toward an IV bag, "they just told me the doctor wants to increase the pain dosage in the morning so she'll be in, like, a semi-coma for a few days. It's supposed to make it easier for her." Tears were forming in his eyes again, "I want it to be easier for her." He shook he head sadly, then pulled himself together and went on, "even now, she may not be able to say anything."

I sat and waited, watching Georgia's face for any sign of movement. Ten minutes went by. Suddenly Georgia blinked her eyes open. She'd been so still that the rapid change startled both Adam and me.

Adam said, "Georgia, honey, this is Maggie Gale. Do you remember her? She was in the conference room." Georgia's eyes focused on my face. The drugs had slackened her features. She tried to concentrate through the fog of meds.

"Oh," she said very quietly. Her eyes became brighter.

Adam said with mild surprise, "She knows who you are."

Georgia moved her head to face me more directly. She opened her mouth to speak, but the breathy sound that came out was so slight I couldn't hear her. She became agitated. She wanted to tell me something. I leaned very close so that her mouth was at my ear. She whispered each syllable slowly and separately, but what she said didn't make any sense. It sounded like, "Carl's macaroni's can." She stopped and nodded slightly. As if to encourage me. As if she was sure I knew what she meant. Then she closed her eyes and drifted off.

"Georgia?" I said in a low voice. She didn't even move. After another few minutes I stood up and walked with Adam out of the room.

"What did she say?" Adam Smith asked brushing his hair from his eyes, wearily.

"It sounded like, 'Carl's macaroni's can'? Does that mean anything to you?"

"No, but it isn't the first time she's said something weird like that. She's slurring her words from the drugs." Adam yawned so widely that I imagined him dislocating his jaw and having to stay that way. His breath was rank. When he finally closed his mouth, he shook his head like a dog. "I'm sorry," he apologized.

Just then two teenaged boys got off the elevator followed by Amanda Knightbridge. The boys were wearing jeans and big sweatshirts and were similar looking except one was a little taller and heavier than the other. Both looked tired and anxious, and as though this tragedy had aged their souls. They came immediately to Adam to ask how their mother was. I took

Amanda Knightbridge aside.

She said, "I'm glad you called me Ms. Gale...oh dear, Adam looks dreadful."

"He needs rest. Maybe one of the boys should go back with him too."

"Send both of the boys back with him, they're all very tired. I have several books, so I can easily be here all night." She glanced at Georgia again, and then focused her bright eyes back on me. "Do you feel Georgia may be in danger?"

"She could be. I think she may know something, but I don't think the... killer... knows that she knows. Regardless, you have to promise me that you'll not let anyone else from the College in the room with Georgia alone." I was impressed that she'd picked up on the possibility Georgia might be a target. "Georgia just mumbled 'Carl's macaroni's can,' to me, does that mean anything to you?"

"No, it doesn't mean anything to me. Do you know who the perpetrator is?"

"No, I don't."

"Yet, you feel I'm not a suspect? You must be going on instinct alone, because I'm sure you have not had time to check my alibi. Perhaps you should call Kathryn Anthony to confirm my story..."

I just smiled at her.

She smiled back and said, "I'll not leave Georgia's side."

"Good. I'm going to arrange with President Bouchet for a guard. I'll call you here to tell you when the guard will arrive and how to identify him or her, OK?"

"Yes, that will be fine."

Georgia Smith's sons went home with Adam. I had assured them all that not only would Amanda Knightbridge stay, but that Georgia would feel secure with her there. The boys looked relieved, Adam looked worried. Whether they would get any rest, I couldn't say.

Chapter 18

The President's Mansion was lit up like a Christmas tree. Every window blazed. The house was obviously full of people. Miranda Juarez answered the door. She looked neat and efficient in a crisp gray suit and ivory blouse, but there was an undercurrent of stress in her voice and her hand shook slightly when she opened the door to a cozy room near the back of the house.

I said, "You're here late...have you been here all day?"

"No, I was in my temporary office this morning working on reconstructing files that were damaged in the fire, then I had some errands to run for the President. Would you like coffee?"

When I said no, she left to get Bouchet. I pulled my laptop out of my bag and made some notes. Less than a minute later, Max Bouchet came in and closed the door. His dark Armani suit was wrinkled and he'd loosened his red striped power tie.

"Has something else happened?" he asked anxiously. Stress was running high. No wonder. People were falling off balconies, getting blown up, and being killed by flying paperweights. Things weren't going well at Bouchet's College.

"No, nothing new, except information." He visibly relaxed and sank into an armchair as I told him about seeing Georgia Smith. He readily OKed a round the clock guard for her, so I paused to make a quick call to a security company I often use, to set it up.

"Max, Skylar Carvelle wanted to talk to me today, but when I got there it was too late. Had he said anything to you?"

Bouchet sighed and leaned back in his chair. "Carvelle was always telling me things about the other faculty, sometimes petty things, sometimes serious."

"A tattletale?"

"Exactly, but I hadn't spoken to him for several days, and I can't think of anything he's said that might have to do with Carl's death. I'm sorry I can't be more help on this, I'll try to remember if there was anything else."

I asked Bouchet for access to Carl Rasmus's apartment.

"He lived in Married Student Housing, right on campus. He wanted to be close to his office and he said he didn't care what the place *looked like*. Security has passkeys. Some of the security people are here now." He went out the door and was gone for a few minutes. He came back with four keys on a single ring. "These are pass keys to the whole college. They'll open almost every door in the place. I have no idea how many people have these. That's why I had Carl's office padlocked," he said shaking his head.

"You have no idea who has pass keys to the college? So anyone could have had a key to Carl's office or to the door to the fatal balcony? Why didn't you tell me this?"

"I know, I know, I just found this out myself. The whole college has been on the same key system for at least twenty years. It's a security nightmare," he groaned with exasperation. "Skylar's death wasn't on Campus...and classes and exams are over, most of the students have gone...and I've had undercover guards on campus since yesterday morning."

"Yeah, I saw them in the Administration Building."

"You did? But..." Bouchet was shocked I'd noticed his guys when they were supposed to be incognito.

"It's my job to notice, and it's not as if they look like college students."

"Oh, yes, well," he conceded.

"Max, students may not be at risk, but faculty have certainly been targeted, do you think it's wise to..."

"Maggie, I know I may be making a mistake but if we close, we may never solve any of these crimes, and that could close the College forever."

It was my turn to groan, but I did it inwardly, then I asked, "Is there anyone here, now, who could corroborate where you were today?" The sound of Kathryn Anthony's voice saying, "Trust no one," had just flitted through my brain, again. I was pretty confident about Bouchet's honesty, but I needed to be sure.

"Um, yes," Bouchet understood the implication but didn't complain. He leaned out the door and called out, "Sam! Angus!"

Two big guys from the College Security Squad came into the room and answered my questions. Bouchet had been in the President's House from 9:00 AM until about 12:30 PM when he and the guys had gone to the College Tavern for lunch.

When they'd gone Bouchet asked me, "Have you narrowed the suspects?"

"Well, in a way." I replied, "It's pretty obvious Skylar didn't kill himself.

Georgia and Bart are out because they were in the hospital when Skylar was killed and Amanda Knightbridge seems to have an alibi for Skylar's murder, too. Because I think the two deaths are related, Dan Cohen's out because he was away during Carl's death, as was Kathryn Anthony, but I'm adding someone to the original list. So barring the *unknown factor*, I have five suspects. I haven't had much luck finding anyone with a clear motive and I need to check alibies for this morning. I already know that Jimmy Harmon doesn't have one. I'm going to Carl's apartment now, then the police station to make a statement. Anything new about that organization...Carl's beneficiary?"

"No, nothing so far." Max Bouchet continued with genuine concern, "Maggie, the police told me Skylar's killer shot at you today."

"Wild shot. Just to scare me. I don't think the killer is much of a marksman."

"Never-the-less, be careful," he rumbled sincerely.

****

All the Irwin dorms are in the same part of the campus, so I stopped first at an undergrad dorm to speak to Mike Jacobsen, the student who'd been using the recording studio the day Carl was killed.

Mike Jacobsen's dorm door was open. His computer screen had just frozen on a music writing program and he was clicking the mouse repeatedly in frustration. "Shit," he said resignedly poking the escape key and pushing long brown hair out of his eyes at the same time.

"Mike? I'm investigating the death of Carl Rasmus. May I speak with you for a minute?"

Jacobsen turned in his desk chair, "Investigating Dr. Rasmus? Like for insurance or something," he asked focusing on my investigator license, I'd held out for him to read.

"Something like that...I just need to know one thing. Jack Leavitt said he thought you might have heard a phone ringing over the mic when you were recording on the day Dr. Rasmus died. Did you?"

"I don't remember much, it was a bad day. Um...yeah, I heard ringing, I guess it was a phone. Probably Dr. Rasmus's because it wasn't from the phone in the booth or any of our cells. It didn't ring for long."

"How many rings?"

"One or two times. Kinda hard to tell, but the sound was there and it ruined that part of the take. It sucked because Caitlyn had sung awesome."

"What time were the rings? Do you know?"

Mike thought for a minute. "Well, we had to stop the recording. I think I clocked the redub at 12:58 PM. It was just before 1:00 PM," he replied with certainty.

Chapter 19

On my way out of the undergrad dorm, my cell phone rang. It was Lt. Ed O'Brien. He tried to be polite, but basically he said, "Get your ass down here, now!" So instead of going to Carl's Apartment, I drove downtown and gave Ed my statement. On my way to the police station, I called the hospital and got through to Amanda Knightbridge on the particulars about the guard for Georgia.

When Ed let me go, it was 10:00 PM. I went to Carl's apartment to see if maybe he kept clues in an old Spaghetti-Os can.

Carl's place in Married Student Housing was on the ground floor near the front door. I let myself in with one of the passkeys. Up until that point, all the Irwin buildings I'd visited had been works of architectural art, but Married Student Housing was just as grim and depressing as I'd remembered it. I'd been there a few years before to see a beautiful poetry professor, with whom I'd had a brief fling.

Carl's apartment in MSH had cement block walls painted institutional green, green indoor--outdoor carpeting, three particle board kitchen cabinets, a counter the size of a door mat, harsh overhead fluorescent lighting and low end industrially made furniture in dull colors that showed extensive wear. And these were its *best* features. This dorm was the ugliest building at Irwin with the ugliest interior decoration. It was an abomination. It was as though the college was punishing students for being in long-term relationships.

Carl's apartment had even less furniture than most. Probably to make it easier for him to get around. There was no art on the walls, no mirrors, no floor lamps and no printed books, although I found some Braille ones by his bed. I looked in every drawer and cabinet, and the one closet. I even turned up the mattress. I pulled out drawers and checked their undersides. I checked the undersurfaces of the chairs and the tiny kitchen table. Nothing.

In the food cabinet, there were two boxes of cereal, a can of tomato soup, and some condiments. There was a box of saltines that were stale, and a box of Devil Dogs three-packs that weren't. Hey, I hadn't had dinner, OK? I didn't think Carl would mind if I ate some more of his Devil Dogs. In fact, since I seemed to be the only one trying to find out who killed him, I figured Carl would have welcomed me a nosh.

The small refrigerator offered a big bottle of diet Pepsi, some American cheese squares individually wrapped, a bag of brown slimy lettuce, some mushy apples, and cartons of milk and orange juice. The milk was bad; the OJ was on the edge. There were jars of mayonnaise and mustard, a squeeze bottle of ketchup and a six-pack of Sam Adams. I contemplated opening a bottle of ale but decided against it, it was unprofessional enough that I was eating a dead guy's Devil Dogs. Taking up most of the space was a half eaten angel food cake that was covered with green mold. I stared at it for a long time. Moldy cake equals sad lonely feeling.

Everything had Braille labels. It made the space seem more personal and human and much more heartbreaking. This was his food. These were his things. But Carl was never coming back to finish his cake. It made me think of Mickey Murphy all alone in jail. I wondered what was rotting in Mickey's refrigerator.

I sighed as I moved to the bathroom. I checked the medicine cabinet. It was neat. No prescriptions or weird over the counter stuff. Just standard medicine cabinet fare. I checked the drawers and cabinet under the sink; extra toilet paper rolls, a new bar of soap, some shampoo, etc. Nothing with a secret compartment or a hidden message. The cover of the toilet tank had nothing taped to the underside. The drain had nothing stuck in it. The light fixture had a light bulb and that was all.

The only thing Carl had in the apartment of any interest was a huge sound system with hundreds and hundreds of CDs. The CD's had Braille labels too. I even found the little electronic Braille label machine. He had every kind of music and sound recording anyone could ever imagine. I figured the group in his will, Rainbow Youth Symphony would probably get his CDs too. Maybe he'd stored things with his family. I could ask them when I went to Hadesville tomorrow.

Georgia had said, "Carl's macaroni's can," but there were no empty macaroni cans here. There were no full cans of pasta either. There were no boxes of frozen macaroni or any kind of noodles. I even looked in the garbage to see if he'd thrown any away. Nothing.

I decided to look at every CD. Maybe there was a recording that was related. I searched my brain for pasta related song titles. Yankee Doodle called his cap Macaroni, was the only thing I could come up with. I looked through the CDs for an hour. Nothing there either. I felt frustrated.

"Carl," I called softly, standing in the middle of the room, "give me a sign!"

His phone rang...I jumped two feet barking, "Holy Shit!"

I looked at my watch. It was almost midnight. Everybody knew Carl was dead. Who'd be calling now? I picked up the phone on the second ring, and said very softly, "Hello?"

There was only breathing, then a hang up.

I waited a minute, then hung up too. I star 89ed the phone and asked the operator to give me the number of the person who'd just called, but the caller had used a pay phone. That's the only way to make a truly anonymous call these days. There's no way to trace a pay phone call. You can't even call the pay phone and just hope someone answers and ask them where the phone is any more, because most incoming pay phone calls are blocked to keep drug dealers from using them to avoid tapped lines. So what the hell? Had this been for me, or Carl, or was it just a wrong number?

I realized there was an answering machine cord hooking the phone to a machine on a shelf under the phone stand. I pressed the replay button. Carl's voice said, "Carl Rasmus...please leave a message at the beep and I'll get back to you." Huh, so that was what Carl sounded like. Nice voice. The machine's mechanical voice then said there were six messages stored. I hit the play-back button.

Call #1: Beep..."Carl, this is Kathryn Anthony, I have the rest of the information you need for your grant proposal. I'll be back from Seattle tomorrow. I could give it to you then, or fax it to you now, if you need it today. You can reach me on my cell. OK? Bye."

Call #2: Beep..."Carl? It's Jim Harmon...we have to talk...um, soon, OK?..."

Call #3: Beep..."Carl Rasmus?" a staccato voice said. "This is Rowlina Roth-Holtzmann. I dislike machines. I must speak with you. I must clear up this misunderstanding. I am concerned you have the wrong idea."

Call #4: Beep... "Dr. Rasmus, this is Miranda Juarez. I have several pieces of information of which the President would like you to become aware immediately. I also wish to confer with you about the matter we began to discuss yesterday regarding the grant money. Please call me at your earliest convenience. Thank you."

Call #5 Beep... "Hello... Dr. Rasmus? This is Connie Robinson," said Connie in a nervous voice. "They told me at church I have to talk to you? OK? I'll try you at your office."

Call #6: Beep... "Hey Carl, it's Leo. Leo Getty. Hey, son, I need to talk to you about before, the grant stuff, OK... I'll try you later, or maybe we can talk tomorrow?"

I rewound the machine and listened to all the messages again. I'd just asked Carl for a sign. He'd sent me the answering machine full of cryptic messages from the group of people who'd had the best chance to kill him. Not to mention the odd little *wrong number*. Creepy. Carl's machine was not set to indicate the time and date that calls came in. The people calling him all seemed to want to speak with him urgently. Except Kathryn. And they were calling him at home, which means they couldn't get him in his office. Maybe he was ducking people.

I unplugged the answering machine, wrapped the cord around it, and tucked it under my arm. It seemed too important to leave behind. I turned out the lights and locked up the apartment. I hadn't found a macaroni can stuffed with clues, but I did find out that a bunch of people from the college wanted to talk to Carl not long before he died. Furthermore, whatever it was they wanted to talk about, they didn't want to leave a message on the phone machine.

****

It was late; nearly midnight and very dark. The hallway of Married Student Housing, with its unattractive glaring lights and prison-like cement walls, was very reminiscent of 1960s housing projects. Most of those 60s projects have been torn down or rebuilt.

Max needs to bulldoze this building, I thought.

Five minutes on the street in my van and I realized someone was following me. It was a compact sedan; American made, probably. I couldn't see the model clearly. I certainly couldn't see the plate number. Was it the person who'd just called Carl's apartment? Hmmm, this was becoming interesting.

In Fenchester, there's a traffic light or stop sign at nearly every intersection. I stopped at a sign. The tail car stayed back in the shadows, allowing a SUV to get in between us. I turned right on 14th and sped up to Hamilton, turned left and went 4 blocks, then hung a quick left at 10th. I sped half way down the block, then squealed a left into an alley next to the Stonewall bar. Needless to say, it's a gay bar. I sped behind the bar and came around the other side heading toward 10th. The little sedan hadn't seen me turn.

I switched off my lights and idled next to a gaggle of garbage cans. The sedan came slowly along 10th Street. I edged out, still with my lights off. To the left, I could see the sedan waiting for the light to change at 10th and Linden Street.

Linden is one way going uptown, so the sedan could either go straight ahead on 10th, or go to the left. I figured the sedan would go to the left because it couldn't see me straight ahead. I was correct. The sedan turned onto Linden, I followed. I was chasing my tail. It was fun. No wonder dogs do it.

Just in case, I reached in my shoulder bag and took out my gun, placing it within reach on the passenger seat. The sedan picked up speed. As it passed under a bright streetlight, I got a better look. Maybe a Chevy Neon? Dark color; blue, gray or black. I couldn't get close enough to read the plates without giving myself away and losing my chance to tail the tail.

The Neon was about two blocks ahead, it made a quick right on 12th. I hung back and watched. In two more blocks the Neon would be in the Mews. It drove along the west end of the Mews on 12th all the way to Liberty, then made a right turn and traced the Mews to 10th street again turning right. It stopped next to a fire hydrant, close to the southeast corner of the square. It idled with lights out, like an animal waiting for prey. Exhaust steam rose from its butt.

I peered into the dark. No one got out. I was stopped with my lights out a block back on 10th, behind a full sized van. Weird. It idled there for a full ten minutes but this wasn't where I lived. So what was it doing here after following me? I glanced at the rowhouse facades, they were dark. Even the Hampshire Apartment building had no lighted windows. Everyone in the Mews had called it a night.

The Neon started up again and turned right onto Washington Street. I followed it several blocks, back toward Irwin College, past the Administration Building toward the Student Union. Then it turned right onto College Street. College Street is the mid street between 15th and 16th. I followed on College but there were no other cars, so I had to drive with my lights out. The Neon drove slowly past a few buildings that were very dark, and then sped up. I turned on my lights and sped after it.

The Neon cornered onto Liberty and ripped up the street running a red light at 16th. Opposing traffic screeched to a twisting halt. It cornered right and zoomed toward Fen Street. I couldn't see where it went next. I was stuck behind traffic. The Neon was gone. *Damn.*

I drove back to my building taking arbitrary turns now and then to be sure nobody was dogging me. I parked in my garage. It's a huge loading dock area in the back of the first floor. The ten-horse power motor shrieks and groans when it raises the huge garage door. Sorry neighbors, but I felt safer with my minivan inside tonight.

I came into the building through the garage and up the three flights to my loft. I was tired but I forced myself to exercise. I have an extensive workout space on the top floor above my living area. I lifted weights and used the elliptical for an hour. I've read fiction where the woman detective runs on the beach or goes to the gym and then extols the joys of exercise. The character insists it makes her feel happy and exhilarated. Well, I'm here to tell you, that's crap. I hate exercise. I hate it when I'm planning to do it. I hate it when I'm doing it. It never makes me feel exhilarated. It rarely lessens my stress. It never makes me feel happy with the world. That's a lot of hooey.

Exercising makes you stronger in the long run and tired in the short. I'll concede that like PF Flyers, exercise makes you able to run faster and jump higher and I'll admit it makes you sleep better. Being able to lift a lot of weight gives you an edge in a fight, which may elevate your self-esteem, but if you want to do something that makes you happy, I'd suggest eating chocolate or having sex. Probably not in that order.

I took Carl's Voice Transcription Software Instruction Manual to bed with me. Talk about a non-habit forming soporific. I was out in seconds.

Chapter 20

Morning came fast. I'd called ahead to make some appointments with people at Hadesville High School and with Carl's siblings. And, I was aware of the meeting I was scheduled to have with Kathryn Anthony in the evening. So I wore my newest black jeans, my cleanest polo shirt, and my best sweater. It wasn't as if I was going to have a date with Kathryn. This was business. On the other hand, you never know what might happen, so I wore new underwear, too. Needless to say, I'm not a big Boy Scouts fan, but I like the motto: Be Prepared.

After eating a bowl of cereal, I loaded the CD with the Voice Transcription System program and all of Carl's files right into my laptop. I hoisted my shoulder bag, tucked the laptop under my arm, grabbed an apple and a juice box of OJ, and headed for my garage. It was 7:30 AM.

Once on the road, it would take me about two and a half hours to get to Hadesville, which is on the other side of Harrisburg. Half of Hadesville is actually the campus of St. Bonaventure College, the largest Catholic college in the state. It was where Leo Getty used to be football coach. In fact, as far as I knew the football team at St. Bonnie's was just about the only thing at the college to *write home about.* People in PA got as het up about St. Bonnie's games as they did about Penn State games. The two colleges were in different conferences so they never played each other. Just as well. Riots would ensue.

I wondered why Leo Getty had left his coaching position at St. Bonnie's when he still seemed so into the game. Of course, many would judge that being the Dean of Students at an old and prestigious private college, is much more impressive than being a football coach. On the flip side, about the same number of folks probably never heard of Irwin college, had no idea what a Dean of Students did, but would kill for a seat at a St. Bonnie's game, even if they had to sit on a frozen bleacher in 10 degree weather, watching the action during a blizzard. Leo seemed more like the latter kind of guy, but maybe he had just gotten tired of coaching bratty prima donna football stars who felt they shouldn't have to go to class just to pass a course.

I plugged my computer into the van power source. I prefer to call it a power source rather than a cigarette lighter, because it has never lit a cigarette and never will. My father died of emphysema. I hate smoking. I hate tobacco companies. There is no cigarette lighter in my van. It's a power source.

The laptop began to read me the tutorial for the voice transcription software. It called itself VTS for short. I told it it could call me Maggie. The VTS introduction began by telling me how wonderful it was. Nothing humble about this program. If it had a horn sound effect, it would blow its own.

The VTS insisted that if I did everything right, I could talk at a rate of 175 word per minute and it would transcribe the words into a text document. Cool. All I would have to do is read five short stories into the mic. The program would record how I said all the words and then it would recognize those words when I said them again and write them down. Even if the words were different from those in the stories, the general word sounds would be about the same and the program would still be able to figure them out.

I listened to the entire tutorial. It described all the separate features that made the program work even better than I could ever imagine. It explained how I could adjust for background noise and voice level. It explained that one must speak slowly and clearly. It said I could set up key word abbreviations called micros or macros. A *micro* would change my words into an abbreviation. Like if I said, United Nations, the computer would change it to UN. Or if I frequently included an address or contact information at the end of an email, for example, I could record a *macro* key word. When I said the key word, the whole address or all the contact information would appear.

It explained that the computer might *hear* certain words wrong. If it does, it's up to the user to find the mistake and then retype the word so the computer would know the word the next time.

Using the speak text program to read text out loud was the easiest of all. All you had to do was copy and paste any text document onto a VTS page. Then hit a key, or even just use your voice to command it, and it would speak the text.

Some of the voice modes sounded like men, some women. One sounded like the robot on *Lost in Space*. One sounded like a slide guitar. The voice that had been reading this all to me was called Angelica. Even though all the voices were different, they were all flatly electronic. No one could ever mistake them for real people.

I pulled into the Hadesville High parking lot at 10:00 AM. My appointment with the Assistant Principal wasn't until 11:00 AM. So I tried to enter my voice into the VTS voice recognition file. At first it wouldn't recognize me at all. As I read a paragraph, each word I said was supposed to be highlighted as the computer *heard* it. It wasn't getting anything I said. Finally, I got the hang of it, but certain words were a problem. When I got to the word *system*, I had to say it 59 times before the computer accepted it. Maybe I have a speech impediment that no one has ever mentioned. I read two of the stories into it then I shut the computer down, hid it under the van seat, and headed for the entrance to the school.

Boys have baggier pants, shorter hair and more piercings than when I was in High School, girls wear tighter clothes and have more piercings. Otherwise kids all look about the same. Hadesville High was definitely big. There must have been several thousand students. The inside had the odor of industrial cleaner and teen hormones.

These days, people walking around schools without an ID around their necks are considered terrorists or pedophiles. So I went directly to the main office to check in. At a big counter I showed a middle-aged assistant my Private Investigator License and told her I was investigating the death of a former student.

"Who died?" she asked leaning her large frame over the counter.

"Carl Rasmus. He was blind?" It might be hard to remember even a bright student from that long ago, but a blind student would be rare.

"I saw that on the news." She was resting her chin on her fist, thinking, "He killed himself, right? I do remember him. Really good at music? He played the piano?"

"Right. That was Carl. I have an appointment." I gave her one of my cards.

"Well, it must be with Mr. Goldenberger, you can't really see anybody without talking to Vice Principal Goldenberger first. And he's been here 20 years!" She took my card with her and went back behind her desk into an office with an open door, then came back without the card.

"You can come in." She pressed a buzzer that unlocked a gate. Whether you're 15 or 35 or 75, being called into the Vice Principal's office can strike fear into the heart of anyone who has ever been in High School. I reminded myself I was a tough private eye.

Larry Goldenberger was a short, bald guy with a fringe of gray hair. He was wearing a gray suit and small gold rimmed glasses. I strongly hoped

Goldenberger wasn't going to be a little Napoleon who'd give me a hard time just because he could.

"Mr. Goldenberger, my name is Maggie Gale. I'm a private investigator working for Irwin College."

He was standing there reading my card. He looked up from it to me, paused and then said emphatically, "A private investigator...cool!"

Whew, that broke the ice.

"What can I do you for?" he asked sitting down behind his desk and motioning me to a chair.

"You've probably heard about Carl Rasmus killing himself at Irwin College about ten days ago? I've been asked to look into the circumstances of his death. The lady at the desk told me you were here when Carl was a student. Do you remember him?"

"Wait, wait...the news said Carl killed himself by jumping off a building right?"

I nodded.

Goldenberger eyed me for a moment then asked, "Yes, they said that, or yes, that's what happened to him?" Astute question, but after all this guy was a pro; he had to get the truth out of dozens of closed mouthed teenagers, every day.

"Candidly, some evidence may suggest there was more to Dr. Rasmus's death than a despondent person taking his own life. I don't know what really happened. That's why I'm here. I'm trying to figure out what kind of a person Carl Rasmus was."

"I can't show you his file..." said Goldenberger more to himself than me. He was thinking it over, then he said decisively, "I'm not supposed to give out confidential information about former students. But let's face it, the kid's dead. Let me look at what we have." He got up and went out to talk with one of the secretaries then came back.

"It'll take a while to get the file. Meanwhile, I'll tell you what I remember," said Goldenberger helpfully. "Carl was a good kid. He played the clarinet in the jazz band. He wrote music too, and the band and orchestra performed it. I wrote him a recommendation for college myself. I think he went to Julliard, and then went on to get a Ph.D. and teach at Irwin. I wrote him a recommendation for that job too because he came back to Hadesville to do presentations now and then and even helped with one of the summer music programs. I think it was *Fiddler on the Roof.*"

A woman came in with a print-out. Goldenberger thanked her, looked it over then said, "Here's the short version. He got good grades. Took a lot of music classes. He was in musical productions and everyone seemed to like him."

"I was told he was thrown out of Hadesville High School for bad behavior..."

Goldenberger frowned at that, "He wasn't thrown out of here. He was...he left a different high school in the second semester of his sophomore year and *came* here."

"He was thrown out of a different school and ended up here?" I asked, now I was surprised.

"I'm not supposed to say *thrown out*, but yeah, that's what happened."

"Why?"

"Doesn't say why in the file. His transcript from the previous school was fine, excellent in fact. It wasn't grades."

"What was the previous school?"

"St. Bonaventure High School, it's adjacent to the College." Goldenberger leaned back in his chair drumming his fingers on his desk. "OK, look, I'll be honest. I knew Carl as a student fairly well. I remember the whole thing. Bit of a scandal...would have been nothing in a public school, today. Really didn't mean much to us then... You probably already know that Carl was gay..." I nodded for Goldenberger to continue, "and, St. Bonnie's High School is mighty conservative, and well, Carl got thrown out because he..." Goldenberger gave a short laugh, then shook his head, "I'm sorry, it just seems so stupid now...he got caught kissing a boy under the bleachers in the field house."

"Really!?!" Now *I* was laughing, but then I realized it probably wasn't funny for Carl.

"Yeah," Goldenberger went on, "see, private schools can expel a student without explanation. In fact, a private school could even deny matriculation to a blind student by requiring the student do something he wouldn't be able to do. Like read something from a paper. Religious schools have all sorts of rules that could never be applied to public school. As I remember it, I think Carl could probably have calmed things down if he'd just said it was a mistake and that he wasn't gay, but he wasn't that kind of kid. And I think he really cared about the other boy."

"What happened to him?"

"The other boy? I don't know anything about him."

I typed the information into my laptop. "Do you think Carl might have killed himself because he hated being gay?"

"Nope," said Goldenberger emphatically shaking his head. "Not unless

Carl changed a lot. When he was a student here, Carl was *out*...the first out gay kid we had...he wasn't depressed that he was gay and he wasn't depressed because he was blind. He was what he was."

I told Goldenberger there would be a memorial service for Carl on Sunday morning at the Irwin Chapel. He said he'd try to come, and then he shook my hand.

So Carl got tossed out of Catholic School for kissing a boy. It sounded like the kind of thing gay characters on a sitcom would brag about, but it must have been very painful in real life.

Next stop, Carl's siblings. My appointments with them weren't for an hour, so I tried to amuse myself by reading some more stories into the VTS program, but I kept thinking about Carl being thrown out of Catholic High School. I was glad my family hadn't tried to force an anti-gay religion on me. Life is hard enough for teens.

Chapter 21

"Mrs. Crenshaw, thank you for letting me talk to you about your brother Carl," I said as I waded through wall-to-wall plastic toys, to perch on the arm of a pine frame easy chair. Its Revolutionary War theme upholstered seat was covered with Duplo blocks. If you think about it, bloody battle scenes on the easy chairs are kind of an odd choice for suburban living room furniture.

Eileen Crenshaw was in her early 30s. She was wearing a pink sweat suit with Care Bears on it. Mrs. Crenshaw's light brown hair was pulled back in a ponytail. She was my height but had a few pounds on me. A little kid also dressed in pink, 3-years-old, clung to the back of her leg. I figured it was a girl because its been my experience that while parents seem to have no qualms about occasionally dressing a little girl in blue, they would rather dip a boy in mud than dare dress him in pink.

A little peek-shihtz-oodle-eeze style dog, that had been yapping since I'd rung the *Avon Calling* doorbell, skidded around the living room. I wondered why anyone who had a three-year-old would want that kind of animal. Both like to run the house. The dog was probably there first.

"Carl's dead," said Eileen Crenshaw flatly.

"I know," I said sympathetically, "I've been hired by Irwin College to look into his death."

"Why? ...Buttons, shut up!" said Eileen Crenshaw, except she pronounced the dog's name *Bah-ins*. "The house is kind of a mess," she said looking at the living room floor as though seeing it for the first time. In the corner was a huge Christmas tree decorated with every Precious Moments ornament ever made. There were a few presents under it. The rest of the haul was no doubt stashed in a closet to be spread out after the kid hit the sheets on Christmas Eve.

Eileen Crenshaw plopped down on the couch and put her feet up on a heavy pine coffee table.

"Mrs. Crenshaw..."

"Cindy, you stop that! Stop that right now, or I'll tell Santa not to bring you anything!" The little girl ignored her mother and continued taking ornaments off the tree and carrying them to a plastic dollhouse in another corner of the room. There was no way in heck that Santa wasn't going to fork over that closet full of presents. Mommy knew it and somehow, so did the kid. At the tender age of three, little Cindy had already learned the meaning of the term *idle threat.*

"Mrs. Crenshaw," I started again, "I just have a few questions."

"Waa? Oh yeah, OK."

"Mrs. Crenshaw, Carl was made to leave high school. Did that make him depressed?"

"Oh, no, not Carl. *He* never was unhappy and *he* never got in trouble. He wanted to go to a different school," she quipped with surprising bitterness.

"Why?"

"Didn't like St. Bonnie's. I mean, if he'd just tried to be normal, he would have been just fine there, but no, *he* wanted to be different."

"Well, he was different wasn't he?"

"Huh?" she said distractedly biting the side of her fingernail, focusing on the dog as it sniffed at the Christmas tree's base.

"Well, he was different from other children, wasn't he?"

"You mean because he was good at music? Yeah, Carl got all the talent, it was so easy for him. He got all the breaks." *I guessed she meant all the breaks, like being blind.*

"Did you and your brother take music classes?"

"Sure I took... but I wasn't any good. Same with Kevin."

"About Carl..."

"Thrown out cuz he was queer with another boy and they caught him," she stage whispered so Cindy and *Bah-ins* wouldn't hear. "My mother was really pissed at the Sisters, but it was, you know, the rule. All Carl had to do was like, you know...say it was all a mistake and go to confession. If he'd just said, you know, that it was a sin and that he wouldn't do it again, they woulda let him stay...but oh no, he wouldn't. And Mom stuck up for him."

I had to shake that rant off before I could focus on my next question. It's interesting that people like Eileen Crenshaw assume everyone in the world thought just as she did. I coughed, then took a deep breath, and went on. "Mrs. Crenshaw, are you familiar with an organization called Rainbow Youth Symphony?"

"No, what's that?"

"Carl designated that organization as recipient of his insurance benefits and the proceeds of his estate in his will."

"What do you mean? I thought everything goes to, you know, his waddahya call...next of kin?" For the first time she spoke with concern.

"Well, I'm not a lawyer but a person can designate anyone they want to get their money."

"But, but, I mean, we're family. Family gets the money. Everybody knows that," she insisted.

"I think if someone designates..."

She jumped up and poked buttons on the phone. When someone answered she said, "Janie? Is Kevin home?... Shit, well where is he?... Tell him to call me right away when he comes back! I'll try his cell..."

She whipped back to me and bellowed in a coarse voice that made Cindy cower and Buh-ins whimper, "We have a right to that money!" Then her expression shifted to calculation. She said, "Maybe I should call a lawyer, do you think I should call a lawyer?"

"I don't know...um, I'd like to talk to your brother, Kevin..." I tried to ask her a few more things, but she was way too distracted to pay any attention to me. I left her my card, but firmly hoped she'd never call me.

At this time of year in Fenchester a variety of Christmas decorations, ranging from tasteful wreaths to onslaughts of giant inflated snowmen, Santa's and Scoobydoos in red hats, jockey for the attention of innocent passersby. White skeletal frames of reindeer and sleds compete with garish plastic armies of elves and full-sized mannequins decked out like carolers. Front doors featuring metallic wrapping paper are disguised as huge faux gifts. I love this. Christmas over-decoration is far more fun than an amusement park for me. It's American kitch at its most exhilarating. It's straight people actually succeeding at camp...of course 90% of them don't realize it.

But Hadesville was the Scrooge of Pennsylvania towns. Not a decoration in site. The breeze had turned very cold; the sky was as gray as flagstone. I zipped up my jacket.

Kevin Rasmus lived just a block away from his sister Eileen. I already knew he wasn't there, but I figured I might be able to get something out of his wife. A nice-looking woman wearing jeans and a sweater opened the door without even peeking out the curtains when I rang the bell. I held out my card and said, "Mrs. Rasmus? I'm Maggie Gale. I was just talking to your sister-in-law about Carl Rasmus's death?"

She took my card and read it while I was talking; "You're investigating Carl's death?" she interpreted.

"Yes."

"And you were just talking to Eileen? Well, that must have been interesting. Did you tell her she might not get his money?"

"I may have mentioned..."

She let out a chuckle and said, "Oh, do come in, I just have to hear all about this." Janie Rasmus had straight dark blonde hair to her shoulders and light brown eyes. Her living room was plastic toy and yapping dog free, but there was sterility about the place that made it seem more like a house than a home.

"Please... sit," she said motioning toward the couch as she took a chair. "Coffee?"

"No, I'm fine Mrs. Rasmus..."

"Call me Janie, I'm still imagining Eileen's face...and wait until Kevin hears..." she laughed again lightly. "Kevin's on a job, he's a roofer, he's just doing a patch job but he won't be home until," she looked at her watch, "about 5:00 PM." She went on, "I'll be honest with you, Carl's siblings weren't very fond of him, but I liked Carl. I'm sorry he's gone."

"Why didn't his brother and sister care for him?"

"Simple, Carl was a successful, happy person, they bombed. They grew up being taught gay was bad by their school and their church and then along came baby brother Carl who was everything they weren't. Including blind and gay, and their mother supported him. I liked her too. Her name was Annalee. She died three years ago. I miss her." Janie Rasmus looked out the window. "Did you know Carl?" she asked after a while.

"No, I didn't...there's going to be a memorial service for him on Sunday at 11:00 AM at Irwin."

"I'm going to get a divorce," she said suddenly.

"Oh...um...I'm sorry to hear that..."

"No, no, don't be. It's just as well. I start a new job on the West Coast in a few weeks. I've told Kevin but he doesn't believe I'll go," she sighed then went on, "it was so much easier when Annalee was alive. She loved Carl. Carl cared about her...and now he's dead too." I could see tears in Janie Rasmus's eyes. She was the first person I'd seen cry for Carl.

"Did Carl seem unhappy to you lately?"

"I'm ashamed to admit, I hadn't seen him in a long time, not since Annalee died. He was so sad about her going that way. It was cancer. She was only 60. Carl didn't get along well with Kevin or Eileen, or Eileen's husband Morley for that matter. They're all asses. Here Carl knocked himself out... of course they never acknowledged that he practiced ten hours a day, studied, worked hard, did all sorts of civic work. Took care of Annalee too."

"Janie, Carl's will leaves everything to a group called Rainbow Youth Symphony. Heard of it?"

She shook her head.

"I don't think I'll be able to wait to speak to your... to Kevin, so maybe I can ask you, were you around when Carl was in high school?"

"I didn't know Carl until after he graduated from college. I play the piano a little too. We would do these duets..." she laughed to herself remembering, then shook her head gently.

"Did he have any friends around here that I could speak with?"

"Um, no I can't think of anyone...all his friends went to college and then on to other places. Oh, wait, Barbara Getty, next door. She's older but..."

"Is she related to Leo Getty?" I asked remembering Getty had said he'd lived near Carl's family.

Janie Rasmus nodded, "They were married. Barbara divorced Leo. Oh, but she's at work at the library until 7:00 PM."

"I didn't know they were divorced." I wanted to ask if she knew why they divorced. More a matter of nosiness for me than anything else.

"She doesn't talk about it, much. Things don't always work out...People's values change...that kind of thing, I guess," she said fastening on her own future, then she said, "did you say you were investigating Carl? Why? Do you think he might not have killed himself?"

"I'm trying to get all the information I can..."

"I'm ashamed to say I didn't really consider...but, of course he never would have. He wasn't that kind of man. Maybe it was an accident?"

"Maybe," I said getting up to leave. I didn't have the heart to suggest to Janie Rasmus that Carl's death was murder. She seemed nice and she wasn't up to it.

While Carl's brother and sister had a small monetary motive to bump him off, I had a hard time imaging they also killed Skylar and somehow rigged a bottle in the conference room. No, even though I'd like to have been able to pin this crime on these unpleasant people, chances were greatest that this was an inside - the - college job.

A gust of cold wind shook the van as I was getting in. I was glad the Mazda heater worked well. It was almost 3:00 PM. If I didn't hit any traffic I could make it to Kathryn's office by 6:00 PM. If I missed Kathryn Anthony this time, it might blow my chances with her all together. I didn't even want to think about that. Luckily the gods were with me; I made it back to Fenchester by 5:45 PM.

Chapter 22

It was getting dark when I pulled into a parking place in front of the Irwin College Administration Building. An icy wind stiffened every muscle. I flipped my parka hood up against the cold and began walking.

Suddenly I realized, that I really had no idea where Kathryn Anthony's office was. I needed to find it fast. Somebody must know, after all, everyone had to take English, but the sidewalks were empty. There was no one to ask.

I was thinking, you can never find one of those, *You Are Here* maps when you need one, when I rounded a corner and ran full tilt into one. I found the Language Arts Building on the map and started down a path that went between the Administration building and the Biology Lab into the quad.

The building I sought was the first one on the left. I looked up at its dark windows. Suddenly I was gripped with the realization that it was almost 6:00 PM, and that there was a good chance Kathryn had already gone home. In fact, it seemed ridiculous to imagine she would still be in her office. What college professor in their right mind would have late office hours on a Friday?

I felt a wave of disappointment. I'd been looking forward to seeing her all day. I'd been confident that getting shot at was a pretty good excuse for tardiness. Actually being hit by a bullet was a better excuse, but I wasn't willing to go that far, even for Kathryn. Well, maybe being grazed. Now, however, I understood the chances of seeing her were very slim and I was bummed.

The door to the building had one of those brass handles with a release at the top that you depress with your thumb. For a moment I was afraid it would be locked. But it opened, making that squeaking noise that every school door crafted between 1910 and 1960 makes. The door banged shut, producing a crashing echo that everyone in the building probably heard. If there *was* anyone in the building.

The directory on the wall said Dr. Kathryn Anthony's office was on the second floor. Number 208. My footsteps made a shuffling tap sound common to stairways made of slabs of marble, slate steps and tile walls.

At the top of the stairs I pushed the brass bar on the fire door and let myself into a dimly lit hallway. Low wattage wall sconces with stained glass shades cast a pale yellow light. The walls were terra cotta tile. Blue, green and yellow figural Moravian squares, decorated with sheaves of wheat, corn cobs, sickles, or plows, dotted the wall at regular intervals. I slowed to look at them carefully, forestalling what I now felt sure was going to be disappointment.

When this building was built by WPA artisans in the 1930s, it had been a dorm for male students. The dorm rooms were now offices. The doors were evenly spaced down each side of the hallway, even numbers on the left. Their windows faced away from the quad, toward the College Street side, directly across the street from Clymer house where Amanda Knightbridge's office was. So I couldn't have seen Kathryn's window from the quad side. I was absurdly elated by this glimmer of hope.

"Geez, am I really this hot for this babe?" I whispered to myself.

The door to office number 208 was slightly open. There was a light on and there was someone typing on a computer keyboard inside. I could have jumped up in the air and cheered. Instead, I knocked on the door lightly.

"Come in... Please take a seat. I just have to finish this," said Kathryn Anthony as she continued to type. She was facing away from the door, looking intently at her computer screen, rapidly spell-checking an email.

What an attractive woman, even from the back, I thought. Her auburn hair looked thick and satiny; there was a gentle strength in her shoulders, and her voice... commanding, assured, but still soft and sexy. I was getting an answer to my own question about being hot. I could feel it in the pit of my stomach, and a little lower, too.

She hadn't turned to see who'd come in. She seemed to think I was someone else. I sat down in a leather chair in the corner of the small office. Just as I was thinking I should say something, the phone rang. She sent the email, then picked up the phone, still with her back to me.

"Kathryn Anthony," she said into the phone. "Yes, yes, Paul I sent the entire proposal at 5:30 PM and I just sent the edited letter of support from the Chancellor a second ago. No... the letter from Temple went... Paul, I've been sitting here working on this since 7:00 this morning...Yes, I am to... I think it will too."

She still faced the computer screen while she spoke. She held the phone in one hand and reached to knead tight muscles in her neck with the other.

I took a moment to look around the room. It was wall-to-wall oak bookcases with some comfortable leather easy chairs and a few framed pieces of art here and there. One was a Klimt print of two women hugging. One was a Frieda Kahlo self-portrait reproduction. One was a small landscape in Maxfield Parrish's style. It looked like a real watercolor, not a print. On a wall shelf just behind her desk was a ten inch bronze figure of a seated nude woman reaching in the air with one hand. A lyrical tilt to the bronze head made the figure seem animated. It was a nice comfortable office, sensitively decorated by someone who planned to spend a lot of time in it.

As she finished the phone conversation, Kathryn slowly swiveled her chair back toward the front of the room. Occasionally her voice ran lyrically up and down the scale when she spoke, but most of the time it was a deep low tone. She sounded wonderful and she was just talking to some guy about a grant or something. What would she sound like if she were talking about...

"OK Paul, I'm tired, I'm stiff as a board. I have an appointment with a student now and I have another call coming in." She clicked the call waiting button and said her name into the phone, then turned her chair more rapidly toward me. She raised her eyebrows when she saw me; she'd expected someone else, but that person was on the other end of the phone line. Her eyes narrowed more with interest than surprise and that excited feeling I'd felt a few minutes before increased.

She said to the caller, "Mr. Fields, your appointment was for 5:30... No, not tomorrow. Monday? All right then, Monday at 4:00 PM. Mr. Fields, next time you cancel an appointment, please do so before you're already late for it. I'm not always...flexible." She was looking right at me as she said it. I got the message. She hung up the phone and said evenly, "I'd almost given up on you."

"Oh, dear, I hope not. You said evening and," I looked at my watch, "it isn't even 6." I insisted with amusement.

"I am still unhappy with you about yesterday." She leaned back in her chair. She wanted to be stern but her voice had a gentle deep undertone. At least she wasn't frowning at me.

"I need to talk to you about the people who were at the meeting..." *Oh crap, that sounded much too official.*

"Ah," she said, in a formal clipped tone.

"But please...please let, me explain why I was late..." I sounded so pathetic, I surprised myself, but her formal gaze softened. Maybe she liked begging.

Chapter 23

"Honestly?" she said raising an eyebrow.

"Yeah." I'd told Kathryn about Skylar and the police. Now, she was resting her head on the high back of her chair. I was appreciating how terrific she looked.

She said, "When Max called me yesterday he was in a hurry, I guess he was just trying to alert everyone. We didn't speak long but I wish he'd told me about you being there. I'm sorry I was so angry with you. How selfish of me..." I could just barely see she was blushing.

"Forget it," I said lightly.

"Do you have any idea who killed Skylar?" she asked seriously.

"I've learned that there are a few people who couldn't have done it. ...I'd like to get your impressions. Do you have time now?" Her eyes were tired but that fascinating glint was back in them.

"I've been working on that grant proposal since early this morning. I'm tired of being here. Unfortunately for me, the laundry room at the Hampshire has been out of order for a week. So tonight, I have to go to the laundromat because I'm out of clean clothes. And I haven't really had anything to eat all day. I just don't think I could concentrate. I wouldn't be of any use to you. Did I mention that I hate laundromats?" she shook her head sighing.

I couldn't let her get away; my brain went into high gear... "Well then, I have a deal for you. I have a washer and dryer at my place. You can do your laundry there and we'll order some take-out food to be delivered, my treat. We can talk over dinner and you can wash your clothes without having to go to the laundromat. How about that?"

Even as I outlined my proposal she was still shaking her head no. She'd made up her mind and was too tired to change it. Unconsciously she'd put her hand on her shoulder again, kneading a place that was stiff from eleven hours of computer work.

"And... I'll give you a massage," I threw in.

She stopped shaking her head and looked up at me. The half smile was back. So was the voice tone I'd been longing to hear, a hint of a melodic humming growl before each sentence. If there was a Disney cartoon with a female panther, it would be Kathryn Anthony's voice they'd use.

"A real massage?" she asked softly, dropping her hand from her shoulder and drawing her fingers down slowly to rest at the opening of her shirt collar. She pushed herself up and walked around to the front of her desk. She leaned against it as she waited for my reply.

I nodded. The little voice in my head was singing, "Yeah baby, you found the right bait for this panther."

She lifted her chin and said with academic precision, "I'm serious, I want specific information, you are offering me: a place to wash my clothes, some dinner, and you will give me a full massage?"

"And we talk about the case over dinner," I added watching her carefully, hoping she'd give in.

She clearly didn't care what we talked about, she knew what she wanted, she pressed, "Not just a three minute shoulder rub? The real thing?"

"Yes, the real thing, as long as you want and...I'm good at it," I said confidently in a lower tone.

"Hmmm, I like a woman who's sure of her skills."

"So it's a deal?"

She crossed her arms and said, "Yes, it's a deal, but I will be very disappointed if I don't get a good massage, because I'm already looking forward to it."

"You won't be disappointed," I said casually. "Are you ready to go now?"

She got her jacket and a small leather knapsack from the closet and followed me into the hall, pulling the door shut. It locked with a click. She walked down the echoing hallway ahead of me. One of the many occupational habits of my business is sizing up people. About 5'7", the shoes are adding an inch, probably 140 lbs, hard to tell with the sweater and jacket. Pretty trim. Wonder if the hair color is natural.

She opened the stairwell door and gracefully gestured me through first. Maybe she wanted a chance to look *me* over from the back.

"To get to your place...?" She made it a question as we went down the stairs. We both paused at the ground level door.

"It's just off the Mews. You can follow me, it's only a few blocks."

"No, I have to go to my apartment and get my laundry, but it will only take me a little while. I'm just around the corner at the Hampshire."

"I remember," I smiled. "My building is near the corner of 12th and

Gordon Streets, 1206, right across the street from Moyer and Jones lumberyard. Do you know where that is?"

"That little Thai restaurant is near there, isn't it?"

"Right. Thai Kitchen is about five buildings up the block. Mine is a converted factory. There are offices downstairs. I live on the third floor. The building is the tallest in that part of the neighborhood, you can't miss it."

"Sounds interesting." She was considering me intently, with her head tilted just a little to the side. "It's a loft? The top floor of an old factory building?"

"The two top floors, but I've only finished one of them. There are two doors in the front. The one on the left is white. That one goes to the first floor. The one on the right is red. That's my door. There are two doorbell buttons by the side of the door. The bottom one is for the law firm. Ring the top bell and I'll buzz you into the lobby. Here's my card," I said fishing one out of my pocket and putting it in her hand, "call me if you can't find it."

"Red door, top button. I think I can handle it. Is there parking?"

Good question. The whole area of Washington Mews is notorious for lack of parking, especially in the evenings and weekends.

"There are private parking places right in front, nobody will be using them at this hour so you'll have no problem. My van will be parked there. You can park right next to me."

"All right then, I'll see you in about half an hour." She gave the brass bar on the door a push.

"Wait," I said calling her back.

She turned with the door slightly open. She'd zipped up her jacket and tossed her red scarf once around her neck. Her eyes flashed with a curious energy.

"You're hungry," I went on, "how about something from Thai Kitchen. I could order it? They deliver. It should be there by the time you arrive." She was nodding her head enthusiastically, I asked, "What would you like?"

"I'm so hungry just talking about food is going to make my stomach hurt. Hmm, *pad Thai* with shrimp, papaya salad or if they don't have that, the regular salad with peanut dressing." She sighed shaking her head and then laughed, "I'm desperate, I'll eat anything they have."

"Fine, I'll order it and see you soon." We both went out into the city wind, with our heads down, going separate ways.

I took out my phone and speed dialed Thai Kitchen. I go there so much I have an account and am on a first name basis with the family who owns it.

Kathryn Anthony had taken my breath away, literally. I'm hyperventilating, I thought, I have to control myself or I'll have to put a paper bag over my head. No, wait I should breathe into a bag. Yeah, that would be safer than trying to drive with my head *inside* a bag. I was frantic that I may have left my place in a total mess. I was racked my brain to remember if I'd left a pile of dishes in the sink.

It was very dark in my small parking lot, with a few slushy snow piles here and there. I let myself in and made sure to turn on the front door light so the parking lot would be illuminated. I ran up the stairs taking two steps at a time. I'm in pretty good shape, but I was gasping when I got to the second floor entrance of Sara and Emma's offices. Slow down and get a grip, I had to tell myself again, you don't want to have a breakdown just before she gets here.

Emma Strong, bundled up in coat and hat, was just leaving the office. "Whoa, what's your hurry," she asked as I dodged crashing into her. She took a step closer peering into my eyes with the calculation of a hot dog trial lawyer, then straightened up with an in-drawn breath. "Maggie, you have a date! And it's a hot one...too. Aren't you cute when you're excited!"

"Well, I..."

"Don't bother to deny it, I see that glint in your eye," she said smiling. "Good for you honey. I have a date too, and I'm late. Oh, the list of people who were at Daria's apartment came back from the credit checking service. Nothing much, but it would be good if you could look it over." She stepped back into the office, grabbed the list, and handed it to me. "Will the criminal information be here by Monday?"

"Probably by Sunday, I rushed them. I'll check over both lists. Daria was a social worker right? These were people she worked with?"

"Mm hmm, from the office, the counseling clinic and the homeless shelter, but don't work on this tonight Maggie, concentrate on the task at... hand." She glanced up the stairs, "Is she coming here? I'm going to want details," Emma teased as she locked the office door.

"I'll have the lists for you by Monday and I don't know if there'll be any...details."

"We can always hope!" Emma called after me as I turned and sped up the next flight.

As I reached the third floor landing, I suddenly realized it might have been a tactical error to give Kathryn my card. Now she had my number so she could call to cancel if she really felt too tired. *Damn.* I'd already begun to imagine the massage. I had to take a very deep breath to compose myself. The disappointment would be crushing if she didn't appear. On the other hand, she agreed it was *a deal.* She didn't seem like the type to bail after making a deal. In fact, if she was, I'd be less interested.

I'd gotten this building as payment from a grateful client. I'd solved the case, but almost lost my life in the process. I'd thought he was kidding about the building, but he really did it. It was scary taking on a big piece of real estate after years of renting an apartment in a high rise, but things seemed to be working out, knock-on-wood.

Before I let myself into the loft, I sent the freight elevator down to the ground floor. Once inside, I ran over to the kitchen area. I took my breakfast dishes out of the sink and put them in the dishwasher. The laundry room is through my bedroom so I straightened out the quilt and fluffed the pillows on my king-sized bed. Thinking again, I decided to change the sheets. *Be prepared.* That done I scanned the room for other telltale signs of disorganization, then proceeded to the bathroom.

There are two bathrooms in the loft. One next to the guest room that's rarely used, so I figured it was clean. But the bathroom off my bedroom, the one I use every day, needed a quick once over. Scrub, wipe, flush, arrange, done. In the laundry room next to the bathroom I checked for giant lint bunnies in the machines. Everything seemed fine in there.

Back in the bathroom again, a dozen things flashed through my mind. Could I take a shower in three minutes? Sure, my hair is short, it would dry. I speed showered, used the blow dryer and changed clothes. I put on a soft button down shirt. I think buttons are sexy.

"What else?" I said out loud.

A few days before, I'd been working on some watercolor sketches. The paints, paper, and unfinished work were still on the long dining table. They were pretty good. I decided to leave them there. Instead, I cleared some books off the smaller kitchen table near the windows and flipped a tablecloth of light purple cotton over it.

Good china or Fiesta? Is that a gay question or what? I opted for Fiestaware, better color choices. Dark green dinner plate and salmon colored salad plate with a bright yellow napkin for her. For me, light green dinner plate with a dark blue salad plate and a bright orange napkin. *Hey, I went to art school, it's what I do.* I set out silverware and water glasses, and put wine glasses on the counter. I picked two different kinds of white wine and put the bottles in the refrigerator, I left some red wine on the counter. I made a few lighting decisions, but decided against candles. Too obvious.

I looked around again and tried to take a calming breath, which ended up stuttering down my throat. I figured I was ready if I could just breathe like a normal person.

I looked out the window into the parking lot below. A blue and white BMW Mini Cooper had pulled into one of the spaces. I had the vague feeling I'd seen that Mini before. Kathryn was opening the hatch back, getting out her laundry basket. She had really arrived. I let out a sigh of relief.

The doorbell rang. I pressed the intercom button, "Kathryn?"

"Yes," she called.

"I'll buzz you in. Just wait a minute in the foyer, I'll be right there."

I pressed the buzzer, then sped down the stairs. I tried to compose myself when I got to the landing. There she was, looking up at me, with that half smile and eyes I felt touching my soul.

"Hello," she said smiling radiantly. She'd set her laundry basket and a duffel bag on the floor. Her small leather knapsack was over her shoulder. She reached to pick up the laundry basket.

"Here, let me open the elevator door," I said walking down the rest of the flight. "It's slower, but easier than climbing the stairs. There are a lot of them."

"It would be nice not to have to climb any more stairs today. Not only is the laundry out of order at the Hampshire, but now it seems the elevator has also broken down. I'm beginning to hate that place."

Through the window next to the foyer door I caught a glimpse of someone carrying a white paper bag. "Oh good, Kenny's here with the food," I said as I went to let him in. "Kenny, you're right on time." I took the bag from him and pulled out the bill.

Kenny Sakda is the youngest son of the family who owns Thai Kitchen. He just started high school. He works in the restaurant most evenings, and when he's not working, he's there doing his homework. I help him sometimes. There's a good chance he's gay. I think he's working up the nerve to talk to me about it. He'd just gone through a growth spurt and is about my height now. Like a lot of teenage boys, he has the metabolism of a mosquito. Eats all the time, but thin as a rail. His short brown mop of hair was carefully uncombed and he was wearing his Fenchester High School letter jacket.

"The *me krob* is bangin," he grinned, "Mom just made it."

Kenny caught sight of Kathryn, then saw the basket of laundry. He glanced back at Kathryn and covertly eyed her up and down. He grinned at me again even harder this time. I felt myself blush.

"This is Dr. Anthony, she's new to the neighborhood," I said formally.

I turned to Kathryn, "This is Kenny Sakda, his family owns Thai Kitchen."

With the duffel bag now in her arms Kathryn couldn't shake hands, but she said in a charming voice, "It's very nice to meet you. Please tell your family I enjoy their restaurant very much."

"Awesome, I'll tell 'em. Have a good dinner." He walked to the door, but as he passed me he whispered, "Hottie," just loud enough for me to hear.

I pushed opened the elevator doors, then stepped in, and put the bag of Thai food on the shelf. I got Kathryn's basket and put that on the shelf too. I'd built it in the elevator for this very reason. All elevators should have shelves. Especially the ones whose doors require two hands to close.

Stretching to push the gate all the way up I explained, "The elevator is very slow, we could walk to the third floor faster than the elevator can make it to the second, and for some reason it's even slower going down." Kathryn stepped beside me. I pulled down the safety gate, then reached up and pulled the strap on the metal door. Half came down from the ceiling. The other half came up from the floor clanking together in the middle. I swung the locking mechanism in place. "If I don't do this all correctly the elevator won't go. It took me a month to learn. It looks old, but it's safe." I twisted the control lever.

"I've worked in many old buildings and ridden in all sorts of contraptions. This is palatial...and in contrast to the Hampshire, it works!" she said leaning against the shelf. Her eyes showed weariness, but they also had an amused gleam.

"So you have a Mini Cooper? I love those cars, what's it like to drive?"

"I sort of fell into it, it was my brother's. He owns a restaurant in Portland. I was visiting him and he was complaining that the Cooper was too small. I was saying that my car didn't get good mileage. So we traded," she said conversationally. "It's fun to drive, but it's the smallest car in the world. At times I think it should only be driven with clowns stuffed in the back seat. Fortunately, I rarely need a bigger car. The food smells wonderful. The kid seems nice..."

"Oh yeah, Kenny and I are pals. I'm sure he's running home to tell his mom all about you."

"Really? So is Thai Kitchen the gossip nerve center of Washington Mews?"

"It's a major relay."

"And is who you're having dinner with a news flash?" she asked. Gentle laugh lines appeared at the corners of her eyes.

"Kenny thinks you're hot," I said watching the floor numbers.

"Hah," she snorted. She paused, then said, "How long have you lived here?"

"About six months. It was pretty raw when I moved in but I've put a lot of work into it. I still have more to do, but I like the space."

"Do you have a long term lease?"

"Well I guess you could say that. I own the building."

"Really?" She was impressed.

"Yeah, it's still hard for me to believe. I got it in exchange for solving a case."

"You must be some crackerjack private eye."

It was my turn to snort, "Yeah, I'm a pistol."

Chapter 24

We'd come to the third floor. I was easing off the control lever, trying to stop the elevator in the right place. I didn't want to do that up and down finagling thing, central to movie comedy bits in 1930s hotel scenes. I managed to come within an inch of being even with the floor. *Whew.*

I pulled down on the strap and the horizontal metal doors blinked into the entrance area like giant eyelids. I'd left the double doors into the loft wide open so the whole space was in view.

The big room in front of the elevator door is about 2000 square feet. The far wall is floor to ceiling windows overlooking Washington Mews. I'd left the space dark, so the bright moonlight streaming through the windows would seem more dramatic. Christmas lights decorating Mews homes twinkled along with the stars above the dark silhouettes of rooftops and tree branches. It was the best view in the city.

I brought up the lights. Part of the wall to the left also consists of floor to ceiling windows. The rest of the north wall has a long kitchen counter with cabinets below and above it, with a built-in double oven and dishwasher and refrigerator at the end. In front of that is another counter island with a stovetop range, double sink and more under counter cabinets. All the appliances are stainless steel. They'd come with the place when I took possession, but were still in the crates when I'd moved in. It was a great kitchen, beyond my wildest dreams. In fact, I'd rarely dreamed about kitchens before, but if I had, they wouldn't have been as sweet as this.

To the right, in the middle of the south wall is an antique marble and brass fireplace with glass doors. I purchased it at an outdoor antique show and installed it with Farrel's help. In front of the fireplace I'd built a one-foot high platform and covered it with soft carpet. There are a variety of pillows on the platform to make a place to lie in front of the fire. Around the platform are a couch and two easy chairs. When friends are sitting on those, we use the platform as a big low coffee table. To the right of the fireplace is the door to my bedroom.

The hardwood flooring is maple. There's one big Asian carpet in the middle in muted tones of red and blue and a few other smaller Asian rugs scattered around in appropriate places. The ceilings are 11 feet high. I'd turned up the heat. It was comfortably warm.

When I'd opened the elevator doors Kathryn had whispered, "Oh!" Any hesitation I'd ever harbored about taking on this building or rehabbing this loft was forever erased at that moment.

"This is..." She stood still, looking. She put the laundry bag down on the floor, took several steps, then turned slowly around. She paused to look at the bookcases on the wall beside the kitchen. She ran her hand over the pine dinning table and glanced over my sketches. She took in the fireplace and the large slightly abstract Mexican landscape painting over it. She walked around the arrangement of small couch and chair that sit directly in front of the windows overlooking the Mews. She looked out the windows then back around the room for several moments. I didn't say anything. I just let her look. It was fun to watch her.

Finally, she turned back to me with an unreadable expression, she said, "You did all of this?"

"Well, the view was already here." She laughed at that. I was really scoring on getting her to laugh. "Friends helped," I added.

Across the room, past the bedroom door a large spiral staircase circled up into the ceiling. She pointed, "What's up there?"

"Still working on that."

"I want to see it." There was a demand in her voice that was kind of provocative.

"Too dark, too cold, not finished. I'll let you see it sometime in the daylight."

"Promise?"

I nodded.

"You've made me several promises tonight that I sincerely expect you to keep." She was using that deep deliberate tone that made me ache again.

"I keep promises," I assured her.

She paused considering me for a moment, then took a deep breath and said in another half whisper, "Seeing this loft has been the best part of my week."

"What a nice thing to say." I privately hoped she'd revise that statement after the rest of the evening's promises had been kept. "Let me help you get the laundry started and then I can get the dinner on the table, OK?" I picked up her laundry basket, she grabbed the duffel bag.

I led her through the bedroom toward the laundry room. She stopped for a moment to take in the bedroom space. The fireplace is also open on the bedroom side of the wall. She took a step closer to look at the large photographs of August Rodin's bronze lesbian sculptures.

"Goodness, where did you get these?" she asked eyeing the swirling erotic forms of women making love, that were done by the sculptor who created "The Thinker."

"I took the pictures myself at a special show of his sculpture a few years ago."

She tilted her head to the side staring for a minute at the organic flowing hair and bodies. She said absently, "I know a lot of women who'd love to have copies of these in their bedrooms."

"Do you?" I teased leading her into the laundry room.

My laundry room is brilliant, if I do say so myself. I wanted a washer and dryer right next to my clothes closet. Only people who don't have to do laundry decide to put the washer and dryer in the basement, two floors from the place where the dirty clothes start and the clean clothes are supposed to end up. Besides the machines, I had an area with a tile floor and a drain with rods over it to hang wet clothes.

"This is one of those high capacity machines," I said, "you're supposed to be able to put 16 bath towels in one load."

She was opening the duffel bag, "Well then, I guess I just have one white load and one dark. I didn't want to be a complete leech, I brought my own soap."

I showed her how to use the machines, then went back to the kitchen to get the food ready. I couldn't help grinning at the effect the loft had had on her. It was completely worth the six months of backbreaking labor.

I put the *pad Thai* in a bowl and heated it up in the microwave. I dished the salad onto plates. The crunchy sweet *me krob* went into a serving bowl with a big spoon, with the plate of spring rolls next to it.

I went back toward the laundry room to ask her what she'd like to drink, and found her standing in front of my bedroom bookcases. She had her hand on the spine of some volume, but it was too dark in the room to see which one.

She turned toward me, a little guiltily. "I'm sorry, I can't pass a bookcase without looking to see what's in it. It's an occupational hazard."

"When you're in my occupation, you can barely walk by a wallet without looking to see what's in it." I could see her eyebrows rise, even in the dim light.

"Well, I do try to control myself. Come and have something to eat. What would you like to drink?" I told her what I had available.

"I'm torn. I'd love a glass of wine, but I think I need coffee," she sighed, "or maybe tea would be better with dinner."

"How about tea now with dinner and glass of wine later?" I suggested leading her back to the kitchen area.

"Good idea. Shall I sit here?" She sat down at the end of the table, idly picking up a fork and looking at the pattern of the handle. "Sterling? Etruscan?"

"Yes it is, good for you. I have antique dealer friends who insist I buy sterling for tableware. They say it's cheaper than new stainless steel at Macy's and it tastes better," I explained as I got out the teapot.

I put boiling hot water in the pot to warm it, then threw that out and put more boiling water in.

"Oolong or Darjeeling?"

"Darjeeling please."

I put loose tea leaves in the pot. When the tea had steeped, I used a little strainer to hold over the cups to catch the used leaves.

Kathryn watched me as I went though each step, "I've only seen people make tea that way in England." She made graceful gestures with her hand now and then to punctuate her sentences.

"A friend whose parents were Canadian taught me," I explained. I brought the teapot and two large cups to the table.

"Milk, sugar, lemon?"

"Just lemon," she said reaching for her cup.

I got a lemon from the refrigerator, cut some wedges and put them on a plate. She was pouring the tea into both cups when I brought the plate to the table with a sterling lemon fork on its side. We dug into the food.

"Thank you for ordering this. I was so hungry, you may have saved my life..." said Kathryn breaking her food focused concentration to smile at me.

"Tell me about the grant you were working on today."

She outlined what the grant was for, then said, "It's part of the satellite campus funding and the best part about it is that I'm done with it." She took a sip of tea, then explained that it was part of her job right now to help various department heads finish grant applications by the end of the term. She added, "This is really dull. You couldn't be interested in this."

While she was talking her hand went to knead her shoulder again, she'd tried to turn her head to look out the window and had reacted to the stiffness in her neck.

"No vale la pena?" I said looking at her hand on her shoulder.

She smiled, "I can get by pretty well with German and Russian, but I'm ashamed to say my Spanish is terrible. Something about not going through pain?"

"It means, *It's not worth the pain*," I said nodding at her shoulder.

She stopped, looked at her hand and flexed it, "I seem to do that all the time... did you know the hat makers of London went mad in the mid-1800s because the paint they detailed the hats with had lead in it? They licked the brushes every few minutes to bring the bristles to a fine point. They ingested so much lead it destroyed their brains. That was the source of the Mad Hatter character in Alice in Wonderland," she shook her head and went on, "and now in the 21st century, workers will go mad from the constant pain of the repetitive motion from keyboard typing in awkward positions. I forget about it for a while and then I move my head... "

She turned her head to the right, cursed gently, and touched the bridge of her nose. "It gives me a headache too."

"How about we try a temporary maneuver?"

"Anything," she said, watching me closely. "What shall I do?"

I moved behind her, putting my hands on the outsides of her shoulders. The black flannel of her shirt was thin and worn to a comfortable softness. Like pajamas. Her sweater vest was way too thick to massage through. She'd have to take it off later. Wondering if she'd take off all her clothes for the massage distracted me for a moment. Shaking my head slightly I came back to the task at hand.

"Sit back and up straight."

The chair is the swiveling office kind on casters; the type executives lean back in at fancy desks. All my dining room chairs are like that.

I put my palm against the left side of her face, just in front of her ear. Her skin felt soft and warm. I noticed her perfume. She hadn't had that scent in her office. She must have put it on when she went back to her apartment. It was stimulating to imagine she'd done this sensual thing for me. I inhaled again and realized it was her shampoo. Her hair was slightly damp. She'd taken a shower when she'd gone home too, that was even more stimulating.

"Turn your head against my left hand," I said as I guided the movement with my right, "harder, keep going." I held my hand steady as she pushed against it. My foot braced the chair's casters so it wouldn't roll away. She groaned in effort as she did it. I was surprised at how strong she was.

"Just a little more," I coaxed, my lips near her ear, "OK, stop now." I took my hands away. She gingerly moved her head back and forth. She touched her shoulder again. "Better?" I asked.

"Ah... it is," she said in a surprised tone. "So, you do know what you're doing. Mmm, how nice."

"You were in doubt?" I said with mock sarcasm as I picked up the dishes.

She just laughed lightly. I put the dishes in the dishwasher and the empty food containers in the trash. I got my laptop and sat back down to look at my notes.

"You were telling me about the grant part of your job. What's the rest of it?"

She turned to the window. With her elbow on the table, she rested her chin in her hand. "Let's see, Max Bouchet needed someone to check the grant driven programs," she faced me and smiled, "and ask stupid questions."

"I don't get it."

"Well you see, everybody running a grant program expects the rest of the College to be familiar with it. There have been several serious... *disagreements*...when someone doing an evaluation asked an ignorant question and the program leader blew up in exasperation. Since I've been working away from the campus for so many years, Max figures I can ask anything and nobody will be too annoyed."

"Of the people who were at the meeting, which of them have been working on grants?"

"As heads of departments, all of them are. I'm really like a grant information sherpa. I carry the data to a central place. Check credentials and personnel working on the grant...look over financial figures. I'm not particularly interested in the job. I won't be doing it next semester."

"What will you be doing?"

"Research for a basic art history textbook on women artists, which will grow into a major course of study for students here at Irwin."

"That sounds fabulous," I said earnestly. "Will you teach in the program?"

"I guess I'll probably *run* the program, but the research part will be fairly quiet. I need a little time off from traveling around. I find that kind of research relaxing."

"This might be kind of personal but I'm dying to know how you got to be a full professor at your age."

"Easy, I slept my way to the top," she kidded, "...don't you believe me?"

"Well...it's not that I think you don't have the charms but..."

"Actually, it was a very hard time in my life. Did you hear about the Central Western University professors who were fired for dissertation fraud about 10 years ago?"

"Yes, I read about it. Quite a story. They plagiarized their research and then backed each other up?"

"I was the one who uncovered the fraud. These men were really scum. They not only faked their own work and lined their own pockets with grant money, they were terribly powerful and extraordinarily hypocritical. They routinely persecuted doctoral candidates, stealing their research and sometimes sexually harassing them."

"And you exposed them?"

"I did. I had to. I had several friends who were being torn apart by these bastards. I was up for tenure and promotion to Associate Professor due to some research I'd published and also because the University system had vastly benefited from some grants I'd secured. Not being tenured is a tough position for any college teacher. You walk on eggshells every day. You do anything to avoid making waves, but I just couldn't stand what these people were doing to the students. When I voiced concern in a minor way, they attacked me academically. They were foolish to do so," she said sardonically.

"What did you do?"

"Found reams of evidence exposing their bogus research and grant manipulation. I took it all to the State Chancellor of Education, who brought charges. Really CWU is a good institution, a number of Irwin profs have studied there, Skylar did, so did Georgia Smith and Leo Getty, Max did a year there and I think Rolina Roth-Holtzman did a year there as an undergrad. I didn't want the whole place to go down in flames. The University System was very embarrassed and didn't want the publicity, so we all made a deal. Frankly, I really didn't want to be branded a troublemaker. Not at that stage of my career anyway," she smiled briefly, "they fired the worst of them, but the University didn't publicly admit to its own gross negligence. I insisted the student files were made right. They also had to institute a checks and balances system on research and grants. The kind of thing I've been doing here."

"But, how did you get the professorship? Was that part of the deal?"

"Oh well, I passed the tenure and promotion board. So I was an Associate Professor, but there was a lot of political pressure to support reforms throughout the state system. The Chancellor suggested I chair the Governor's committee, but also pointed out to the University that I really should be a full professor if I were going to lead this important panel. I didn't want to work at CWU any more, so I got a leave, the promotion and the reigns to a committee that was more work than anyone could imagine." She shook her head, "I worked 20 hours a day for months on that thing. We did a good job though.

After a year and a half, the reforms were in place and I applied for this opening at Irwin."

She stopped talking, lost in thought, after a long moment she said, "It wasn't fun, believe me. One of the people who was fired was a major force in college basketball. There was a chaplain involved to, who tried to make an issue of my sexual orientation. There were threats from their supporters, but you know, the threats just made me stand fast."

"It all sounds very hard," I said sympathetically.

"Long time ago," she shrugged. Her hand went to her shoulder.

"More tea?" I asked lifting the pot. She nodded, so I poured. "I'm sorry I have to tax you with this case."

"It's all right, go ahead," she said more formally, sitting up squarely in her chair.

I looked into her eyes for a long moment, then I said, "I'm going to be very candid with you. I think someone at the Tenure Committee meeting set a fire bomb that caused the explosion."

"No!" she said shocked, "...tell me."

I told her what Daniel Cohen and his fire inspectors had determined. She listened carefully, her eyes growing wider. She said when I finished, "So one of them did it... it couldn't have been an outsider. My God... who?"

Chapter 25

I scrolled to the Committee list on my laptop and recited, "Daniel Cohen, Leo Getty, Rowlina Roth-Holtzmann, Georgia Smith, Jimmy Harmon, Amanda Knightbridge, Skylar Carvelle, Bart Edgar and you, but of course you weren't at the meeting. Also at the meeting were Max Bouchet, Miranda Juarez, Connie Robinson. Skylar Carvelle is dead. Of the rest of those people, only you and Daniel Cohen have airtight alibis for Carl's death. If we assume that this is all tied together and that Carl was murdered, that let's you and Cohen out of the loop."

"Thank you," she said wryly.

"I wouldn't be telling you this if I thought you were a suspect," I smiled. "I'd like your opinion on these people, I need to get more insight into them. If you were doing candid evaluations on them tell me what you'd write. Start with Skylar Carvelle because he wanted to talk to me about something important and someone killed him. Any ideas?"

"I'd say that Skylar was a bit of a weasel because he seemed to revel in being a first class snitch, but if I said that, I'd be doing what I was blaming Skylar for doing. Though, if Skylar had managed to...um ...spill the beans to you, he might still be alive. I guess there's a moral in there somewhere?" she asked with raised eyebrows.

"Yes, the moral is you must answer all my questions with veridicality and alacrity."

She snorted, "And I must do this because you have a large vocabulary?"

"No Kathryn, do it because I'm the detective trying to stop the killer," I said frankly.

She drew in breath at that and nodded, "Yes, OK. I'll try. Um, I really can't think of any reason why Skylar called you."

"OK, then let's talk about Bart Edgar."

"Bart's a fuck-up," she said flatly.

"You'd write that on an evaluation?" I snorted.

"I don't often use language like that. It demonstrates a lack of vocabulary, but it does seem to concisely describe the man."

"What happened that day, when he picked you up at the airport?"

"Oh, my... well... Miranda instructed him to wait on a bench at the bottom of the main escalator. I finally found him on bench at the bottom of a different staircase."

"Hey, he was close..."

"Uh huh," she said dubiously. "We went to the baggage claim area..."

"Did you talk about anything?"

"It's impossible to have a conversation with that man. He... oh rats, I sound like a bitch saying this..."

"Your candid opinion..."

She shook her head in dismay, "I'll just tell you what happened. He tried to make conversation, but I couldn't follow what he was talking about. He starts every sentence in the middle. I tuned him out. My cell rang. It was the Governor's office, so I asked Bart to watch for my two bags, a huge brief case and my suitcase, each are blue with a big red stripe... very easy to identify. I wandered away, taking the call."

I nodded.

"So when I was done, I came over to the baggage carousel. Both my bags were circling around and Bart was staring off into space. Bart asked me if I wanted him to look for my bags and what color they were," she said with exasperation. "It was like the Twilight Zone." I laughed. She went on, shaking her head slightly, "he kept getting in the way, so I asked him to get me a Cafalatte. He looked at me blankly. I explained it was a drink and that I'd seen them at the snack stand. I gave him the money. He scurried off and came back with a Diet Iced Tea."

"You're kidding," I snickered, she was telling it with comic timing.

"Nope...it's true. So then he got lost on the way home, even though the Airport is, what, five miles from here? When Max nearly suggested Bart drive me to Harrisburg, I almost passed out..."

"I saw the look on your face," I said smiling. Then I went on more seriously, "Did you know that Jimmy Harmon almost hit Bart?"

"Yes, I heard about that. You think Jimmy might be guilty, don't you?"

"Well..." I responded slowly, "he had opportunity for Carl and Skylar and the fire bomb and he seems to have a motive."

"A motive? What motive?" she demanded. "A bad temper? Anyone would want to hit Bart!" Her blue eyes darkened defensively and I felt a bit jealous.

"Kathryn, you didn't hit Bart when he annoyed you and Bart is one thing, but ...Jimmy almost hitting a blind man ...for little reason?"

"I'm sorry. It's just that Jimmy is, well, he's a sweet guy," she paused considering, then added, "he was on this allergy medication..."

I told her I knew all about Jimmy's allergy meds. I said, "Jimmy seems to be guilt ridden. I think there was something between Jimmy and Carl that Jimmy isn't talking about."

Kathryn thought, then said speculatively, "One time in the Student Union I heard Carl arguing with Jimmy about a piece of music he'd wanted Jimmy's agent to hear. Carl said something to Jimmy like, 'It's not that hard to write popular music, and you're not the only one who can do it.'"

"What did Jimmy say?"

"Um...well, some obscenity."

I made a note of that then said, "Amanda Knightbridge says she was with you in your class yesterday morning?"

"Yes, my grad seminar. I'd asked her to help me with a presentation. First she'd said she couldn't, but then just before class she called to see if I might still need her. I was glad because I was...a little tired after a late night," she said alluding to our snowy encounter in the Mews.

"Uh huh," I said smiling, "and after the seminar?"

"We went over to the Student Union for lunch. She left and Jimmy came in. You came in right after that."

"So Amanda left at...?" I asked.

"About 1:35 PM or maybe 1:40, Jimmy came in about 5 minutes after that. What does this all mean?"

"It alibis Amanda and you, and not Jimmy. Now tell me about Carl."

She said all the things everyone else had said. Nice guy, good at his work, but acted squirrelly lately. She finished with, "OK, here it is, I don't care how confused he seemed lately, I don't think he wrote that note. The words...they weren't his words." She said this as though stating an indisputable fact.

"Rowlina Roth-Holtzmann. Do you know her?"

Kathryn shrugged, "She speaks at least five languages, masterfully, she might construct sentences in a Germanic way, but I've never heard her make a grammatical error. I think..she likes to go to conferences because she likes the superficial relationships. You see people you barely know, but you go out to dinner with them because everybody has to go somewhere to eat. You sit with people, have a drink, meet at the buffet breakfast, go to the lectures, and then it's all over in a few days. I think she likes the cheerful lack of connection."

"How do you feel about those types of connections?" I asked using a more personal tone.

"Not my style. Life's too short."

I privately agreed. "Rowlina seems very unhappy to me..."

"It was ridiculous for her to marry Josef Holtzmann. He needed US citizenship and personally I think he's kind of shady, though I can't put my finger on why, maybe because he's in the import business which always sounds like pirates to me. Lina married him last year and they haven't seen each other since. I can't believe the INS hasn't questioned it. As far as Lina is concerned, she may have thought the marriage would quash speculation about her sexual orientation," Kathryn shook her head, she added," I don't understand why people make so much trouble for themselves."

"Rowlina seemed to have some serious disagreements with Carl," I suggested.

"It's odd though, she had no idea what he was angry about. Of course, Lina doesn't have good interpersonal communication skills. Her self-recriminations seem to literally be cramping her body. She must have neck tension ten times worse than mine." Kathryn had just become aware that she was kneading her shoulder again. She moved her hand away with irritation.

I changed the subject, "I went to Hadesville today. I found out that Carl was thrown out of a Catholic high school because he was gay. He was caught kissing another boy after school under the bleachers."

"Sounds like a cliché."

"It does doesn't it?" I told her the rest of Carl's high school story then I scrolled my notes. "Um...Miranda Juarez?"

"She's kind of an enigma isn't she?" said Kathryn leaning back in a more relaxed way. "She's a fantasy secretary. Has a troublesome ex-husband. What's his name...?"

"Shel Druckenmacher."

"Yes, that's right...and a son and a daughter. The daughter is married and lives in Fenchester, I think she's about 28. The son's two years older and lives in Seattle," Kathryn remembered something, "you know, when I was in Seattle, just before I went to England, I saw Miranda's son Enrique. As a matter of fact, I also saw Leo Getty's son. That was even more of a coincidence."

"Miranda asked you to get in touch with her son?"

"Yes, she gave me a little book to give to him. He came to my hotel and offered to take me to lunch, I suggested we just have coffee. He asked me anxiously how Miranda was. Then, he asked if Druckenmacher had been around. He obviously doesn't have much regard for his father."

"So everybody thinks Shel Druckenmacher is a bad egg..." I typed a note, "You happened to see Leo Getty's son in Seattle too?"

"I'd gone to a restaurant for dinner with my friend Christine, she's a friend from grad school who lives in Seattle. It was a gay-owned dinner club. Very trendy. We were standing in the lobby waiting for a table and Christine asked me if I was going to try to make a home in Fenchester. This nice looking man standing behind me with a group of three other people said, 'Excuse me, are you from Fenchester, Pennsylvania?' When I said I worked at Irwin, he told me his father, Leo Getty, worked there too. I didn't get to speak to him at length, but I would bet he was gay."

"No kidding? Leo doesn't seem to know. He told me his sons were married and had kids. He even has pictures of them in his office complete with wives and grandchildren. The pictures look pretty old though. Things change..." I mused, "I'm sorry, go on."

"Leo's son enthusiastically told me they'd all just come from a performance of a jazz symphony that he'd written and conducted. Then Christine and I were called for a table, so I said goodbye."

I thought about that for a moment then realized I'd been grilling Kathryn with questions without being a good host. Shame on me. I stood up and said, "Shall we have a glass of wine?"

"That would be nice."

"I have a Chardonnay and a Sauvignon Blanc, and I have a Shiraz and a Pinot Noir. Which would you like?"

"Too many choices," she sighed with amusement. I was taken with how she looked smiling and sitting there at my table. The dark windows reflected her like a mirror. I could see myself in the reflection too. She said, "I lean toward the reds."

"So, let's have the Shiraz, it's supposed to be a nice one." I filled her glass, she held it up to the light, studying the color. Then I said, "Leo doesn't seem like he'd be too keen on having a gay son. Did you mention seeing his son to him?" I asked after taking a sip of wine. It was a good bottle, satiny finish, rich but easy to drink.

"I did. I'd gone to Seattle to the Union of Art Colleges Convention. I came back the day after Carl died. The College was in turmoil. Everyone was so sad. I had to go to London almost immediately. I only had one day here, but I saw Leo in the elevator of the administration building before I left and I told him I'd met his son in Seattle."

"What did he say?"

"That's exactly what Leo said, he said, 'What did he say?' I told him we'd had a quick chat and that people on campus should know about him and all he's done. Then the elevator doors opened and I got out."

"And... what did you answer Christine?"

"About?"

"About whether you'd try to make a home in Fenchester?"

"I said...I said I wasn't sure, but that I was tired of traveling."

I nodded, feeling pleased.

She wanted to know what had happened at Skylar's so I gave her the short version, downplaying the details, then I asked, "Do you think Connie Robinson could kill someone by whacking them with a glass paperweight?"

"No, not the type.... but she did do all those surprising things during the fire," Kathryn took a sip of wine then said, "Connie's family goes to a very conservative church. She's in conflict over it. She just moved into her own apartment in the last few days. The church... the way they present information... those horrible, bogus pamphlets saying we're all pedophiles, it virtually justifies violence."

"What did you say?"

"I told her self-identified gay people are statistically far less likely to commit child abuse than heterosexuals."

"How did she take that?"

"With confusion...she wanted more information. I explained that every reputable medical and psychiatric organization in the country refutes the junk in the pamphlet. She said the Bible was against it. I told her to read the story of Ruth and Naomi in the Old Testament."

"Whither thou goest..."

Kathryn nodded.

"Did she hear you or just look at you blankly?"

Kathryn shrugged, "She's not stupid. I think that's why she's so confused. She's not really the type to hate people just because someone tells her to."

I made some notes about Connie and wrote down the things I needed to check. Then I said, "Georgia Smith?"

"It must be terrible for her. Have you seen her?"

I told Kathryn about Georgia in the hospital room, that she'd said something about a macaroni can.

"I brought Carl's laptop home. I went over the instruction manual for the voice transcription program during free moments today. I'm fairly clear on how the program is supposed to work, but the program has a much better opinion of itself than I do. I read my own voice into the system so now it's supposed to transcribe what I say into text."

I got the laptop from a table near the door and placed the open screen so Kathryn and I could both see it, "Check this out." I booted up the program and adjusted the mic. I said, "This is what the computer will write if I say this."

The computer studiously wrote: *this is " Cox computers " practical sixth hikes people looking upset*

Kathryn laughed out loud.

So I spoke into the computer again: *"No really, this is what the computer will write if I say this."*

Word by word the computer slowly wrote: *"No leaps the income input MACBETH kaput brokers REPAIR unpalatable."*

"Oh no, stop, stop," said Kathryn laughing with abandon, as each word popped onto the screen. "Why is it doing that?" she asked when she finally caught her breath.

"I don't know. It says in the manual that if it makes a mistake, and you correct it, then it will remember the correction. So I tried saying the same sentence over and over today and it came out wrong every time, even though I corrected it continuously. And get this; the manual says it will actually type 175 words a minute! It doesn't mention that they'll be 175 *wrong* words. I guess the manufacturer didn't want to be a stickler for technicalities."

Kathryn began laughing again each time she looked back at the screen, finally wiping her eyes, she insisted, "Carl used this program every day. I'm sure it worked better than this for him."

"He must have had a more sensitive mic than the cheap one I'm using. Miranda Juarez also said that the main thing he used it for was reading back text out loud."

"Show me."

So I typed in the words: *This is how I sound when I am reading in an electronic voice.* I pressed the read-back command and a robotic sounding voice pronounced each word precisely, but emotionlessly.

"No, problem there," she said.

I looked at my watch. A little after 8:30. Still early. Picking up the wine bottle, I glanced at her questioningly. She nodded so I added wine to her glass. She was leaning back in her chair in a relaxed way watching me with that half smile and an intriguing expression I couldn't quite read.

She rested her elbow on the chair arm holding her glass. "This wine has a wonderful smell. Like chocolate and...cherries. Is it something very special?"

"Actually," I said, "I have a few simple wine criteria. First and most important, it has to be cheaper than a large pizza," she chuckled as I went on, "second, there has to be a sign next to it at the wine store saying it's good."

"Is there a third criterion?" she asked in an amused voice.

"I'll think a third one up...um... to be the very best, it has to make beautiful women swoon with joy."

"Does this wine meet your criteria?" Her voice tone had changed to something slightly more dangerous.

"It meets one and two, but since you seem to be swoon free, it hasn't met the third."

"Hmm," she colored a little, then said, "where can you find wines that even fit criteria one and two?"

"I go to a tax free discount wine store in Sturbridge, Mass. Near the big outdoor antique show in Brimfield. Have you heard of that show?"

"Brimfield? Yes, I've been there."

"Really, do you go to the big shows?"

"Whenever I'm traveling."

"Did you go to Portobello Road when you were in London?"

"I managed a little time there and I went to Manchester," she said mentioning a huge British outdoor show.

"What was that like? Did you find anything special?"

"Absolutely enormous. I walked around the booths for days. I did find some lovely little things."

She was into the chase. Collectors love to stalk the prize. For a person with a Mini Cooper, I wondered how she reconciled the lust for antiques with the need for portability. I also wondered abstractly how hard she'd be willing to pursue something she wanted. I wondered just what it was she wanted from me. I was fairly clear on some of the things I wanted from her. I'm into the chase too.

"Well, have I given you enough information? Are we done with the questions now? Because if we are, I'd like to ask you some."

"You're entitled."

"How old are you?" she said raising her eyebrows a little.

"I'll be 36 in February. How old are you?"

"I'm 37, but it's my turn to ask the questions."

I gestured silently, inviting her to go on.

"Are you from Fenchester?"

"No, I was born in Western New York and I grew up there." I told her the two-minute version of my personal history.

"Why did you choose art school?"

"My mother was a painter and I guess you could say her other passion was advocating for disenfranchised people. She taught me to find solutions to problems in creative ways. Design, composition, visualization. Studying art and going into law enforcement both seemed natural extensions of those early lessons. Natural to me anyway."

She nodded. "Are those your watercolors? Do you paint regularly?" She motioned toward the big dining table.

"As much as I can. I like to do at least a few drawings a week...keeps me sane. May I do a portrait of you sometime?"

"I'd like that," she said still leaning back, swiveling the chair slightly from side to side. She didn't seem tired any more, she looked so fabulous, eyes bright, skin clear and smooth, her soft dark red hair curving in toward her throat...and the voice. Keep talking to me, I mentally begged.

We both paused, then I said, "Anything else?"

"Uh huh," she said looking directly into my eyes, "I want my massage now. I have to put my laundry in the dryer and use the bathroom first." She drank the last of the wine in her glass, stood up, gave me the enchanting half smile again. I watched her slowly cross the room.

Chapter 26

I put our wine glasses in the dishwasher, then followed her into the laundry room, "I need this," I said, pulling a folded sheet off a shelf of linens.

"Wait," she ordered.

I turned to listen.

She'd put her clothes in the dryer and set the dial. Leaning back against the machine, she tilted her chin up and said in a business like way, "I have some ground rules. Just two...to begin with. First, I'm not going to take off my clothes." She paused looking at me a little defiantly.

I have to admit, I was a bit disappointed. I'd already begun to imagine the feeling of her skin, but I was undaunted.

"Fine, that's up to you. I can still do a good job. What's the other rule?"

"Um," she hesitated, then said with a wry smile, "no... *surprises*."

"And by way of clarification, you mean no *passes*?"

"Exactly."

"*Surprises* would get in the way of the massage ...and so will your sweater vest, it's too thick. You'll have to take that off... and your shoes. You can leave everything else on. Deal?" I could be businesslike too, even while negotiating with a beautiful woman how much clothing she would remove.

She nodded once in agreement.

I went back to the big room to arrange pillows on the platform in front of the fireplace. I put some large flat rectangular ones in a row, then covered them with the sheet. I opened the glass doors of the fireplace and laid a fire. The kindling was burning in no time. Living across the street from a millworks means that I'm set for life with firewood. Culling the dumpster now and then beats chopping logs in the forest anytime.

She came back into the room just as I was lowering the lights. The flames beginning to gather strength in the fireplace made the area inviting and warm. She'd taken off her wool vest. Her flannel shirt wasn't thick fabric. I could see the contour of her breasts pressing against the material. They were a little larger and fuller than I'd imagined. She was also a bit thinner than I'd guessed.

She was slipping out of her shoes, which made her an inch shorter. That, I'd estimated correctly. She seemed a tad self-conscious. For the first time during the evening she was uncomfortable meeting my eyes. She looked instead at the pillows and the fireplace.

"This is for me?"

"Yes, lie down on your stomach."

"Tell me what you're going to do to me," she said quietly as she eased herself a little stiffly onto the pillows.

My mind reeled for a minute. A bouquet of responses came to mine. Oh, yeah, I remembered, she's talking about the massage.

"First I'm going to find out where it hurts." I stroked firmly from her shoulders down to the small of her back, then explored with my fingers. There were several places that were particularly tight. "Then I'm just going to massage all this tension away. You'll like it, it will make you feel better."

I reached under her shoulder to lift it a little, but at the same time she moved to lift it for me. "Kathryn, don't help me," I whispered, "just lie there and relax. Let me move you, otherwise you're working against me."

"I'm not very good at giving up control." She had that quiet growl back in her voice, like distant thunder underscoring her words.

"You've given up the control of your body to stress, that's why your shoulders hurt. Concentrate on letting go."

"That's going to be hard," she said wearily.

"We'll work on it together."

"Mm, OK."

I worked on the knotted muscles of her shoulders until they began to loosen and ease. I asked, "Am I hurting you? Tell me if I do."

"No, it feels wonderful," she said in a far away voice. "Please... don't stop."

"I've just begun." I'd realized with each stroke that besides her captivating face and bewitching voice she had a fantastic body. Firm and strong muscles, but soft and yielding curves. The last thing I wanted to do was *stop* touching her.

I moved to straddle her hips, repositioning myself above her, so I could concentrate long even strokes in the areas of her back where she needed it most. At one point she sighed spontaneously as though slipping into a warm bath. She seemed more supple now, more able to move freely. In fact, her movements had become catlike. An occasional long stretch, a graceful stirring of her head, the motion of her hand as she shifted it slightly, were all deliciously feline.

She'd been under so much stress, I knew rubbing her head would practically hypnotize her. I began by stroking lightly behind her ears. She was getting an erotic pleasure from it that was pretty satisfying to me too. I could see her smiling unconsciously. Her lips parted. She breathed deeply. I stroked the back of her neck gently, then ran my fingers slowly up through her hair, delicately massaging her head for a long time. She seemed to enjoy every minute of it. I did. She'd drifted off to another plane where there was only my touch and her response to it.

After a while she said lazily, "Please tell me that this is not the last time you'll ever do this to me ... it's exquisite."

"Any time you want," I whispered in an undertone, then even more quietly, "but, no clothes next time."

Later, with one of my fingers stroking behind her ear, and my other hand rubbing her shoulder, I asked, "Do you still have a headache?"

A few moments went by. She finally answered softly, "I don't know." By then I'd forgotten the question. I think she had too.

The soft flannel collar of her shirt covered the lower part of her neck, but I reached under the material to touch her skin directly. She shifted slightly, tilting her head, allowing me more access. I drew my fingers slowly along the edge of her collarbone in a careful gesture of exploration. I caressed the side of her throat lightly with my fingertips. Her lips parted again. Her lovely face was showing me just what she enjoyed.

I went back to rubbing her back with long luxurious strokes, which made her sigh contentedly again. I traced the waistband of her jeans, acutely aware that her clothes were just plain *in the way* of the kind of more intimate massage I wanted to offer at that moment. I wondered if she was feeling the same way.

After a while I shifted off her and sat to her side. My hands glided down her hips and slipped to the backs of her thighs. I considered parting her legs and stroking their inner surfaces, but I decided it would be too forward. *No surprises,* I'd promised. So I just rubbed slowly down her legs to her calves. They were strong from all the walking she did.

I'd given her back more than an hour of sensuous attention, drawing from her a number of pleasure sighs and grateful comments. It was time for something else. "OK, I'm done with your back. Turn over. I'm going to stoke the fire so you won't be cold. Don't rush, take your time."

She began to move leisurely as I poked up the fire and put more wood on the glowing embers.

"This is better than sex," she said as an involuntary stretch rippled through her from head to toe.

"Nah, it's just different." The fire's glow cast dancing shadows over her beautiful face and frame. The light from the flames in the hearth seemed to lick her breasts and thighs. I watched with envy.

The buzzer on the dryer went off, as unwanted as an alarm clock at 5:00 AM.

"Oh, I'll get that," said Kathryn straining to sit up.

"No, no, I'll do it. Just lie on your back and relax." I walked into the laundry room, took the dry clothes out of the machine, folded them quickly and put them in the basket. The rest were towels that were still damp. I set the dryer for forty minutes more.

When I came back into the big room, Kathryn was lying on her back in front of what was now a blazing fire. She'd raised her arm and had one hand covering her eyes. I sat back down beside her, close to her hip, feeling the warmth of the fire and the warmth of her body at the same time.

"Are you OK?" I asked her.

"I feel wonderful, but, aren't you getting tired of doing this?" she said taking her hand away from her eyes and turning her head slowly to look at me.

"I'm not tired ... are you getting bored? I still have more to do, but would you rather I stop now?" I asked, willing that she'd let me continue. She didn't disappoint.

She searched my eyes for a long moment. I wondered what she was looking for. Then she said slowly with the firelight in her eyes, "No, I'm not bored. I was hoping you'd say you still had more to do. This is really glorious. In fact, I can't think of a time in my life when someone made so much effort to...to make my body feel this good."

"Really? Wait a minute, I thought you said you went to Smith. I bet you had women lining up for a chance to, *make your body feel good.*"

She snorted softly, "Well, it *was* kind of like a candy store, but college students don't... well, most students always seem to be in a hurry."

"Hmm, what a shame. You said in your *life* though..."

"It may have more to do with me than... it may have been I who was always in too much of a hurry. I haven't given myself much time to, *smell the roses.*" She turned her head toward the fire and said, "I haven't lain next to a wood fireplace since I was a kid. I grew up in Maine. We had a vacation cabin with only a fireplace for heat. We'd go there during the summer.

Sometimes the nights were cold, so we'd lie by the fire all night. It was ...comforting."

I laid my hand on her stomach and began to rub slowly back and forth. It was an affectionate intimate gesture. Like petting a cat or maybe taming a panther?

She looked back up at me and said with that hint of panther growl, "Tell me what you're going to do to me...now."

Oh man, she'd said it again. There was nothing tame about Kathryn Anthony.

"I'm going to stretch you."

I moved around to her head, then I lifted her arms, extending them toward me. I grasped each of her wrists and slowly leaned back, stretching the entire length of her body.

She groaned sensually as I did it. When I stopped she demanded in a low voice, "Do that again."

I pulled a little harder this time using my own body weight to coax her to her fullest reach. She responded with a growling moan of pleasure. It's hard to express what she looked like extended that way, on her back, moaning. But the sound made me tingle from head to toe.

I replaced her arms by her sides as she said with pleasant surprise, "Umm, that was satisfying,"

I moved to her side, touching her throat with just my fingertips then let them trail out to her shoulders. Placing my palms on each shoulder, I evenly pressed her back into the pillow, holding her there for several long moments.

She groaned again, but in a more sultry way this time. "This might be too good," she said in a throaty voice.

I moved down to the end of the platform and massaged her calves for a few minutes. I pulled gently on her legs one at a time and then together.

"Feel a little taller?"

"Mmm, that all felt wonderful..."

"You should have someone do that to you every day," I said massaging her left shoulder, then stroking down to her hand.

"Would you do it to me...every day?" she murmured.

"Shhh...be still." I lifted her wrist, resting her forearm in my lap. I held her hand with both of mine and said seriously, "You know, the way your computer is set up you're buying yourself a one way ticket down the carpal tunnel."

"I know it's all wrong, I've put in a request to the computer tech department to make my typing station ergonomic. They said they'd do it, but

I have a feeling I'm on a two-year waiting list."

I began on her hand. I was more than willing to give her a massage without any kind of return on my investment other than the discussion of the case, but she must have been aware that I was doing my best to put her in the mood for something more than muscle relaxing.

Massaging someone's hands can be extremely intimate. Years ago, when I was in high school, I had a boyfriend who was a little older than I and who had a full-time job and a lot of disposable income. I was becoming aware of my true sexual orientation and not very interested in having sex with him, which was what he wanted to do all the time.

Instead we would go to the movies. Which was fine by me, I like movies. To keep him at bay, I'd hold his hand in my lap and trace pictures in his palm. It wasn't very taxing on me, but frankly, that kind of stimulation can be a direct conduit to areas below the belt. Much later he got in touch with me to say he was still in love with me. Unfortunately for him I'd been a confirmed and committed and contented lesbian for years. I really think it was the hand massages that made him remember me more than all the girls he'd slept with.

I slowly rubbed Kathryn's left palm with my thumbs. I stretched her fingers and rubbed her wrist. I ran my fingers lightly over the back of her hand and then I finished by tracing a figure in her palm. Her lifeline and heart line were very strong.

"You're left-handed?" I asked.

"Uh huh, can you tell just by looking?"

"By looking and by feeling the muscles in your forearms." I was musing on the extraordinary advantages of having a left-handed lesbian lover. Really...think about it.

"Professional sleuth," she said, "although I think this should be your career."

"Massage therapist? Nope, I'll sleuth for almost anybody who can meet my price, but I'm very selective about whom I massage."

"Any woman would pay you to do this to her."

"I'm a better sleuth than I am a masseuse."

"I can only testify to your skill at massage. You've proved it. How do you show people you're good at being a detective?"

"Well..." I placed her left hand back down by her side and began on her right. I massaged her palm and each finger with firm caresses. "Well, Kathryn, one of the things that sleuths do is investigate ...stalkers."

She blinked up at me, a smile played at the corners of her mouth and danced in her eyes. "Oh?"

"Uh huh," I continued to stroke her hand. She was feeling it throughout her body. I could tell. "You know, it's important for a detective to be trained in observation. Do you know what I observed on Wednesday night?"

"Tell me," she whispered.

"I observed three cars driving through the Mews while I was shoveling the snow. One was a Chrysler PT Cruiser, one was a Ford Focus, ... and one ...was a blue and white BMW Mini Cooper, with a Maine license plate." I ran my fingers lightly over her palm in slow sensuous circles.

"Really?" she breathed, closing her eyes, savoring my touch.

"Yes, and as a matter of fact, I'm sure the woman driving the car saw me quite well, because her headlights shined in my face. I couldn't really see her, but she would certainly have known exactly whom she would meet, if she chose to go for a walk in the moonlight."

She closed her hand on mine. It was just a light squeeze. "You win," she laughed softly.

Not yet, I thought.

She seemed very relaxed. The windows to her soul were closed, but her lips were parted slightly. I came very close to kissing her right that second, but then she let go of my hand.

I took two cushions from the pile on the floor. I put one under her knees and one under her feet.

"What's this for?" she asked raising her head to look.

"I'm going to massage your feet now. Maybe do some reflexology."

"How did you learn how to do all this? Do you have formal training? You must."

"Some training, some experience, an artist's knowledge of anatomy, and a lot of empathy. I know what it's like to have body pain. I know where it comes from, and I know a few tricks to make it go away."

"Have you been hurt in the line of duty?" she asked raising her head again.

"Once or twice, but so have you, and this is about you, not me. Put your head down and relax or you'll mess up all the work I've already done," I said with mock severity.

"OK...no wait."

I stopped arranging the pillows and glanced up.

"Um, one thing... I'm very ticklish." It was a simple statement, but her voice was suggestive, causing me to look carefully at her face to gauge her expression. But her eyes were closed again.

I said deliberately, "I haven't noticed that so far."

"It's not a general sensitivity, it's... my feet. When my brothers wanted to force me to tell secrets, they would torture me by holding me down and using a feather on the soles of my feet." She still had her eyes closed as she told me this. I was glad she couldn't see my cheeks flush.

"Was that a turn-on for them?" I asked, as I lifted her legs and placed another pillow under her ankles.

She paused to think and then said, "Probably," with a little laugh.

"And ...was it for you?" I asked slowly in a low voice.

She paused to consider even longer... she made a throat clearing noise, "Probably," she admitted softly.

"Hmm," I wasn't sure if she was cautioning me or trying to encourage something. "If you feel that I'm tickling you, tell me and I'll stop." I said as I put my hand on her right instep. I looked down. "Wow, these are some socks, are they cashmere?" They were black knit and incredibly soft.

"Yes, aren't they great? A student gave them to me as a present. I really love them."

"And they say there are no perks to teaching," I said. "Did this student know that she or he ...?"

"She."

"Did she know that she was giving you a sensuous gift or was she just pawning off a dull holiday present from Aunt Gladys?" I was working gently on the soles of her feet now, stroking and kneading. It was having an affect on her. I could see a slight, almost imperceptible movement in her hips. Hey, I'm a detective. I notice these things. Especially at moments like this.

" ...Um....I think the former. I think she knew...she...knew just what she was doing," Kathryn answered, having trouble concentrating on what she was saying. Her face was flushed.

"And did you get anything...else...from her?" It was my turn to be suggestive. I caressed the cashmere more slowly watching her reactions carefully.

"She...she... was one of my research assistants...and...um...ah... she did a lot of research...more than what the average student would do."

Kathryn lifted her head, opened her eyes and looked at me. I stopped for a moment and looked back. She went on, "I stay away from romantic involvement with students. Besides the impropriety, I'm not interested in women that young."

I eyed her steadily for a long moment. "Lie back down and relax," I commanded in a low voice. She closed her eyes and laid her head back on the pillow. I began working on the other foot. "Do you have a lot of students chasing after you?"

"I've heard the student's nickname for me is, *The Ice Queen*."

"Really? Do you think that's apt?" I said incredulously.

"Um...well...Kenny thinks I'm hot."

"He's not the only one," I said in a stage whisper.

"Hmm," she murmured.

I went back to gently massaging the sole of her foot. The movement in her body was more pronounced. She was losing herself in it, moving her hips rhythmically. She raised her hand to her throat and turned her head part way to the fire. The firelight flickered across her face. A flame was lighting in me too. She wasn't relaxed any more. Her stomach muscles were taut. The tendons in her neck were more pronounced. She surprised me and herself by suddenly arching her back off the pillows. She thrust her head back and opened her mouth for just an instant. She gave a quiet grunt followed by a small but audible gasp. These weren't huge dramatic movements, but they were totally visible to me and she knew it.

Well, well, well, I thought, *that was interesting.* I rested her foot back on the pillow but continued to hold it gently. After she'd relaxed just a bit, I asked softly, "Do you want me to stop?"

She began making a sound that could only be characterized as purring. Her eyes studied mine. We held each other's gaze.

Frankly, I was pretty happy with the way things had turned out, but I'd vowed *no surprises*, and I was going to stick to it. If she wanted something more from me, it would have to be up to her. In fact, I wanted her to ask for it. I wanted her to make the move. I wanted her to tell me that she wanted me.

"How about if I do something else for a while? I'm going to touch your face, so I'll wash my hands first." I got up and went across the room to the kitchen sink. I'd done it to make her wait. I took my time. She turned on her side and watched me silently.

The contours of her body were silhouetted against the ever-changing flames in the fireplace. After what had just happened, I needed a minute to catch my breath but this alluring tableau did nothing to ease my breathing. On the platform in front of the fire, she seemed to be waiting for a ritual to begin. I dried my hands and went slowly back to her.

I sat down beside her as she shifted to her back. I reached down to rub her temples. She closed her eyes and her breathing slowed. I could see the muscles in her hips relax. I wondered if she was as wet as I was.

I traced the contours of her ears delicately, then stroked her throat more gently until my fingertips were just barely touching her. She was a beautiful sleek panther responding to my hands. She was making that noise that sounded like purring again and I was burning with desire. I traced my fingers over her forehead at her hairline, appreciating the elegant shape of her brow. Her expression was totally, radiantly relaxed. I stroked the rest of her face very lightly, following the outline of her eyes to her cheekbones and then her jaw. I ended the massage by touching her lips, just brushing across them several times with the soft pad of my thumb as my fingers caressed her cheek. She was lying very still.

"I'm done," I said quietly. "Is there anything...else you'd like me to do?"

She opened her eyes and searched my face. Momentarily her forehead showed creases of deep concentration. I just looked back into her eyes passively.

"Would you push on my shoulders again?"

"Sure," I said sliding closer to her and placing one hand on the front of each of her shoulders. I pressed each back in turn, then both at the same time. She watched me with her eyes wide open. She moaned a little, enjoying the pressure. And then there was that purring noise, an mmmmm sound.

I held her shoulders back for quite a while, like pinning her to the platform. It had an aggressive feel to it. She stared into my eyes as it was happening. I stared back. When I finally moved my hands away, she lifted her left arm to partly cover her eyes with her palm. I just sat beside her, watching her move, wondering what would happen next. It was hard to resist kissing her, in fact, I could barely control my breathing. My heart was pounding so hard I suspected she could hear it.

She moved her hand from her eyes and slipped it behind her head, propping herself up slightly. She said looking up at me with that half smile... "You have a lot of intimate knowledge of my body now. It's making this relationship a little uneven."

"Relationship," I repeated. I was silent and still. I just stayed where I was, looking deeply into her eyes, with just a hint of a smile.

She whispered, "You're going to make me beg, aren't you?"

I exhaled softly and slightly nodded my head. There were 24,000 cubic feet of space in the room, and every inch was full of the sexual tension between us, circling around us, drawing us together.

I said in a low voice, "You made the ground rules my dear, changing them...is up to you."

Finally after several long moments of searching my eyes she whispered, "All right then, I have another rule, which modifies the first two."

"Yes?"

"It has to be safe." She reached to touch my cheek and the dryer buzzer went off again. She pushed herself up a little and I shifted back. "I'll go and deal with that," she said sitting up. And then she was out of the room, gone from between my arms. The moment seemed lost. I wasn't sure what she'd meant exactly. I felt a wave of dismay. Have I mentioned that I had a nagging pain between my legs? I sat on the edge of the platform waiting, hoping for her to come back.

"Maggie," she called after a few minutes, it was the first time she'd used my first name.

"Yeah?"

"Would you come here?"

She was standing in the dark bedroom next to the window looking out at the Mews. I could see her only by the moonlight streaming through the glass.

"Show me where the river is."

I came up beside her. I could smell her scent. It wasn't just Chanel anymore, it was desire, and it was coming from me too. The moonlight shimmered in her eyes.

"You can just see a corner of it... over there." I pointed to a space between the Hampshire and Dakota.

She looked at the little piece of the river that showed through the trees. Then she turned toward me and said in a voice that was mostly whisper and sigh, "Do you seduce all your women by giving them wonderful massages like that?"

It doesn't always work, would have been the most accurate thing to say, but instead I answered, "I don't know yet."

She faced me for what seemed like an age, but what was probably a second. She took a breath, then she made a soft demand, "Undress me."

That's something you'll be remembering for the rest of your life, flashed through my mind. I hadn't expected anything so specific. My legs almost gave way. I reached for the top button of her shirt. My hands were trembling. I undid two. She put her hand on the back of my neck and pulled me toward her for a long passionate kiss. Her lips were deliciously soft. She tasted wonderful, like everything I'd ever wanted.

Yeah, this is going really well, I thought to myself and that was the last coherent thought I had.

I had all her buttons undone. I moved the shirt off her shoulders and slid it down her arms. She let me undo her bra without helping at all. Her breasts were firm and perfect and I longed to touch them but I held back for just a while longer. Her skin was more tempting than I could have imagined. I unzipped her jeans and gently pushed her back a step to the edge of the bed. I looked down at her body and couldn't keep from saying, "Wow," as I pulled her jeans and underwear down and she stepped out of them.

I said, "Are you finally going to touch *me* now?"

"Yes...and I'm good at it," she said confidently.

"I like a woman who's sure of her skills," I whispered.

Chapter 27

I'd testify in front of a grand jury that Dr. Kathryn Anthony was no ice queen! That woman was hotter than a branding iron, a 400 amp service and a handful of habañero peppers rolled into one. And she was more than accurate when she said she was *good at it*. Damn, that was an understatement!

Kathryn had done some things to me, that I hadn't actually believed possible. Once I had her undressed, she'd pushed me onto the bed and had my clothes off in no time.

I just had to say, "Tell me what you're going to do to me."

She laughed.

I'd figured that when she'd said, *It has to be safe,* she'd meant safe sex. We both knew that it would be statistically easier for a lesbian to win the powerball lottery six times in a row, than to give her lover AIDS, but there are some skin to skin transmitted things like herpes that anyone can get if their partner is infected. So we used latex to be safe.

In fact, it was fun. I'd gotten, as a loft-warming gift, a whole bunch of safe sex protection from a friend at the health department. I hadn't had a lover since I'd moved in. Truthfully, it'd been longer than that. Kathryn teased me for having the sex stuff in a drawer right by my bed.

She used some of the latex gloves, and a dental dam. She took her rapture filled time. When I became desperate for release, she made me have three separate earth shattering orgasms. The last one had been so intense, I'd blacked out for a moment. When it was my turn to try to satisfy her, I was a little intimidated, but her body was so supple and responsive I felt encouraged. I used the latex too. She led me exactly where she wanted to go. The only word she said was, *slowly*. She said it twice. So I slowed. It was magnificently sweet.

Finally she was so ready that using the latex glove was smooth and sensual. I used my other hand to stimulate her. When she came, she gave a long low groan that started out quietly and built to a surprising crescendo.

Her body arched suddenly as if a bolt of lightning had hit her. She grabbed my shoulder and held on so hard I nearly cried out. Her climax lasted a very long time and seemed to surge in waves. She finally gasped, "Yes," then let go in complete exhaustion.

I knew a woman once who would fall asleep the minute her orgasm ended, but Kathryn was taking long deep breaths. She wasn't asleep.

She said, "Oh Maggie," and reached out to me. I put my arms around her and felt her body tremble. I leaned my head back to look at her face. She was crying.

"Kathryn?"

She turned to me and smiled, she sighed, "It's all right...I...it's just that ... it's been so long."

It happens that way sometimes, after a long period alone. That huge rush of release can bring uncontrollable tears. I held her in my arms and stroked her hair.

She brushed my cheek softly with her fingers. Watching me closely, searching my eyes, she touched my mouth. She held her hand there until I slowly parted my lips and bit the tip of her finger. She immediately put both her hands on the sides of my face and drew me to her in another deeply passionate kiss. Where did she learn to kiss like that? Maybe they had a course at Smith. We began all over.

We'd gone into the bedroom fairly early in the evening. Even with many hours of love making, we had much of the night left over to sleep. Which was a blessing because by then we were both totally exhausted.

I woke from a dreamless doze at about 6:00 AM. I heard Kathryn's soft rhythmic breathing beside me. I could feel her warmth. I wanted to wake her up and tell her how happy I was. I wanted to make love to her again. I let her sleep. I looked at the changing colors of the sky through the wall of windows.

I was propped on a pillow against the headboard with my head turned to the right looking out at the sunrise. Kathryn stirred. She touched my bare shoulder. Her hand was soft and warm. She was so beautiful I could barely believe she was lying next to me. We both smiled but didn't speak. She took one of the small pillows and put it on my stomach resting her chin on it so she could watch the sky too. I reached down and touched her hair.

After a while she shifted her body to lie along side me. She kissed the side of my neck. I was suddenly afraid she was going to leave. I was afraid it might all have been just a one-time adventure for her. I put my arms around her and didn't want to let her go. Her hand trailed over my sheet-covered body and made me shiver.

"I want you to tell me everything about yourself," she whispered in my ear.

"I feel the same way about you," I whispered back.

"That's a good start..." she murmured on the edge of sleep.

She leaned her head on my shoulder. I could feel her relax and become heavy.

I thought, She can fall asleep in my arms and she wants to know everything about me. Yeah, it is a good start,

I fell asleep too.

The clock said 9:00 AM when we woke again. I was a little stiff because we were still lying in each other's arms. The sun was much higher in the sky. It cast a warm square of light across the bed.

Kathryn whispered with delight, "Look, there's a rainbow."

I shifted my attention from her to the sky. I saw it. A pale rainbow clearly visible in the morning sky.

"Make a wish," she whispered, "rainbows are better at granting wishes than stars. Stars are over worked." I made a silent wish.

I had to go to the bathroom. So I slipped out of her arms. She watched me cross the room. I pulled on a T-shirt and shorts before I came back.

In the bedroom, Kathryn was propped on a pillow against the headboard. She'd pulled on her flannel shirt. "What are we going to do now?" she said cheerfully.

I slipped back into bed with her and said, "It depends on what you mean by now...as in: Do we have coffee now? Do we have breakfast now? Do we make passionate love again now? Do we rent a UHaul now? Do we try to take over the world now?"

"I think, A, B, and C and we can talk about the rest later..."

"A, B and C in what order?" I grinned.

"First, I have to use the bathroom, then I think, C, A and B. How does that sound?"

"Very nice...I left a new toothbrush and some towels next to the sink for you," I called after her.

When she lay back down beside me she said, "What's that scar on your back?" She looked concerned.

I didn't want to talk about my gun shot wounds, but she'd seen the evidence. I couldn't pretend they were bee stings. I pulled off my T-shirt and lay on my side facing away from her so she could see. I felt her fingers touching the older scar on my shoulder. The one near my waist was newer and still pink, although it didn't hurt much anymore. The bullet had gone all the way through at my waist, so there were two scars there. Entry and exit.

"The shoulder one was *friendly fire*, as they say."

"You mean you were shot by another police officer?" she asked in a quiet but shocked voice.

"Yeah, he said it was an accident. That was when I was in the state police in Indiana."

Then she traced a path with her finger to the other, more recent scar. "And this one?" she sounded sorry and sad.

"The price I paid for this building."

"Oh Maggie," she said with profound concern, "you paid too much."

"I don't want you to think this kind of thing happens to me all the time." I turned toward her and pulled her closer.

"Someone shot at you two days ago!" she said pushing me back with her palms, to look at me directly.

"Kathryn..." I said seriously, "sometimes people are threatened by what I do. Everyone who tries to make change sometimes puts themselves in danger. I help people who need my help. I can't stop doing it because someone might hurt me. You do what you do, and people threaten you. You've told to me that threats made you double your efforts, that you couldn't compromise your commitment."

She touched my face softly, "Oh Maggie, I've just found you and the thought of losing you..." she held my hand in hers. "But you're right, I wouldn't compromise. I can't ask you to...I like who you are." She kissed the back of my hand, then she said very seriously, "So far, you've kept all your promises to me. Will you promise me that you'll be as careful as you can be?"

"Yes, I can promise you that." I lifted her hand to my lips, then said, "There's something else, since we're on the topic of health and welfare... and being careful. When I was in the hospital last spring, I had them do a full screen for STDs and everything else. I was free of everything. I haven't been with anyone since then, so..."

"So, we don't have to use latex?" she said smiling. "Well, I'm clear of everything too. I had a full check-up before I went to Europe in September, and I've been *alone* longer than you have."

Kathryn's tone became more sensual, "But had you ever used those things before?" her half smile was returning, "did you...enjoy them...?"

"You mean the gloves and stuff, no I've never used them before, but honey after last night I think from now on just the smell of latex is going to make me wet," I laughed.

"Hah!" she laughed too. Then she noticed my other shoulder, "What about these bruises?

"Yeah, well, you did that to me last night. What an iron grip! It just goes to show that injury can come when you least expect it."

She looked horrified. "Oh, I'm so sorry! I don't remember..."

"If you don't remember, then I'll take it to mean I was doing a good job."

Her voice dropped to that deep register, "You were wonderful to me last night..."

"Kathryn, some of the marvelous things you did to me ...I've only read about them in books..."

"Well," she laughed, "I am a literature professor."

"Hah!" I pulled her closer and kissed her. Then slipped down along her body under the covers. We spent a while doing an abbreviated version of the night before. Variations on a theme, *sans latex*.

Chapter 28

"I'm hungry," Kathryn confided as we lay together in the tangled sheets.

"I'll turn on the coffee," I said pulling my T-shirt and shorts back on. "We can go out to eat or I can make you something."

She'd gone into the bathroom. I could hear the shower running. I opened the refrigerator to see what I could pull together. The phone buzzed, it was the building intercom. I picked up the mobile.

"Hi... it's me, who's up there with you?" My nosy sister Sara.

"Hold on," I said.

Kathryn had called from the bathroom. I went in the bedroom to answer her, carrying the phone. I raised my voice and asked through the closed bathroom door, "What did you say?"

"Do you have a blow dryer?"

"Second drawer in the sink cabinet."

I heard her open the cabinet and turn on the dryer.

"What?" I sat on the bed and said in a low voice back into the phone.

"Who's up there?" Sara whispered.

"Are you downstairs?"

"Of course. I'm in my office. I saw the purple dot and ...I just heard the shower." Now who was being Nancy Drew?

"It's a friend..."

"A friend you just fucked or you'd be telling me who she is," Sara chided, "is it...."

She named someone so far fetched I snapped, "Of course not, will you get real!"

"Then who? I really want to know...I'll come up and find out if you don't tell me."

This is what it's like having a younger sister. On the other hand, maybe they aren't all as nosy. Both my sisters Sara and Rosa are notorious snoops. They should be the P.I.s. They have to know everything. Sara wasn't kidding when she said she'd come up here.

"OK, I'll tell you, but be nice...it's Kathryn Anthony..."

"Woo hoo! I want to see her. Is she great looking? She works at the College, doesn't she? Has she been there all night? Hey, I got bakery croissants and donuts. I left them at the door. I didn't come in... Hello?...Maggie?"

I'd stopped because Kathryn was standing in the doorway to the bathroom watching me talking on the phone. She had one elbow resting on the door frame, with her head against her fist. She was wearing her black flannel shirt again and nothing else. I could see the swell of her breasts at the open vee of the collar; the material clung to the contours of her damp body. Her shirttail hung to mid-thigh. She was smirking at me with mock exasperation.

I said to Sara, "Gotta go," and disconnected.

"Lesbian chivalry is dead?" Kathryn said shaking her head. She folded her arms and began walking toward me.

"I've been bad and you're going to punish me?" I asked with amusement.

She pushed me hard onto the bed and climbed on top of me, straddling me at the hips. She was leaning over me laughing and saying, "You're shameless! The minute I turn my back, you call a friend to kiss and tell?"

I was laughing too and saying, "No, no..." in protest. She had her hands on my shoulders pushing me back against the bed. She was trying to pin my arms down.

"Listen," I said, "you're gonna have to learn to trust me and you're gonna have to face an unpleasant fact..."

"What?"

I dropped my hands to the soles of her feet and tickled. She squealed, shifting her balance. I easily flipped her off me and was on top in a second. Marshal arts training comes in handy in many situations.

Now I was straddling her. I held her wrists pinned over her head with one hand. The look in her eye was encouraging, her breathing deepened. I undid the first button of her shirt. She didn't complain so I kept talking as I unbuttoned.

"I come with family baggage. See, that was my sister, and I didn't call her, she called me on the intercom phone. The phone buzzed while you were in the shower. Her office is downstairs and sometimes when she has to work on weekends, she brings her laundry over here to do," I undid the last button, "and we have breakfast together. She has a key and just comes in, but she knew someone was here so she didn't...interrupt us...until she heard the shower running..." I explained while spreading Kathryn's shirt open and brushing my fingers over her lightly from throat to navel. She enjoyed the sensation. She arched into it.

"But, how did she know I was here?" asked Kathryn who was panting now because I'd begun to caress her breast.

"Well," I said a little sheepishly," I left a colored magnet on the outside of the fire door. It's a signal not to come in..." I was teasing her nipple between my thumb and forefinger.

"You mean it's like a red sign saying Do Not Disturb?" she gasped trying to keep up the conversation, struggling against the tickle of my touch and savoring it at the same time. That nipple had grown full and erect, so I began to work on the other one.

"Not exactly. A red sign means Do Not Disturb, but I used the purple dot, which means I Have A Date In Here, and believe me, if I'd just used the red sign she would have come in anyway. Sleeping late is not enough to keep her out." I stopped talking and leaned down to suck one nipple while I rubbed the other with my hand, then I said, "Sara brought assorted croissants, she left them at the door. I think she said donuts too but..."

"Your sister brought donuts!?!" Kathryn wriggled out from under me and jumped out of bed. I could hear her making her way to the entrance door.

"Wait," I shouted, "don't go out there!" I was too late though, I heard the door open, then Kathryn picking up the bakery box. I could hear my sister hoot loudly all the way from downstairs. Kathryn came back into the bedroom looking in the box. Her shirt still wide open. Her nipples still very erect.

"Oh, no," I groaned.

The phone started to buzz. Kathryn looked at it.

I said, "It's my sister again. She just saw you come out of the door on the closed circuit TV."

Kathryn glanced down at her open shirt, then she looked at me and really began to laugh. "And that's her on the phone? How's she going to feel about a mostly naked woman reaching out the door of your loft?

"Well since she's a lesbian, I think she'll feel *privileged* to have seen you, like that," I said sarcastically.

The phone buzzed again.

"Answer it," nodded Kathryn.

I picked it up. "Yeah?"

"Woo Wooo Baby!!!"

"Shut up."

Kathryn called, "Tell her to come up and have breakfast with us!"

Sara said, "OK, I'll be right there..." and hung up before I could respond.

"Oh shit," I said, pressing the intercom button. I yelled at the floor, "Pick it up!!!"

Sara answered, "What?"

"Please give us 20 minutes, I haven't even taken a shower. OK!?!"

"OK," Sara conceded.

I hung up the phone and looked at Kathryn, she was laughing at me. She said, "If you can't beat 'em..."

"Geez...OK, look, she's going to be here in like, ten minutes, I.."

"You said twenty."

"She's a lawyer, she writes her own rules. I have an appointment in a little while, I'll have to go," I was touched to see disappointment register on Kathryn's face.

I went on, but with hesitation, "I...I...will you have dinner with me tonight? Is it too, *lesbian relationship overkill?*"

"Maggie, we *are* lesbians, of course I want to have dinner with you..."

"And stay over again... I mean, if you want to?" I asked quietly.

She smiled and nodded.

I grinned, "I don't know how long the appointment will take, may I come to your apartment when I'm through...?"

"Sure, it's 319, but I think I'll go to my office, so could you come there when you're ready? Dinner will be my treat, it's my turn."

"I think we're pretty even on the treats."

She laughed deep in her throat. Then she went toward the laundry room saying, "This is one of the rare occasions when the illicit paramour doesn't have to wear the same clothes in the morning that she came in in the evening. I have all my clean clothes here!"

"Illicit paramour is not the right character designation," I called.

She leaned out the bathroom door and tilted her head to the side... "What is the right characterization?"

"Well, we could have talked about that, but you decided instead that it would be a good idea to invite my extremely nosy sister to breakfast!" I said with exasperation.

"Can we talk about it tonight?" she said with a sweet smile.

"Let's talk about everything tonight," I said smiling back. Kathryn went to get some of her clean clothes from the laundry room. I turned on the shower again, then went into the closet to grab what I needed while the water got warm. I could see Kathryn pulling on her jeans in the laundry room.

She looked up and said, "That is the finest shower in the world. Did you design it? The tile bench is inspired."

"I did design it, I haven't been able to get the handheld part on the hose to work though, but it's really the rain showerhead that makes it so special," I said as I went back into the bathroom.

Kathryn was in the kitchen area when I'd finished dressing and came into the big room. She was setting the kitchen table with plates and silverware for breakfast. She'd put the butter dish on the table.

"I'll be right there," I called across the room to her.

I opened a closet near the entrance door where the security equipment was and rapidly changed the recordable DVD in the security recorder and erased the digital files. I took the old DVD over to the kitchen counter and cut it in half with some heavy kitchen shears. I folded the pieces and threw them in the garbage.

"What are you doing?" asked Kathryn curiously.

"Protecting you from distribution ...watch what Sara does the minute she gets in here. She'll try to be subtle, but watch."

Exactly eleven minutes after I'd told Sara to give us twenty, there was a knock and she unlocked the door and walked in singing, "Good Morning!" Then she fumbled around with her jacket and casually walked over to the closet, acting like she was going to hang it up.

"I erased the files and cut up the old DVD," I called out as she reached for the doorknob to the closet with the video equipment.

"Damn!" she exclaimed laughing. Kathryn laughed too. I stood there with my arms folded.

"You are so bad," I said shaking my head.

Sara came over to me, kissed me on the cheek, then said very rapidly, *"Buena mañana, querida. ¿Entonces donde conociste esta chica caliente y cuán fue en la cama? ¿Le sobra algo para mi?"*

"Callate maleriada, recuerda que todavia te puedo dar una tremenda pela. Si, la miras no mas, te boto de aqui," I said in a menacing voice.

"Despues de haber hecho lo que yo sospecho, la noche entera, seguro que esta demasiado casada para manejar eso," she teased.

"E'tate quieta Sara, de veras," I said threateningly.

Translation:
> Sara came over to me, kissed me on the cheek then said very rapidly, "Good Morning, sweetie. So where did you get this hot babe and how was she in bed? Does she have any left over for me?"

"Shut up you brat, remember I can spank the crap out of you. If you so much as look at her, I'll kick your butt out of here," I said in a menacing voice.

"After what I suspect you've been doing all night, I doubt you'd have the energy to manage it," she teased.

"Quit it, Sara. I mean it," I said threateningly.

Sara said, "Hey, if I'd known I could use donuts to lure naked lesbians into my clutches, I'd have a girlfriend by now. I'm changing my whole approach." She extended her hand and said sincerely, "Hello Kathryn, I'm just teasing my sister. This is no reflection on you. I'm very glad to meet you."

"Sara, thank you for the baked goods. They were just what I wanted." Sara was still holding on to Kathryn's hand even after they'd finished speaking.

"Let go of her, Sara!" I commanded.

My sister smiled at me sweetly and said, "Do you have any orange juice?"

Sara was wearing paint stained pants and a turtleneck shirt with a ratty sweatshirt over it.

"Professional outfit," I teased.

"At least I *have* clothes on," she quipped under her breath.

"I heard that," said Kathryn laughing again, "and someday, I'll have to know what you were just saying to each other."

I got orange juice from the refrigerator and some glasses. Kathryn put coffee cups and a carton of half and half on the counter.

Although Sara drives me crazy, I love her very much. She and Rosa and their mother are the only family I have in the world, other than Farrel and Jessie, who are family I chose. It was very important to me that they all liked Kathryn. Sara would be the hardest sell. Sara has been known to say on more than one occasion, "I hate new people," but Kathryn was being so charming to her, Sara was trapped. It was making me a tiny bit jealous, because I'm always aware that even in scruffy clothes, Sara is very attractive to just about everybody. And Kathryn was flirting with her.

Intellectually I knew Kathryn was doing it to be diplomatic, but it's amazing how just one night in bed creates a powerful possessiveness. They chatted personably through several croissants and cups of coffee. I ate a donut and watched.

I knew I was going to have a hard time concentrating on the case during the rest of the afternoon, but I needed to interview Bart Edgar at noon. That gave me about thirty minutes before I had to leave. If I wanted to spend those thirty minutes alone with Kathryn, I might have to physically throw Sara out.

"So Kathryn, where are you from?" cross-examined Sara.

"I grew up in Portland, Maine."

"You don't sound like you grew up in Maine," said Sara at the zenith of snoopery. "Did you have voice training?"

Kathryn laughed, "I guess that's a compliment. I can speak like a Northern New Englander, *Ya can't get they'ah from he'ah.* You're right though, I trained in theater classes and I sing a little too. I wanted to have a voice that could carry to the back of the lecture hall."

Most of the donuts were gone, but Sara was still mercilessly pumping Kathryn with questions. While Kathryn was doing just fine holding her own in the conversation, I was wondering what it would be like to have Kathryn sing to me.

"How do you feel about same-sex marriage?" asked Sara pointedly.

"I feel annoyed and discriminated against because it's not legal in this state"

"Uh huh... but how do you feel about it personally?"

"Fine," said Kathryn without skipping a beat.

"So, tell us your coming out story, Kathryn," said Sara leaning back in her chair.

"No," I said to both of them, "we can talk about that later if Kathryn wants to, but right now, I have to go in a few minutes and I want to talk to Kathryn alone, so go back to your office right *now.*" I gave Sara such a look that she actually did it, after politely saying goodbye.

I turned to Kathryn after Sara left and said, "I thought she'd never leave. I'm sorry she was so pushy."

"Maggie, my twin bother Kiernan is just like her, and he's gay too. Believe me, I understand. I can also see she loves you very much. It's important to you that she approves of me isn't it?"

"If she doesn't approve, don't worry, I can beat her up," I said in the time honored fashion of an older sister, "Kathryn, I have to leave soon..."

In response, she leaned across the corner of the table and gave me a tender kiss. She said sweetly, "I want to talk to you about lots of things tonight. Shall we do that?"

"That will be nice. At the moment there is only one thing in the world I can imagine that would be more exciting than *talking* to you." She kissed me again.

After a while I said, "You don't have to go, you can stay here if you want."

"No, I'll go get some work done, then we'll have plenty of time to be together. I have to look over two late thesis proposals and, if it's all right with you, I'd like to take the instruction manual to Carl's Voice Transcription System. I woke up in the night thinking about it. I don't understand why it's working so poorly."

"Sure, take it." I got up from the table, found the manual and brought it back to her. "I'll come to your office as soon as I can, but I have several people to interview, starting with Bart."

"Oh dear, that will be trying."

"Quite...I'll be at your office between 6:30 and 7:00. You get to decide where we'll have dinner." We kissed again.

"And...then we'll have *all* night," said Kathryn. Her expression was so delicious, I began to ache all over again.

Chapter 29

On my way down the building stairs, Sara called out to me as I passed her office. "How can you leave that lovely woman alone after what was obviously a very hot evening? Maybe I should go back upstairs and keep her company?"

"Sara, listen..." I said with irritation.

"OK, OK, I'll stop, it's just so fun to tease you about your girlfriends and you have to admit you haven't given me much chance over the last... how long has it been?" Smiling she came to the door, "Honestly Maggie, she seems like a good catch. Or was this just a one night kind of thing?"

"You think she's all right?" I asked earnestly. Sara nodded smiling, so I went on, "I'm not sure where this is going, but we have a date for tonight. I'm kind of amazed this is all happening. I feel like a lucky pup."

"Maggie, she's the lucky one, don't think for a minute you're not a damn good catch, too," said Sara squeezing my arm. "You better get going, you're probably late for your appointment already. I just wanted to go over the list from the Daria Webster party. Have you checked it yet?"

"Emma just gave me the credit information last night, she said there wasn't much to it and ...I've been kinda busy," I said glancing back up the stairs. "I haven't looked at it yet. I put a rush on the criminal checks, they should be here tomorrow."

"Good, we have to have all the evidence for Mickey's hearing by the beginning of the week."

"OK, if there's anything important in the criminal stuff, I'll call you right away." I kissed Sara on the cheek, "Thanks for saying Kathryn's OK," then I tweaked her cheek lightly, "and that's for being a bratty little sister."

****

Though the city was cold and gray, the combination of Kathryn in general and the fabulous sex we'd had after such a long dry spell, made me feel like a teenager. I had to fight off a goofy grin. Just the mildest recollection of last night created a personal condition that threatened to make my pants freeze in the December wind.

Bart's place was in a residential block of row houses west of the Mews. I rang the bell and peered though the front door into the vestibule. Bart peeked out his apartment door, hesitated, and then came out to let me in. His right hand was heavily bandaged. He made an unsuccessful effort to hold it up and not run it into the wall. Without the pain meds he would have screamed. I wondered how they'd affect his already lacking ability to communicate.

Bart Edgar bobbed his head hello as he led me into his living room. I'd imagined Edgar's apartment would be a mess and it was, but there were some nicely placed art objects throughout the space that counterbalanced the disorganization.

"Did you decorate this all yourself, Mr. Edgar?" I asked noticing a nonrepresentational sculpture on the mantel and a beautiful Asian style flower arrangement on a table near the door.

He nodded but said, "No."

"No?"

"A friend, she lives next door."

"Marry her Mr. Edgar," I said immediately.

He looked shocked. He clearly hadn't thought about it before. I felt sorry for the woman, but hey, maybe they would *complement each other*, as Amanda Knightbridge might say.

The doorbell rang. Bart went to get it. He came back into the apartment followed by a young woman carrying a brown grocery bag.

"Oh, hello," she said, "I'm Bart's friend Nancy, let me just put this in the kitchen."

When she came back, Bart was obviously not going to introduce us, so I did the honors, ending with, "I'm here to ask Mr. Edgar about the explosion."

"Perhaps I should leave?" she asked standing up.

Since she was by far the smartest part of Bart Edgar anyone had ever encountered, I said, "No, please do stay. You might be able to help."

She nodded, then looked at Bart indulgently, "Did you take your pill?" She sounded like a kindergarten teacher, but then again, everybody spoke to him that way. Maybe she really was a kindergarten teacher. Might be a perfect match, in a grotesque kind of way.

He stared, then shook his head. She got up, went to the bathroom, got the pill, went to the kitchen, got a glass of water, came back and stood there as he swallowed it, then she sat down next to him again. I watched the entire thing with *car wreck* fascination.

I asked him about the day of the fire. Bart did best with yes or no questions, which meant I didn't get much information. Finally I asked, "Mr. Edgar, did Skylar Carvelle say anything to you when he came into the rest room?"

In the book *The Wizard of OZ*, when the Scarecrow thought hard, the needles and pins the Wizard put in his sack head, *to make him sharp,* always stuck out. I imagined at any minute Bart's head would extrude pointy things. I doubted, however, that sharpness would ensue.

Finally he said, "Yes."

Yes, what, you idiot!?! I wanted to scream, but instead I asked, "And what did Dr. Carvelle say?"

Bart's face became blank with concentration, or maybe the lack of it. Finally he began to speak, encouraged by Nancy's nodding. "Um, he said that Leo stunk of cheap cologne."

"Stank," said Nancy.

"Huh?" said Bart.

"Never mind," said Nancy.

"Did he say anything else?" I asked.

"Dr. Carvelle said that, um... Jimmy Harmon spilled grape soda on him and that he wanted to wash it off because... his jacket was crash...smear."

"Cashmere," said Nancy.

"Yeah," said Bart happily nodding at Nancy.

"Good, good. That's helpful," I said, finding myself nodding along too. Nancy beamed as though Bart had just won the spelling bee.

"OK so, right after that you went into the conference room. On the way in you passed Georgia Smith. Do you remember that?"

He nodded tentatively.

"OK, now...why did you go back into the conference room?"

He thought for a long time. "I went in to..." A dark cloud passed over Bart's face. He shook his head in mid-sentence and said, "I don't remember."

"Come on now...you went back into the roommm..." I coaxed. I noticed Nancy's mouth had dropped open for a second but now she assumed a countenance of stony silence. She looked angry, but she was mad at Bart, not me.

"Please try to think Mr. Edgar..." I insisted. But stick a fork in him, Edgar was done. He wouldn't say anything else.

Nancy was fuming; the same look Kathryn had when I was late to lunch.

No...Nancy was more pissed.

Nancy followed me to the kitchen. I left my business card on Bart's refrigerator under a magnet. I said, "This is my contact information, if Mr. Edgar thinks of anything else important, please call me. Please."

Nancy nodded once, then said sympathetically, "I hope Bart isn't your only lead, that would be like putting all your eggs in one basket."

As I left, I tried in vain to imagine Bart calling me with something important. Maybe Nancy the earnest girlfriend with the good taste in art would help him. I wondered if she was putting all *her* eggs in Bart's basket.

What if your best prospect was Bart Edgar? I frequently thank my lucky stars I'm a lesbian.

Chapter 30

It was only 1:00 PM. Visions of Kathryn swirled around my brain. I needed to think about the case. I sat in my van for a while with the motor running and the heat on full blast, entering some notes and reading through what I'd already written. I took a drawing pad out of my bag and began a sketch.

I drew three baskets. The first represented Carl's murder, the second the bombing and a third for Skylar Carvelle's murder. At the top of the page, I sketched 12 eggs, decorated with a symbol for each of the suspects. A musical note for Jimmy Harmon, a cross for Connie Robinson, a football helmet for Leo Getty, and so forth. In each of the *crime baskets*, I drew the suspect eggs that couldn't be eliminated.

I stared at the finished drawings, then snagging my cell I called Miranda Juarez. She answered on the second ring.

"Ms. Juarez, this is Maggie Gale, I need to ask you something. On Thursday morning, I was in Skylar Carvelle's office when Connie Robinson came in. She had a problem and I encouraged her to call you about it?"

"Yes, I remember."

"What time did Connie get back to your office?

"I cannot say...I had some errands to do. I did not return until 2:00 PM. Connie was here when I came back."

I asked Miranda if she knew what kind of car each of the people who were in the conference room had. Amazingly, she reeled them off efficiently; as I listened I began to sketch an egg representing Connie in the *Skylar Murder* basket. No Neons. Miranda drove a Camry. Connie a Geo.

I disconnected and punched in Max Bouchet's number. "Just a few things," I said quickly when Max picked it up on the third ring, "at the meeting, do you remember who went up first to get their drink?"

Bouchet's voice rumbled deeply as he considered, "I think it was Bart, then Rowlina, then uh, either Jimmy Harmon or Skylar Carvelle ...no Skylar was with Leo Getty, so it must have been Jimmy next, then Skylar and Leo and then Amanda Knightbridge. Is that the way you remember it?"

"Yes, that's the order I remember. Now, do you remember anyone carrying two bottles back to their seat, or doing anything that might have concealed a bottle?"

Max Bouchet thought carefully, probably seeing the scene in his mind, considering each character. At last he said, "No, I don't. Do you?"

"Nope, I can't remember anything like that. Amanda Knightbridge confirms that Leo, Skylar and Jimmy didn't carry a bottle back to the table with them other than their own drink...she couldn't see Rowlina Roth-Holtzmann."

"Well, I suppose someone could have hidden it somehow. Dropped it on the floor? Put it...what...up their sleeve?" Bouchet said only half joking. "Maybe it *was* just a gas pipe blast...Have you checked the alibi's for Skylar's murder?"

"Everyone's except Leo Getty and Rowlina Roth-Holtzmann. But it's not just the alibis that concern me. It's who knew I was going to Carvelle's condo. Jimmy Harmon, Leo Getty and Connie Robinson were actually in Carvelle's office, and Rowlina Roth-Holtzmann was right outside. And Max, forget the pipe, it was a bottle bomb."

Max sighed, "So the list is narrowed down to four?"

"There's one more. Miranda Juarez was on the phone to Connie and could have overheard that I was going to Carvelle's."

"Miranda? But, she didn't get a drink during the meeting," said Bouchet connecting the dots.

"Miranda was so involved with the beverages that she may have been able to set up the explosive without actually putting the drink on the table herself. Or, she could have had help..."

"But why, what's her motive?"

"I don't know that. But I think we have to consider her a suspect. Look Max, this is all speculation, but, I have a feeling something's about to break... and it might be bad. Please, keep up the security around campus, OK?"

"Guards and security are working round the clock," he assured me. "Twelve guards will be covering Carl's memorial service tomorrow. You'll be there, won't you?"

"Yes, and I'd guess everyone else will be too. I'll see you then."

After I disconnected with Bouchet, I sketched another egg with a question mark on it in the Skylar basket, while I called the numbers I had for both Rowlina Roth-Holtzmann and Leo Getty. The egg could represent Miranda, but also any unknown factor I hadn't considered. Neither Leo nor Rowlina answered. I left simple messages on their machines to call me back as soon as possible. I thought maybe Leo would, but figured Rowlina was as likely to call me as put a big old rainbow bumper sticker on her car.

I phoned Connie Robinson. Kathryn had told me that Connie was moving to her own apartment, but the number Miranda had given me must have been old. The person who answered was obviously Connie's mother. She was orneriness personified. I had to pry out of her that Connie was working a volunteer shift at the soup kitchen on lower Hamilton Street.

"Mrs. Robinson, is there a way I can reach Connie now?"

"Now? Why now?" croaked Mrs. Robinson in a cigarette raspy voice, "She's doing the Lord's work now, even if it is in that place of sin."

Huh? This was getting to be too much. "Does Connie have a cell phone?"

"She does have one of those things, but for the life of me I can't guess why, it's not like she has any friends to call."

What a bitch, no wonder Connie moved out. "Do you have the number?" I asked sweetly.

"I don't even know you..." she snapped back.

"Oh, I understand Mrs. Robinson, it's no wonder Connie won't give you the number, after all, she's a young woman on her own now. She wouldn't feel she needed to give her private information to you..."

"Well, I certainly do have the number!" she barked. She reeled off the digits in rapid fire to show me just how wrong I was. "Connie can't keep things from me! Honor thy parents, that's what she's been taught to do, when these young girls today stop listening to their pastors and their mothers, well, that's when they..."

Coo coo ka choo, Mrs Robinson. I could barely keep from ending with *bite me,* but I just said, "Thanks," and hung up. I wondered if Connie was as psychologically damaged, as a movie-of-the-week-teen who had a mother like that would have been. I punched in Connie's cell number.

"Hello?" said Connie adenoidally.

"Hi Connie, this is Maggie Gale, may I come over to the soup kitchen and talk to you for a few minutes?" I asked directly. Time was a-wastin' and I had someplace to be later...

"Now?"

"Yes, now."

"Oh, um... well, I guess...."

"I'll be there in about ten minutes." I hung up before she could think up a reason to say no.

I called Kathryn in her office. She answered on the first ring, with a tone that reminded me of dark chocolate. We exchanged erotic suggestions and she ended the conversation with, "Don't use up all your energy working."

****

It might be a good idea for all people to do work in homeless shelters now and then. Then more people would understand that homelessness doesn't happen to people because they're lazy.

When I entered the fluorescently lit, clorine scented lobby, I headed for the check-in desk. There was no evidence this shelter was a religious place. No bleeding Jesuses were stapled over the door. No Bible verses were painted on the wall. The posters Scotch-taped all over the place skipped preaching and concentrated on information. Everything from childcare, to senior services to AIDS testing was covered.

Several men of all shapes, sizes and races were standing near the door. They eyed me when I came in, so I eyed them back. Surprisingly, one of them was that bully Shel Druckenmacher, Miranda Juarez's ex-husband. When he recognized me he hawked like he was going to spit on me. I moved out of range.

A big sign making it clear that drugs and guns were not allowed in the building, hung behind the check-in desk. The man seated at said desk was decidedly sectarian. He beckoned me over with a large hand and an expressionless face. There were several lists on the desk. The headings included: Volunteers, Rules, Officials, Shelter Residents, Children under 18, and a big paper that just had the word NO at the top.

"I'm Maggie Gale, I'm here to speak with Connie Robinson." I held up my laminated PI license. The guy took it and looked it over as I said, "Connie's doing a volunteer shift. I just spoke to her on her cell phone."

"Connie has a cell phone?...Huh." Was his immediate response. His name badge said Arturo Murcielago. He was balding and heavy with a dark brown mustache, dark skin tones and a savvy look. He spoke slowly in measured rhythm. He didn't smile, but he wasn't being rude, just incredulous.

"So, may I see her?"

"Oh, yeah... she's in the kitchen." He copied my name, address and phone number onto the paper headed Volunteers. "Connie's washing dishes, you can help her."

I guess he thought I'd balk but it wasn't like washing toilets, or washing other people's butts. There are a lot worse things to do in the world than washing dishes "Okey doke," I agreed.

Arturo placidly called a lanky teenage boy named Taylor over to lead me to the kitchen.

"New volunteer?" Taylor asked quietly as we went down a hall, then pushed through double doors marked *Kitchen.*

"For today anyway," I nodded.

"Hey, Connie," Taylor shouted across the room. She didn't hear him. "Earbuds," he shrugged as he turned to leave.

A thin earphones wire snaked up from Connie's pocket and disappeared under fluffy blond hair pulled back in a ponytail. I hate when this happens. If I shouted to get her attention, it would scare the shit out of her. If I tapped her on the arm she'd probably scream. I found the switch to the ceiling lights and flicked it on and off. Connie wheeled around and saw me. She was startled but at least she didn't drop a plate, or worst yet, throw one at me.

"Hi, hope I didn't scare you."

"Oh, hi, yeah, no, you didn't." She couldn't decide whether to be pleased or nervous that I was there.

"Arturo signed me up to help you. So, what do we do?"

"Oh wow, you're a volunteer? That's great, yeah, I could really use some help." She glanced at a dozen piles of dirty dishes along the counter. She showed me how to operate the commercial hot water hoses and we started working. It was kind of fun. We developed a rhythm after a while. Near the end, as we got a little tired, we were squealing and laughing and fooling around. When we were all done with the stacks, I high-fived her.

We grabbed rags and bleach cleanser to wipe down the counters.

She asked idly, "How did you know I was here?"

"I called the number Miranda had for you and your mother answered..."

Her head snapped up, "You talked to my mother!?!"

"Why? What's the big deal?"

"Well, she's always... she doesn't like me working here. It's not *Christian* ... she thinks people who don't go to our church are hell-bound."

"She's entitled to her opinion."

"It's not just her opinion, it's in the Bible," Connie held her cleaning rag in mid air as she waited curiously for my reply.

"It's in the Bible that everybody has to go to your mother's church? C'mon Connie, you don't really believe that, do you?"

She didn't say anything for several moments, intently rubbing the same four inches of counter. Then she erupted. Religion questions gushed out of her like beer from a broken keg.

Finally she cried, "Do you know the part about Hagar? Why does God say Sarah is wrong for being angry with Abraham for sleeping with the maid? Why is it OK? Because that was a long time ago?"

"It was thousands of years ago, and he wanted to have a male child," I said, watching Connie's forehead crease with consternation. She was having one of those crises of faith you hear about. I went on gently, "Are you wondering if that means people get to pick and choose what to believe in the Bible?"

"Well, yeah!" she nearly shouted, "yeah, why isn't that true for everything?"

I said simply "Connie, I think each person has to decide what's right and what's wrong."

"But how do you know what sin is!?!" she demanded.

"I'll tell you what I think, but you have to make up your own mind. OK?"

She nodded, near tears.

"I don't think right and wrong is arbitrary. I think that a sin is something that causes harm. Stealing, killing, bullying people, being cruel, polluting the environment, abusing animals, you know what I mean? The Bible has all sorts of good messages like, Love Thy Neighbor, but it also has what some people call *legalistic* sins, that are interpreted to keep women from being ministers, or people from eating shrimp or pork, or that wearing a gold ring is bad, or even that a person from a different religion is a sinner. They aren't about something that hurts someone and I don't think they apply to the world the way it is today."

Connie was still wiping the same patch of counter. She said, "Pastor Mason read an article about Dr. Rasmus... this was before Dr. Rasmus killed himself... and the pastor asked me if I knew Dr. Rasmus from work. He said I should get him to come to church so they could make him to stop being gay. So, I called him, Dr. Rasmus, at his apartment. He wasn't there so I left a message." She laughed nervously. Connie had just answered my question as to what her message on Carl's answering machine was about.

Connie said, "But, after I called, I started to think that I couldn't come up with a good reason for him to stop being gay...I used to talk to Daria about this kind of stuff..."

"Daria Webster? You knew her?"

"She worked here, well, she was here part of the time for her job...she got, she...um...died, right after her party. I'd just seen her... I feel so sad...there's nobody to talk to about anything..."

Of course Connie had known Daria, and been at Daria's party just before she was murdered. Daria had invited everyone from work. Poor Connie, so many things happening in her young life all at once and no friends to talk to. I said softly, "Maybe you should find a church that helps you work things out in a more positive way."

"Are there churches like that?" she asked in disbelief.

"Sure," I named some progressive denominations. She nodded her head, but the fog didn't clear.

I said gently, "I think it's good you're asking yourself these questions, the worst thing is believing things just because people tell you to..." She was staring off into space, folding the rag she was holding absentmindedly.

"Connie?" I said trying to get her attention again.

"Huh?"

"About the day of the fire..."

"What?" she asked tensely.

Why was she so anxious about this? She was a hero during the fire. You'd think a kid this age would be telling the story ad-nauseum. I forced Farrel and Jessie to listen to me tell it twice while they fought off the nearly unbearable stench of *eau de burnt ceiling tile*.

"You had to put the drinks on the table, right?" I asked.

She just stood there looking at me. Finally she whined, "I heard Dr. Bouchet say it might have been a bomb to one of the security men, he talks so loud... I wasn't, like, eavesdropping or anything...but really I don't know anything. It wasn't my fault."

"I'm not saying it was your fault, I just need to know what happened. Haven't the police already interviewed you?"

"I guess... I answered their questions, they didn't ask much." Her voice was shaking.

"What's the whole story, Connie? Tell me everything that happened."

She frowned, trying to recall, "You and Dr. Anthony, Mr. Edgar and Miranda, went into the President's office. I had a list of the beverages that I was supposed to get ready. I also had some typing to finish so I...yeah...I did that until Dean Getty and Dr. Carvelle came in. President Bouchet had told me to unlock the conference room when the people started to come, so I did and they went in and sat down..."

I nodded for her to go on.

"OK, so I...I went into the...um...I can't..." she strained to recall, squeezing her eyes shut trying to visualize the sequence, "OK, yeah, then Miranda came out of the President's office and she went into her office. She looked into the conference room and I guess I figured the meeting would start soon, so I went into the storage room to get the drinks. I got out the tray and wiped it off and put one of those white paper mats on it." She stopped, biting her lip, "Then I got another tray. I got the cookies out of the refrigerator. We keep them in there so bugs won't get in them."

I nodded and she went on, "I dumped the cookies on a plate and arranged them a little and then I opened the fridge to get the drinks. But...I forgot the list. I'd left it on my desk. So I went back to get it and I saw that Dr. Knightbridge and Professor Harmon were in the Conference Room. The elevator doors were opening and I'm pretty sure Dr. Roth-Holtzmann was getting out. Anyway, I got the list from my desk and went back in the storage room."

"This is really good, Connie, tell me the rest," I encouraged.

"Um, so I read the list and I got all the drinks, and that's all," she ended abruptly.

"Do you remember which drinks you put on first?"

"No, why?" she shot back nervously.

There was something about the drinks eating her. "Connie, think hard. Bart Edgar and Georgia Smith were seriously hurt. Dr. Carvelle is dead. Everyone at the College is ..."

"Dr. Carvelle? What does he got to...I didn't ...you mean he got killed by the person who...who put the fire bomb...but..."

"Connie, what is it? Tell me," I spoke sternly. She looked up at me on the verge of tears, torn by indecision.

She sniffed twice and then asked, "Did the person who killed Dr. Carvelle set the bomb?"

"It looks that way," I said simply.

"I don't know what to do... I lied to the police. Will they put me in jail?" she sobbed.

I pulled one of those course brown paper towels out of a wall dispenser and handed it to her to wipe her nose. "Connie, just tell me what happened."

She took a deep breath then said rapidly, her voice rising with every word, "I looked at the list and I took the bottles out and I checked them ...against the list, ya know? I was supposed to buy all the drinks and I thought I did, but I missed one. This thing I'd never heard of. Hoohoo. It's chocolate milk."

"It's called Yoohoo and it isn't really chocolate milk."

"It's not? Miranda said it was. Um, well, this was the first time we were going to do the drink thing. President Bouchet and Miranda wanted it to work good, so I was afraid to tell them I messed up. I didn't know what to do, so I just put another drink on the tray."

"Which one?" I asked, suspecting the response.

"It had a funny name. I'd never heard of it either."

"Grape Nehi?"

"Uh huh, that was it. Do you think it was the drink that had the bomb in it? Was it my fault? What is it anyway?"

Gee, doesn't this kid watch TV? Well, I guess she's too young to have seen MASH.

"No, Mr. Harmon drank the Grape Nehi. It didn't have the bomb in it." This took so much weight off Connie, I could see her shoulders rise an inch. "But why did you think it did?"

"I told someone I messed up and then he said that it was all my fault. He said the police would arrest me for lying. They would arrest me even just for... omission."

"Who told you that?"

"Mr. Druckenmacher. Miranda's husband. He works here, fixes the lights and like that. Well, he did until about two weeks ago. He talked to me, he asked me about Miranda and my job. He seemed nice... so I decided to tell him what happened and ask him what I should do, but he just laughed at me. He said he'd tell the police I lied unless I...um..." She turned beet red from her neck to the tops of her ears like a human thermometer.

"Unless you what?"

"Unless I did sex with him, then he wouldn't tell. He said...blow him... but I told him I wouldn't, not ever. So he said to give him money. Now, every time I see him, he ...you know ...he gets this look and then he... rubs himself." She glanced down to her own crotch area in explanation.

"I saw him here today. If he doesn't work here any more, why is he hanging around?" I was so pissed at this dirty scumbag that I was all set to make sure he wouldn't hang around here any more.

"He stays here sometimes... Yeah, he's always here."

"Connie, do *you* volunteer here every day?" I asked incredulously.

"Oh no, just Thursday, Friday and Saturday, washing dishes," she said as though that was nothing. A twenty-year-old kid, with a full-time job, giving up her weekends for the homeless. I vowed to at least put an end to Shel Druckenmacher's blackmail career.

"Connie, I'll make sure Druckenmacher doesn't bother you any more and I'm going to explain about the Nehi to President Bouchet and Miranda too. I think you should too. They won't be mad at you." I won't let them, I decided privately. "Listen, aren't there any volunteer jobs where you could work with some people your age?"

Connie was so relieved she looked like she was about to do a cheer. Instead, she thanked me twenty times as I got ready to leave.

Unless Connie had the theatrical gifts of Meryl Streep, she was innocent of the bombing and Skylar's murder. There was just no way she could have made up her story and performed it that well. Abstractly, Connie had been the most likely suspect because of her control of the beverage bottles, but now she was out of the running. Without Connie, the list of suspects was down to four.

In the lobby, Arturo Murcielago was still seated behind the desk, watching the action inscrutably. I went up to him. "You run this place don't you?"

"Executive Director," he nodded.

"Mr. Murcielago, Connie Robinson just now told me that Shel Druckenmacher," I nodded toward the group of men near the door where Druckenmacher was still hanging, "has been trying to blackmail her."

"Really?" said Arturo Murcielago in an even voice, "that might be great news. I hate that guy. Finally fired his ass just a little while ago. I want him out of here, but I need a reason."

"Has Druckenmacher been a problem here?"

"I've had three reports that he's selling drugs, but no hard evidence."

"OK, so what would be a *good reason* to ban him from this shelter?" I asked curiously.

"Starting a fight, punching somebody..." Murcielago suggested matter-of-factly.

"Do I *have* to let him hit me?"

"You look like you could take it," he grinned suddenly, then his face became unemotional again.

"Geez," I said resignedly, shaking my head and turning toward the group of guys still standing at the door.

"Mr. Druckenmacher, may I speak with you a moment please?" I said loudly, but politely.

Shel Druckenmacher swaggered out of the group toward me. He smelled of liquor, which was in my favor. When he was quite close I began speaking in a low tone, "You have been trying to blackmail a friend of mine. Get out of here and don't come back." I added under my breath, "I've already removed you from one place. You should be tossed out of here, too."

He didn't like women telling him what to do. With a furious expression he drew back his arm to throw a right at my face. I stepped close into him and took it short on my shoulder, drawing gasps and a few screams from some of the people in the lobby. Everyone in the place turned to watch. His punch had looked hard but since he hadn't had a chance to get any weight behind it it didn't hurt more than a slap on the back. The movement had thrown him off balance so I just hit the side of his knee with my own, sending him sprawling onto the floor. This was accompanied by gales of humiliating laughter from his (now former) friends.

Arturo Murcielago got to his feet and ambled toward us with a cell phone to his ear. He was phoning the cops. I just stood there looking innocent. Druckenmacher had had too much to drink to realize he was out-matched. All he could see was me and red. He scrambled around to get to a standing position, then reached in his pocket and fumbled out a flick knife. West Side Story in slow motion.

Druckenmacher yelled, "Fuckin' dyke!" at me and began to lunge. I spun to the side. As the knife slashed past me, I high kicked his hand. Not only knocking the knife to the floor but breaking three of his fingers with a satisfying triple snap. He screamed and fell on his knees in agony.

Surprisingly fast for a man of his size, Arturo Murcielago made a lightning grab for the knife, scooping it up in one movement. Druckenmacher was in no condition to try to get it back.

By then, the cops were arriving. Fenchester police response time is very fast, and it didn't hurt that the police station was just a block away. I think the guys ran over. Tito Rodriguez and Jim Trexler were part of the pack that showed up. Pals from my years on the force. In fact, I rode with Tito as a partner for a while. They both took one look at me and began to chuckle.

"Officers," I said formally.

They both snorted in unison, then turned their attention to Murcielago, who patiently explained that Mr. Druckenmacher had punched me, then pulled a knife in a threatening manner and lunged at me, calling me a derogatory name in the process. Five or six witnesses corroborated the story, including Taylor the teenager, who kept saying *awesome*.

Under Pennsylvania's Ethnic Intimidation Law, the yelling of a minority class name during attempted murder could make this a hate crime, which would elevate the sentence. I considered that as I promised the police I'd press charges to the fullest. When all that was over, it was 5:00 PM. From my van I called Miranda Juarez, asking to come and see her.

Five minutes later I found her waiting at her foyer door in a small apartment building near the College. Work had seemed to be her whole life, but the inside of the apartment showed otherwise. Pictures of her son and daughter at all ages, her daughter's wedding, and dozens of pictures of her grandchildren were everywhere. Miranda asked if I wanted coffee. Though I did, I said no. This wasn't a social call. We sat on the couch in the living room while I told her about Connie and her Yoohoo vs. Nehi mistake.

Miranda shook her head, tsking with disdain. "It is hard to train people today, they do not take the job seriously."

That fried me. The pressure she'd put on Connie had caused a great deal of this evening's problems and I didn't need her holier secretary than thou attitude.

"Honestly Miranda, get down off your pedestal and give the kid a break. Connie's twenty and inexperienced but she takes her job and the rest of her life very seriously. If the College wanted a super-secretary they should have hired another you and paid for it." Miranda stared at me wide-eyed.

I softened my tone, "Druckenmacher's been blackmailing Connie. And Connie was tough enough to say no to Shel, though she thought it would mean losing her job and going to jail. She seems pretty brave to me, even if her efficiency level isn't all it could be."

Miranda covered her mouth and turned her face to the wall. She didn't want to hear any more but I wasn't going to let her off the hook just because she was uncomfortable. Connie had dealt with this nightmare for three days, Miranda could take it for at least five more minutes.

"Shel gave Connie two options, money or oral sex," I told Miranda, who shook her head, but didn't look up. "Less than an hour ago Druckenmacher hit me and lunged at me with a knife. He's in jail, arrested for assault and attempted assault with a deadly weapon. He will call you to post bail. He'll only get one phone call today. The caller ID will say Fenchester City Jail. DON'T ANSWER IT! Turn off your message machine. Ignore him."

I sat staring at her. Finally Miranda lifted her head. "He had not been around for a long time," she said plaintively. "Then...last week, like the bad penny, he was at my office. Very angry, very upset, demanding money. When we were married, he... there was a lot of debt. I have worked for a long time to reestablish my credit. I do not have much, but I gave him what I had. I thought he would leave me and the children alone, but the last few days, he has contacted me often, in a desperate way. I had no more to give him."

Maybe Shel Druckenmacher's drug selling sideline was getting him in trouble with a local gang, or even more likely, he owed some supplier a bundle of cash. He probably wanted money to help himself get out of town.

"Why do you put up with him?" I asked her softly.

A long moment passed before she answered, "He is not the father of my son, Enrique. He has threatened me that he will tell both my daughter and Enrique. They will not...I am afraid they will not understand."

"Miranda," I said looking directly into her eyes, "deal with this now. Conference call your son and daughter immediately and tell them. I'll bet Enrique will be relieved that Druckenmacher isn't his father."

"I don't think I..."

"Do it, Miranda. You're a strong woman. Do it now. Then he'll have nothing to hold over you." I slid the phone across the coffee table, then pushed myself up from the couch and left her apartment, clicking the door shut. Out in the silent hall I waited, crossing my fingers, listening at the door.

Miranda Juarez the super personal assistant, could set up a three-way conference call in seconds, and she did. She spoke Spanish to her two adult children, confessing her darkest secret to the dearest people in her life. Miranda's love for her children rang in her voice, but I wondered if she would be able to break the cycle of abuse she'd endured from Shel Druckenmacher all these years.

I sat in my van for a few minutes, typing notes on the *Connie, Shel and Miranda Triangle*. Then took off. It was 6:00 PM. Images of Kathryn flooded my mind.

Chapter 31

I parked next to Kathryn's car in the Language Arts Building parking lot on College Street. It was freezing out. The air deposited a penetrating layer of frigid mist on my skin and then blew on it. On the sidewalk, I bumped into Leo Getty. Literally, he slammed into me. It was dark and he wasn't paying attention. He gasped in surprise and grabbed his chest with both hands.

"I'm terribly sorry Dr. Getty," I said as sincerely as possible, although it was his fault, he'd really whacked into me. His thick fireplug body was harder than I thought.

"Oh, um, yeah, Maggie, howya been," he said mechanically. He was wearing a dark brown down jacket that came well below his waist. With no hat, he had maraschino ears. His breath puffed clouds of steam that fogged his glasses. He'd shoved his cold hands into his pockets. Instead of gesturing with them while he talked, he moved them inside his pockets, pulling his jacket askew with each phrase he wanted to emphasize. He looked up and down the street saying absently, "This really has been a tough week hasn't it? I was just thinking about Bart and Georgia...and Carl. You gonna be at that thing for Carl tomorrow?"

"Yes, I'll be there. You?"

"Oh yeah, sure." He looked around again distractedly, making idle small talk. "Ha...I can't remember where I parked, must be up the block. I guess I'm more shook up than I thought, you know? Oh, there it is. He focused on a SUV farther along College Street. "Hey, what are you doing on Campus anyway?" He'd gotten back some of his bluff personality.

"Just checking some things. Dr. Getty, may I ask you something? Two things actually."

"Oh yeah, sure."

"First, do you remember where you went after leaving Skylar Carvelle's office on Thursday morning?"

"Thursday, Thursday." Jacket twist, jacket twist. Then with shock he recalled, "That was when Skylar was killed!"

I nodded.

"Oh, well, um I... I went back to my office and then I went home to have breakfast. You have to have a good breakfast, even if it's late, right? I had an evening meeting with the admissions staff and I decided to take a little *comp time* beforehand, *if you know what I mean.*" Then he eyes widened, "Wait, you mean...you think I ...whoa now, hold on." His face got as red as his ears.

"Dr. Getty please, I'm just trying to confirm where everyone was."

He paused, taking several deep breaths, steam rising in a jet from his nose. A car went up College Street, after it had gone by Leo Getty said less tightly, though his face didn't get any less red, "Uh huh, that's right. Yeah, I know, I'm sorry Maggie. I just feel bad about everything that's happened. Skylar was my friend and Carl...I really miss him... Thursday, yeah, I called my secretary about some stats we had to file with the state."

"About what time?"

"Just before I went back to the office. Maybe about 1:30."

Not really a great alibi, but if he was innocent why bother to set one up?

"Dr. Getty, I went to Hadesville High School yesterday and I found out that Carl actually was thrown out of St. Bonaventure High School, not the public High School..."

"Yeah, so? Oh, I get it. I guess I said it wrong. Yeah, I'm sorry. I was so busy with the team in those days," jacket twist, "it was hard to pay attention to other things. I stand corrected," he laughed heartily. He seemed to be itching to slap me on the back. I took a small step backward.

"Just one more thing."

"Shoot."

"You left a message on Carl's home answering machine saying you wanted to speak to him, and you asked him not to mention it to anyone else? Something about a grant? Do you remember what that was about?"

"Oh... yeah sure, it didn't have anything to do with me...Carl was trying to get a grant as part of that satellite thing and I didn't want him to mention it because, well, I didn't want him to jinx it for the College. You know how it is, sometimes you talk about something and people get all excited about it and then it doesn't come through and people get upset...truth is, I'd heard on the grapevine that Carl's grant might not work out, never know how true that kind of info is, but it's better to be safe than sorry. Geez, it's getting cold and it's way dark, huh? I better be getting home."

He smiled, said goodbye and walked across the street. I turned and headed for the Language Arts Building door, skipping up the stairs, then down the hall to room 208. The door was closed. I rapped twice and Kathryn's extraordinary voice called out, "Who is it?"

"Emily Dickinson."

Kathryn opened the door, grabbed a handful of my shirt, pulled me into the room, reached around my shoulder with her other hand and slammed the door shut. She pushed me up against it and gave me a kiss that made my toes curl. I did my best to keep up.

"So what does the Belle of Amherst have to say for herself?" asked Kathryn when we paused to catch our breath.

I recited:

Wild Nights -- Wild Nights!
Were I with thee
Wild Nights should be
Our luxury!

Futile -- the Winds --
To a Heart in port --
Done with the Compass --
Done with the Chart!

Rowing in Eden --
Ah, the Sea!
Might I but moor -- Tonight --
In Thee!

"Oh, very good," she laughed. She was wearing her outdoor jacket unzipped, with a dark purple sweater under it. She looked wonderful, but kind of bundled up. "I've been thinking about you all day," she said holding me by the shoulders.

"*What* have you been thinking?" I whispered in her ear. She laughed, we kissed again, this time more slowly. The dull ache below my belt was becoming more acute by the second.

"Oh Kathryn, I want..." I began passionately, but then came to my senses. I said in a reasonable voice, "I'd love to roll around on the floor with you right at this very moment, driven by desperate desire... but it's so damn cold in here! How could you stand this all afternoon? Klondike bars wouldn't melt in this room! It's colder than outside."

"Terrible isn't it? There's a timer on the building heating system, it goes down to 50 on the weekends. I have a little space heater under my desk that helps. I even got quite a bit of work done, but I am so cold. I feel like I'll never thaw." Her voice became lower, "If you take me someplace warm and give me something to eat, I'll gladly do anything you want."

"Anything?"

"Mm hmm."

"Interesting dinner conversation topic...and it's your turn to choose the place."

"How about Casa Mexicana?

"I will take you there, where it is warm, and get you something to eat right now."

She grabbed her knapsack, slipped the manual for Carl's Voice Transcription program in it and we went quickly into the hall, and down the stairs.

"How about taking my van and leaving your car here? My engine is warm, the heat will work right away." I leaned to whisper in her ear, "I want to be able to have you in a warm place as soon as possible, because I want to see if later you really will do anything I want."

"I'm very glad to hear *your engine is warm*, but, have I placed my virtue in peril?" she said in a low voice.

"You certainly have," I growled back. "Is it safe to leave your car here overnight?" I asked looking up and down the empty street.

"It's as safe here as it is in the Hampshire parking lot. Probably safer. Campus security knows it. Hold on, I have some things I want to bring with me." She opened the hatchback of her Mini Cooper and took out a garment bag. We got into the van and I turned on the motor, cranking up the heat full blast.

"Oh that's wonderful," said Kathryn putting both hands over the warm air vent. She looked up through the windshield, "Rats, I left a light on in my office."

I could see it clearly. It was the only lighted window in the building, "I'll go turn it off," I volunteered gallantly.

"No, no, it doesn't matter, it's not dangerous. It's the wall light, not a high intensity one or anything like that. I'll call campus security and they'll turn it off." She was still looking up at the window, leaning forward slightly, with her chin tilted up, her graceful throat exposed.

"Kathryn, I'm so glad to be with you," I said spontaneously. She reached over and touched my arm, sliding her fingers up to my face. We leaned across the space between the seats and kissed deeply. We both forgot about the light in her office, which turned out to cause several serious problems later that night.

I drove down Liberty and across on 12th to my building. As usual, it was easier to park there and walk over to the restaurant.

La Casa Mexicana is an authentic Mexican restaurant just off the Mews on 11th Street, around the corner from Liberty. I put my arm through Kathryn's as we walked together. She was still shivering.

"Tell me everything you did today," I said as we walked to the Mexicana.

"Um, let's see...Went to the Hampshire for something to wear to Carl's service. Went to my office. Read two boring thesis proposals. Worked on some seminar notes. Called my bother Kiernan to say hi and Paul Erickson to talk about his grant. After that, I spent two hours reading Carl's voice program manual, during which I nodded off twice and dreamed about you."

"Sweet dreams?"

"Not exactly sweet, but certainly stimulating."

La Casa Mexicana is a double 1890s row house that was rehabbed in the 1990s by the Estevez family into a restaurant, Mexican grocery and bakery. The restaurant wasn't famous for fast service, just great food. Enticing smells wafted from the kitchen. We chose a small table in a corner.

"What did you do?" Kathryn asked placing her hand on top of mine, lightly tracing her fingers over my knuckles.

"I spent the whole day... imagining what it would be like later, when I have the chance to get you out of your...socks!"

"Oh no!" she laughed out loud then said, "I swear I didn't know that was going to happen...it's never happened before."

"Oh, really? So all the foot massages women have given you in the past haven't produced the same results?"

"*You* have the magic touch. I wonder if you'll be able to do it again?" she winked at me.

"We'll see," I said just as Rafael the waiter appeared.

"Hola Maggie, como estas?" He handed us both menus.

Rafael, doesn't speak much English. I know him and the rest of the Estevez family well. He placed a huge basket of fresh tortilla chips and four kinds of homemade salsa on the table in front of us.

"Hola chico. Como estas? Por favor, conozca mi amiga. Ella se llama Kathryn Anthony. Ella es una nueva persona en la vecindad," I said, introducing him to Kathryn and telling him she was new in the neighborhood.

"O, sí ella es tu nueva amiga la doctora, no?" said Rafael.

"Sí, pero quién le dijo eso?" I asked.

"Mariana me dijo. Que quieren comer? Quieren mas tiempo?" he said.

I turned to Kathryn and asked, "Do you know what you'd like, or do you want to see the specials?"

Rafael said, *"Sí, los especiales,"* and scurried off to get the small marker board he was supposed to have set up next to our table. We considered the choices.

Kathryn said, "I'll have the Veggie Combo, with the *chile relleno,* cheese *enchilada* and *chalupa.*"

I ordered the Shrimp *Fajitas* with sides of *nopalito* salad and sweet fried bananas. I also ordered a *Molcajete con Guacamole.* Rafael went off to put in the order.

"*Nopalito* salad? And what was the special *guacamole, molca...?*" Kathryn asked curiously.

"*Nopalitos* are marinated cactus. They taste kind of like marinated roasted red peppers. A *molcajete* is a mortar made out of lava rock, they use it to make the *guacamole* and then serve it in the *molcajete.* It's the best *guacamole* ever. I don't know how they do it. Even Jessie can't make it that way."

"Is she a good cook?"

"Excellent."

"What was Rafael saying to you? Something about me being a doctor? He spoke so rapidly, I can usually read Spanish fairly well, but..."

"It seems the nerve center of Mews gossip has done its job. I told Rafael you were a new person in the neighborhood and he asked if you were my new friend *the doctor.*"

Kathryn snorted, "Who told him?"

"Mariana. She's the owner."

"But how did she know?"

"Kathryn, it's a small neighborhood, and the news runs through the women." Rafael put the *molcajete* on the table and brought us a new basket of chips. Kathryn tried the guacamole and leaned back in delight. I loved watching her, I reached to hold her hand, but her cheerful expression began to fade.

"I have something to tell you."

An *uh oh* flag waved in my brain. She was going to tell me something about herself that she thought would make me feel differently about her.

"Go ahead Kathryn, nothing you can say will chase me away," I reassured her. But that was a lie. After all, I knew very little about her and there *were* things that could make a difference. Hey, I'm not just being shallow, what if she told me she was... a member of the 700 club, or that she liked to hunt bunnies, or that she voted for...

She went on, "Last year, I was living in California and Irwin College was interviewing for Max's position. The board wanted me to be in on some of the interviews. As it turned out later, Max ended up being the star candidate and since I knew him, I couldn't be impartial..." she stalled, taking a sip of water, "anyway, I came here in the early spring. I sat in on some interviews. Then one evening I was asked to take some of the board members out to dinner. So...I brought them here."

"Here to the Mexicana?" I asked.

"We sat over there," she indicated a large table in another dark corner. "They were all corporate types. Big business, very eager to talk about high finance. Nothing that interested me, but they didn't mind, they had each other to talk to."

I nodded.

"So, I sat in the corner and I thought about my solo life, and ... your friends Farrel and Jessie, came in. Of course I recognized Farrel from the College. I could tell they were deeply in love and I felt a bit jealous of them. I was alone, wasting a Saturday night with three dull bureaucrats," she paused and took another sip of water. "Then, you came. You hugged them and gave them a present. You laughed and congratulated them and at the end you picked up the check."

The memory of that evening flooded in and I *had* noticed her briefly, sitting in the back corner. "I remember the night," I said softly looking steadily into her eyes.

"You do?"

"It was Farrel and Jessie's anniversary. But, this is your story, go on."

"And you were alone too, so...I cast you in my fantasy," she smiled self consciously, "and though I didn't know you, I thought about you even when I went back to California."

She went on, "I came back to Fenchester and suddenly there you were, in Max's office. I wanted to know you. That's why I went out to see you in the snow. But, I've made all sorts of assumptions that were unfair to make. I have to be honest with you..." she stopped and started again, "last night was wonderful, really wonderful, but if sex now and then is all you're looking for, well, I can't...I need..." she stopped talking and finally looked up at me.

She'd shown her vulnerable side. Not something an *Ice Queen* would ordinarily do. I gathered her hands in mine gently, "Kathryn, I'm so happy you're telling me this, because my biggest fear in the last 24 hours was that you were going to pat me on the head, say: *thanks that was fun,* and disappear. I know things have to progress at their own pace, but if this can work out...Is it too much to ask you to go steady on the second date?"

She said brightly, beginning to relax, "This is our third date, if you count our night in the park, which you have artfully discerned was premeditated, at least by me...and yes, I'd be delighted to go steady with you. Do I get a sorority pin?" she asked smiling at last.

"I'll think of something," I smiled back.

Rafael brought a dozen dishes to the table and while we ate, I told Kathryn about my day. When I got to the part about Bart Edgar's girlfriend Nancy, Kathryn said immediately, "He should marry her, did you tell him that?"

"Yup, first thing. Do you think we sound like Amanda Knightbridge?"

"Oh my," she smirked, "what did she say to *you*? Did she say..."

"That we would..." I added.

"Complement each other?" we both said in unison laughing.

I went on talking about the day's events. When I got to the part about Connie's Yoohoo/Nehi confession, Kathryn's face clouded at the Shel Druckenmacher blackmail attempt.

"That poor girl. She has far more moxie than I'd ever have thought. Do you think she was telling the truth about the whole thing?"

"Yeah, she'd have to have been Dame Judy Dench to have pulled off that story. I think she's out of the running as a suspect."

"Was she a suspect?"

"*Trust no one...*" I said in a low voice.

Kathryn laughed, "...but, really?"

"Sure. In some ways she was the best suspect because she had the best opportunity. Now it has to be that the person who set the fire bomb somehow had to manage juggling the extra bottle back to his or her seat without anyone noticing."

"Is there anything you can do to stop Shel from bothering Connie?"

"Shel's in jail," I said idly as I carefully filled another flour tortilla with shrimp and some of Kathryn's black beans.

"But how did..?"

I told her about the plan Arturo Murcielago roped me into and about the police coming to make the arrest.

Her fork clattered to her plate. "Shel tried to stab you?" she said flatly. She seemed angry. "You promised me you'd be careful."

"Kathryn, please understand that a mostly drunk guy in a situation like that is not a big threat to me. I didn't get hurt, I didn't even get winded. I really wasn't in any danger," I explained calmly.

"Really?" she said doubtfully.

"Yes, really. I have a black belt in karate and ten times more hours in marshal arts training than you probably spent on your dissertation. Believe me, I wouldn't have done it if I'd been in danger. Trust me Kathryn, there are some physical things I can do quite well."

"Well, I have to concede that," she smiled.

We were both full and there was still a ton of food on the table. I asked Rafael for some take-home cartons. While we were putting the leftovers into boxes Kathryn asked, "So you spoke to Bart, Connie and Miranda, was that everyone?"

"I left both Rowlina and Leo phone messages. No word from Rowlina but I bumped into Leo in front of your building. He's upset about Carl."

"Oh, that reminds me, I read most of Carl's VTS manual. It certainly does have a high opinion of itself and dull directions. I wasn't kidding when I said I nodded off twice. Of course, I had a lot of exercise last night..." Kathryn smiled mischievously. "Anyway... I think the way Carl was able to get it to work so well was by frequently using the *keyword macro function*. Did you read about that?"

"Uh huh."

"The manual says you can do a *needs scan* for any of the user based files. That might be a way to find Carl's password. Also I think you're right about Carl having a high sensitivity microphone. Did you speak to Jimmy about that argument I overheard? The one he had with Carl?"

"No, but I'll set something up."

I could tell Kathryn wanted Jimmy to be cleared. I took out my cell phone, punched in Jimmy's number and got him on the third ring. He hemmed and hawed, but I insisted on a meeting the next morning, before Carl's memorial service. He finally agreed to 10:00 AM.

Rafael brought us a big plastic bag to carry the boxes of leftovers. He also brought Kathryn back her change. She left him a very generous tip. That was another plus in her column. I'm suspicious of tip cheapskates.

As we were just about to leave, my cell phone rang. I peered at the tiny screen. "Oh gee, it's Cora Martin, Farrel and Jessie's senior citizen neighbor who's watching their house while they're away. I'm sorry I have to get this...Cora?" I said into the phone.

"Maggie? It's Cora, dahling. I'm so glad you're home."

"Well, I'm on the cell phone Cora. I'm at the Mexicana."

"You are, dahling? Say hello to Mrs. Estevez for me."

"Cora, do you need me to do something?" I looked at Kathryn who was chuckling softly while picking up her water glass.

"Oh yes, dahling, yes. I was at Farrel and Jessie's. There's an electrical problem there. I want you to look at it, dear."

"Electrical? What happened?"

"I went to feed the kitties and I turned on the light in the front hall and the bulb exploded. To death it scared me."

"Exploded...you mean the glass broke? Or it just popped and went out?" I asked patiently.

"Well, it was a big pop. Do you think it just burned out? I could go and put in a new one. I'd have to stand on a chair."

"No, no Cora, don't stand on a chair!" I put my hand over the receiver and mouthed, *she's very short,* to Kathryn who smiled broadly. "Cora, I'll go and fix it right now. I can do it on my way home, I have their key."

"Oh good dahling, I don't want the girls to come home and be in the dark. ...So, Maggie, Mrs. McCourt tells me you have a new *friend*...and that she's a doctor!"

I looked right into Kathryn's eyes while I said clearly to Cora, "Yes, I do, but she's not a medical doctor Cora, she's a professor at the College."

Kathryn nearly choked on her water. Her look of astonishment was hilarious.

After I'd said goodbye to Cora, Kathryn demanded in amazement, "Who told her?"

"Mrs. McCourt...she's the head housekeeper at the Dakota."

Chapter 32

We said good night to Raphael and I asked him to be sure to tell Mariana Estevez hello from Cora Martin and me.

Outside, a cold December wind swept snowflakes off tree branches and window ledges. They clung to our hair as we crossed the park toward Farrel and Jessie's.

"The food and the heat in the restaurant helped, Maggie, but I'm still cold," shivered Kathryn, "if you're expecting to get *anything you want,* you're going to have to do better."

"I like a challenge, especially when the prize is so lavish. I'm sorry we have to make a stop on the way home, but trust me, it's not good to disappoint Cora."

We got to Farrel and Jessie's in no time. I managed to let us in and turn off the alarm without setting it off. Kathryn bent down to pet Griswold and Wagner as they wove their bodies around our legs.

Griswold said, "Merf."

Wagner said, "Ow."

I turned on the lights and Kathryn looked at the house eagerly. "This is very nice," she said, turning in a circle, viewing the living room.

The hanging light just inside the front door was out. I left Kathryn busily examining the ornate oak woodwork, while I got a new bulb and screwed it in. I called Cora and told her it was all fixed. She was pleased, but didn't want to chat because "Judge Judy" was on.

A stained glass window at the front of the house had diverted Kathryn's attention. "Is this original?" she asked. "How old is the house?" Clearly appreciating the architectural fine-points of buildings was a scholarly and passionate pursuit for Kathryn.

I explained that the house was really two rowhouses combined into one and that Farrel had done most of the rehab work. "They're still working on it. Farrel just finished this solid walnut staircase."

Kathryn was swept away. She moved toward the back of the house where the large dining room and kitchen open into each other. Kathryn looked out the dining room window toward the space between the *Old Side* and *New Side* houses. I pointed out the addition that joined the two original kitchens into one, leaving a small enclosed courtyard in the middle.

"Farrel and her friend Barb built that deck," I explained as I took Kathryn into the addition. She looked out the bay window facing the lovely backyard. We could see tiny white lights illuminating the garden.

"This is amazing," Kathryn breathed at seeing the koi ponds Farrel had built for Jessie.

"Wait until you see it in the daylight, see that staircase at the back, it goes to the garage rooftop gardens, they have raised vegetable beds up there. And those are all fruit trees." I pointed to the side of the yard.

"I want to see the whole house," Kathryn demanded, her eyes flashing. Interesting spaces beat a path to this woman's heart. Her excitement was making my blood run faster.

"I knew you'd say that. I hate to dampen your architectural ardor, but I can't show you the house unless Farrel and Jessie are here. They'd never forgive me. Don't worry, they'll let you see it another time, they like to show it off."

Her face showed disappointment. "Maggie, you're a shameless tease. You thrill me with an interesting place like this, and then interrupt full gratification?" She was beginning to tease me, now.

I pointed through the French doors, "Look carefully," I suggested.

She turned and looked into the interior courtyard. A leafless tree in a tub strung with tiny purple lights romantically illuminated the snow-covered space.

She focused on something. "What's that," she asked pointing to a large rectangular shape rising about a foot above the deck.

"I'm so glad you asked...it's...a hot tub. Take off your clothes," I said in a forceful whisper.

"Really?"

"There's nothing better to chase the chill away than several hundred gallons of 104 degree bath water."

"Is it deep?" she asked with interest.

"Deceptively. It's about 40 inches deep. You can float in it. There's a little bathroom over there," I nodded toward the far end of the kitchen, "I'll get us some towels." When I got back, I went out into the courtyard, cleared the snow off the tub cover and folded it back onto the deck. Steam rose from the water's surface. I turned off the kitchen lights so only the purple lights and the stars illuminated the courtyard.

Kathryn stood barefooted in her shirt and jeans. She watched me as I pulled off my sweater, stepped out of my shoes and socks, and then took off my pants. I put my arms around her. She kissed me, but I could feel her shivering. I didn't hesitate. I pulled off the rest of my clothes and put them all in a pile on one of the chairs in front of the bay window. I slipped Kathryn's jeans down her legs as she unbuttoned her shirt and undid her bra. She clearly felt self-conscious standing naked in a stranger's kitchen... who could blame her?

"Now, this is the hard part," I explained, "the three-seconds of naked December exposure before you make it to the water. There are seats in the corners, step down there. Watch me."

"I can't take my eyes off you," she whispered.

I slipped out the door, took two steps barefooted on snow, then stepped carefully into the tub.

Kathryn hesitated, then came out the door and sped into the tub, steadying herself with one hand on the brick wall.

"Oh, oh, oh...it feels so hot." She eased in, like Bugs Bunny lowering himself into a soup pot.

"Give it a minute, you'll get used to it. Lean your head back and look at the stars. Try not to get your hair too wet or it will freeze."

After a moment Kathryn stated simply, "This is heaven."

Farrel once told me that making love in a hot tub was like being weightless. Now I could see what she meant. I could wrap myself around Kathryn. I could hold her in my arms or on my lap. I could raise her hips to my mouth gently. And she could do all of the same to me, effortlessly. And we did, for quite a while. When I coaxed her to climax, she called out at the height of her pleasure. I tried not to think about Cora next door, hearing the sound and wondering what was going on over here. I'd thought it would be hard for me to be satisfied in the water, but it was so easy with Kathryn.

"Are you warm now?

"Mmm hmmm," she said in a deep relaxed voice.

"Have I met all your demands?"

She opened her eyes wide realizing that she was in debt, "Uh oh," she said apprehensively, "um... just what will the *anything you want* be?"

"We shall see...later."

Suddenly a bright light went on in the backyard behind the house. The light shined through the bay window, across the kitchen addition and through the French doors to the hot tub.

"Oops," I mumbled.

"What? What's happening?" asked Kathryn in bewilderment.

"I guess Farrel and Jessie are coming home early," I explained in what I hoped was a casual voice.

Kathryn was laughing, but she was also vexed, "Oh, for heaven's sake Maggie! Why must I meet all of your friends and family when I'm naked?"

"Well, it is your best outfit..." I said while I realized with increasing embarrassment we hadn't even brought the towels outside with us. "It'll be OK. They aren't nearly as likely to tease us as Sara."

Kathryn covered her face with her hand and shook her head. I turned the aerator up so the clarity of the water changed to cloudy white. Through the windows we could see two middle-aged women wearing heavy winter jackets coming from the garage door.

Jessie, who is several inches shorter than Farrel, came first, carrying two pillows under her arm and a food cooler in one hand. Farrel trailed behind her carrying two travel bags over her broad shoulders and a large plastic storage box in her arms. Jessie's cheeks were pink from the cold, contrasting the white highlights in her hair. She unlocked the kitchen door and Farrel followed her in, each pausing to knock the snow from their heavy shoes on the outdoor mat.

They turned on a bright kitchen light, further illuminating the hot tub and its contents. We could see them moving around the kitchen, pulling off their heavy jackets. They seemed tired. I saw Farrel stretch when she put down the plastic container. I was facing the French doors. I felt Kathryn creep behind me.

I heard Jessie say with concern, "Why isn't the warning alarm beeping?"

Farrel turned and noticed our piles of clothing on the chairs. She walked over to them, then turned and looked out the French doors at the tub. "I think we just caught two lovely young mermaids in our courtyard lagoon," said Farrel with amusement.

Jessie asked in surprise, "Who?"

We could hear a murmured reply. Then Farrel said in a loud voice, "Maybe we should go away for a few hours?"

I called out, "Maybe you could just go upstairs for about 15 minutes?

I saw Jessie plug the coffee maker in and turn it on; an instant later they were gone. I said to Kathryn, "See they aren't teasing us."

"And that's supposed to make me less embarrassed?" said Kathryn sarcastically.

I jumped out of the tub and got the towels. Kathryn took her clothes into the bathroom while I put the cover back on the tub and then dressed hurriedly in the kitchen. I hadn't thought we would be disturbed at all, but at least we hadn't been interrupted in the throes of passion. That might have been too much for Kathryn to bear.

I went to the backstairs and called up, "We're out of the tub now."

"Kathryn?" I said turning back to the bathroom door. She pushed it open with one hand, standing there fully clothed, shaking her head at me, with that half smile playing across her lips.

"I just love it when you look at me that way," I laughed. "Am I going to get a spanking when we get back to the loft?"

"You should be so lucky!" she said sardonically.

Farrel and Jessie had come down the walnut staircase into the dining room. Griswold and Wagner were swirling around their legs doing variations on their merf--ow routine.

"Jessie, this is Kathryn Anthony. Farrel, you know Kathryn," I said casually, as though we hadn't just been caught frolicking naked in their spa.

Jessie said hello to Kathryn graciously. She and Farrel were trying very hard not to burst into grins.

I broke the ice by raising my voice to say, "What the hell are you guys doing coming home tonight!?!" Everyone laughed.

"We just set up for a few days. We did so well we left early, instead of staying for the rest of the weekend. The show management was thrilled, they resold our booth space before we were even off the field," said Farrel.

"We wanted to be back for Carl Rasmus's memorial service. We called people from the road and told them we'd have a brunch afterwards. So, we had to be back to get that ready," Jessie said. She was smiling at Kathryn and me. I knew they both wanted the story. After all, the last time I'd seen them, I'd been asking if they thought Kathryn might be a lesbian. I guess the verdict on that was definitely in.

I explained, "Cora called to say there was a light bulb out here and she wanted me to fix it. So we stopped by and..."

"And I was cold..." added Kathryn.

"And Maggie had the perfect cure for that?" smirked Farrel.

Jessie sensed that the situation was getting too silly for everyone. "Kathryn," she said sensibly, "your hair is wet, why don't you come upstairs with me so you can use a hair dryer. If you go outside like that your hair will turn to icicles. And when we come back down we can have some cake. Farrel, get that angel food cake out of the freezer."

Kathryn smiled at Jessie with gratitude. I heard her say to Jessie as they headed toward the front stairs, "Your house is so wonderful, will you show me some of the rest of it?"

Jessie Wiggins was brilliant. She wanted to know about Kathryn and me but she knew I wouldn't talk if we were all together. Now that Farrel and I were alone, I'd spill the beans and Jessie could get the details from Farrel later.

"So, how long has this been going on?" grinned Farrel, as she pulled a foil covered package from the freezer.

"Since last night," I grinned back.

"Is it serious?"

I nodded.

"You don't look very serious with that goofy grin...but you do seem to be glowing. I don't know that I've ever seen you look this way before. Does Kathryn agree that this is serious?"

"I asked her to go steady and she said yes."

Farrel snorted, "Are you going to give her your letter jacket? I glanced at the stairs, thinking that Kathryn and Jessie might come back any minute. "Don't worry, Jessie will keep her occupied for a while. She wants me to get all the inside information. Maggie, I hope you don't take this the wrong way but... I've heard people around campus refer to Kathryn as the *Ice Queen*. Have you...um...?"

"Oh yeah, uh huh...four times last night, no five...and twice this morning and..." I glanced back at the hot tub.

"Five times in one night? Yow, Maggie," Farrel chuckled, "don't let her get away! She's so attractive, and that voice! Smart, successful at her job... are her politics OK? Is she *out* enough?"

"Yeah, everything. I keep wondering if I'm dreaming."

"Does Sara know?"

I told her an abbreviated version of Sara and the security cam. Farrel burst out laughing, I grabbed her arm. "Shhh, please don't say anything. Kathryn was a good sport about it, and now, tonight..." I glanced back at the hot tub.

"I'm sorry we walked in on you. We called your message machine to ask you to come to the brunch tomorrow. Bring Kathryn too, of course. I'm sure Jessie's inviting her right now."

"I'm not sure I'll be able to come, I'll be working on Carl's case, but Kathryn might come. Would that be all right? Whom else did you invite?" She listed a few names including Sara and Emma. We could hear Jessie and Kathryn coming back downstairs.

"Did you see everything?" I asked Kathryn.

"Some. Jessie said I could see the rest of it tomorrow in the daylight...when we come to brunch?"

Jessie removed the foil from a large piece of angel food cake and put it in a bowl. She took a jar of strawberries in light syrup from the refrigerator and placed it, with a large spoon on the dining room table. Farrel had gotten bowls, utensils and coffee mugs. When we sat down, I explained to Kathryn that I would probably have to work much of the day on Carl's case, but that if she wanted to come for brunch, I could meet her here later.

"Would it be all right for me to come?" Kathryn asked Jessie, who was already nodding. Kathryn turned to Farrel, "Jessie told me to ask you about the antique and flea markets."

"There's Lambertville and Adamstown, Jessie or I go every Sunday morning. I really have to go tomorrow because we sold a ton of stuff at Metrolina. We need merch. Do you want to go to the markets sometime?"

I said, "Kathryn shopped Mansfield when she was in England in September. She goes to Brimfield too."

"Really?" said Farrel with interest, "would you like to come with me to Adamstown tomorrow? I have to warn you, I leave very, very early."

I was floored when Kathryn said yes. Farrel told her what I already knew, that flea markets are the *before dawn* part of the antique business and that since it took about an hour to drive there, she'd be leaving at 5:30 AM. Kathryn was unfazed. She wanted to go. So Farrel said she'd pick Kathryn up in front of my building and that they should be back in plenty of time for Carl's memorial service at eleven.

Farrel looked at me, "Are you going to go?"

"No, I can't, I have an appointment." I was astounded that Kathryn was going to do this. On the other hand, I figured Farrel would take the two hour drive time to grill Kathryn to be sure she was good enough for me. I wanted Farrel to like Kathryn and to approve, but I also wanted to know her opinion on our chances for something long term.

It's often tough to face your new girlfriend's best pals for the first time *with* your girlfriend, but to face them all on one's own could be more than sticky. I wondered why Kathryn was so eager to throw herself to the potential lions this soon. Then I remembered what she'd done when faced with Sara. Maybe she'd figured out that these were the people in my life that I would expect her to endure and was diving in head first to see if she could handle them. This woman was very brave.

"Oh, I forgot," said Farrel getting up and opening the refrigerator again.

She came back to the table with an armload of Devil Dog cakes. "We're eating angel food cake because it was one of Carl's favorites. He loved Devil Dogs, too. He used to give Devil Dogs out to all the people sitting around him at the Symphony during intermission. He said he was cultivating it as his trademark eccentric behavior, that and eating angel food cake. So..." she unwrapped a Devil Dog and took a bite, "here's to Carl!"

Chapter 33

We'd left soon after, with our bag full of restaurant leftovers and additional food from Jessie's kitchen. As we walked toward my building I said to Kathryn with amusement, "Let me just see if I completely understand this, you're going to leave my bed in the dark of night, to go off with another woman...who happens to be my best friend?"

She laughed, "Maggie, I have some serious shopping to do. Christmas is less than two weeks away. I can get everything I need at the antique markets. I'm a speed shopper. You wouldn't want me to have to do something truly terrible like...go to the mall!"

"No," I agreed gravely, "that would be terrible. Um, are you aware that Farrel...and Jessie too...tend to be a little *parental* when it comes to me?"

"You mean Farrel might ask me to explain my intentions toward you? Oh yes, I know that very well. I also fully understood that Jessie took me out of the room so you could tell Farrel what's going on between us. What did you tell her?"

"What's going on between us." Kathryn turned to me with raised eyebrows. "The short version," I assured her.

"I told Jessie I was worried about you because a man had hit you at the homeless shelter today. Was it all right that I told her that?" asked Kathryn.

"Uh huh."

"Jessie said to tell you to show me the top floor of your building and that you should...*show off for me*. That's really what she said, that you should, *show off for me*. What did she mean?"

"That I can take care of myself."

We'd entered the foyer. I turned off the burglar alarm by pressing in a code. Then stopped Kathryn saying, "I have something for you." I wrote some numbers on a piece of paper and handed it to her, "This is the combination that opens the front door and the door to the loft. And this is an *easy to remember* alarm code. It will be, 2929...your birthday twice. OK?"

I showed her how to open the combination lock and then how to enter the code to turn on and off the alarm. "We leave the alarm on at night and weekends, it covers the doors and foyer. We'll turn it off here, but there's a keypad on the third floor to turn it back on. I'll show you when we get up there."

"Is this my sorority pin?" she asked holding up the paper.

"Part one of it," I kissed her lightly. We made our way to the third floor and she practiced rearming the alarm.

"Jessie said you have to show me the upstairs," Kathryn insisted as soon as we got inside.

"OK, OK. I have to get some things. Don't take your jacket off, it's not very warm up there." I went into the dressing room and grabbed a pair of shorts. Then I took her hand, "Come with me."

We climbed up the big spiral staircase and I opened the door into the top floor. I threw a big electrical switch that turned on all the lights at once. The space seems much bigger than the third floor because there were no solid walls and the ceiling was about twice as high. Every exterior wall was windows. There were some studded interior walls without sheet rock on them, dividing the space into four areas that were roughly the same size. Electrical wires and plumbing ran through the skeletal stud walls.

One corner was obviously my art studio. I'd laid out sheets of block-printed paper to dry on most of the tables. There were several storage units and a huge old card catalog cabinet, each drawer labeled with the art supplies it contained.

Next to the studio was a big framed open rectangle with windows on two sides, waiting for usage decisions to be made. Across from that area were storage closets and the access to the elevator and main stairs. In the corner at the top of the spiral stairs stood a ton, well literally far more than a ton, of fitness equipment. Treadmill, stair master, weight machine, a speed punching bag and a floor-mounted heavy bag, a high chinning bar, rowing machine, and a variety of other stuff like that.

In front of a wide floor to ceiling mirror, there was even a frame that allowed barbell freeweight lifting without the danger of being crushed accidentally. Jessie, a former top administrator in a rehab hospital, had made me put that in. She'd started out as a physical therapist and had told me she'd seen the results of too many accidents to have to be worrying about me getting my neck broken under a barbell.

Kathryn walked into the center of the space and looked around silently. She noticed a small sheet rock finished room set between the workout space and the art studio. She just pointed to it.

"Bathroom," I explained.

"Then she noticed a door that went out to a roof area. She walked over to it, unlocked it and pulled it open. A freezing wind blew in. She closed it hurriedly.

"There's a deck out there," I said.

Once again, Kathryn was speechless. Finally she said, "What will that be?" pointing to framed northwest corner.

"Don't know...yet."

Kathryn turned back to the fitness equipment. "Show off," she demanded.

"I have to change clothes."

"May I look around the studio?" called Kathryn.

I nodded. When I came out of the bathroom in shorts and sports bra, Kathryn was in the studio looking in the art supply drawer marked brushes. I came to her side. She reached into the drawer and took out a new two-inch round watercolor brush. She looked me up and down, then touched the soft brush lightly to the hollow of my throat and drew it slowly down between my breasts with a look that made me feel weak.

I shook off the weakness and led her, still holding the brush, to a stool in front of the big mirror. She sat and gave me her full attention.

I did several standard stretching moves then sat down at the weight machine, set the weights fairly light and warmed up fast with leg presses, arm curls and other lifts. It was a thrill to have Kathryn watching my every move.

"Now for the impressive part," I said catching her eye. She hadn't been looking at my face. I pressed 250 pounds ten times with my legs. I got up and went over to the free weight frame. I lifted a 150 lbs barbell over my head several times. Fueled by Kathryn's evident admiration, I decided to risk some particularly difficult moves. I sat down on a gym mat, my legs straight in front of me, my body in a perfect L shape. I slowly lay my torso flat over my legs touching my nose to my knee, then I sat up straight again and grasping my heel, I lifted one leg straight up along side my head. I resumed the L position, put my palms on the floor and flexed, lifting my body and legs off the floor still in the L. I slowly leaned my head toward the mat, drawing my legs back through my arms, finally muscling up into a handstand.

"Oh my God," gasped Kathryn. She clapped her hands. I was really glad she'd been impressed because it had been damn hard for this nearly 36 year-old body to manage. I tipped myself backward and landed on my feet smoothly. I leaned over again and did another handstand, then lifted one hand off the floor and balanced for several seconds. I put my hand back on the floor and did a light handspring back into a standing position.

I looked Kathryn in the eye. She was speechless.

At the chinning bar, I put some chalk on my hands, stepped on the foothold, then reached over and hung from the bar. I chinned myself up, kicked out and piked my legs straight up. I swung three times, piking on the back swing and then spun all the way around the bar three times in full extension. In my youth I could have done a flip dismount, but these days I'm not quite so willing to press my luck. How cool would breaking my leg be? Instead I flew forward off the bar in a spilt, touching my toes then stuck a standing dismount.

She was staring at me in disbelief with her mouth open. After a long moment she said, "Show me how you kicked Shel Druckenmacher."

I did three *Bruce Lee* style high kicks in a row and then a double one, jumping four feet off the floor and landing the force of it on the heavy bag. I bounced off into one of those rolling dives ending up on my feet at the end. Then I ran up the wall near her and back flipped, swinging another few kicks into the heavy bag. It was just like a Jackie Chan movie. For the finale, I walked slowly toward her, picking up a towel that was draped over the stair machine, wiping the sweat from my face and chest.

When I got close to her I whispered menacingly, "Stand up and don't move." I reached around her and pulled the stool out of the way. I pushed her firmly against the wall mirror. With my hands at her waist, I lifted her straight up against the mirror fully extending my arms. I made it look like I wasn't even straining.

"Oh," she exclaimed. I lowered her very slowly into my kiss. When I drew away, she pulled me back to her and kissed me again passionately. At last, she pushed me gently away holding me at arms length. She slowly began to touch me. I was playing it to the hilt, tensing my muscles to rock hardness. She felt my biceps and shoulders. She dropped her hands and felt the hard muscles in my thighs sliding up slowly. When her fingers felt the top of my hipbones, one side was tender, but I didn't let it show.

She made a fist and lightly punched me in the middle of my stomach. No yield at all.

"Harder," I whispered, she did it a little more aggressively. I was like stone. She extended her fingers and traced the muscles of my bare stomach that were pumped into a pretty good-looking washboard.

"OK, I get it now. By the way, this is quite a turn on...how could I have imagined this? I mean, I knew you were in good shape but...I work in a land of paunchy couch potatoes...well, not all of them, but some of them. Who would have known you were...I mean nobody...I've never seen any..." She was babbling, not something I imagined she did often. I kissed her to shut her up.

"Let's go downstairs," I suggested, taking her by the hand, "and bring the paint brush."

As she followed me down the spiral stairs she said, "So, I must presume that if we wrestle, you will always win?"

"Kathryn, if we wrestle physically, I will always win...unless I want you to, and I'm sure I will sometimes. But there are all sorts of ways to wrestle. You have the edge by far when it comes to mental gymnastics."

****

I took a shower. Kathryn had forgotten her garment bag and went down to get it out of the van. She got to practice the alarm system again, which was now no problem for her.

I was quick in the shower. I stepped out and was toweling off when I realized Kathryn was in the bathroom watching me. She'd taken off her clothes and was wearing a terry cloth robe. She was leaning against the sink counter facing me. She'd let the neckline of the robe fall open, creating a deep vee that showed the swell of her breasts.

"I couldn't wait to see you again," she said with that rumble of distant thunder in her voice.

I pulled on my own robe, replying, "You've seen plenty of me. I want to see you. I haven't seen your body in this kind of light."

"It can't compete with yours."

"I'll be the judge of that. There's something I have to know." I loosened her sash and pulled the robe open. She was marvelous in every way.

"What did you want to know?"

"If your hair color is natural. And, I see it is."

Chapter 34

We decided to sit on the couch in the bedroom and have a glass of wine. We talked about everything. Our families, our lives, our work. How we felt about pets, where we chose to live, whether either of us wanted kids. We covered politics, religion, marriage, and a dozen other subjects. No conflicts, no attitudes that were diametrically opposed. Everything seemed to click, and it was so much fun listening to her.

"Does everyone call you Kathryn?"

"Kiernan calls me Kath. People who don't know me sometimes call me Kathy. What's Maggie short for?"

I told her the story of my abbreviated name, which amused her.

"There's something else I think you should know about me," she said, "I occasionally have insomnia."

"How does that affect you?"

"I can't sleep."

"*Yeah, I know what it means*, but what do you do when you can't sleep? Do you toss around in the bed? Do you get up and roam the halls? Do you putter around the kitchen? Does it go on for night after night? Do you know the cause of it?"

She smirked at me and then answered in rapid fire..."I don't toss and turn. I get up and read. It doesn't go on for too many days. I don't know what causes it. It's not usually tied to an obvious source of stress. I guess that's what annoys me most."

"OK, OK, I just wanted to know...come here." She moved closer to me along the couch. I took her in my arms and held her tightly, kissing her hair, "When you have it, is there anything I can do to help it go away?"

"I'm not sure about that either. No one has ever asked me that before," she said in a softer tone, relaxing in my arms and kissing my neck softly. "Did I thank you for giving me that wonderful massage last night? It was...please don't take this the wrong way...but it was almost as nice as making love. I only woke up once. That's rare for me."

I let go of her and got up. I took a soft pillow from the bed and sat back down with the pillow in my lap. "Lie down on your back and put your head on the pillow."

"Is this just a comfortable place for me to lie, or do you have something special in mind?" she said easing onto her back.

"If I stroke your face with this paint brush, will it relax you or will it tickle you and make you tense?"

"Do it."

I gently brushed the curves and contours of her face and throat for a long time. I could feel her head become heavier as her neck muscles eased. I concentrated on the beautiful lines of her face, the firm jaw, the elegant hairline, expressive eyes, her nose, her lips, and those cheekbones.

"What are you thinking about?" she asked lazily.

"About painting you. I'm thinking about how I would use the color and shadow to capture your mood and expression."

"Tell me what you'd be doing," she said quietly.

So as I moved the brush over the contours of her face, I described what each brush stroke would achieve. She enjoyed the narrative as much as the sensation; I'd have to remember that.

The firelight cast a golden glow over her features. As her expression changed from relaxation to anticipation, I used the paintbrush to trace along her clavicle and down her sternum. I opened her robe and used the brush on her breasts. She exhaled sharply as I discarded the brush and caressed her with my hand. When I reached down her body and slipped my fingers into the soft hair between her thighs, she responded at once. I stroked her slowly, taking my time. I whispered, "Come to me," in her ear. She began to make pleasure noises. Then she moaned softly, but just as she was close to letting go, the phone rang.

I cursed quietly.

Her eyes blinked open, she groaned with exasperation, "Buzzers and bells may be the death of us both."

It was after 11:00 PM. The answering machine clicked on but I could hear Max Bouchet's voice say it was an emergency. I got up and picked up the phone. Kathryn sat up, staring at me with concern.

"Yes, what is it Max? Rowlina Roth-Holtzmann? Is she dead? What hospital? Are the police there? Well, why not? Where are you?...Uh huh...Is the security guard that found her still with you? Uh huh...OK, I'll be there soon."

Bouchet had told me that Rowlina Roth-Holtzmann was found injured on one of the Irwin Campus sidewalks about 45 minutes ago, by a security guard. When the guard knelt down by her, she mumbled to him that she'd been shot. He'd immediately called the paramedics and campus security headquarters. They'd called Bouchet. Bouchet was at the hospital now.

Bouchet said Rowlina was not seriously hurt but there was a bullet hole through her coat. An exit wound seemed to show that the bullet had just passed through the folds of material, not even grazing her. The doctors had determined that she'd fainted and hit her head on the sidewalk. There'd been minor bleeding from a small cut, but no serious damage other than a possible concussion.

I relayed all this information to Kathryn who listened with her chin propped on her arm on the back of the couch. "Where was she?" she asked.

"On the east side of College Street, not far from Washington."

"Can she speak? What was she doing out in the middle of the night?"

"Rowlina was very upset and not very coherent. I have to go. I'm so sorry...and just when you were about to..."

"I'll hold the thought," she smiled the half smile. We moved together for a lingering goodbye kiss, which made me even less eager to leave.

As I drove my van to the hospital, I had a very bad feeling about this latest incident. It wasn't just that another person had been hurt. It was something else I couldn't name. It was there though, bubbling in my stomach, a nasty sensation that was much scarier than Rowlina being used for target practice. But I couldn't put it all together. Not yet.

****

The hospital lobby was hushed by the night. Dr. Rowlina Roth-Holtzmann was in room 410, barely awake. Max Bouchet and the security guard who'd found her, were waiting with her.

"Maggie, it's good you're here," said Max in an impossibly loud whisper.

"Max, I'll talk to her and look at her coat with the bullet hole, but we have to call the police, it doesn't matter that she wasn't seriously hurt. I'm obligated to report it," I said this all very quietly so the other people in the room couldn't overhear. Bouchet nodded.

I went over to the bed where Rowlina lay under the covers in a hospital gown, "Dr. Roth-Holtzmann, I must ask you some questions, and you must answer as fully as possible."

She stared up at me fearfully. She nodded but it hurt her head. She closed her eyes against the pain.

"Tell me what happened?"

She opened her eyes again and slowly began, "I was coming out of the building when I heard a shot. I turned around quickly and stumbled..." she said in a papery voice.

"Did you see or hear anyone?"

"No."

"What were you doing on campus so late?"

Rowlina glanced nervously at Max Bouchet and remained silent. I said, "Max, would you step out of the room and make that call? Oh, and would you take the guard with you? "

He wasn't happy about it, but he did it.

"Why were you on Campus so late?"

She closed her eyes for a moment, took a breath and said haltingly, "I had wanted...to speak to...someone...about a problem...a personal problem and from my car on College Street, the light of Kathryn Anthony, I had seen."

Kathryn's office light, her car in the Language Arts parking lot and her habit of *burning the midnight oil*, would cause anyone to think she was in her office. Probably, over the years, many lesbian coeds had gazed with desire at Kathryn's late night office lights. Had Rowlina hoped for a midnight tryst with Kathryn? I'll admit to a certain smugness in knowing that Kathryn was resting her beautiful head in my lap, while Rowlina prowled the night looking for her.

"What did you want to see her about?"

"A serious problem I have with...government officials...and as she knows the Governor..." Rowlina touched the bandage on her head. She went on, "but that has nothing to do with this. I don't know why..." she stopped again, "perhaps a robbery? There is no reason why anyone would want to shoot me. Perhaps it is that I merely imagined it?"

I opened the closet door. A dark gray suit and an acid green polyester blouse hung on hangers with her billowy dark wool coat and red shawl. Brown leather low-heeled shoes were on the floor. On a shelf was her ridiculous fox fur hat. One side of the hat was covered with blood, a grotesque wearable rendering of highway roadkill. Maybe she'd get rid of it now.

"What do you mean, you're in trouble with the government?" I asked inspecting the coat with my back to her.

"It is the Immigration...they do not think...but it has nothing to do with me..." she sobbed.

Fear had seeped out of all the creepy little corners of her life and it had begun to push her over the edge. She was barreling toward a breakdown. I inspected her coat. Through the outer right side, at the top of a wide pocket, was a bullet hole. Another hole in the back on the right side, showed the exit path. I folded the material and could easily imagine how the bullet could have passed through without hitting her. We needed the cops to comb the area to find the bullet. If it matched the one in Skylar Carvelle's wall, it would be an important piece of evidence.

"Tell me what you did, step by step, from the time you got in the area of the office building. Where had you come from?"

She said more alertly, "I parked my car at the Architecture Department in my regular space."

"Why did you park so far from Dr. Anthony's office?"

"I always park there. It is my spot, and it is not so very far away..." It was her parking place, she always parked there. Routine was part of her identity.

"I walked through the quad...and went into the...Language Arts Building through the quad side door. To the second floor offices, I went. But there was no answer when I knocked at the door of 208. Might Kathryn have been harmed in her office and that was why she did not..."

"No, she's not been harmed." Except when I bit her shoulder in the hot tub. I mentally slapped myself. *Pay attention.*

Rowlina slumped back against a pillow. "That is all right then. Ah, and so...I came down the front stairs of the building..."

"Why did you come down a different way?"

Her head moved sluggishly as she did her best to form an answer, "Because it...had been very dark in the quad. I had not been safe-feeling and so on the street with lights, I wanted to walk."

She licked her lips. Finally she said, "So, then...when I came out, there was a shot and I turned around and fell...and then I woke when the guard was there."

"Tell me about the shot...did you hear anything before that?"

"Before the shot. Before...?" she looked bewildered but tried to think, "Yes, yes, so...I heard a click and then another louder click. ...I turned a little toward it, like so." Her eyes went to the left, " and then bang and then I think maybe running footsteps."

"You turned toward Washington Street? Straight along College Street toward Washington Street?" I asked leaning over the bed with my face close to hers, forcing her to keep eye contact.

"Yes, but a little back...toward the quad." She yawned fiercely. Her stale, smoke-tinged breath made me draw back sharply.

She was nearly asleep now. A nurse came in to check her vital signs. I went into the corridor to find Bouchet. He and the security guard were sitting on a couch down the hall. They both stood up expectantly. I spoke to the guard briefly who hadn't actually seen or heard anything but a small scream from Rowlina. I told him he could go, but that the police might want to speak with him.

I said to Bouchet, "She didn't see who shot her. The bullet holes in her coat are small. I'd say they're from a twenty-two. No powder burns, so the shooter had to be a few feet away. That jives with her story. She says she wanted to talk to Kathryn about a personal problem."

"What? I want to know. I won't tell," he said boyishly.

"Well, OK, Immigration may be after Rowlina because she married that guy on the West Coast to get him citizenship." I felt a little sorry for her. She hadn't married Holtzmann to break the law, just to close the closet door on herself. I wondered if she was being blackmailed on top of it all. Which of course made my mind flit to our resident blackmailer, Shel Druckenmacher. "Max, I need to go back to the College and see exactly where Rowlina was when this happened."

Bouchet said the police were on their way and I'd better get going. "I didn't mention you were here," he assured me.

"Good, show them the bullet holes in Rowlina's coat and suggest they go to the scene and search for the slug and spent shell. If it matches the bullet that killed Skylar Carvelle, then we'll have a clear link.

I left by the stairs, checking the lobby through the landing door window for police. I ducked when I caught sight of Ed O'Brien and two detectives striding across the lobby. They sped past the desk flashing their badges officially, on their way to the elevator.

When I heard the ding and swish of the elevator doors closing, I high-tailed it across the lobby to the exit.

****

Was it just my imagination or did it seemed darker on College Street than usual? I parked next to Kathryn's Mini Cooper and surveyed the entire scene though my windshield.

It *was* darker...the bulb over the Language Arts Building door had been smashed. I looked up. The light in Kathryn's office was still on. The street was deserted. A cold gust of wind shook the van. I felt vulnerable sitting there in full view of anyone. I started the engine and drove to the Architectural Design Building, where Rowlina Roth-Holtzmann's office was. Her car was in the spot with her nameplate.

I parked in a dark corner. Unlike Rowlina, I felt safer in the dark. I took out my gun, undid the safety and held it down at my side as I walked toward the Language Arts Building, following a path through the quad that had been kept clear of snow by the overhanging roofs. I took my time, somehow managing to keep my mind off Kathryn, who was waiting for me in my nice warm bed. Playing hide and seek with someone who might shoot you is not the time for your mind to wander.

When I finally got to the path that went around to the front of the Language Arts Building, I moved more slowly, sensing every noise, shadow and smell. There was an odor of something cloying. Just a whiff, then it was gone. I could see where the shooter probably waited. There were bushes to the left of the entrance, there was even a low window ledge where someone could sit and watch the door. Below it were footprint indentations. Nothing very clear, too much mulch around the bushes and too little snow because of the overhanging roof.

So, I figured, the killer shot and missed, but he or she didn't finish Rowlina off because when she fell, the killer probably thought she was dead, and then heard the guard coming. If Rowlina had been shot at by the killer, then the suspect list was down to just three...and the ever-possible wild card. It might also be possible that Rowlina set this whole thing up herself. It would divert suspicion from her and after all, she wasn't hurt and nobody saw the shooter. Oh shit, this is so damn complicated. Why does there have to be all this intrigue? Give me a gang drive-by anytime. Those are a breeze to figure out. Hell, the perps brag all over the street about them.

I tried to imagine each suspect waiting here in the cold dark night to kill Rowlina. But why kill her? Why even try to scare her? She was scared enough already. Whomever it was would have had to follow her here, watch her go in and then wait for her to come out. It didn't make sense. In the back of my mind parts of an idea were beginning to take form. If I could just get the outer edge done, maybe I could finish this jigsaw puzzle.

Chapter 35

When I got back to the loft, I managed to turn off the alarm before it even started its warning beep. I let myself in quietly. The door to the bedroom was ajar. I pushed it gently. Kathryn had fallen asleep while reading in bed, her book lay open on her lap. How nice it was to come home to her. Low dancing flames were alive in the fireplace grate. Kathryn's fascinating face was relaxed, rapid eye movements under her lids hinted at her dreams.

I went back into the big room, got my laptop and a drawing pad, brought them back to the bedroom and sat in an easy chair. Propping my feet on the edge of the bed, I quietly entered some case notes about Rowlina's attack. I scrolled through the other notes thinking about all the facts I had, then closed the computer and put it aside.

I opened the drawing pad and made a small overhead sketch of the Language Arts Building entrance. I added all the walkways that would ultimately lead to the place where I'd figured the attacker had been. I stared at the sketch and tried to image someone walking there, sitting on the window ledge, taking out a gun...No lightning flashes of insight hit me, just a deep nagging memory that wouldn't surface.

I gazed at Kathryn. Flipping to a new page, I began a quick sketch of her. Just a gesture. The position of her head was particularly interesting. I did another fast sketch from a slightly different angle. I turned the page again and began a drawing with more detail, beginning with her hairline, her closed eyes, her nose, the shadows cast by her hair. I was just beginning to shade the contours of her mouth, when her eyes blinked open.

Without shifting her body her eyes swept the room, to the door, to the clock, to the fireplace. When she caught sight of me at the far corner of the bed in the shadows, her face broke into a radiant smile.

"There you are, I was just dreaming about you. How long have you been here? Why didn't you wake me?"

"You were so lovely sleeping, I just wanted to look at you."

She lifted welcoming arms toward me. I crawled across the bed, into her embrace.

"Take off your clothes and finish what you were doing before you left," she demanded softly.

I did as I was told. Absence had certainly made the heart grow fonder; making her wait had also stoked her ardor. She watched me undress with fire in her eyes, then pressed me onto my back and slid on top of me, shrugging out of her robe in one fluid movement.

"I understand there are times you may have to leave me in the night, but I don't like to be kept waiting, Maggie. I want you, now," she whispered.

I pushed up gently and rolled on top of her, "Professor Anthony, I've learned how dangerous it is to keep you waiting." I trailed lingering kisses down her body, "Now, I'm going to teach you that patience has it rewards. Are you paying attention?"

"Yes, yes," she moaned as I began a lesson that went on for quite a while and ended very successfully.

Kathryn took a slow deep breath and said languidly, "That was worth waiting for.

"Don't you have something you'd like to teach me?" I asked feeling the need for her keenly. She answered me with a searing look that made me ache. She took me slowly but with an intensity that made my head swim. When I was finally able to catch my breath I managed to murmur, "You certainly deserved that full professorship."

After those delightful tasks had been tended to, we lay together comfortably in each other's arms. Kathryn asked me what had happened at the hospital. I told her all the details.

"So the INS has caught up with Rowlina," said Kathryn thoughtfully.

"Seems like it."

"What does she think I could do about it?"

"Talk to the Governor?"

"That would be a stretch, INS cases are a federal issue, not state...but I don't see what that has to do with this whole thing. Why would someone shoot her?"

"I don't get it either...what would happen if she died...would Holtzmann still retain citizenship?" I wondered.

"Probably, but think of the investigation that would come up...and it was such a clumsy attempt."

Yes...Kathryn was right, it was a clumsy attempt at Rowlina's life. Far more like what happened at Skylar's, than a professional hit.

Moments later Kathryn said, "We didn't really finish our conversation before. I should have asked, is there anything I should know about you?"

I thought for a while, "I have nightmares sometimes. They can be very vivid."

"Are they recurrent? Do you...are they frightening?"

"When I was a child I dreamed about my mother dying, or sometimes I dreamed about things suddenly disappearing, like my teddy bear, or my room, or our cat. I guess those were really about my mother too. Juana, my stepmother, always told me my dreams were very creative. Each dream is always different. I don't have them as much as I used to. Now they tend to be about problems I'm trying to work out. The scary thing is that the ones I have now, sometimes they're...portentous or prophetic. I don't scream or anything like that. They wake me up, though."

Kathryn reached for my hand and held it. "Prophetic? Really?"

"Sounds arrogant, doesn't it."

"No, just...well...interesting, and I can see why you'd feel that was scary." She brought my hand to her lips, kissing my fingertips lightly, "You won't be alone if you have a bad dream. Not tonight anyway."

I hugged her to me, "You have to get up in about four hours, you should go to sleep," I yawned.

I turned out the light and we both drifted off. It seemed as if the alarm went off two minutes later, but it was really 5:00 AM. Kathryn slipped out of bed and went into the bathroom. I fell asleep again, vaguely aware of the sound of the shower. Soon she was kissing me goodbye, and telling me she'd see me later. The scent of her drifted into my senses through my sleep soggy brain.

"Maggie, please be careful," she said gently.

"I will," I murmured more than half asleep, "I love you."

She leaned in very close and whispered something in my ear and then she was gone.

Moments later my eyes opened with a start. Had I really said, *I love you?* Or had that been part of a dream? And had I dreamed her reply? What was her reply? I thought carefully and remembered her warm breath in my ear saying something that felt good, but I couldn't remember exactly what it was. Hm. I burrowed back down under the warm covers, pulling her pillow to me. Hmmm. I smiled as I drifted off again.

I woke at 7:45 AM. I figured I'd skipped real workouts for too many days. Making love with Kathryn could be energetic, which might take care of aerobics, but I needed more weight bearing efforts to stay in shape to fight bad guys. I went upstairs and worked out for an hour, then came down and took a shower. I dressed in dark gray pants, a gray turtleneck and a black blazer. It was a funeral after all, and I needed the blazer to hide my holster.

I got to the Music building just before 10:00 AM. The door was locked, but one of the Bouchet's passkeys fit it. I let myself in, locking the door behind me. I took the stairs. My steps echoed as I made my way to the recording studio floor where Jimmy Harmon had said he'd meet me.

"Jimmy?" I called out when I opened the door to the big room. Nobody there. It was dark. Empty as a tomb I thought and then shivered at the allusion.

The padlock was still in place on Carl's office door. Inside, I decided to snag Carl's high sensitivity microphone and try to use it with his laptop at home. I unplugged it and put it in my shoulder bag. I sat at Carl's desk for about 10 minutes, straining to pick up a vibe. I tried to imagine what happened the day he got on the elevator and went up to the balcony. The students had heard a phone ring. So suppose somebody called him and told him to come up to the sixth floor.

I closed my eyes. "Ringggg," I whispered. I groped for the phone, picked it up and held it to my ear. "Carl Rasmus," I said. What would the voice on the other end say?...maybe: "Carl this is so and so, listen, I have something to show you"...no they wouldn't say *show you*... "Carl, I have something to talk to you about, alone. Come to the sixth floor...I'll be waiting at the door"? Well sure, that would work if it were someone he knew. So I got up, still with my eyes closed and began to move toward the door. But Carl would do this much more easily than I could, so I opened my eyes.

I jumped, gasping. There stood Jimmy Harmon in the doorway. I may be a big tough private eye, but I'd be fibbing to say the look on his face wasn't frightening. He looked down right maniacal. I instinctively stepped back.

"What the fuck are you doing?" he demanded in a loud rasping voice.

"Why the fuck are you looking at me like that?" I said with equal force.

"Just get to the point OK, what do you want me to say?"

"Jimmy, you're kind of starting in the middle of the conversation. Let's ease up."

He was so red in the face it looked like he had either been running a mile, was pissed as hell or about to cry. His face could have adequately expressed all three. Abruptly, he spun on his heel and walked out. I called his name but he didn't answer.

I quickly locked up Carl's office and followed Jimmy, but by the time I got to the stairs, he was nowhere in sight. The building seemed eerily quiet.

Where had he gone? Maybe up? And then, as if to confirm my suspicion, I heard a noise in the stairwell above.

I went up, I could see a light coming from the window in the sixth floor-landing door. I opened it as carefully as possible and distinctly heard another door, somewhere on that level, click shut. I reached under my jacket into my shoulder holster and drew out my gun. Flattening myself against the wall in a shadowy corner, I moved slowly along the corridor, my parka making a swishing noise against the wall. "Jimmy," I called quietly.

There were doors to various music rooms to my right. Some had choir risers; others were smaller rooms with upright pianos or groups of music stands.

I passed the glass doors to the balcony where Carl had fallen. The curtains were drawn, but clearly one of the doors was open. A cold wind was luffing the door curtain like a sail turned into the wind. No question about it, someone had just opened this door. The wet, foggy, outside air hadn't made the hallway cold enough for it to have been open very long. I didn't want to lean out there to see if someone was hiding around the balcony corner. I waited, listening.

Several minutes went by. I figured either I was alone, or the crazed maniac who wanted to kill me, simply had more patience than I did. If it turned out to be the latter, it would mean I had less patience than a crazed maniac. Not exactly something to include on a resume.

The empty hallway had many windows but all were curtained, making the area dim. Across the hall from the balcony door, double doors to a small dark practice room were open. In it I could make out an upright piano, two metal folding chairs and two black metal music stands.

The stillness was getting to me. Time for action. I pushed the balcony door open as quietly and as slowly as I could. I drew the curtain back and looked out. I couldn't see anyone, but there could still be someone hiding to the side of the door. Shit, I hate this kind of stuff. I got down lower and duck-walked onto the balcony. The wind was briskly blowing icy December cold through my clothes. There was nobody out there.

Suddenly, I heard a sound like a huge bowling ball rolling down an alley. It was a runaway piano headed right toward me at full speed, whatever full speed for a piano was, aiming to crush me or push me over the edge of the balcony.

I leapt up on top of it without thinking twice and grabbed hold of the door lintel. The piano slid smoothly under me, crashing into the balcony's cement railing, dislodging a huge chunk that went tumbling down the side of the building. It made an echoing clunk noise on the sidewalk below. The piano dangled one wheel over the edge, but the opening in the railing wasn't big enough to let it fall.

I dropped to the floor, rolling to the far wall of the hall. I could distinctly hear someone running. Jumping up, I ran to the stairway at the other end of the building. I could hear footsteps far below. I threw open the door and followed, staying as close to the wall as possible, keeping myself from being an easy target. If this was the killer, why had he used a piano rather than the gun...maybe he was out of bullets?

When I got to the ground floor, I had to give up. Whoever had just tried to flatten me was gone. There were too many paths leading in too many directions to figure out which way.

It was 10:45 AM. Cars were lining the streets, parking for Carl's memorial service. I made my way to the Chapel along with dozens of people. Students were everywhere. Some had stayed on campus for the funeral, others had come back just for the day. All of them looked sad missing Carl and feeling the terrible, incomprehensible loss and despair that suicide makes people, especially young people, feel. I wondered how their feelings might change when they learned this was a case of murder not suicide.

Worming my way through the crowds and into a side door, I found stairs to a choir balcony overlooking the sanctuary. The crowd coming in was growing. People were desperately looking around for friends or acquaintances to sit with. Nobody wants to sit by themselves at a funeral. I climbed to the choir loft.

In my bag was my small pair of high-powered binoculars. My father and stepmother had given them to me when I went to Europe in my junior year of college. I still carry them with me everywhere. They've come in handy more times than I can count. The choir loft was a perfect vantage point to see everything at once without anyone seeing me. I stepped into a dark corner and studied the room.

Max Bouchet came in with his lovely wife Shanna. He walked down the aisle with her, encouraged her to sit in a pew near the front, then went back to the entrance to greet people. Miranda Juarez was already in place there, to help Bouchet remember names. I could see Bouchet reaching in his pocket for his cell phone. My phone vibrated in my pocket, it was Bouchet calling me.

"Maggie, are you here?"

"Yes, I'm in the choir loft. I have a pretty good view."

"Excellent. I received the report on the attack on Rowlina from the police.

We should go over it after the service. You can come to the mansion, can't you?"

I said, "I have people to speak to after the service, but I'll come over right after I do." Bouchet agreed and resumed his meet and greet.

Daniel Cohen came in with an attractive woman I recognized as his wife, from the picture on his desk. They sat near the back row. Soon after, several younger people came in and sat in Cohen's row, greeting Daniel deferentially. Must have been his current students. Immediately after that three more young people came in and greeted Cohen affectionately. They must be graduates who were now making a ton of money based on the skills Cohen had taught them.

A large crowd pushed through the door with Jimmy Harmon in the lead. A woman and three redheaded kids, obviously his family, were with him. A group of music students and musicians followed, including Jack Leavitt and Mike Jacobsen. I stared at Jimmy with the binoculars. Did he look like a guy who'd use a piano as a deadly weapon? He looked agitated, but then that was his general song and dance.

The numbers of people entering began to swell. It was five minutes to eleven. I saw Farrel and Jessie come in a side entrance, with their friend Judith Levi. Kathryn was with them. Her presence made my heart leap and other parts of my body tingle.

Farrel and Jessie found a seat halfway along the aisle. Kathryn took off her coat and placed it next to them, but walked to the entrance to say a few words to Max. She clasped his hand and nodded while speaking. Judith Levi had seen Cora Martin, they were long time chums and about the same age. Judith sat down with Cora and Doug Scribner, another friend who'd be at the brunch later. Sara and Emma were sliding into a pew two rows behind Farrel and Jessie. They sat with some other people, I recognized them as other members of the Arts Commission. Leo Getty came in by himself. He shook hands with Max, and then walked slowly down the aisle. His face was still as red as it had been when I'd seen him last. Spying an empty seat, he stooped to cross himself before he slumped into it.

Kathryn walked slowly back down the aisle. She had on a dark suit, with a skirt that reached just below her knees. I realized that seeing her formally dressed was stimulating, but then, everything about Kathryn was stimulating. She'd stopped to talk to someone. It was Connie Robinson wearing a short winter jacket over a dark blue dress that was a little too tight for her. She was talking earnestly to Kathryn, then she hugged her. Kathryn hugged Connie back in a consoling way, patting her back. Connie was crying.

Back at the entrance, Bart Edgar came in with Nancy. She led him to a pew on the left aisle and they slid into place. I would talk to them after the service.

I saw Adam Smith, Georgia's husband, sitting with her two sons. He looked tired, but not as tired as he had when I'd seen him in the hospital.

No sign of Carl's sister Eileen Crenshaw. I doubted whether she or Carl's brother Kevin Rasmus would bother to attend. So far they were the most unpleasant characters in this scenario and they had the best motive because of the money they thought they'd inherit. Unfortunately, there was no way I could pin the crimes on them. Everything that had happened really required someone who was on the spot and they were just too far out of the picture.

Sweeping the crowd with my binoculars I picked out Janie Rasmus, way in the back in a dark corner, sitting with an older woman and a blond young man. I was glad she was there, for Carl's sake. I wondered if Janie had actually walked out on Kevin yet and I speculated on who the people she was sitting with were. I noticed Vice Principal Goldenberger of Hadesville High sitting right behind them. Good for him for showing up.

Everyone was settling down now. Kathryn sat next to Jessie who had Farrel on her other side. I yearned to know what Farrel and Kathryn had talked about on their trip to the antique markets.

Max Bouchet came back up the aisle and sat with Shanna, signaling that things would begin soon. Amanda Knightbridge came through the entrance as the ushers were closing the doors. She sailed down the aisle not seeming to notice anyone until she stopped next to Kathryn. Kathryn invited her to sit down next to her, bidding Farrel and Jessie to move over. I watched with the binoculars in fascination as Amanda Knightbridge, who seemed to be quite pleased, spoke to Kathryn. I would swear Kathryn blushed as she shook her head. Amanda asked her something else and Kathryn shook her head *no* again.

Amanda looked around the room for just a second, then peered toward the choir loft directly at me, even though it was so dark where I was standing it must have been impossible for her to actually see me. Amanda bent her head to Kathryn's ear. Kathryn leaned forward and looked up to where I was standing in the balcony. I leaned into the light for just a second so she could see me. She didn't wave or give me away; she just smiled, then turned to face the front of the church. I noticed Amanda Knightbridge's face had taken on an attitude of sublime satisfaction. That woman was downright scary.

The College Chaplain spoke from the heart about Carl. Unlike many funerals the person delivering the eulogy had really known the one who died.

I flashed on the main doors again, one was opening slightly to let in Rowlina Roth-Holtzmann. I was wondering if the hospital would hold her, there hadn't seemed much reason to. Thank goodness she wasn't wearing that dead animal on her head. Her new overcoat billowed as she twitched into a pew at the back. The police must have kept her bullet pierced one as evidence.

Doors behind the Chaplain sprang open and an orchestra entered. Not a quartet, or a small band, but a full fledged strings and brass orchestra. There was even a grand piano being pushed in. I gulped. Rolling pianos had suddenly become my new phobia, I wondered how long that would last. A hundred people, all toting their instruments, chairs and music stands clattered themselves around the apse and waited.

Jimmy Harmon got up from his seat and walked slowly down the aisle to lead the group. He turned to the *audience* and said simply, "Carl wrote many fine pieces of music. We will play one of his sonatas; the Sonata in E Flat, his *Concerto for Piano*, and a contemporary piece called, *I Can See*."

Jimmy was total concentration. He became one with the group and they played the sweetest music I've ever heard. Each of the pieces was honest and pure. The song at the end was sung by Caitlyn Zale, who'd been at the recording studio the day Carl died. She sang like an angel, holding the listeners in the palm of her hand.

Carl's song, *I Can See*, had both the lines *I'm a blind man* and *I'm a gay man,* in it. I was glad Carl's true self was being celebrated on this day that had been set-aside just for him. During each piece, I watched the room with the binoculars. By the end of the concerto, most people were teary. I saw Kathryn wipe her eyes several times. As Caitlyn progressed through Carl's song, everyone was blinking back tears. Janie Rasmus, and the woman and young man with her, were crying like babies. Farrel was too. She's such a sap. Yet, I have to admit, I wiped my eyes a few times too. It was all very moving; beautiful, sad, and hopeful all at the same time.

At the end of the music, Max Bouchet was at the podium saying that we should all celebrate Carl's life and strive to emulate his courage. I made another silent vow to Carl, I'll find out who killed you, and bring him or her to justice.

Since this was the regular campus Sunday service, the Chaplain was up again telling folks they could all come up and receive communion. People began to queue.

Kathryn had told Farrel I was up here in the loft. Farrel caught my eye and gestured subtly with a slight head toss for me to come down and join them. I ran down the steps, then skirted the room coming around to the far side of the pew. A student had stopped to speak to Kathryn. She didn't notice as I slipped in along side of Farrel.

"Well?" I said impatiently.

Farrel grinned, then glanced at Kathryn who was still turned away. Jessie had noticed me and reached across Farrel to squeeze my hand, then she leaned a little forward making it impossible for Kathryn to see me. Allowing me and Farrel to talk for a moment without interruption.

"Well?" I demanded more urgently.

"OK, OK...she's falling for you, honey, that's pretty damn clear. So don't screw this up, because she may be the *one*."

"But what did she say?" I couldn't help grinning either.

"I grilled her and frankly she grilled me right back. About you. Look we can talk about this some other time -- but here's the 60 second version: I think you two are very well suited..."

"But?" I asked.

"Well, she likes to be in control and I'll bet she can be very stubborn. If you and she argue, it's going to be pretty intense, and you aren't going to win. Um...I think she's going to need her own space...at least some space that's all her own...and she may want a little more attention than you have time to give her. And...this might just be my erotic imagination but, she seems to be extraordinarily hot for you."

"Farrel, I can't imagine not paying attention to her."

"I can see that."

"What did she say that made you think...I mean, that she's...you know... hot?" I reddened a little.

Farrel snickered, "You don't need me to explain that."

Just then, Jessie leaned back and I found myself looking directly into Kathryn's eyes. They were electric. Her half smile twitched for just a second. Causing me to feel instantaneous lust. I winked slowly at her, then turned back to Farrel exhaling.

I said, "Bouchet wants me to look at some papers, so could you please take Kathryn to your house after the service? I'll see you all as soon as I can." People were still going up the aisle for communion so I slid back out of the pew and worked my way around the inside of the building again, managing to find Bart Edgar and Nancy.

I sat down next to Nancy with Bart on her other side. I didn't even bother to speak to him, I just asked her point blank... "What bottle did Bart pick up in the conference room?"

Nancy exhaled through her nose in an exasperated way. "He says he went to get coffee," she spit out with supreme irritation. I figured he'd better hurry up and marry her or he'd lose her to annoyance.

"But the coffee pot is in the waiting room," I pointed out.

"I know," said Nancy flatly.

"But..." I began, ...Nancy just shook her head stiffly. This was Bart's story and for now, he wasn't going to budge. Maybe he really did forget where the coffeemaker was. I looked beyond Nancy into Bart's foggy eyes. He nodded for no reason. Punching him in the nose fluttered through my mental suggestion box. I decided it wouldn't help.

The line of people getting communion had almost ended. I left Bart and Nancy and made my way to Max and Shanna Bouchet.

"Things seem OK, here," I said to Max after I'd slid in to the pew behind him. I didn't want to get into the piano incident right then.

He turned around and nodded, "The closing prayer is about to start, I have to be with the Chaplain to shake hands with people as they leave. Maggie, you can't see the security today, can you? We worked on their undercover disguises yesterday."

I turned and glanced around the room, easily picking out four of the security guards. I'd noticed all of them when I'd been in the choir loft. I said to Bouchet, "No, can't see them...good job."

He beamed, then got up to make his way to the entrance.

I moved to the back of the Chapel near the door so I could scout all these folks one more time. Jimmy Harmon was gone. When he'd finished directing the musical piece he'd walked right down the aisle. I'd thought he was going back to his seat, but he wasn't there. He was acting like such a squirrel today. Maybe that was an understatement since there was more than a 50/50 chance that he'd just tried to kill me with a loaded piano.

I made my way to his family, stooping down to speak to his wife. Her name was, I searched my brain....Linda. "Excuse me, Linda?" I said as though I knew her.

"I'm sorry...?" she said courteously. She didn't know who the hell I was, but this kind of thing probably happened to her all the time, since Jimmy was a celebrity.

"Yeah, hi, I was supposed to help Jimmy with the instruments," I said vaguely, "Where'd he go?"

She had a slightly worried look, but mixed with it was the knowledge that Jimmy was always disappearing and then turning up later, doing something creative. "I don't know," she said, "after the pieces he walked back here, but he just kept going up the aisle."

"What kind of car did you come in? Maybe he's out in the parking lot?" I suggested in a helpful tone...but I really wanted to know if Jimmy had an extra car that happened to look like a Neon.

"We all came in the minivan...Oh golly, I hope he didn't take it." She glanced at the three cute little redheaded kids sitting with her. They were being really good considering they'd just sat through a long church service.

The Chaplain said loudly, "Let us sing." Everybody flipped pages. It was that rainbow song that they do at the Metropolitan Community Church. Rainbows, underscoring that Carl was a gay guy. I liked that. There were a heck of a lot of gay people there, transgender people too. And they were singing their hearts out. I wondered if this 100-year-old Chapel had ever had dozens of gay, lesbian, bisexual and transgender people singing a gay hymn in honor of a gay man, with such fervor. Maybe. There have always been gay people in the world, it's just that now, we no longer buy into pretending we're the same as the majority, just so the majority won't be uncomfortable.

I eased out the side door and found a spot near some bushes where I'd be able to see people coming out of both the main entrance and the side. The people exiting from the front were going to have to bottleneck at the handshaking *reception line*. The side door would be used by the folks who were either incognito or wanted to speed off to a local diner for an artery hardening brunch. At this very moment however, people were still singing inside. No one had bolted for the doors yet. The old stone sidewalks, which had been shoveled clear of snow and ice, waited silently for Carl's mourners.

The morning ground fog had all but cleared and the sky was a brilliant blue with puffy white clouds that looked distinctly like pieces of angel food cake, passing only occasionally in front of a bright yellow sun. Patches of pale grass showed around the snow covered lawn. The air was crisp and clear. It was a beautiful day for Carl's funeral, which made me suddenly very sad. This was the kind of day that inspired people to want to write music. Carl was one of the rare individuals on earth who could actually do such things well. The edge of a cloud passed in front of the sun, and a perfect rainbow appeared directly over the music building. I made a wish that it stayed in the sky for all Carl's mourners to see.

Bouchet stepped out with the Chaplain, then the main doors burst open and humanity flowed through. The Cohens, Jimmy Harmon's family, Bart and Nancy, and Rowlina Roth-Holtzmann were mixed in the crowd. Farrel and Jessie came through the door with Kathryn. Farrel saw the rainbow and pointed it out to Jessie and Kathryn. Then Farrel introduced Jessie to Max

Bouchet. I watched Kathryn's every graceful move. Farrel, Jessie and Kathryn moved along, then stopped just beyond Bouchet to talk to Amanda Knightbridge, who had also spied the rainbow and was pointing it out to others around her. Cora Martin had joined them, so had Judith Levi and Doug Scribner. Sara and Emma exchanged a few words with them, then left for the parking lot.

"Um...Ms. Gale?" Connie Robinson was calling to me, she jogged over to where I was standing.

"Hi Connie, What's up?"

"Uh, you know that guy Shel?" Connie was still deeply worried about Druckenmacher, it showed in her face.

"He's in jail Connie, and I'll do my best to keep him from bothering you any more," I said firmly.

"Really, can you do that? That would be really good." She was clearly relieved but there was something else on her mind. She said, "I wish I'd stood up to him more."

"You did Connie, you told him no. That took a lot of guts."

"Oh yeah, um, but that was just me, I mean when he was picking on *her*, when everyone was there, she was in that little kitchen, she wanted somebody to stop him."

"Who? Miranda? Miranda was with Shel in the storage kitchen in the Arts Building? When?" This was something new.

Connie shook her head then focused on me. "Oh no, I'm sorry for being such an airhead. Not Miranda, I was talking about that party, not at the College and this was about Shel selling drugs, too."

"Oh," I said hiding disappointment that this wasn't going to be a clue to the bombing. If Shel was linked to the drink bottles, he and Miranda would have moved to top suspects as a team, but I'd jumped ahead. That wasn't what Connie was saying at all. I said to Connie, "I'm sure Druckenmacher harassed other women in the shelter kitchen, I'm not surprised about that..."

We were both startled by a commotion across the lawn. The young man who'd been sitting with Janie Rasmus was calling out, "Dad! Please!..." to Leo Getty, who was on the sidewalk. Leo just waved him off without looking at him.

Janie Rasmus stood by as the woman she'd been sitting with shouted, "You're really a fucking asshole, Leo!"

Leo whirled around in anger. I left Connie without saying goodbye and sped toward the group. Leo turned beet red, he looked like a cartoon character who'd drunk a bottle of Tabasco and was about to blow flames out his ears. There are not that many types of personal relationships that could cause that kind of ire. Obviously, this woman was Leo's ex-wife Barbara. I guessed the phrase *amicable divorce* wasn't in either of their vocabularies.

Leo stared angrily at his ex-wife and son, then turned toward Bouchet with the same hate-filled expression. Then he turned again and hurried off toward the parking lot without looking back.

Janie Rasmus, Barbara Getty and Leo's son got into a car parked at the sidewalk. They sped off before I could run half way across the lawn. Damn, I'd wanted to talk to them, but the Hadesville crowd didn't seem to have any direct link to the murders. I decided there were better uses for my time.

Out of the corner of my eye, I saw Miranda Juarez looking worriedly toward a group of cars. I was afraid Shel Druckenmacher might have made bail and was ducking around over there, but it wasn't Shel, it was Jimmy Harmon walking unevenly in the parking lot. He looked like he was crying. He bounced off a parked SUV. I ran after Jimmy, but he got into the passenger side of a minivan and it drove away. At least he'd found the wife and kids. Crap, I was missing everybody.

I went to my van, pulled my little laptop out of my shoulder bag, booted it up and entered some notes to the case file about the piano incident, Jimmy ,and Leo. Especially that I had to talk to Jimmy soon, and I added: Bart says he wanted coffee, but is probably lying. Rowlina was well enough to attend. Connie is relieved about Shel Druckenmacher, who had harassed other women at shelter events. Amanda Knightbridge was getting to be way too clairvoyant. Nancy, Bart's girlfriend may be coming to the end of her rope.

And, I thought, This little private eye is hungry and wants to see her gal, but has to talk to the client first.

Chapter 36

"Good grief, Max! How did you manage to get the lab to process the bullet so fast? It's been less than 24 hours! We were seated at the dining room table in the President's mansion, the police papers spread out in front of us.

"Well, I do have some pull..." he said.

And tons of money, I thought.

"So they found a bullet in a tree near the Language Arts Building door and it matched the one at Skylar's, and..." I flipped forward to look at another page again, "there were no powder burns on Rowlina's coat." Nothing in the report surprised me.

"We can take this to mean that the person who killed Skylar, shot at Rowlina, which removes her from the suspect list...correct?" rumbled Max.

"Possibly...probably," I nodded, "but suppose this was Rowlina trying to distract suspicion from herself. She sees Kathryn's light on and assumes she's there. Rowlina parks, comes down to the Language Arts Building, she shoots the gun right below Kathryn's window, assuming Kathryn will hear it and call the police. Kathryn isn't there, but a security guard hears the commotion and comes running. Rowlina falls down hitting her head, calls out and the guard finds her."

"But, what happened to the gun? It wasn't on her and the police searched the area," said Bouchet shaking his head.

"Yeah, you're right, it's a stupid theory. The thing is, I can't come up with any good reason for someone to shoot at Rowlina, and because I can't, I'm thinking of all sorts of outlandish possibilities. I'm not sure why Skylar was killed either, although it was probably because he had information about the bombing."

"I need you to figure this out, Maggie. The inquest is Tuesday..." Bouchet was fidgeting with his collar nervously, displaying an uncommon lack of self possession. He was getting desperate.

"Max, it's all coming together, but I can't promise I'll figure it out by

Tuesday. That's less than two days away!"

"I know, I know...but try, OK?" Max rumbled sincerely.

****

After parking at my building, I walked over to Farrel and Jessie's and went right in rather than ringing the bell. These people were my closest friends and family. Most of them were sitting around the big dining table. Doug Scribner and Judith Levi were discussing a play. Cora Martin was talking over her shoulder to Farrel, who was clearing empty dishes from the table. My darling and sometimes annoying sister Sara and her business partner and pal Emma, had their heads together trading secrets. Jessie was at the stove. Griswold and Wagner were absent. No doubt Farrel had stashed them in an upstairs bedroom. Otherwise, they'd insist on being the center of attention.

Kathryn was helping Jessie and Farrel clean up the kitchen. When Kathryn looked up and saw me standing in the doorway of the dining room, she put down a dishtowel, fixed her eyes on me and walked slowly forward. Everyone stopped talking. Kathryn put both her hands behind my head and pulled me into a flagrantly sexual kiss. Not to be undone, I tipped her back to make the whole moment more dramatic.

Everyone either laughed or hooted or both. Kathryn breathed in my ear, "After all I've had to endure in last two days, I just had to embarrass you a little in front of your friends."

I whispered back, "Feel free to kiss me like that anytime."

Emma said in a low voice to Sara, "Kathryn's like that woman on Star Trek, the captain with the sexy voice."

Cora said to Judith, "Who is that actress she reminds me of? Patricia Neal?"

Judith responded with, "I've been thinking Katherine Hepburn, but more substantial."

I said hello to everyone, kissing Doug on the cheek because I hadn't seen him for a while. Then I went into the kitchen with Kathryn to see if Jessie had anything leftover for me to eat. I was starving. Jessie scooped up a helping of egg casserole baked in a crisp hash brown potato crust, layered with cheese, and topped with thick bacon and roasted red peppers. On the side she slipped two light fluffy waffles, which I topped with maple syrup.

"We haven't had dessert yet," said Jessie, "so hurry up and eat this so you can have some. Look, I have some andouille for you, just a little piece." She dropped a chunk of my favorite sausage on my plate, then shooed both me and Kathryn out of her kitchen.

"Did you get enough to eat?" I asked Kathryn as we sat down at the table.

"I'm so full, I'll never be able to eat again, you should have warned me," she groaned. I noticed there was a half full Cafalatte bottle at her place.

"I told you she was the best cook ever."

Everyone at the brunch had known Carl in one way or another, except me. Though now I felt I knew him well. Judith and Cora were both docents at the symphony and had chatted with Carl when they were on duty. Farrel and Kathryn had known him from the College, and Jessie had met him on several occasions at Irwin musical events. Doug, who was gay and who was about Carl's age, had been in a play at the local community theater for which Carl had been musical director. It turned out they'd spent quite a bit of time together during the run.

I finished the last bite of waffle and put my fork aside. I was staring out the window into the courtyard when Kathryn reached under the table and squeezed my hand.

"What are you thinking about?" she whispered.

"Carl," I said simply. She smiled sadly and nodded.

As if on cue, Farrel looked around to be sure everyone had something to drink, then raising her glass, she said simply, "Let's toast Carl."

We all raised our glasses, saying Carl's name. I was moved by the sincere expression on each face. Before the silence threatened to become oppressive, Jessie said, "I thought we should have angel food cake for dessert. Carl liked it. I have strawberries to go with it."

Kathryn asked me quietly, "Does she always cook like this?"

I turned to the crowd, "Kathryn wants to know if Jessie always cooks like this?"

Jessie said, "No, no."

Everyone else said, "Yes," in unison.

Farrel added confidentially, "I used to be a lot thinner." Then she turned to Jessie and said, "Do you want me to get the pies now?" Jessie nodded.

Farrel brought out a sizable dish filled with half moon shaped pastries.

"These are really something, but they're kind of rich," she said. They were light pie dough filled with apple, blueberry or cherry pie filling, deep fried and covered with a sugar glaze. I'd had them before. They were habit forming.

I took a blueberry pie and shared part of it with Kathryn, who moaned appreciatively at first bite. I rapidly finished the rest trying not to imagine myself expanding into a giant blueberry like Violet Beauregard in the Willy

Wonka movie. The others were groaning that they were too full, but I noticed they all took helpings of the fluffy angel food and strawberries and most took at least one of the small pies.

Farrel sat down again helping herself to cake, then said, "Judith, tell that story you told me the other day." When Judith looked blank, Farrel said, "You know..." then leaned in, reminding Judith in an undertone. Farrel had known Judith for almost thirty years. Judith had been Farrel's English teacher when Farrel was a college sophomore. They'd eventually become friends and when Farrel had taken the job at Irwin she'd encouraged Judith to join Irwin's English department. Now in her mid-70s, Judith was long retired. Farrel and Jessie treated her like a beloved aunt. They considered her family, so by extension, she was part of my family too.

Judith waved her hand saying, "Oh well, that was really nothing...not really a story, just...what are you always calling it, Farrel? *A brush with fame?*" She went on to tell a fascinating story about meeting *Yardbird* at a jazz club in New York in the 1950s. Judith had actually been on the radio in her early career and had a wonderful speaking voice.

Emma asked in awe, "You hung out with...Charlie Parker?"

Farrel was grinning and nodding.

Judith nodded, "He was very nice. Quite amazing music..."

"Hard to top," said Kathryn under her breath, so only I could hear.

"She always is," I whispered back.

"Oh, I forgot something," said Doug heading for the pantry.

Sara caught my eye and asked softly, "Did you get the list back?" She meant the criminal checklist of people who'd gone to Daria's party. Emma was listening for my response.

I shook my head. "It might be there now. I'll call you if there's anything."

Sara and Emma nodded, then Sara went on in a more conversational tone, "Oh, I have to tell you all this thing Emma and I found out about our office window in the back." By now everyone was listening. "If you look down and a little to the right, you can see right into the bedroom window of..." she named a prominent conservative elected official whom she usually referred to as Mayor McCheese, though he wasn't the Mayor. "And, well, you all know, I'm a notorious peeker."

"Really?" said Kathryn with mock curiosity. Several people at the table barked laughter.

Sara just wiggled her eyebrows at Kathryn. I would have kicked her under the table but she was too far away. Sara proceeded to tell an interesting story about a *bedroom meeting* McCheese had had just the night before. It solicited several, "Well, well, well," comments from the fascinated listeners.

Doug came back into the dining room carrying a large platter piled high with Devil Dogs, still in their clear plastic wrappers.

"Carl loved these," said Doug. "He used to bring them to the symphony and hand them out to everyone in the aisle he was sitting in, whether he knew them or not. You're all probably too full, but take some home."

Farrel picked up a package and looked at it. "Was it Devil Dogs or Yankee Doodles in that old commercial? You know, the guy came on...an adult guy talking about when he was a kid. Some kind of New York accent and he said something about...oh geez, when I was a kid I saw that commercial so many times I could recite it with the TV. He'd say, 'I lived across from the playground. I was in every game. They couldn't leave me out.' And then he'd pick up the package and you could see there were three cakes in there and he'd say, 'One for me, one for my brother, ...save the third one for later.' Did you see that commercial, or was it only people who were my age?"

Farrel had an incredible memory for trivial details. Like Nero Wolfe's Archie Goodwin, she could repeat a conversation, usually word for word, and she was always amazed when other people couldn't do it. She looked around the room, but nobody acknowledged that they'd even heard of Devil Dogs, much less some repetitive commercial on TV 30 or 40 years ago.

"It is kind of curious that they're in a three pack. I wonder why?" said Doug shrugging.

Farrel, always loving a trivia quiz, questioned, "What else comes in three packs?"

"Um, I know...tennis balls," I volunteered.

"Fleichman's Yeast," said Jessie, "and it's silly too, because you never ever come across a recipe for three packages of yeast. They're always for two. So then you always have the third pack left over."

"Oh, oh," said Doug, "condoms come in three packs now."

"Why?" asked Cora and Judith in unison. Everyone laughed. Nobody knew the answer.

"Cafalatte comes in three packs," said Kathryn joining in the game. "I think I'm the only one who drinks them at the College. Thank you so much for getting some for me, Jessie. How did you know?"

"You had one in Adamstown. When I called Jessie to say we were coming home," explained Farrel, "I mentioned it to her."

Typical of Jessie to run out minutes before a party just to pick up a special beverage for someone. I was touched that she'd gone to so much trouble for Kathryn. I thought about the leftover Cafalattes in Jessie and Farrell's refrigerator for a long time.

The brunch was winding down. People were thanking Jessie and preparing to leave. Kathryn found her coat and began to gather up the bags and packages she'd brought home from the flea markets. I was impressed by the sheer number of them. I hugged Farrel and Jessie goodbye and so did Kathryn.

I carried half of Kathryn's purchases as we made our careful way down the icy steps of Farrel and Jessie's house and out into the cold gray December afternoon. When we got onto the sidewalk, I started up the street, but Kathryn hesitated. I turned to look at her. She stared into my eyes for a moment. I raised my eyebrows, wondering what was making her pause, then tossed my head in the direction of my loft and smiled. She smiled back and we began walking together.

Chapter 37

"I stopped at my office to pick up the faxed criminal check list from Daria's party. In the loft, as I stored my gun in the safe, Kathryn was singing *Who Knows Where or When* in a beautiful voice.

"Don't stop...that was lovely," I said sincerely.

"I'm out of practice...I need a piano," she said putting her packages on the long dining table and taking off her coat. The skirt of her suit must have been cut on the bias because it fell in graceful folds just below her knees. She still had on the high heels.

"Kathryn, you look lovely in that outfit, you have such terrific legs..."

"Do you think so?" She turned a little to the side and lifted her skirt to mid-thigh. Terrific had suddenly become a puny adjective.

"Stop," I laughed fanning myself with my hand, "you're giving me the vapors. And such a *come hither* look!" I put the rest of the packages on the table and took her in my arms, kissing her deeply.

With her palms on my shoulders, she pushed me back a little and peered intently into my face. I looked back, unsure of what she was thinking. She stroked my cheek with the back of her fingers.

Finally I said gently, "Show me the stuff you bought today. Did you get anything great?"

"That's exactly what Farrel asked. 'Did you get anything great?' Is that what antique dealers always say?"

"Yup."

"I want to wrap these so I can get them in the mail tomorrow. I have some wrapping paper." She let go of me and faced the table.

"I'll get you some tape and scissors. I even have left-handed ones." I went to the tape and a pair of shears.

"Left-handed? Great, that will be a relief," she said putting the shears on the table and sitting down.

"Speaking of relief, did you really walk around the markets for hours in those heels?"

"No, I meant it when I said I was a speed shopper. I had a pair of sneakers. They're comfortable for walking but they didn't go well with this outfit. I changed before I got to the Chapel," she explained. I was glad I didn't have to wear uncomfortable shoes for my job. I made some tea, then came to sit next to her.

She put all of her purchases on the table in a row while she told me whom they'd be for. There was an especially nice 19th century coin silver snuffbox with an ornate etched decoration of a log cabin. The date in the inscription was 1811. Kathryn was going to give it to her father as a pillbox.

She'd found many other beautiful things. She told me about each one. I was impressed by her taste and knowledge.

"Let's see, what else...oh, look at this. She pulled a very small plastic switch-back pin out of a little bag. Switch-backs came in gum machines and candy boxes in the 50s and 60s and showed a picture of one thing when you held it at one angle, then the picture changed when you tilted it. This one, however, was unique.

"Where did you get this! Is this Christine Jorgensen? This must have cost a fortune!" I said looking at the switching male and female figure of Jorgensen, who was the first person in the world to have a "sex-change" operation.

"Yes, isn't it amazing? My brother Kiernan has a collection of gay and transgender historical memorabilia. He has a display case full of significant artifacts in the lobby of his restaurant. Affectionate tin types, those old pictures from the 1880s of gay men holding hands, 1930s documents from the Hayes office, 1950s body building magazines, photographs from some of the first gay rights marches in the 60s. He even has part of a manuscript signed by Kinsey. He has a Life magazine article about Christine Jorgensen."

She took the pin from me and looked at it. "This really is a piece of history. What would it be like to have your life exploited to the point that your gender identity was emblazoned on a Cracker Jack prize? She must have been very brave..."

Kathryn showed me a bronze and sterling decorated box. The ornamentation was very *Mission-Style*. I picked it up for a closer look. "Nice..." I murmured inspecting it closely.

"That's for my brother Ryan."

She'd told me the night before that Ryan was three years older than she and her twin brother Kiernan. She'd confided that Ryan was the most difficult member of her family, other than her mother whom she rarely saw. Ryan was the arguing kind. "It's hard to know what Ryan thinks about my life," she'd said frankly. "One minute he seems fine and says all the right things, the next minute he comes out with something totally negative."

Kathryn was wrapping everything in red and black Art Deco patterned gift paper.

"Oh, here's a present for you. Farrel said you'd like it, I hope she wasn't teasing me. There was a booth in the field that had a pile of new art supplies." She pulled out a bag and handed it to me. "Open it, I hope this isn't too silly." It was a huge set of little cans of bright colored plastic clay. There were twenty-four different colors.

"Wow, these are really neat," I took each of the cans out of the bag, paying careful attention to each different hue. "Um...Kathryn? Did Farrel happen to mention that art supplies...turn me on?" I asked barely able to tear my eyes from all the colors.

"I thought she was kidding."

"She wasn't," I said exhaling heat.

Kathryn snorted softly. She began fitting a few of the wrapped gifts into a larger mailing box as we talked about the brunch. She'd liked the people there. I was glad she'd enjoyed herself.

"And all that food. Do you get to eat at Jessie's table often? What a treat!"

"Yeah, they're very sweet to me. I spend Sundays and most holidays with them...Um, about this morning, did Farrel *quiz* you?"

"Didn't she already make a full report in the Chapel?" said Kathryn distractedly, fitting a small china figurine into a cardboard container.

"She said she likes you and she told me not to do anything to mess this up."

"Good advice," Kathryn said with amusement, "Farrel mentioned she was one of your professors when you were at Baltimore."

"I took woodworking with her."

"Did you have a crush on her?"

"Wouldn't you have?"

Kathryn thought for a moment then chuckled, "When I was in college...you bet I would have."

"Farrel was actually already with Jessie then. So I got over it pretty fast. We became friends. Jessie's always been sweet to me. They were why I came to Fenchester. Did *you* often fall for your teachers?"

Kathryn continued wrapping. She said offhandedly, "I've been in two serious relationships. The last one was with a woman who had been one of my grad school professors."

"Did it last a long time?"

"Five years."

"That's a long time...did you live together?"

"Now and then."

"Would you rather not talk about this?" I asked seriously.

"Hm? Oh, no, it's not that." Kathryn stopped what she was doing and smiled. "We haven't really spoken about the people in our past have we? Well, how can I put this...it was am important relationship to me. I wanted it to work out and I tried for a long time, but it was doomed from the start because we didn't want the same things. I'd probably still be with her, if it had all mattered less to me. When I got this job at Irwin, I realized that my leaving really didn't matter to her. As long as I came back to visit now and then, she was content. I didn't want that kind of relationship."

Kathryn held a small box delicately in her fingers, turning it end over end as she spoke, "And...she let me know she didn't care whether I was faithful to her or not. Which bothered me most of all." There was sadness in her voice. I was immediately angry that Kathryn had been hurt. How could anyone be such a fool as to be indifferent to this fascinating woman?

Kathryn shook her head a little, then said, "There was never any passion... I was so young when it started, I thought it was a normal way for relationships to be...passionless. Maybe it is for some people...but..." Kathryn gave me a searing look and lowered her voice, "I like passion." She went back to working on the presents. She said, "Tell me about the women in *your* past."

"I've had two serious relationships. One that began during graduate school that lasted about two years and another that ended several years ago."

"Do you want to talk about them?"

"No, not really. Sometime, but not right now," I smiled.

She looked at me curiously with her head to the side. After a long moment she said evenly, "I guess it's time for me to go home."

I felt the bottom fall out of my stomach, that sudden sinking feeling. "Why do you say that? Do you want to leave?"

"Maggie, I know you have a lot of work to do. You have this case to work on and you're arguing with yourself about me being here. I can practically see the miniature angel on one shoulder and the devil on the other. Both are whispering in your ears."

I laughed in relief, then said honestly, "I assure you that's not at all what I'm arguing with myself about. My two little voices are both devils trying to figure out the best and fastest way to get you into bed. I do have the case, in fact I have two cases, but if you left, all I'd do is think about you. Don't go...unless you have to."

She turned her chair toward me and said, "What a flatterer you are." She seemed pleased. She went on in a low voice with more than a hint of lust, "Is there anything I can do to help you...work?"

The scent of her made me ache. "What do you have in mind?" I whispered.

She sat back in her chair, aware that her closeness was fueling my desire. "Maybe we should try positive reinforcement. I'll tell you what, how about I offer a little reward? You work on the case and get things sorted out, and when you get some of your work done, I'll..."

"Reward me?"

"Mmm, yes, exactly."

"All I have to do is sort things out and I get a prize for that? What if I figure out something important? What if I solve it? Are there various levels of compensation?"

"There now, you're warming to the idea already. I'd like to watch you work. Do you just sit back and think, like English detectives in murder mysteries, or do you have a different technique? Will my being here cramp your style?"

"I have a non-traditional way of working and I think you watching me will enhance my style, but we're getting away from your incentive program. You should tell me what the reward would be. Don't you think it would fuel my efforts to know what's...at the end of the rainbow?"

She smiled her most devilish half smile and leaned closer. "Turn your head," she murmured, stroking my jaw lightly as I looked away from her. "Hold still."

She used both hands to hold my head steady, one cupping my chin and one at the back of my neck. She brought her lips very close to my ear. I thought she was going to whisper some suggestive method or technique, but she surprised me. She breathed warm air into my ear, then gently bit the lob, sliding her tongue very lightly up to the outer shell. She nibbled, the silkiness of her tongue continuing to tease the surface, then kissed just behind my ear.

"Oh," I moaned involuntarily, breathing in deeply, feeling an electric charge from head to toe. The sensation was so sweet I froze in place, hoping she'd go on and on.

But she pulled back, lightly trailing her fingers down my throat, whispering, "Get to work, you know I'll make it worth your while. I'll spend the whole time planning erotic thrills for you."

"This is supposed to help me concentrate on the case?" I groaned. I turned to her, lifting my hand to touch her face. "I want you even more now."

"Well, my dear, you can't have me now...but if you get some of your work done, I'll make you very glad you did. I have an extensive imagination, I'll think up something very special for you."

Now I was making the purring noise. "Is this the way you get your students to get their work done?"

"No, no. For students, I'm the Ice Queen, remember? Only you are eligible for this reward." I could see a smile twitch at the corners of her mouth, but the look in her eyes was firm. I wasn't going to get any more *attention* from her until I did my duty. So I took several deep breaths and began to concentrate.

Kathryn moved to the other side of the table and went back to wrapping her presents. I pulled my laptop from my bag and booted it up. I fished out the two checklists of the people from Daria's party and put them on the table in front of me. Finally, I took out the drawings I'd done of the baskets with the *suspect eggs* and looked them over carefully.

Kathryn watched me, then asked, "If we talk, will it bother you?

"No. When I was on the police force, we'd always talk cases over with our partners. I miss that."

"What are those?" asked Kathryn glancing at the lists. "Did you say you were working on two cases?"

"I'm also working on the Daria Webster murder. Sara and Emma are the defense counselors. Did you read about it?"

"Daria Webster? That young woman who was assaulted and murdered? It was all over the papers, but the way the police presented it, it sounded as though they had the murderer and the case was closed."

"It's not. Mickey Murphy, the guy they have in custody, is innocent..." I explained some of the situation to Kathryn. "The reporters should have mentioned that the D.A.'s case is built on a confession pressured out of a man with the mental capacity of a child of 8 and the fear quotient and quirky memory of a child of 4," I said emphatically. "He lives in a landscape of pinball machines, peopled with cartoon characters. I think he confessed because he feels guilty for not protecting Daria. He didn't kill her."

"What a terrible thing. That poor young man. He's lucky he has you and Sara and Emma as friends...but the police said he was covered with defense bruises."

"They didn't know Mickey," I explained to Kathryn that playing pinball is a contact sport.

"Do you think Mickey actually saw the murderer? Maybe that was why he was so afraid when the police found him. What does he say about that night?" she asked.

"Very little. Mostly he says, 'I can't remember'." I thought back to that day at the jail. "He said something about Batman, Robin, Chief O'Hara, Spiderman, the Sandman and *the rest of the people*." I began to explain about the cartoon character names as I added shading to the egg basket sketch. Kathryn couldn't help but be amused.

"Storm because your name is Gale? Makes sense," said Kathryn cutting a sheet of wrapping paper. "What are some of the other nicknames?"

I put the sketch aside and started a new one on a fresh piece of paper. It was of the conference room table. As I told Kathryn about She-ra and Wonder Woman, I opened some of the little cans of plastic clay Kathryn had just given me and began to make a series of different colored figures, each representing someone who got a drink in the conference room before the bomb went off. "The names can be very hard to figure out. Mickey calls Farrel Case *Fur Ball*."

Kathryn paused, looking up at the ceiling considering, then smiled, "I've got it! Furball was that *feral* cat on that Tiny Toons show, wasn't he?"

I thought about it, "Yes, yes, of course, very good Kathryn! Ha! I can't wait to tell Farrel." I shook my head. "It's astounding that Mickey even understands what the word *feral* means, but then, he has that Rainman - Savant kind of thing going on..."

"I feel so proud of myself. Honestly, I'd really be insufferable if I actually solved some complex case," said Kathryn with amusement. All the gifts were wrapped. She stood up stretching her arms over her head, which I paused to appreciate. She picked up my sketch of the egg basket.

"These are the suspects in Carl's murder, aren't they? The football-helmeted egg is Leo, the one with the musical note is Jimmy, the one with the cross is...um, Connie?" I nodded as she asked, "and what's drawn on this one? Is it a door?"

"It's a closet door."

"Ah, Rowlina...and the one with the *X*?"

"I think of that one as the unknown factor."

"Bouchet? Miranda? Me?"

"Not you or Bouchet, both of you have alibis. Possibly Miranda, but she seems to have an alibi for the bombing. It's just to remind me that there could be someone else I haven't considered at all."

"I can't imagine any of them as killers. Does the drawing help you look at the case more abstractly?"

"I guess you could say that," I said, working with the clay again, making tiny little bottles.

"I'm going to change my clothes," said Kathryn moving toward the bedroom.

"You mean put on something more *comfortable*? Goody," I chuckled.

"Keep working," she tossed over her shoulder in a husky tone, "remember, you have to earn it."

"Mmmmmm," I groaned. I picked up the lists from Daria's party and read through them quickly. Three bankruptcies and two car repos on the credit sheet. Several DUIs on the criminal sheet. Nothing to call Sara about. The only interesting thing was that Arturo Murcielago had been arrested for loitering during a Union demonstration 15 years before, which meant he was part of either a sit-in or some kind of protest. Of course, just because none of these people had a criminal record for rape or murder, didn't mean that none of them could have killed Daria. In fact, crimes in some states don't show up on these record lists at all. At least I could tell that none of these people had an assault record in Pennsylvania, at least not under these names.

I put the lists aside and began to move the clay figures around the drawing of the table. Kathryn came back, dressed in jeans and a sweater. Her hair was loose; she pushed it back behind her ears as she came to sit next to me again.

"I forgot to ask you," she said, "what happened this morning? Did you talk to Jimmy?"

"Well, kind of." I explained that Jimmy had blown me off at the Music Building, and then ran out of the Chapel later. I also told her about the dust-up between Leo and his ex-wife. I didn't mention the run away piano incident. "What did Connie Robinson say to you in the Chapel?"

"Just that she was sorry she'd made foolish assumptions. She wanted to apologize."

We talked about the service and the exceptional music. "Do you think that's what made Jimmy run out?" I asked.

"You mean because the music was so moving? Maybe, maybe. Do you want me to talk to him?"

"No, I don't," I said more sternly than I'd meant to.

She looked up, responding to my directive tone, "I'm sorry?" she said sharply.

"Oh Kathryn, it's not that I don't want you to help me, or even that I don't think you could do a better job than I could, it's just that..." I hesitated.

Her face softened to concern, "It's that you think Jimmy could be a murderer and you'd rather I didn't mix with that kind of crowd?"

"Yeah," I said simply.

"OK, I'll leave the potential bad guys to you...but I can take care of myself you know." She smiled that suggestive half smile that made my heart leap and my underpants moist. Then she got up and moved to the other side of the table. I laughed out loud.

"Well, I'm supposed to be helping you, not distracting you, so I'll stay over here," she explained, "may I look at this list, or is it confidential?"

"Sure, read it over. It's information anyone can get. Do you know any of those people? Read them to me."

Kathryn read each name off the list. It began with Daria Webster, then listed each person who'd attended the party Daria had given just hours before she was killed.

"Taylor Johnson. Odd, he has no credit rating at all. Oh, I see, he's only 16."

"I met him at the homeless shelter. I guess Daria invited everyone who worked or volunteered there. Connie's on the list, too."

"Yes, Constance P. Robinson. I wonder what the "P" stands for?"

"Knowing her family situation, I wouldn't be surprised with Prudence."

Kathryn read a few more names and then said, "Cedrick S. Druckenmacher, also C. Sheldon Druckenmacher, also Shel Druckenmacher. Miranda's ex-husband?" she asked with raised eyebrows. I nodded. She flipped over the page, then looked at the other list. "He's such a low life, you'd think there'd be more about him. He doesn't seem to have a record though, just a low credit rating, and that could happen to anyone. Hmm, well, he seems to have three low credit ratings, one for each configuration of his name."

"Giving a new meaning to the term creative financing?" I suggested.

Kathryn stood, and began to walk around the room, still looking over one of the lists. She glanced out the window. The late afternoon sun was beginning to set, making the sky redden and casting a pink hue on the house facades. I watched her as she turned and walked back toward the fireplace and bookcases, idly looking over the objects on the shelves. She picked up a big conch shell a friend had given me as a house-warming present. She noticed me watching her. "Shall I light a fire?" she asked nodding at the fireplace. I smiled, she'd been lighting a fire in me all afternoon.

"Is that everyone on the list?" I said trying to sound businesslike.

She scanned the paper while holding the shell in her other hand. "Here's a man whose last name is Murci..."

"Murcielago," I pronounced it for her, "Arturo. He's the Executive Director of the shelter."

"I've never heard that surname before..."

"I was just thinking that it's a strange last name, it means, um...*bat* in Spanish." I vaguely wondered who else might have known that.

Kathryn put down the list and began to run the tip of her finger over the smooth surface of the opening of the shell, tracing the folds sensually, touching it like it was part of a woman's body. Then catching my eye and holding my gaze, she brought the flowing organic shape closer to her mouth.

I thought, If she starts to lick the inside surface, I may faint. Kathryn smiled devilishly, then simply held the object to her ear, listening for the sea. And it was only a seashell, again. Sea...shell.

"Batman and Robin," I said aloud. I bolted out of my chair knocking it over. I grabbed the other list of names, scanning intently.

"Maggie, what is it?" asked Kathryn in alarm.

I held my hand up, frozen in thought. Then scooping up my cell phone I scrolled to Connie Robinson's number. "Connie?" I nearly shouted when she answered, "This is Maggie Gale. You were at the party at Daria Webster's, right? That's what you were talking to me about today wasn't it? You know Mickey Murphy? Yes, he lived next door. Did he call you Robin? And Arturo was...Batman? He called Daria...yes, yes. You heard him? Connie, listen carefully, who was...The Sandman?"

Chapter 38

"Hello, Emma? I tried to reach Sara, but her cell isn't on."

"She's here, we're in my office going over Mickey's case. What is it?" said Emma.

"It's about Mickey. I think I know...come upstairs, now!"

I'd tried to call Sara the minute I'd gotten off the phone with Arturo Murcielago, whom I called for more information after I spoke to Connie. Now I could hear Sara and Emma's footsteps clattering up the stairwell. I turned to look at Kathryn. She sat comfortably in an easy chair near the fireplace, watching my every move with a look of fascination in her eyes. I stared back at her for a moment, exchanging a spark. Most people would have asked me what I'd figured out. It was interesting that Kathryn was content to wait and let things unfold.

I opened the door. Emma and Sara burst into the room and then stood there, not knowing what to say. Emma noticed Kathryn and smirked, "Is this still your first date?"

Kathryn shook her head smiling, "Technically it's our fourth."

"Great," said Sara, "because you know, if people like each other, usually the fourth date is when they..." she glanced toward the bedroom.

"I've heard that," said Emma snickering.

"Will you women stop flirting and pay attention, this is important," I said firmly.

Sara faced me and could see I meant it, "What is it Maggie, go ahead."

"Kathryn can listen to this, can't she?" I asked.

"As long as what you're going to tell us has to do with clearing Mickey. If you're going to say he's guilty, she'll have to leave," said Emma seriously.

"No, this is good," I picked up the lists of partygoers and gave one to Sara and one to Emma. "Look at the names and remember what Mickey told us about the day he was arrested. He said, 'I remember the police guy, Chief O'Hara, and Batman and Robin, and there was The Sandman...he's one of

Spiderman's enemies, he shot me.' We know Mickey assigns cartoon character names to real people..."

"Maggie, Mickey doesn't always make sense," said Sara.

"He doesn't always make sense to rest of us, but I think he always makes sense to himself. He just can't explain it, or sometimes, he can't remember it. But let's figure that these are real people. Chief O'Hara the police Chief of Gotham City is easy, it's Lt. Ed O'Brien. We know he was there on the scene later that night, but earlier at the party, Mickey saw Batman and Robin. Robin is Connie Robinson, she confirmed that on the phone to me a few minutes ago. And Batman, is Arturo Murcielago."

Sara was looking at the list of names, "How could Mickey have known that Murcielago means bat in Spanish?"

"I just called Arturo at the shelter, he said he told Mickey about his name when Mickey was doing volunteer work there one time. That's secondary, though, more importantly, Daria is...was...Spiderman."

"And you know this because?" asked Emma.

"Her name was Webster," I explained simply.

Sara was looking more intently at the lists, "And..." she pressed.

"And Spiderman's arch enemy is The Sandman. I think Mickey dubbed Cedrick Sheldon Druckenmacher, as The Sandman. Oddly," I went on, "he's indirectly part of the Carl Rasmus case, too."

"Druckenmacher?" wondered Emma.

"No, *Shel*. Look at the list, C. Sheldon...get it seashell?"

"Well, that's a possibility, but I don't think it will hold up in court," said Sara with concern.

"But there's more. Druckenmacher was suspected by more than one person of selling drugs at the Shelter. Arturo Murcielago wanted to fire him for it. Daria told Connie she wanted to get rid of the drug dealers at the Shelter. Connie had seen Shel arguing with Daria in an aggressive way. She just confirmed that to me on the phone. Murcielago just told me that Daria asked him for a meeting for the day after the party, to talk about illegal drug issues. Murcielago believes that Daria was going to give him the name of the pusher. He even told the cops about it, but when they arrested Mickey, they stopped worrying about other suspects. So it fits. Druckenmacher had motive, and a history of abuse toward women. He was at the party being aggressive toward Daria, and then there's Mickey's ID of him as the Sandman."

"OK, let's work from there. We can follow this up, but why did Mickey say that the Sandman *shot him*?" asked Emma.

"The water! The water on the floor. It's just a theory but let's say Shel comes back to Daria's apartment after the party when she's cleaning up. He tries to frighten her into giving up the evidence she has about his drug dealing. He bullies women physically, it's his pattern, but Daria won't tell him where the evidence is. He tries to force her by assaulting her, then he chokes her with the rolling pin. He may have gone too far by mistake, or he may have killed her on purpose, knowing that she could identify him to the police."

"But Mickey said he *shot* him?" insisted Sara.

"I'm getting to that...OK, so Shel uses the Lucite rolling pin to choke Daria. When he realizes she's dead, he takes the rolling pin to the sink to wash off his fingerprints. Daria may even have scratched him, there might have been his own blood on the rolling pin. So there Shel is, standing at the sink, washing the pin with the sink hose and Mickey walks in. Shel aims the hose at Mickey and squirts him by pulling the hose trigger. The shock of the water and seeing Daria dead on the floor scares the hell, and all coherent memory, out of Mickey. He runs back to his apartment terrified and hides," I looked at Kathryn, who was nodding.

Kathryn said, "Didn't the papers say that Mickey was found in his underwear? That would explain why. His clothes were wet so he took them off. The police couldn't find any blood or semen stains on Mickey's clothes, because they were only *stained* with water. By the time the police searched Mickey's things, the water had dried."

We all looked at Kathryn, who was leaning forward. She was right on the mark. I said, "Yes, exactly."

Sara whispered, "Brava."

Emma snapped back into lawyer mode, "OK, so, where is Shel Druckenmacher? The police need to get him into custody."

"Luckily," I replied, "the police have him in custody. He's been in jail since yesterday, when he tried to stick me with a flick knife."

Sara turned back to me and said in a louder voice, "Brava!"

"Good," said Emma, "but we have to be sure the police keep him there. I'll call the top guys I know and alert them to this. I think I'll call the DA's office too. Cracking the case this way, by getting a drug dealer, maybe even getting him to cop on other dealers, will be much better PR for them than convicting poor defenseless Mickey Murphy. And now that they'll have a real suspect, they'll be more likely to link the DNA connections."

Sara said, "I'll go to the jail and talk with Mickey. If I take a picture of Shel and he identifies him as the Sandman, we'll be clear to move ahead. Mickey may be able to tell us something more. I'll talk to Arturo Murcielago in person; he may be able to tell me what kind of evidence Daria might have had to prove Shel was dealing. It could still be in Daria's things, maybe in her office."

Minutes later Sara and Emma were off tying the loose ends of Mickey's defense together and I was alone again with Kathryn.

"Aren't you sexy when you're being a detective?" she said putting an arm around my waist.

"You're not so bad yourself. You really impressed Sara and Emma, I loved that."

"It was so intense, when everything was clicking into place, so satisfying, almost physical. Is it always that way?"

"Well, it can be, but there are downsides. All sorts of them, and while you're working you constantly wonder, *What if I can't figure this out.*"

"But you did figure it out, and it looks like Mickey will get out of jail, and probably the real killer will be caught. You did that. It was exciting. I'm very impressed," she held me closer, my breathing began to deepen.

"Are you? That sounds promising. So do I...get a reward? Or are you going to punish me for all the naughty situations I got you into this week?"

"Hmm, reward I think...any special requests?" asked Kathryn, drawing her fingers down my throat and along my collarbone.

"I remember some mention of erotic thrills?"

She laughed. "Give me a few minutes, I'll call you when...I'm ready."

I watched her disappear through the door. I was beginning to crave her calling me to the bedroom. Waiting for her voice built heat in me that could have been measured in BTUs, and frankly the adrenalin that pumped up from figuring out part of Mickey's case had stoked my fires. I sat still, floating in the sweet sea of anticipation.

"Maggie." Just that one word, but her voice held the promise of all things sensual. I heard the shower running. On the bed was a large note that said, "Undress and join me." I realized I was breathing like a marathon runner.

I left my clothes in a pile and opened the bathroom door. Steam billowed, clouding the room. I moved to the shower door, peering into the large tiled enclosure. Kathryn stood under the wide circular showerhead, a torrent of hot rain coursing over her beautiful body. She tilted her head up, letting the water stream over her face, washing down her torso in swirling rivers.

She felt my presence, shook the water from her eyes with a toss of her head and held out her hand to me. In a low sultry voice she said, "Come hither."

She drew me into her arms, the water flowed and eddied between our bodies. I ran my lips along her throat, drinking in the wet taste of her skin. She held my hand to her mouth, gently sucking the ends of my fingers.

"Oh, Kathryn," I murmured as my desire grew.

"Oh, yes," she answered. She pressed the shampoo dispenser on the shelf and began to massage the liquid soap over me in fluid strokes, rubbing it slowly over my breasts, then teasingly soaping between my legs. "Sit down," she said, pressing me back onto the tile bench built into the corner of the large stall.

"This has been quite a reward," I smiled. "I have some wonderful massage oil that's perfect after a shower."

"There's more to this shower," she said unhooking the handheld nozzle and straightening its hose. "You need to be...*rinsed* off." Before I could mention that the hose wasn't working, she twisted its dial and a gentle gush of warm water spilled out of a dozen holes at its head.

"I fixed it," she explained.

"Your talents are boundless," I said as she trained the tickling stream over me, rinsing the suds off my shoulders.

"This unit has its own boundless talents," she said as she twisted the dial again. A pulsating cht - cht - cht, of water throbbed out of the head. "Relax, Maggie, you'll enjoy this."

She spread my knees apart. Before I could react, she aimed the water at the area just below my navel, then let the stream drop slowly toward a more sensitive place. She pushed against my thighs, urging me open fully, then ran the pulsing current to its mark.

I'd never felt anything like it, hard, vibrating, almost painful, relentless stimulation, narrowly focused just where I needed it. I squirmed and shifted as she pressed the nozzle against me and dialed the control to speed the pulse. I thrust my head back into the tile corner, bracing myself for the volcanic climax that was erupting in my body.

She dialed the pulse to slow, then drew the showerhead away as I regained my senses. She rubbed a soapy hand slowly between my legs easing my shuddering gasps. I leaned my head back soothed by her touch, but her fingers explored, finding the faint beginnings of another orgasm. She began teasing it to the surface, still holding me wide open.

Sooner than I could have imaged possible, I was ready again. This time she held the showerhead in place beginning with a very gentle stream. She took her time dialing it to a pounding pulse, while she worked on other sensitive areas with her free hand. As I felt the waves of sensation flow through me, the sound I made when I came echoed off the tile walls like an explosion.

After a few minutes of incoherent bliss I realized that while my need for her had been satisfied, I wanted her even more.

"It's time for part two of this adventure, don't you think," I said when I could finally speak, then pulling her to me I added, "you must be so ready for this." She nodded slightly, her half smile bewitchingly inviting.

I moved her around and guided her onto the corner bench. I flipped the metal hose, the showerhead slid into my grasp. Kneeling before her, I lifted one of her legs so the inside of her knee rested on my shoulder.

Dialing the showerhead to hard pulse with my thumb, I reached with my free hand to make her ready. Teasing her, I let the jet of water play against the inner surfaces of her thighs, but her fingers twisting unconsciously in my hair let me know she couldn't wait any longer. Holding her firmly, I did what she'd done to me. She began to climax almost immediately, gasping and arching as I pressed the spray closer.

"There, yes," she moaned, then voicing a cry of complete release, she finally slipped off the bench into my arms, ravenously kissing me as waves of pleasure continued to make her tremble.

Druckenmacher had used a stream of water to scare Mickey and wash away evidence after a horrible murder. We'd used a stream of water to make love. Everything can seem sordid if you let it. Or, you can celebrate the simplicity of joy by firmly separating it from cruelty. After all, what's more life-affirming than the intimate sharing of sexual love?

****

We lay in the bed under the covers, dry now, but still a little pruney, even after the body oil. "That was fun," sighed Kathryn.

"That was an understatement," I said languidly. "Did I mention that there's a security camera in the shower?"

"Well, I hope it caught everything."

"Would it spoil the moment to say I'm rabidly hungry?"

"For more sex?" asked Kathryn lifting her head from my shoulder.

"For pizza."

"Me too! It's still early, I'll order it," said Kathryn finding her cell phone and calling for a delivery, as she sat on the edge of the bed. "What's this bruise?" said Kathryn touching the top of my hip, just to the left of my navel, "Did I do that to you?"

I looked down at the half-dollar-sized black and blue bruise. "Huh, I don't know, maybe I bumped myself on the chinning bar. It doesn't hurt though," I was fibbing, it was painfully tender, but I didn't want to seem like a wuss to my girlfriend.

We pulled on clothes. A few minutes later, the bell rang and Kathryn buzzed the delivery person up. I recognized Donna the regular delivery woman carrying the pizza box. She took a long look at me, eyeing my bare feet, then said something I didn't catch as Kathryn was paying her.

I filled wine glasses and got a stack of napkins. We sat in front of the fireplace and each took a piece of the pie.

"What did Donna say to you?" I asked.

"Just two words."

"Let me guess...'Nice catch?' or maybe...'Hot babe?'"

"Nope, she said, 'Bout time!'" said Kathryn laughing.

"Well, I guess that's that," I said laughing along. "News has traveled from Thailand to Mexico to Italy in just two days."

"And then there's the Dakota," said Kathryn starting another piece.

"Kathryn, I've had more *satisfaction* with you in three days than I've had in the last...ten years all put together. You're wonderful. Will it be like this every night?"

"Sure..." she yawned, "every single night...from now on. Are you up to it?"

"I'm game if you are," I said cheerfully. "Shall we do the whole thing over again right now?"

She looked up at me in amazement, then saw I was smiling devilishly.

She said, "If you really want to do it all again, I'll accommodate you to the best of my ability, but in all earnestness, right now I'd like to just fall asleep in your arms...I have to admit...I'm knackered." Kathryn snuggled up to me, sighing with contentment. I stroked her hair and kissed her cheek.

"Me too, as soon as I finish another piece of pizza," I yawned.

In bed soon after, we both drifted off easily. It was warm and relaxing at first. There's nothing like great sex to produce an overwhelming sense of triumphant, self-assured, well-being that eases into rapturous sleep. Good pizza and wine didn't hurt either. I floated in nirvana for what seemed like a long time...but then a dam burst. Something that had been churning in a distant corner of my mind all day began to grow into a nagging idea just out of my reach. Suddenly the dream parade began.

The Dream:

I was at a door trying to turn the knob, but the door

wouldn't open. Walking down a hall behind me was a man with a white cane. He was holding a can of elbow pasta. When I looked up at his face he had no features other than a mouth full of macaroni that was flooding out like vomit.

I ran down the stairs, bumping into Rowlina Roth-Holtzmann. She had a live fox draped over her head with its tail curved around her neck. The fox looked rabid, it was gnawing her just above her collar, causing bright red blood to flow over her shoulders. I screamed, but no sound came out.

Jimmy Harmon raised his hand to slap me, but a disembodied arm held him back. Behind it, a door opened and three men stepped into the room. One was Max Bouchet in a wet, sooty pinstripe suit. One was Leo Getty wearing a bumpy purple robe and a football helmet, and the third was Skylar Carvelle with a bloody glass paperweight stuck in his head.

The three men were joined by Jimmy Harmon. Each man removed something from his pocket and put it in a pile on a desk. The pile became a small silver gun, which burst into flames. Daniel Cohen appeared with a bucket of water and doused it out. Leo Getty looked over his shoulder at the wall behind him where empty picture frames hung. He took one off the wall, Christine Jorgensen took it from him and looked at it closely, though there was nothing in it.

Miranda Juarez stood one step behind Bouchet. She threw a wad of paper money over her shoulder in a perfect arc behind. Shel Druckenmacher leaned through a door, he was covered with sand. He caught the money with a bloody hand, then darted back out of view.

Jimmy Harmon pulled some sheet music out of his sleeve and tried to walk away with it. Behind him was Carl Rasmus again, with a cane and dark glasses. Next to Carl was Kathryn. Carl grabbed the music from Jimmy as Kathryn watched. Jimmy grabbed it back.

A phone rang. Carl tried to answer it but his mouth was still full of macaroni. He spat it out on the desk. It landed in a disgusting mass on a computer keyboard. He answered the phone. Carl walked to the window and fell out. Kathryn looked after him with tears in her eyes.

Connie Robinson came in running. She picked up

something large that became a huge stack of dishes. A piano sped by her through some French windows, crashing to the ground. I looked out and saw a blind man's body crumpled on the sidewalk in a fetal position, illuminated by a doorway light, which blinked once and fizzled out.

Now Connie was holding a package of three Devil Dogs. She took one out of the pack, but another appeared in its place. It happened over and over, then morphed into a can of tennis balls. She handed the can to Kathryn who dropped it because it had grown into a grotesquely large package of Cafalatte bottles. The three bottles falling to the floor sounded like a chunk of cement hitting the sidewalk.

Kathryn put her hand to her neck, blood seeped through her fingers running down both shoulders. I tried to go to her but I couldn't move my feet. Kathryn didn't seem concerned about herself. She was looking at my stomach with profound fear. I looked down. There, stuck in my side, was a knife just above my left hip. The bloodless wound seemed huge. I grasped the handle of the knife and pulled it out. It turned into a small gun. The disembodied hand took it from me and aimed it at Kathryn. I tried to grab it back but I couldn't move fast enough. The gun went off. I screamed.

I bolted upright in bed, dripping with sweat. Kathryn sat up and put a protective arm around me.

"Maggie, what is it?"

I turned and carefully touched her neck. It was smooth and porcelain white. The image of her bleeding faded from my mind. I held up my hand to stop her from speaking. Think...I shook my head to make the pieces fall into place faster, but they were taking their own sweet time. Suddenly, I got a hold of one important piece that slapped me in the face and finished one section of the puzzle.

Carl with pasta in his mouth. Macaroni...macaroni's can, "Oh shit, of course," I said out loud.

I jumped out of bed and ran to get Carl's laptop computer. I brought it back into the bedroom and booted it up. I opened the file with all Carl's programs in it. I selected the Voice Transcription System program, and opened the Macro files. I scanned down the list.

"Look, look," I said to Kathryn, turning the screen toward her and pointing.

"Oh my God," she said staring at the screen. She turned to look at me; her eyes were filled with angry tears. "Who was it? Damn it, who did it?"

"I don't know, um...Connie and Miranda are long shots."

"So...that leaves Jimmy, Leo and Rowlina as those most likely?" she pondered, "Which one?"

I didn't say anything. I wasn't sure. There was something kicking a part of my brain. I knew I had the information to figure this out, but I couldn't fit the puzzle together yet. The solution was on its way though, and for some reason it scared the shit out of me.

"Maggie, you think it was Jimmy don't you?"

I didn't answer, instead I said, "It's time to push the envelope."

I needed to call Bouchet. I got out of bed and went to get dressed. It was 2 :00 AM, but I didn't care. I had firm evidence that Carl was murdered and I needed to tweak the killer out into the light of day. I was working on a plan to make that happen and Bouchet was going to have to play a big part. I was trying to figure out the rest of the dream too, but like so many dreams that fade into dawn, the images were drifting away.

Bouchet was groggy when he answered, but snapped to alertness when I told him I'd found the key to Carl's suicide note. As I was talking to him I noticed that Kathryn had drawn on her robe and was pacing around the bedroom. She seemed racked with emotion. An assortment of expressions crossed her face. Even after I'd disconnected with Bouchet, I watched her. She seemed both enraged and deeply confused.

"Kathryn?"

She stopped abruptly and turned and sat on the bed.

"Maggie, you're talking about prodding a rattlesnake in a shallow hole. You're not even sure who it is. What are you going to do? How can you be safe? This person is a killer with a gun..."

"Kathryn," I began. This was just what I'd been talking about earlier in the evening. When the case was abstract to her, it could be simply exciting, but now that all the players were people she knew.

"No, don't say anything," she said standing up, beginning to pace again, "I have to figure out exactly how I feel about this."

I'd been dealing with crime for more than 15 years. I'd had time to grow a thick skin, to get used to it, but this was all new to Kathryn. Kathryn might not be able to handle this.

****

On my way to Bouchet's house, I was still worrying about the effect this was all having on Kathryn. When I was leaving she'd agreed that we'd talk about it later, but she seemed so distracted. Maybe we would talk about it all night. Or maybe, when I got home...she'd be gone. The possibility squeezed my chest and brought tears to my eyes. I realized at that moment, I was falling in love with Dr. Kathryn Anthony and that if I lost her, it would break my heart.

Chapter 39

It was Monday morning. I was tired but keenly alert. The adrenalin that pumps through cops' veins when they're on the hunt, was coursing through mine. Bouchet and I had worked out a plan. It was fairly simple. He'd agreed to call an emergency meeting of the Tenure Committee, complete with Bart Edgar, Miranda Juarez and Connie Robinson at 10:00 AM. He was to insist. Everybody had to be there, except Georgia Smith who was still in the hospital.

The suspects would be followed after the meeting by the campus security team. I really wanted to get Fenchester Security to give me a few operatives to handle the tails, but there wasn't time to get them in place. I'd have to use Bouchet's people.

I was wearing a bulletproof vest. Really, I was. One of those ultra light Kevlar ones. Since the killer only had a 22mm, the vest would stop it...but of course, the bullet would have to hit me in the vest. I tried not to think about that too hard. I also tried not to think about Kathryn's reaction to the whole thing. She hadn't minced words. She'd said flatly that it was a stupid plan. She had a point. It certainly was a snake prodder.

She and I rode up in the Administration Building elevator together. Leo Getty, Jimmy Harmon, and Rowlina Roth-Holtzmann were all in the elevator with us.

Rowlina touched Kathryn's arm, "I must speak to you sometime very soon," she whispered desperately. Kathryn nodded to her.

Kathryn paid little attention to me but she was deeply concerned about Jimmy. She desperately wanted to believe he was not the killer. She tried in vain to chat with him about Carl's music at the service, hoping to hear innocence in his voice. He just grunted. Leo affably mentioned a minor glitch in his grant application. Kathryn said generously "Leo, I know all about the whole situation. I'll get to you later today. I have to..."

The elevator doors opened. Max Bouchet, who was standing in the hallway, interrupted Kathryn and asked her to come into his office. I went directly to the small conference room with Carl's laptop under my arm and sat near the door.

The small conference room was about half the size of the large conference room down the hall, which was still under restoration. It had a good-sized table with about ten chairs around it. No drinks this time.

Dan Cohen was already seated at the table. He smiled and nodded at me. Jimmy Harmon came in and sat down. He placed a stack of papers on the table and stared blankly at them. Rowlina Roth-Holtzmann found a chair at the far end of the room and began nervously fidgeting with a note pad.

Bart Edgar was already seated. He began to nod his head, his shaggy blond hair flying in all directions. He said, "I'm, ah, not really here," and then giggled. I took that to mean that he was still officially out on leave. He held his bandaged hand in the air in the most conspicuous way possible. In fact, he kept bumping his head into it, as though he had no idea it was there. Maybe now would be a good time to grab him around the neck and squeeze until he told me what happened right before the bomb went off. I decided to do that after the meeting, unless I had a better idea.

Leo Getty came in, no longer bluff and personable. He said nothing to anyone. He hefted his briefcase on the table and sat down, looking blankly around the room. If Jimmy, Leo and Rowlina were indeed the prime suspects, they sure as hell were playing their parts to the hilt. These were three people who couldn't have looked more guilty.

Amanda Knightbridge glided in with an air of quiet celebration. When she looked directly at me, her expression of pleasant expectation turned to concern. She opened her mouth to say something to me, but I shook my head slightly at her. Her face closed up. Connie Robinson and Miranda Juarez came in and sat down. Connie looked nervous, but not nearly as much as she had when I'd seen her on Friday. Compared to most of the rest of the people around the table, she was positively serene. Miranda was totally inscrutable. Having regained her composure after our little talk, she seemed even more emotionless than ever, but tightly wound.

Max Bouchet walked directly to me with a worried face. He leaned over to whisper something in my ear, amazingly for once, modulating his voice so the others could not hear.

Then he said in a clear voice, "I've received a very serious email I think you should see." He put a hard copy of it in front of me. In the subject line was my name and business title. The sender line said:
K.Anthony@Irwin.edu

The text said:

To: President Max Bouchet
From: Kathryn Anthony Ph.D
Dear President Bouchet,

It is a concern to me that the current investigation into the death of Carl Rasmus, is being conducted by Maggie Gale Investigations. While I am sure that Miss Gale is fully capable of investigating minor matters for the college, situations that are like this are too serious and dangerous to be handled by her alone.

As evidence of that, I call to your attention to Miss Gale's risky effort in the fire last Tuesday. Everyone who recalls her efforts to rescue Bart Edgar while he was laying on the floor in the burning conference room, must admit that her attempts, while brave, were needlessly dangerous.

Please reconsider your employment of Miss Gale. Those are my feelings, I do not want to further discuss them with you .

I stared at the note, rereading parts. I looked at everyone else at the table, who were all looking at me. Then spun to Bouchet who was still standing by me.

"Where is she?" I said with undisguised fury.

"Out there, but I don't think..." said Bouchet glancing over his shoulder toward the reception area toward Kathryn, who was standing there with her coat on. Before Bouchet could finish, I was on my feet striding out the door.

Amanda Knightbridge, in an attitude of deep concern, watched my purposeful approach to Kathryn. Dr. Knightbridge craned her neck when I stepped into her sight line, blocking her view. I held the email hard copy in one hand. Dr. Knightbridge could see Kathryn taking it from me as I raised my voice in anger.

Amanda Knightbridge heard me say to Kathryn, "What the hell is this? What do you mean by this?"

Everyone in the small conference room was listening now. They heard Kathryn murmur an answer. She took a step toward the stairwell but I got in front of her, blocking her path. She was shaking her head at me.

Kathryn's severe voice ripped back, "As a matter of fact this is the way I feel and I'm not at all sorry you've seen this. You don't have any right to question my motives. You're being stupidly rude. You're making a mistake and because of it you're putting yourself and the college at risk! I can't support it and I certainly can't support the way you're acting now!"

Amanda heard me respond to Kathryn, "Who do you think you are? You have no right to criticize me or my work at all..." My voice dropped to a lower tone so that the people in the conference room couldn't make out my words, but my expression and gestures conveyed my ire. I was furious.

Kathryn's fury was equal to mine. She hauled off and slapped me across the face. She pushed past me and made for the stairs at top speed. I didn't even bother to look after her. I unconsciously lifted my hand to my face. It hurt like hell, in many more ways than one. I could have cried, but I was too pissed off. I stormed back into the conference room.

Amanda Knightbridge was on her feet, staring at me in horror. She scanned my eyes. I looked fiercely back at her and she sat down.

"President Bouchet, don't bother to call this meeting to order. I'll do it," I said in an angry authoritative voice, "I was hired to investigate Carl Rasmus's murder..." There was a gasp around the table, like my role was a surprise. For Christ sake, the place had been bombed. Skylar Carvelle had been whacked to death in the comfort of his own home, but these people still insisted on hiding in their ivory towers. Even Bouchet had thought it was a game. And now all this with Kathryn! It was too much. I was at the edge.

"Yes, it was murder..." I said savagely. I opened Carl's laptop. The screen lit up. "This laptop has duplicates of Carl's desk top programs and files. I copied them several days ago."

I stopped to survey the room. I pulled Carl's high sensitivity microphone out of my shoulder bag. One end was already plugged into the laptop. I went on in a more controlled voice, "Carl had a program that allowed him to speak text into the computer. It also read text back to him. I've entered my voice into the program so it can understand me as well. The program also has a *macro function*, which allows the user to say a keyword that cues the program to write a designated set of lines." I turned Carl's laptop so it faced everyone in the room.

I picked up the mic and flipped on the switch. I took my cell phone out of my pocket, pressing a button that made it ring. Holding it to my ear, I looked around at everyone and then said clearly, "Carl Rasmus." Immediately words began to appear on the laptop screen. They didn't stop until the whole text of Carl's suicide note appeared.

The effect on the room was formidable. I tried to view everybody's reactions, but Jimmy Harmon pushed himself up and stumbled out of the room. I grabbed Kathryn's email and followed him out.

Jimmy ran down the stairs and was going top speed to the music building. I ran after him. I saw him haul the door to the music building open and sprint up the stairs. He didn't know I was behind him.

He rushed to Carl's office door, grabbing the padlock in his hand, he yanked on it fruitlessly. He pounded the door with his fist and kicked it. Finally, he sank to the floor, sobbing.

"Jimmy, get off the floor and get a hold of yourself," I yelled at the top of my lungs. "Listen to me and answer...what's the deal on the music Carl gave you to show to your agent?"

Jimmy twisted his body around so that his back was against the door and his legs were straight out in front of him. When he raised his head, he was smiling. He hadn't been sobbing, he'd been laughing. It was damn creepy.

"Don't fuck with me Jimmy," I yelled grabbing him by the shirt collar. He was staring at me, his eyes bright. I said fiercely, "You're acting like a rabid squirrel, stop being an asshole and answer me. What the hell is going on? This isn't just because you're on some sinus medication." I shook him by the collar, his head snapped back and forth. "Did you push Carl off the balcony...is that what it is?"

"What! No, no, I didn't, I didn't. I'd never do anything like that. Don't you see, it *wasn't* my fault. All along, I thought...I thought he killed himself because of what I'd done..."

"What did you do!?! I yelled.

"I took his song...and other tunes...and I showed them to my agent and he liked them and said he'd get them published. But that morning, the morning when Carl died...when he got killed, I told him that my agent said his stuff was crap. I was such an asshole. I don't know why, but I just didn't want to admit Carl was good, but he was, everybody loved his stuff. People who are totally hard nose were saying it was the best work ever. I was jealous. I was going to tell him... but, well...he died. I thought he killed himself because I told him ... because he thought everyone was against him."

"You stole his work?" I asked incredulously.

"Huh? Oh no, it wasn't like that. His name was on it. It's not like I told people it was mine. It's just that I wanted it to fail...and when it didn't, I told him it had. I'd have to tell him that all his stuff was going to be published...but I was just so annoyed and I guess insecure... paranoid...and then when he died...I thought he'd done it because of what I'd said. It was so cruel... "

I understood this. I'm an artist. I've lived and worked around artistic types for years. People whose creative work meant everything to them...and who felt the pain and insecurity of rejection to their very soul. While I couldn't condone, in a million years, the mean trick Jimmy had played on Carl...I knew of a dozen parallel instances and clearly Jimmy's meds had added to his insecurity and paranoia.

"Jimmy, why did you run out of the meeting and come here?"

"Because it must have *all* been fake, not just this one note. All those emails. They must have all been sent by someone else...by the person who put the note on his computer! I came over here, because I wanted to see... there must be some trace of the person who did it!"

"Jimmy, read this." I thrust out the copy of the email Bouchet had shown me earlier. I was buying Jimmy's story, most of it rang true, but I had to be sure. The killer had sent me a tool. Now, I had a test for Jimmy. If he passed, then he was in the clear.

Jimmy took the paper and glanced at it.

"No read it...carefully, right now," I insisted.

He looked at it more seriously. "It's from Kathryn? This is the thing Bouchet showed you today? No wonder you were pissed." He read it over again..."Do you really think she wrote it?" He asked trying to hand the paper back to me.

"Why do you say that?" I asked curiously.

"Because..." he flipped the paper back and read some of it again, "...because Kathryn's an English teacher. I've never heard her make a grammatical error, she'd certainly never write one..."

"So?"

"Well...*laying on the floor*...it's incorrect...she'd never," his head snapped up, "oh shit, you think the killer wrote this?"

He was right, Kathryn didn't write the note. The person who wrote it didn't know the difference between lie and lay. The note was from the killer and the killer wasn't Jimmy.

I got out my keys and unlocked the door to Carl's office. I thought maybe Jimmy could find a clue in Carl's computer system, but there was something else happening in my brain. Jimmy struggled to his feet. He bumped against me. The contact irritated the bruise on my hip. What was happening in my brain now felt like the beginnings of a tsunami, but it hadn't hit the shore yet.

I turned on the light. Carl's office was just as I'd left it. No papers and tons of equipment. I idly opened some of the drawers. The little stash of Devil Dog 3-packs was still in place. I looked at them. Devil dogs had been in my dream...I thought about my dream. I froze. Jimmy was watching me. I flashed on the wound in my side in the dream. I touched the top of my hip. It hurt. Rowlina...the fox.. the red blood...The Tsunami crashed on the beach.

"Oh shit! Oh no!" I gasped. I grabbed my cell phone and frantically hit Kathryn's office number. She picked up on the third ring.

"Kathryn, this is an emergency..." I said.

"I'm sorry," she said cutting me off shortly, "I can't speak to you now. I'm busy with someone in my office." She hung up.

Chapter 40

"Shit, shit," I gasped. Fear clutched my stomach. I scrolled to Amanda Knightbridge's office number and punched it in.

"What is it, what's wrong?" yelled Jimmy seeing the terrified look on my face.

"It's Kathryn, there's something wrong in her office."

"Why? Just because she won't talk to you? No offense but you had a pretty big argument with her today."

"It was a sham. We were acting. I told her to slap me. I knew the email was a fake..." Puzzle pieces crashed into position like ice floes slamming together at a dam. "I know who the killer is, and he's been trying to kill Kathryn all along." Articulating the last part made my heart ache physically, but sharpened my senses.

Amanda Knightbridge's secretary answered. I told her to put me through to Dr. Knightbridge immediately.

When Amanda Knightbridge came on the line I said rapidly, "This is Maggie Gale. This is urgent, Dr. Knightbridge. I need you to go to the second floor of your building and see if you can see into Kathryn's office window...now!"

Thank the gods that Amanda Knightbridge could grasp the concept of *urgency*. She hurried up the stairs carrying the phone with her. In a minute she was out of breath, but at the second floor window.

"What am I looking for Ms. Gale?"

"Leo Getty...is Leo Getty in her office with her?"

Jimmy said "Leo!?!" but Amanda Knightbridge said nothing. She was looking.

"There is someone...I can see Kathryn's back...oh thank you Millie...I have some binoculars, just a minute...yes, yes, it's Leo Getty with her."

"Keep watching them Dr. Knightbridge. I'm on my way there."

"Shall I arrange to call the police?"

"No, yes...um..." I said as I ran down the stairs with Jimmy hot on my heels. "Call Lt. Ed O'Brien. Tell him that there is a hostage situation, use my name. Tell him that everything must be calm and quiet. A swarm of sirens will make Leo...Oh God," I said in anguish.

"I understand, I will communicate your directions and concern. I will also call Max Bouchet, and tell him to keep the security people at bay, and I will stay on the line with you." She was a calm spot in the storm but I wasn't paying much attention to her. I was running faster than I ever had in my life.

Why hadn't I seen it before? It was all so clear now. Leo Getty was the killer and he'd already tired to kill Kathryn twice. There was nothing to stop him from trying again. And this time he was in her office, face to face with her and probably holding a gun.

I'm not a religious person, but I found myself trying to make a deal with unknown powers: Please don't let him kill her...Please don't let anything happen to her...Please don't take her from me.

When I got to the door of the Language Arts Building I slowed and opened it quietly. When it squeaked, I winced. Leo was obviously nuttier than squirrel crap, but that didn't make him any less dangerous. He was in her office, and I had to stop him.

When Jimmy and I got to the fire door at the top of the stairs, I spoke to Amanda Knightbridge again as softly as possible, trying to keep the edge of desperation out of my voice.

"Have you seen anything else? Is she still all right?"

"Ms. Gale, get a hold of yourself...you must have all your wits."

Amanda was right, I sounded hysterical...I needed to control myself.

"Yes," I said in a calmer voice into the phone, I took a deep breath, "What do you see?"

"They are talking...she is behind her desk with her back to the window. Leo is sitting across from her. I'm going to tell you this to let you know his state of mind, but you must not overreact, do you understand?"

"What?"

"Her just hit her. It was a backhand slap, but she seems to be all right. She has her hand to her face, but they are still talking."

He hit Kathryn. I filed that away but processed the implications. I'd trained in hostage negotiations. Hitting was bad, but on the other hand, he had a gun, he could have shot her.

"Can you see a gun? Is Leo holding a gun?"

"I believe he has a shiny metal object in his right hand. It could be a gun. He does not seem to have it directly trained on her."

I motioned for Jimmy to follow me, and opened the door to the hallway. It creaked as we slipped in, but not very loud. At the first deserted office door we passed, I took out the set of passkeys Bouchet had given me and tried them in the lock. I found the passkey that opened these doors. All the other keys were the wrong shape or size.

We padded down the hall, making no noise. I cupped my hands to Jimmy's ear and whispered, "Put the key in the knob and turn it to the right. I'll kick the door open and rush in." I reached in my shoulder holster and took out my gun, removed the safety, moved a shell into the chamber and held it ready.

"But...but...should we wait for the cops? If you rush in, he could shoot," whispered Jimmy back into my ear.

"He's too hinky, Jimmy. He's here to kill her. We're on borrowed time as it is."

We could hear Leo ranting things like, "You're the one...bitch...the world's better off...you should all be dead..."

I put the key in the lock myself indicating that Jimmy should turn it.

This was it. I motioned for Jimmy to stand clear. Jimmy reached over and turned the knob. I kicked with all my might, flying low into the room, aiming my gun at Leo. He'd turned his gun on me and was beginning to squeeze off a shot, but Kathryn reached over her shoulder, grabbed the bronze figure on the shelf and roundhoused Leo in the head. Leo's shot hit the bookcase five feet above me. He was knocked to the floor but he still had the gun in his hand, and he was swinging it around in an arc that would end at Kathryn. I threw myself at his arm knocking the gun spinning over his head. It slid into the far corner as Leo scrambled to get it. I right hooked him, which isn't easy to do when you're on the floor, but it did its job.

Instantly cops were pouring into the room. I rolled out of the way and they took charge of Leo, jumping on him, pressing him to the floor and cuffing his hands behind his back. I scrambled to my feet. Kathryn was standing behind her desk, still with the bronze statue in her hand, staring at what was going on. I holstered my gun and made my way around the desk to her, gently taking the statue from her and leaving it on her desk. I circled my arm around her waist and guided her into the hall.

Bouchet was running toward us. He was shouting, "What happened, what happened?"

I just shook my head and he had the good grace to leave us alone. Kathryn's cheek was red where Leo had hit her, which made me sad and sorry, but way glad I'd punched him in about the same spot.

"He had a gun. I hit him with the statue," sputtered Kathryn. Her eyes rolled back, her knees gave way and we sank down to the floor together.

She was conscious, just dazed. We sat there leaning against the hallway wall, me holding her and stroking her hair, her arms tightly around me. After a few moments, Amanda Knightbridge was speaking to us in a calm but commanding tone.

"Kathryn, Maggie...listen to me now," we both turned to her voice, "it's time to go. President Bouchet will take care of the rest of this." She looked at me intently... "The press is coming. It would be best if..." she glanced at Kathryn who was really quite pale, "take her home now, Maggie." Amanda Knightbridge fixed me with the kind of stare that birds of prey use to compel their victims. In this case, it simply made me take Kathryn and go.

****

During the short drive to the loft Kathryn was talking at full throttle. Words spilled out of her like a Texas livestock auctioneer two fisting espressos. Everything made sense, but she was jumping from topic to topic at warp speed. I'd seen this kind of adrenalin rush before. It happens to rookie cops after their first car chase or stand off. I'd had it to a lesser degree after the fire.

Kathryn said that after she'd left the administration building she went directly to her office. She'd felt horrible after hitting me, even though I'd insisted in a whisper that she must.

She paused for the sixth time in the story to say, "I'm so sorry, does it hurt? I'm so sorry."

I gently told her yet again that she should stop worrying about it. I didn't mention it had hurt like heck, because it didn't matter. I was so proud of her. I'd known at once that Kathryn hadn't written the email. She and Bouchet had already conferred about it in his office. When I stepped up to her, she fell into the necessary role immediately. It was complicated. She'd had to be angry at what I was saying without admitting she'd written the text, because the killer would suspect her if she pretended she had. She'd managed splendidly. My part was easy. It wasn't hard for me to act annoyed, I was violently angry at the killer for using Kathryn in this way, but I hadn't understood that the killer was actually after Kathryn. Not at that moment anyway. Not consciously.

Kathryn said she'd been behind her desk when her office door suddenly opened and Getty walked in. She was surprised, since she thought the door had been locked. It turned out that Getty, being the Dean of Students, had kept passkeys to the entire campus for years.

"In the first seconds I wasn't too concerned to see Leo. I'd mentioned I needed to talk to him when I'd seen him in the elevator. I certainly didn't think he'd come there to kill me..." said Kathryn in a way that would have seemed casual if she hadn't been talking at 45 rpm in a voice an octave higher than usual. "But then I saw the gun!" she sped on, "I thought there was supposed to be security following Leo?"

We found out later that the security guard Bouchet had assigned to tail Getty had lost him in the first three minutes. Getty had managed to get on the elevator by himself, then avoided the security men in the building lobby by taking the elevator to the second floor and walking down the stairs to the basement. He'd used one of his keys to open a stairwell that exited from the back of the building behind some bushes. Getty had made it to Kathryn's office in just a few minutes.

"He began waving the gun around, yelling that I was a meddling dyke bitch and that all the problems of the world were due to homosexuals," recounted Kathryn. "It was what I'd said to him in the elevator that made him come after me. Remember when I'd said, *I'll get to you?* Well, he thought I was threatening him."

I was relieved at that. I'd felt very guilty that it was my little dog and pony show with Carl's laptop might have spurred Getty into action.

"I didn't speak much. Most of the time I couldn't understand him," said Kathryn. She paused to yawn but she was still talking fourteen to the dozen.

"The phone rang and it was you, I just said the first thing that came into my mind to you. I was so worried. I knew you'd come charging in to try to save me," she turned to face me, "and you did...you did come charging in, and you did save me!" She smiled at me brilliantly.

"And you saved me, by hitting Leo. We're quite a team." I reached over to hold her hand.

Kathryn squeezed my hand back. Then skipped to another thought. She touched her swollen cheek. "Leo hit me," she said yawning. "He said I'd stuck my nose in where it didn't belong." Yawning again, her words slowed, like a victrola running down. "He...was...so...angry."

We'd arrived at the loft parking lot. Kathryn leaned her head back against the seat. I got out, walked around and opened her door.

"I feel so tired. I ..." She yawned again raising the back of her hand to her mouth, acting like Dorothy in the poppy field. She was tumbling down off her adrenalin high and after all, neither of us had had much sleep in the last few days. I helped her out of the van and into the lobby. I thanked our lucky rainbows that the elevator was at the first floor, because one look at Kathryn told me she'd never make it up the stairs under her own steam.

"Lean against me," I told her, holding her up with one arm as I ran the elevator up to the third floor.

"What's wrong with me? I can't keep my eyes open," she said trying to shake the exhaustion from her head.

"You just need to take a little nap, querida. You've had a hard day." I put ice in a plastic bag for her cheek, then managed to get her into the bedroom without actually having to carry her.

"Will you come too? To take a nap...?" she asked in a far away voice. When she saw the bed, she wanted to drop onto it just as she was. She was wearing a tailored wool suit and silk blouse.

I said gently, "Kathryn, I really think you should put your jammies on."

She looked up at me, barely able to keep her eyes open.

"You do?" she asked in a sleepy whisper.

"Yeah, I'll help you, c'mon." I steered her into the dressing room, leaned her against the wall, found a long tee shirt, helped her out of her clothes and into the sleepwear and then steered her to the bed. I tucked her in and kissed her forehead. She was already asleep. The whole thing would have been pretty adorable, if the preceding event hadn't been so terrifying.

It was still early afternoon. I felt out of it too, but not in the same way. I needed to work out. I knew Kathryn would sleep for at least three hours. When she woke up she was going to be ravenously hungry. I've been there, I know what it's like. So I called The Farmer's Market Deli and asked them to deliver a bunch of sandwiches. Then I called Sara. She was in her office downstairs. I told her what happened and that I figured the cops and press were about to hound us.

"I'll take care of them," said Sara efficiently. "You'll both have to talk to the police, but let's set it up for tonight at 6:00 PM in my office. That will give Kathryn some time to rest and she won't have to leave the building. The press won't be able to get at her here."

As a lawyer, Sara's a shark. Good thing she's on our side. I thanked her, said we'd be there at 6:00 and then went upstairs to spend some time kicking and punching inanimate objects.

Chapter 41

A few days later, Kathryn and I were having dinner at Farrel and Jessie's. We'd been cooped up in the loft dodging the press and were suffering from cabin fever. So we sneaked out the back under cover of winter's early darkness.

Jessie's kitchen was full of good things to eat, as always. The main course was a simmering paella with chicken, sausage and extra large crawfish on a bed of saffron rice. There were crisp rounds of deep fried potatoes on a large platter, and two kinds of homemade salad dressing.

"We've held off on this long enough," said Farrel. "We want to know how you figured this all out!"

"Don't say anything until I get there," said Jessie bringing a large bowl of green salad to the table. "Now, first the suicide note, what made you think of the voice program?"

"Well," I said, "I'm kind of embarrassed about that. Georgia Smith guessed it. She wasn't saying *Carl's macaroni's scan,* she was saying *Carl's Macro Needs Scan.* I just couldn't understand her. Not consciously anyway. Then I dreamed about Carl spitting macaroni on the computer keyboard. Surreal but literal, like a Dali movie sequence. Leo rigged Carl's computer so that when Carl said his name the macro would be the suicide note."

"And how did you know it was Leo?" asked Farrel.

"A lot of things..." I paused, "see, once I realized the intended victim was Kathryn, it eliminated most of the other suspects. For one thing, I figured out that Leo had shot at Rowlina, because he mistook her for Kathryn.

"You're kidding!" said Jessie and Farrel in unison.

"No, really. What he saw was: Same color coat, same red scarf, and to someone as nutty as Leo, Rowlina's fox fur hat was about the same color as Kathryn's hair. Also Leo had broken the light bulb above the Language Arts Building door to give himself more cover, but the darkness made it harder for him to see his victim. He was sure that Kathryn was in her office because the light was on. At that point he wasn't confident enough to go right into her office, so he waited outside. He figured whoever came out, had to be Kathryn. I even caught a whiff of his cheap aftershave still wafting around the building a few hours later. Anyway, since the killer had shot at Rowlina, that ruled Rowlina out as a suspect.

"Was she one?" asked Jessie.

"Sure, she had opportunity but there wasn't much motive. Of course, any of them might have finagled a grant or faked a degree requirement and so would have feared Kathryn because she was checking up on grants and credentials and she had a reputation for exposing fraud in colleges. Rowlina had been acting guilty, but it was because of the INS probe."

"But how did you know the killer was after *Kathryn*?" Farrel asked.

"The clincher for me was seeing the three pack of Devil Dogs. Things that came in three packs were even taunting me in my dream. See, Devil Dogs come in three packs which reminded me that Cafalattes do too, but in the fridge in the Administration Building storage room, there were no open three packs of Cafalatte. I began to consider the importance of that as soon as Kathryn mentioned Caffelattes came in threes, here at the brunch. There should have been an opened package with two bottles in it, if Connie had put a Caffelatte out for Kathryn. So how did a Cafalatte bottle get on the back table without leaving an open pack in the fridge? The answer: Connie didn't put one there, but the killer did."

I looked at Kathryn who was gazing at me with fascination even though she knew the story already. I snorted. She smirked.

I said, "Everybody knows that Cafalatte is Kathryn's drink, heck they stock the College cafeteria with it just for her. Leo must have been carrying that bottle bomb around for days, incredibly dangerous thing to do, even if it wasn't armed. Then he saw his chance. He put the rigged Cafalatte on the table because he assumed Kathryn would be at the meeting and would pick it up. Several people said that they hadn't seen Leo carrying an extra bottle back to his seat, which gave him a bit of an alibi. But it turned out Leo didn't have to spirit the real Cafalatte bottle away, due to Miranda's anal efficiency. See, Connie had gone into the storage room to load a tray with bottles, but she forgot the list of drinks. Meanwhile Miranda, learning that Kathryn was not going to be at the meeting, efficiently crossed off the Cafalatte for Kathryn from the list on Connie's desk. Too bad I didn't just ask Miranda about that, or even Connie. Either could have told me that Kathryn's drink had been crossed off. Anyway that cleared Miranda. She knew Kathryn wasn't coming, so she wouldn't have tried to kill her with the bottle. And

Connie would have known as well, so that let her off."

Did you suspect Miranda?" asked Farrel.

"She'd been a possible suspect...not much of a motive though, especially against Kathryn. By the way, Miranda didn't even try to bail Shel Druckenmacher out of jail, even though he begged her, and it turned out there were several outstanding warrants under different names on him from other states. DNA evidence will probably link him to Daria's murder but Emma and Sara have already found the key. Daria had actually taken some of Shel's drugs to turn in to the police. He needed them to sell, if he didn't produce the cash, the higher-up dealers would kill him. He was desperate to get the drugs back. That was his motive for using deadly force to try to get Daria to tell him where the drugs were. Sara figured out where the drugs were hidden in Daria's office, and Emma found a street source who told her about the dealer pressure on Shel."

"What a terrible man," said Kathryn.

I paused while Farrel filled everyone's wine glass.

"That left only Jimmy and Leo," I went on, "Jimmy was a tough one, he was acting like a guilty psycho, but he knew right away that Kathryn didn't write the note. Since Jimmy could easily have avoided it, he didn't write it. That left Leo, his grammar is terrible."

"And Leo was stalking me," prompted Kathryn.

"Yeah, I literally bumped into Leo in front of Kathryn's office. I'm glad I did, because I guess he was there to...well he had Skylar's gun with him and he'd probably seen Kathryn's light on..." I didn't like to think about how many times Kathryn had just missed being Leo's target. He'd even borrowed his son Leo Jr.'s Neon to stalk Kathryn at her office and me at Carl's apartment and then Kathryn at the Hampshire.

"How do you know he had the gun that night?" asked Jessie.

"It was in his belt and he smashed into me. It left quite a bruise," I unconsciously touched my hip. He was even afraid to take his hands out of his pockets after he bumped me. I must have dislodged the gun and he was holding it under his jacket."

"Were you ever able to find out Bart's reason for going back into the conference room?" asked Kathryn.

"He decided it would be a great idea to get that Cafalatte for you since he'd messed up getting it at the airport, but then he remembered a memo about removing supplies from the building and he felt he'd be admitting to pilfering if he came clean. So he tried to cover it up."

"That man really is a buffoon," said Kathryn to me. "Do you think he even understands right from wrong?"

"I don't think he even understands right from left," I sighed.

"But why? Why did Leo do all this? Was it just because he hates gay people?" asked Jessie.

Kathryn took up the yarn, "It's certainly true that Leo is a rabid homophobe. Homophobia ruined his life...you see, Jay Getty is Leo's *third* son; the one Leo never talks about. Jay was the boy Carl kissed under the bleachers. They were both thrown out of St. Bonaventure High, but Carl had the support of his mother and went on to excel at Hadesville High. Jay was sent away to school, which was very hard for him. The whole thing broke up the Getty family. Ultimately, Barbara Getty came around. She loved and supported Jay, but Leo went over the edge. It's not clear whether St. Bonaventure fired Leo from his coaching position because he had an unrepentant gay son, or if Leo was so embarrassed by his son's sexual orientation that he chose to leave town. Either way, his wife divorced him because he was so horrible to Jay. By the way, Jay Getty is the director of The Rainbow Youth Symphony."

"But there was more to it than just the gay stuff, though," I said.

"Yes, there was," said Kathryn, "you see, Leo faked most of the research for his dissertation. He got his degree by being part of the group of plagiarizing professors I'd exposed years ago. Leo was sure I was about to blow the whistle on him, but really, I didn't have a clue. Monday morning, when I said that I'd see to him, he was sure I was about to turn him in. The thought of losing his current job was bad enough, but to lose it because of a meddling lesbian made him crazy."

"But why did he kill Carl?" asked Farrel.

"Leo confessed this morning to the police. He told them Carl knew all about the dissertation fraud," said Kathryn sadly. "Jay Getty had told Carl that Leo was too busy in those days to do minor research, much less come up with a huge statistical report for publication in a dissertation."

I added, "Unfortunately, Carl confronted Leo. Leo hated Carl anyway, he still insists that Carl *made* his son gay, but Leo managed to suppress his fury while he planned to get rid of Carl. Carl suggested that Leo come clean on the bogus research and try to make amends. Carl even offered to help Leo. While Leo silently raged, Carl suggested Leo reach out to Jay. Harmony was all Carl was thinking about."

"Naive," said Jessie.

"Yeah," I said, "Carl's trying to *help* Leo was a fatal mistake. Leo began a desperate plan to break down Carl's credibility and his self-esteem. He set up fake emails that seemed to come from Carl and altered ones that were sent to Carl. At times Leo was able to intercept an email to Carl and then just change the meaning by altering a few words. Those were the most confusing for everyone."

"Such a risky course of action. After all, the tampering could have become apparent so easily," said Farrel.

"Leo was desperate and don't forget Carl was blind. Leo was able to delete and change things while he was in the room with Carl," I said.

I didn't mention that Leo had confessed that he also tried to squish me with a piano to keep me from prowling around Carl's office and to try to push suspicion off on Jimmy Harmon.

"Also, I have proof that Leo set up a meeting with Carl on the day of his death. It's on Carl's answering machine. The date is apparent by the order of the calls."

"And Skylar Carvelle? Why was he killed?" asked Jessie.

"The gasoline. Leo smelled of it. Skylar noticed the smell on Leo, even over Leo's gallons of cheap cologne. Skylar teased Leo about the rank smell, not realizing he was stepping on a scorpion's tail. Skylar had even been standing fairly close to Leo when Leo set the Cafalatte bomb on the back table. Skylar may have seen something, but he and Leo had known each other for a long time, so I guess Skylar just couldn't imagine Leo as a killer. Then Leo heard in Skylar's office that Skylar wanted to talk to me, Leo figured Skylar was going to turn him in."

"Wait, back to Carl again...How long had the suicide note been set up?" Jessie asked.

"Not long. Leo set it up earlier in the day. Leo had keys that would open Carl's office. See, Leo had thought Carl would just break down after all the painful email he was getting but Carl was a tough guy. He was beginning to figure out that things didn't add up. Then there was that dust up between Carl and Jimmy. A whole class heard Jimmy say Carl's work sucked and that professional people hated it. Leo heard about it on the grapevine and figured he needed to act while Carl seemed depressed."

"So Leo set up the suicide message and then waited for Carl to go to his office? And then what?" asked Jessie.

"Leo called Carl. Carl answered his phone by simply saying his name. Which triggered the macro. Then Carl left his office and went to the top floor to meet Leo. The rest was easy."

The image of Carl's last frightening moments as he was pushed by Leo, flashed through everyone's mind.

After a long moment Kathryn said, "Leo's doctors say he has a serious heart condition. That's why his face gets so red. He's actually been moved to a locked ward at the hospital." She reached for my hand under the table.

"We want you both to come here for Christmas, OK?" Jessie said after several moments. "Everyone's invited. We'll have a big dinner and play games." Jessie looked directly at Kathryn and said, "We always have a fun time." Kathryn nodded smiling, still holding my hand.

Epilogue

Generally:

Over the next few months things at Irwin College slowly got back into a regular rhythm.

Connie Robinson got a raise. Miranda Juarez was rid of Shel. Nancy dumped Bart Edgar who continued to work for the College. There was a memorial service for Skylar Carvelle.

Georgia Smith finally came home from the hospital with a renewed commitment to her husband Adam, which everyone hoped would last. Rowlina Roth divorced Holtzmann and managed to convince the INS she'd been duped by him. She continued to stay in the closet, however, which fueled her need to smoke like a chimney.

Jay Getty mourned Carl. His organization, Rainbow Youth Symphony, inherited all of Carl's worldly possessions despite Carl's sibling's efforts to contest Carl's will. This turned out to be quite a boon for Jay Getty and his youth group, because among Carl's possessions were the rights to Carl's creative work. Jimmy Harmon compiled, arranged, and marketed Carl's compositions and songs, creating some excellent works that were recorded by everybody from JLo to Elton. The royalties poured in.

Jay Getty asked Kathryn to help him set up and administer the Carl Rasmus Trust, which used the royalties to help young musicians. The trust also had a special program to award music scholarships at Irwin for blind kids and gay, lesbian, bisexual and transgender kids. Carl's music will live on, not only for its quality and beauty, but also for the good it will do.

Leo Getty had two small heart attacks, and then just before his trial, a big one that took his life. I was glad Kathryn didn't have to testify, but sorry that Leo's rampant homophobia wasn't publicly exposed for the death and destruction it created. I think what actually killed Leo, was the realization that he couldn't find a lawyer who agreed that his revenge against gays was justified.

Shel Druckenmacher pled guilty to Daria's murder and went state's evidence against some drug connections to beat the death penalty. He got 45 years, minimum. Miranda Juarez didn't attend his trial.

Mickey Murphy was freed, but Sara and Emma still worried about him until Cora Martin offered to let Mickey rent a bedroom in her house.

"I'm tired of being alone," she'd said, "and now I'll have someone to change the light bulbs."

Mickey calls Cora, Cora...which we all thought was a good sign.

Personally:

My stepmother Juana came and stayed at Rosa's for the holidays and joined us all at Farrel and Jessie's on Christmas morning. She loved Kathryn and so did Rosa. That was a great Christmas present for me. Sara, Emma, Judith, Rosa, Rosa's boyfriend Michael, and Doug were there too. Amanda Knightbridge also joined us.

"It seemed obvious to invite her," Jessie had said.

Cora took Mickey with her to visit her son in LA. By then Emma had lost interest in Ingrid but had met another very attractive woman whom she calls Meryl.

There were masses of presents. Among the exchanges:

Sara gave Kathryn a sexy bathrobe, "For times when you really should throw something on," she winked. Everyone laughed.

Kathryn countered immediately by presenting Sara with a pair of tiny, high powered binoculars, "For when peeking just isn't enough!" Kathryn explained. That also got a big laugh.

Farrel and Jessie gave Kathryn a UHAUL gift card.

I gave Farrel and Jessie a set of guest towels...for the hot tub.

With a completely straight face, Farrel gave me a quart of massage oil. Kathryn snorted, then eyed me with *that look*.

I blurted out, "I didn't tell her!" Then I turned suspiciously to Sara who admitted she'd seen an empty bottle by the side of the bed.

"Obviously I was correct in my deduction," said Sara smugly shaking her head. "You two have the worst poker faces I've ever seen! I'd tear you apart on the stand."

I gave Kathryn half a dozen pairs of cashmere socks and the tiny gold pin I got for being on the safety patrol in sixth grade. It was the closest I had to a sorority pin.

Kathryn gave me her senior class pin from Smith. Her father had Fed Exed it from Maine.

Judith leaned to Farrel and explained, "Smith College does not have sororities, it's one of the reasons I went there. A senior student traditionally gives her pin to a junior upon graduation, and then the junior sends it back to her when *she* graduates, usually with a small gift."

I whispered to Kathryn that she'd have to tell me all about the young women she gave her pin to some time. Kathryn just winked at me, then gave me a wonderful traveling watercolor set and an extraordinary book of vintage erotic Japanese prints which Sara had some choice things to say about.

****

Later on Christmas Day, while Kathryn and I were walking back to the loft, I thought about all the complicated arrangements I'd made with Max Bouchet to deliver Kathryn's holiday gift from him.

Bouchet had felt extremely guilty that it had been his plan to make Kathryn survey faculty grants and credentials at Irwin. Kathryn had been pushed right into the lion's den without even knowing it and Leo had almost killed her. I used Max's guilt to pressure him into setting up a very nice present for Kathryn. I figured it should be in the middle of the loft right now.

As we walked along in the cold December night, I thought about what I wanted to say to Kathryn. Should I talk to her tonight? How would she react? I was getting very nervous.

As we went up the stairs I said, "Max is supposed to have delivered a little present for you. It should to be in the loft at this very moment. It's a surprise."

"Really, what is it?"

"A surprise," I laughed. "You'll see in a minute."

"Oh goodness, it's not a dog is it? Or something like that?"

"Well," I said as I opened the door, "it does have four legs, or maybe three."

In the middle of the big room, was a black Steinway baby grand piano. It was even set up with the lid propped open for dramatic effect. One of the track lights was focused right on it. It looked spectacular."

"This is for me?" said Kathryn circling around it, eyes twinkling.

"Here's a card," I said picking it up from the bench.

She read out loud, "Dearest Kathryn, Here is a token of my profound esteem. Fondly, Max."

She ran her fingers over the keys, then sat down on the bench.

"Show off for me," I gently demanded, sitting down at the dining table, ready to watch her play.

"I haven't played in a while," she said stretching her fingers in a professional way. She played a couple of chords, then began a movement of Gershwin's *Rhapsody in Blue*. She played flawlessly. When she was done with that, she changed the mood completely by playing *Maple Leaf Rag*, by Scott Joplin, slowly, the way it was meant to be played. It was totally different from the Gershwin, but just as enchanting.

At the end of that piece, she turned to me. "Any requests?"

"Sing something to me..."

She thought for a moment, looking into space, then played and sang *Someone to Watch Over Me*. She sounded wonderful. When she finished she looked at me again.

"One more?" I asked.

"One more...hmmm." She began a slow torchy swing version of *Save the Last Dance For Me*. The unhurried rhythm was achingly sensuous.

When she got to the last line, she got up from the piano and came over to me with her hand extended. She danced me around the floor singing the last verse of the song in her most seductive voice. When she sang the words about the girl who's asking to take you home, and that you must tell her no, and not to forget who's arms you're going to be in after the last dance, she looked into my eyes with such demanding passion, it made my heart soar.

Kathryn had filled the room with romance. I'd wondered whether she could dance, and she could, even while she was singing. We did some fancy turns and spins and laughed in delight that we fit together so well on the dance floor. She ended the song with an ardent kiss.

This is too good to be true, flitted through my head, but then I remembered my plan.

"Come over here," I said leading her by the hand to the couch. She sat down next to me and grew silent when she saw the earnest look on my face. I was trying to decide how to start.

"Is this going to be something bad?" she whispered.

"I hope not."

She took my hand and stroked my palm.

I looked into her eyes. I said, "Kathryn, one of my greatest fears over the last couple of days has been...that you were going to tell me they'd fixed the laundry room at the Hampshire and you were going home. I know this is all going very fast, but...I don't want you to go..." I looked away, "so, I have three proposals for you."

"Proposals," she repeated without inflection.

"Yeah. I'd like you to stay here and give up your place at the Hampshire. So that's the first one." I glanced back at her. She still held my hand. She nodded slightly. I wasn't sure if she was saying yes, or just encouraging me to go on. So I went on.

"For the second one," I reached in my pocket and pulled out an envelope. "I got this from Max Bouchet yesterday. It's a bonus for the case. I feel half of it belongs to you, I couldn't have figured it out without you, not to mention your quick thinking with the bronze..." I drew the check out of the envelope and showed it to her. "Read it," I said holding it in the light.

"Maggie!" she exclaimed softly at the amount.

"I propose that we spend this money on converting the northeast corner on of the top floor into your own space."

"You mean like an apartment?"

"No!" I snorted, "no way. You still have to sleep with me! ...I mean, like an office. Your own office. One that doesn't go down to 50 degrees on the weekends. Any kind of space you want."

"Could I have my own bathroom?"

"Sure," I said smirking. "That's the first thing you thought of?"

"Well, the first thing I thought of was having a hot tub on the deck."

"We can have that too."

"I have money of my own. I don't have to use your money."

"Kathryn, this check is not even my fee. It's like found money. If you want to use some of your own money, you can buy a nice desk or something."

She still held my hand. Finally she said, "So, what's the third proposal?"

"Well...I thought we might want to find out if we can really manage being in close quarters for an extended period, so I'm proposing we go away to someplace warm together for a few weeks."

"What did you have in mind?"

"Farrel and Jessie's Florida beach house. It's nice there. They won't be using it. We could stay as long as we want..."

She seemed amenable but she hadn't really said yes, which was making me nervous.

I added, "We don't have to fly. It's not really a bad drive. We can take the van. We could walk on the beach, and relax, and make love, and plan your office, talk, read books, eat fresh shrimp at ocean-side cafes, and... um..."

She was just looking at me, not moving or saying anything. Finally I said, "I'll give you a massage every day?"

She broke into laughter.

"OK?" I asked.
Kathryn looked into my eyes and recited:

"Her breast is fit for pearls,
But I was not a "Diver" --
Her brow is fit for thrones
But I have not a crest.
Her heart is fit for home --
I -- a Sparrow -- build there
Sweet of twigs and twine
My perennial nest."

Poems:

A Winter Ride
By Amy Lowell

It Sifts From Leaden Sieves...
By Emily Dickinson

Meeting By Accident...
By Emily Dickinson

Wild Nights...
By Emily Dickinson

Her Breast Is Fit For...
By Emily Dickinson

About the Author

Besides her work as an author of fiction, **Liz Bradbury** has written and had published over 300 nonfiction articles and essays on gay, lesbian, bisexual, and transgender issues. She has regular columns in several GLBT publications and web sites including the *Valley Gay Press*, *PA Diversity Network's web site: www.padiversity.org*, *Panzee Press* and *Gaydar Magazine*. She speaks frequently on GLBT rights. She lives in Allentown, Pennsylvania and Amelia Island, Florida with her partner Patricia Sullivan.

She is currently at work on her next Maggie Gale Mystery - *Being the Steel Drum Man.*

Check Liz Bradbury's web site at www.lizbradbury.boudicapublishing.com or www.boudicapublishing.com for details.

Join the FACEBOOK group:
MAGGIE GALE MYSTERY READERS
for discussions with the author and other readers
and for special inside information

Twenty percent of the net profit from the book sales of *Angel Food and Devil Dogs* goes to benefit Gay, Lesbian, Bisexual, Transgender, and Allied (GLBTA) 501c3 not-for-profit organizations.

If your GLBTA organization seeks a fund raiser opportunity and would like to arrange an *Angel Food and Devil Dogs* reading/booksigning event with the author, contact Boudica Publishing Inc., for details. Email BoudicaPublish@aol.com or call Boudica Publishing at 610-820-3818. See further information at www.boudicapublishing.com.

Book clubs are also encouraged to contact Boudica for "meet the author" opportunities.

BOUDICA PUBLISHING INC.

Learn about Boudica Publishing Inc.'s imprints
at www.boudicapublishing.com
or by calling: 610-820-3818

Wildfire Poetry Press

PURPLE KITES

CHILDRENS BOOKS

LESBIAN MYSTERY BOOKS

Join the FACEBOOK group:
MAGGIE GALE MYSTERY READERS

wf / BR

T 31450

Made in the USA